MW01105859

~Allbooks Reviews~

"Pike Wheeling has to face sorrow and hardship. He fights in the American Civil War, gets captured, and is taken to Andersonville Prison. While in prison, he made some good friends, but many were lost due to the dreadful living conditions in prison. He survives, but leaves the prison with a deadly enemy............

Lori Davis does write a compelling tale. The story shows the differences between good and evil, and the fine line that divides them both. It portrays the gruesome nature of life in Andersonville Prison, war, and malevolent individuals. It also shows the struggles and sorrows individuals suffer during a lifetime, and more importantly, the courage needed to get through those tough times."

For a good read in historical fiction, this book is **highly recommended by: Margaret Orford, Allbooks Reviews**

~Midwest Book Reviews~

"Pike Wheeling survived the living hell that was the Confederate prison camp called Andersonville.......
Second Wind is an original novel that presents its author, Lori Davis, as a skilled storyteller who is able to weave a complex tale of equally complex characters into a fascinating, entertaining, and highly recommended 'theater of the mind' event for its enthusiastic and appreciative readers."

Helen Dumont, Reviewer

SECOND WIND

SECOND WIND

By

Lori Davis

Argus Enterprises International
North Carolina****New Jersey

Second Wind © 2009
All rights reserved by: Lori Davis

A-Argus Better Book Publishers, LLC

For information:
A-Argus Better Book Publishers, LLC
Post Office Box 914
Kernersville, North Carolina 27285
www.a-argusbooks.com

ISBN: 978-0-9842596-1-8
ISBN: 0-9842596-1-9

Illustrations by Lori Davis

Book Cover Art by Dan Shalloe

Printed in the United States of America

DEDICATION

To my mother, Mary Jo, for without her lifetime dedication in bringing forth my great-grandfather's story, this book would never have existed. And I would have lived the rest of my life without realizing I could reach this most personal dream. It is through her faith in me and my abilities that I found my voice and pen. Stemming from her ironclad convictions, she has given me the best gift of all: knowledge.

SPECIAL THANKS

I would be very remiss if I did not thank my stepfather, Dave Carlson. His avid support, expert editing, and computer skills I could never put a price tag on. Thank you so very much. I have thoroughly enjoyed sharing this experience with you.

Also, I would like to thank my husband, Reggie, for his hard work and dedication in shouldering the responsibility of providing for our wonderful family. Without that, I would never have the time to write. To you, a special hug and a kiss from me.

Second Wind
By
Worley/Nestler

There's an old friendly breeze that blows
In the Gulf of Mexico
Somehow it always knows
When I'm feeling low
So, I'm gonna take her down
Wait'll it comes around
Leave the rest of the world behind
Yeah, That's how I'll pass the time
Till I catch my second wind
Get back up and take control again
Find the strength I lost back when
You stopped loving me
I guess I'll just stay out here
Till I know the coast is clear
Sit and watch the tide roll in
Till I get my second wind
There's a peace in the way I feel
When the water's still
And as long as it's calm out here
I've got time to kill
But, as soon as it starts to stir
I'll lose track of the way things were
Float away on the open air
And, I'm not going anywhere
Till I catch my second wind

Prologue

This is more than I can take. More than anyone should have to live through, Pike's mind wailed as the steady rise and fall of the locust's chorus tickled at the fringes of his consciousness while sweat dripped unheeded down his face and back.

I'm going to find Drisco. God, how I want him dead!

And even if Pike found that murderer, and gave him what he so rightly deserved, it would never be enough. *Never!* Not for what Drisco had done to so many. Only Drisco's last victims had personally touched Pike, had in fact devastated him, and it was this loss that sent him out into the heavy blackness to search, to find, to eradicate the blight.

"Easy, boy," Pike called to his huffing gelding, as he calmed himself for the confrontation that lay before him. Exactly where, he didn't yet know. But, it didn't matter as there would be no escape this time. That son-of-a bitch had killed his last victim.

Tuning out all else, Pike focused his mind on finding the hideout in the wild forest, their cabin, their cesspool of destruction. Pike strained, peering into the darkness and waited for the outline to come to him. Sensing he was near the rotting cabin where he would find the killers, Pike straightened himself, loosening his seat, signaling his mount to slow its gait.

Watering ...piercing ...Pike's eyes filtered through the darkness, searching for a glimpse of the cabin while the sliver of the moon provided scant help. But all at once, the outline of the hated cabin rose through the blackness as it contrasted with the oaks enveloping it.

Not able to contain his grief, instantly Pike's back stiffened and his fists clenched, then tears burst from his eyes as his body's grief rocked him - hard. Images he couldn't shut out of Rebecca's bloody body crumpled over the wagon and baby Hope's tiny form lying in the dirt - like a forgotten rag doll - marched through him, leaving fresh hurt in their wake. The agony of watching his brother Amos's eyes close for the last time melded with the other staggering losses as if the shock was still as fresh as when it first hit him like a physical blow, taking his breath away.

With ragged, hitching breaths, uncontrollable sobs wracked him for a time, the flow of a broken dam that couldn't be stopped...wouldn't be stopped, it just felt good to let go. But finally, with several more raw gulps of air, Pike's anger flew back into his chest and consumed all else, stomping its way back in as he angrily swiped the tears from the sandpapery stubble on his chin. He lightly tugged his black gelding to a halt as his thoughts turned bloody. *Here I come, Drisco. You and your bastard cousin will pay for all of those you've laid low. You aren't getting away with it this time. And remember, sometimes, just sometimes, spent gunpowder smells oh-so-sweet.*

Letting go of the residue of his grief, as a few errant tears cut muddy paths along his dirty cheeks, Pike tossed the reins over the nearest bush. And he told himself, *It's your night, Colt!* while he clutched the hefty, forbiddingly cold, six-shooter, to slip with focused stealth into the underbrush of the free-ranging forest. *Just try to stop me,* Pike told Drisco in his head, as butterflies thrashed inside his stomach.

The outline of the cabin grew clearer to Pike as he stalked into the brush, and he could easily see the moon glinting from the metal smokestack, through breaks in the foliage. More careful, more focused, as he released his grief into the universe, Pike sank to his knees to then creep carefully across the talc-like ground, long without rain, as clouds of dust rose in the meager light of the moon. No light shone from the inside of the crudely-built log structure, and Pike was thankful that his arrival would be a complete surprise since he was outnumbered and would need the advantage, and he meant to take full advantage of it.

Sounding in the deep quiet, the only unnatural sound around him, Pike was aware of his ragged breathing while adrenaline from the pure hate - pure vindication, flowed deep within. He was unbridled hatred.

Knowing it best to calm himself so he'd have a steadier hand, Pike took several deep, cleansing breaths as he stared at the cabin windows, looking for a sign his approach had been heard as he collected himself, centering his emotions.

As he began to move forward once again, Pike was halted in his tracks by a horse blowing through its nostrils in fear. That one sound cut through his thoughts, reminding him of his second mission: finding Hank. Now close to the rear of the cabin, Pike peered toward the windows to make sure the occupants had not been wakened, ears sharpened to any sound from within. Relieved there was no movement, and hearing nothing but locusts and his beating heart, he craned his neck in the horse's direction, straining his eyes and praying Hank would be there. It took but a flash to recognize his stolen buckskin.

Hank! Thank the Lord. Drawn as surely as a fly to Sunday's dessert, Pike couldn't suppress the urge to see his old horse in spite of his desire for vengeance. Making his way silently to the dilapidated corral, Pike easily slipped inside the brush barrier, as Hank snorted again.

"It's okay, boy," Pike crooned to soothe his long-time friend. "It's me, remember? Huh, boy?" Pike stepped slowly, holding out the back of his hand for Hank to sniff.

The abused gelding threw up his head and glared, with his ears pinned against his sunken skull. His eyes brimmed white as he lunged menacingly at his one-time buddy.

Praying he could calm Hank and not willing to give up, Pike eased a bit closer. "Boy? Easy now, Hank. . it's . . it's okay. I'm here to help you."

Ears twitching back and forth as Hank pawed with a front hoof, recognition dawned. Then, with one velvet nicker, the horse dropped his head and took a tentative step forward. A few heart beats later, he took a couple more. Finally . . . finally, after all the months of worry, Pike smiled at the warm, familiar breath along his cheek while calmness returned to his being as he relished Hank's warmth. Reaching out a quivering hand, Pike trailed his fingertips softly along the gelding's muzzle and then his forehead. He couldn't help what came next as he laid his face against the soft hair of the buckskin's neck, breathed deep, and released his months of worry.

I never thought I'd get you back, boy.

His right arm slid down Hank's neck to pat the horse's side, instantly, what met Pike's callused fingers were the ragged bumps of Hank's ribs which jutted out a raw angles.

Those bastards!

That was it, he could hold back no longer. Sweet revenge! How he ached with it.

Wheeling about on his boot-heels, Pike stomped, grumbling, his one focus was bringing Drisco to his knees and making him beg for mercy as he cut through the corral. Next came the rough plank door, there was *no more* thought of stealth.

Wham! Well-aged leather kicked open the door, causing a hideous screaming of the hinges. Pike glared across the threshold with the Colt locked in front of him. A soft rustling directed Pike's arms as the two men jumped up from their bunks. Aiming into the blackness in the direction of the sound, he pulled the trigger.

Part I

Pike's Imprisonment

Chapter 1

I know I will run into those Graybacks soon, Pike told himself as he crawled forward, cold wind causing his ears to ache. Almost to the crest of a minor slope, hoping to scan the area just beyond it, Pike gazed, searching for the enemy, those secessionists. But, *What the hell . . .?* blasted into his thoughts, like the Mini' ball had just done as it flew by his left ear - so close he could feel its heat. Instinctively reacting, he jerked his head back below the tops of the waist-high grass, instantly ceasing his crawling. *Now what? Those Sunday soldiers have us. Got to get out of here! Where did those black-guards come from? God, what now?*

But first things first, looking to his right, Pike hoped to find Ben and Tom. No such luck. To try to protect the other three soldiers of his Northern Army scouting group who were likewise snaking through the vestiges of last summer's native grass, he warned, "Boys, the Reb's have got us covered!"

Where's Frank? Pike wondered, chewing the inside of his lips before he whipped his head to the left, catching a glimpse of his tow-headed little brother. Frank's white-fringed eyes were locked on Pike, a question showing there. Pike mouthed, "Get back," hoping Frank would understand.

Lips scrunched in a hard line and brows tightly furrowed, Frank nodded, then his gaze broke its lock on Pike's face. Quickly, Frank swiveled on his belly, all of his movements quick and choppy, fish-like. Still hoping to spot the others, Pike turned back to the right, praying like hell he'd see them, but again, no such luck.

Damn! Now what? Got to do something! "Stay low!" Pike barked louder than he'd liked, "Make double quick for the trees!" The trees and safety were but fifty feet behind them which was not an insurmountable race, or so he hoped.

Taking his own advice to heart, Pike pivoted and even as big a man as he was, he managed the turn swiftly using his innate, coordinated grace. He called on all that skill now, silently thanking God for his abilities as his very life depended on it. Grunting from his exertions, all of the sounds of the struggles around him were blocked out by the blaring drumbeat of his own blood, pounding in his ears with each heart-beat. Boom. Boom. Boom

But his thoughts were just as loud as he fussed at himself. *Why didn't I spot them sooner? Must've been a lookout.* The sounds of his men's efforts then floated to his ears as they struggled to get away - alive. "Just a few more feet," Pike whispered encouragingly. "But hurry!"

Crunch. Snap.

Pike heard the familiar sounds from heavy hooves among the dead limbs scattered on the ground not far from where Pike now lay, panting, his ears still pulsing with blood. Fear licked its icy tongue over the hairs on his neck, causing them to stiffen and fear-bumps rose as quickly. *There they are,* he told himself at the first glimpse of the mounted Rebel soldiers. In response, Pike's stomach clutched as tight as a badger on a velvety rabbit, then it fluttered.

The gray-clad riders trotted forward, guns drawn and pointed in their opponents' direction. Pike and his companions from the New York 12th crazily hoped to vanish into the undulating waves of dry grass, brittle from the sharp February cold.

Wild thoughts careened through Pike's mind. *Are we going to be shot? We're trapped!* While thinking, he took several great gulps of biting air as his lungs heaved, his mind still screaming, *There's no way out!* Panic ran free and unfettered, slicing him to his very core.

One rider pushed forward on a copper-colored

horse, gun leveled, shouting, "Okay, you whore-masters, don't try nothin' or you won't live long enough to regret it." After a few breaths, the leader ordered sharply, with a jerk of his rifle to back it up, "Now, stand up. And I mean for ya to do it slow. Too fast, and I'll shoot yer damn heads off."

His own eyes hard, his brow creased, Pike knew they were lost. *Is there a way out? Maybe so.* He held on to the miniscule hope as he gave his men instructions. Turning, he nodded, signaling them to comply. Together, the trapped soldiers eased their hands heavenward, then began to stand slowly and with care.

Expression wild, Frank's eyes made Pike give him an extra emphatic nod of his head, using the glare of his green eyes to back up his directive. *I can't let Frank pull that pepperbox!,* the one he knew was in the right pocket of his brother's woolen army-issue coat.

Directing the man next to him, the Rebel leader grunted, "Git their weapons." The appointed man tossed his leg over the rump of his furry, dull-looking mount and stomped toward the prisoners. Starting with the youngest, Ben, he patted him all over, taking his pistol and hand-made knife, the one fashioned by his own father and dearly treasured by Ben.

Breathing a sigh of relief, Pike watched Frank let his weapon go, unused, but then flashing up from his very core, anger flared, an ember that had been in his belly rose, wild and uncontrollable. In one swift, practiced motion he bent low, yanking out his large-bladed knife from his right boot. *Get his throat!* was Pike's single thought as he leapt at the Grayback.

The blade plunged deep as Pike used his towering frame to his advantage. But, luck was not to be his as he missed the soft throat for the less tender shoulder. A shot rang his ears unmercifully, erasing his ability to hear as Pike was conscious of the slam to his left upper thigh, spiraling him to the cold ground. Just barely aware of reality, Pike landed on top of the smaller rebel, just before blackness enfolded him in its cloak.

*

His heart vibrated and began to flutter and race at the first sight of Rebecca, his girl back home. Pike didn't realize how absurd it was to see her. His only thought was how good she would feel . . .how lucky he was. Not losing another second in wonder, Pike hopped up from the ground, pumping his legs for all he was worth, racing to his love.

Eyes drinking in every detail, Pike quickly noted the girl's unbound hair and bright eyes, her grin reflecting his own on her rosy face. It took only moments to reach her and he couldn't help but take a second, hard look into Rebecca's eyes as his own flooded in response. The tears felt good because it meant he was alive. Reaching out, Pike wrapped her body with his arms and the first touch of her against his chest sent a shiver of the purest joy right through his center. As Pike drank in Rebecca's familiar lavender scent, he relaxed, letting himself live in this precious moment, this drop of heaven, this most unexpected gift!

Pike said in a husky voice, "I held onto the hope I would see you again. I've kept the watch chain you wove from your hair. The gold watch too. Whenever I felt lonely, I'd hold onto that chain." He pulled back to take another peek at her young, earnest face. "Let's go and see your folks."

With the sun highlighting her hair, making it glow, Rebecca bobbed her head. Clutching her smooth, thin hand, Pike turned to start up the wooden stairs for the front door of the family home. He couldn't help but give Rebecca's hand one more loving squeeze before he glanced back at her. But -- but . . .she was no longer there.

Terror seized Pike's heart as he called after her, "No. Come back!" Panic rang in his voice as he reached out in one mad grasp for her retreating form. Next, he could see a vision of her in the distance, waving at him, a loving grin on her face. Desperate, Pike tried to freeze that picture into his memory just before all became dark once more.

*

First it was the breath of a bitter wind that Pike became aware of - then another, sending a shiver down the length of his spine. Trying to make his mouth work and his eyes open, Pike found he couldn't as he wondered, *Where am I? Am I dead?*

A sliver of pain registered somewhere deep in his brain. Pike was partially aware of the sound coming up the back of his throat just before the sound wave pummeled the back of his lips. Fighting it for a second, Pike's soldier mentality caused him to clamp his lips against letting out what he feared would be a moan, or worse.

But the moan was not to be stopped because he was too weak and he just couldn't fight any more. As the moan burst from his mouth, his eyes fluttered open and then a scream followed in its wake. Clamping his jaws against the sounds, reality went galloping away, like a spring colt, on new-found legs, while warmth returned with the dark cocoon of unconsciousness.

*

With a jerk of his body, mind muddled, consciousness dribbled back. How much time had passed, Pike wasn't sure. Vainly, he shook his head, hoping to clear it as agony erupted, sending many miserable shards up his thigh and right into his guts, twisting them in a flash. He screamed inside, *God, please make it stop! Please let me go back to sleep!* The picture in his head of himself jumping on the Rebel soldier brought him fully back to where he was, causing him to sit bolt upright.

"Whoa there," someone directed. "Better get back down." Friendly hands urged Pike to follow orders by gently pushing against his chest until he lay back on the cold ground. Looking up, Pike recognized Ben's boyish eyes, the youngest of them at seventeen.

God help me, its freezing, Pike thought as a fresh wave of cold rippled through him, adding more misery to his pain. Pike hadn't realized Frank was next to him until he heard him speak.

"Brother, we're captured. Don't know what they are

going to do with us. Need to get you some help. I'll see what I can do. Just hang on." As Frank's hand slipped to his brother's shoulder, he made his plea. "Don't leave me, Brother. You hear me?" Frank knelt down to back up his directive by staring into Pike's pain-riddled face.

It was all Pike could do to get his head to make the appropriate response, but he managed it, somehow, as ice flushed his veins. Now, all he could do was close his eyes and search for unconsciousness. Not able to find the relief he fervently prayed for, his thoughts drifted, drifted back to his home before this ugly war between the Yanks and the Rebs changed his life forever. Drawn like a moth to a flame, his frozen hand drifted, inch by inch, to his pants pocket. Pike knew his most treasured possessions - the hair chain and gold watch - would be there. When his stiff fingers wrapped around the fob, his eyes opened.

The color red captured Pike's attention from the corner of his eye, causing him to turn his head to stare at the blooming patch of crimson. Being intensely trans-fixed by the sight of his wound, Pike felt the warmth of the blood as it ran, soaking his pants. For a time, he gazed as the blood dripped, dripped and dripped, soak-ing the ground. *This can't be happening to me,* was the single notion that ran over and over in his mind as he stared.

Several minutes ticked away while Pike gawked at the gruesome wound, and the stark reality of the situa-tion, stole into his thoughts. Pike pleaded, *God, let me be some other place.* Finding sweet oblivion was far easi-er this time.

*

It wasn't the cold that announced to Pike that he was awake; it was a stranger's voice that penetrated his fog.

"It went clean through but he's lost a lot of blood."

Are they talking about me? Pike wondered as he forced his eyes open through the stubborn crust that had glued them shut. First his eyes looked on Tom,

Frank and a frowning stranger who was kneeling beside him. The intensifying pain let Pike know that the stranger's hands were on his injured leg.

Taking a quick study of the man's face, Pike noted the heavily creased skin, puffy brown eyes, and blood-stained clothes. The worn appearance of the man let him know the doctor had suffered greatly in this never-ending war.

"Okay, son, we're going to do for you what we can." The kindly doctor was obviously trying to be comforting as he patted Pike's arm in a fatherly fashion. "I'm going to clean you up. But don't let on about it. Guess they'd rather see you die. Guess they want you to suffer for what ya done. Maybe that's why they didn't kill you on the spot."

Nodding just perceptibly, Pike let the doctor know that he understood his savior's predicament. With practiced precision, the doctor then directed the stripping of Pike's pants because he couldn't cut them – there were no replacements. A fresh wave of pain lit up every nerve, making it impossible for Pike to focus on anything but the agony as they readied him for treatment, and gratefully, a wave of darkness grasped him again.

*

Frank couldn't help but wince as his brother struggled to control his pain and Frank prayed, *God, you've got to help him!*

"Since the last battle, I've been real busy but, luckily, son," the doctor told Frank, "I'd finished my last surgery when you found me. I'm going to wrap this wound. Take this dressing. Change it daily, 'til you run out. It's the best I can do." Shaking his head, the doctor said softly, "He may die."

It was obvious the doctor's hands were used to this kind of work as it took but few minutes to complete. The surgeon sighed while he shook his head several times, and after sitting back on his heels he uttered, "That's all I can do. He looks feverish already. Put his pants back on."

Once again, Frank felt hopelessness wash over him,

causing him to droop – he felt completely lost. As the surgeon rose, Frank took note of the Rebel doctor's stoop and observed as the man turned back and said, after one last hard stare, "Try to stay warm. And God be with you." Then the doctor lifted his bag to creep silently away, vanishing into the frigid night air without one more look back.

After the doctor disappeared, Frank crouched next to his limp brother, staring, thinking, *What can I do?*

The four prisoners were now alone, without a fire to warm them. Not able to help being transfixed by his brother's limp form, thinking, Frank vowed, *I'll do anything to keep you alive.*

The deep breath into Frank's lungs was frightfully cold, as Frank recalled his earlier pleadings with the Southern surgeon. Frank knew full-well that he'd been lucky, or was it God watching over him, to slip off unnoticed. The darkness must have worked in his favor as no one spotted him leaving the other prisoners. Frank wasn't concerned with being caught as he had one thought on his mind: helping his brother.

Once he had located the single surgeon in this encampment, Frank observed the rather worsted-looking man for several minutes as he finished cleaning himself from the bloody work he must have just completed as dark red liquid was all over his arms, hands and clothes. Without thinking of the consequences, Frank slipped from the dark into the circle of light around the doctor's weak fire, taking advantage of the stranger's hesitation before he recognized the ragged man before him as one of the enemy.

Not waiting for a reaction, Frank had made his case. "Doctor, you've got to help my brother. He's all I've got. He might die." Then after his rush of words, lacking any more, Frank had fallen silent, but he kept his eyes locked on the older man – holding his breath.

The doctor had taken a few beats as he measured his response and Frank knew the next words he heard would most likely be the verdict on whether Pike lived or died. Not saying a word, the surgeon rose and clasped a leather bag in his freshly-washed hand. Not needing any more direction, Frank trotted behind.

Releasing the memory to refocus on the here and now, Frank observed his injured brother as he thought about the exchange with the doctor and his years at home before the war. *I'll always remember that doctor's kindness. What would I do without you, Brother? You've been the one I looked up to. Not Amos.*

Even as a tot, Frank had trailed after his oldest brother, the red-headed, long-limbed man before him. He'd never been close to his middle brother, Amos. Nor had he played much with his two sisters as Frank had been happy to be Pike's shadow.

Walking closer, Frank plopped down behind Pike as his thoughts turned to their home in Baltimore and their days together there before this blasted war. Pike, who, at six foot three, stood head and shoulders above most folks in their hometown, and wherever he went. *You'd never be lost in a crowd would you, big brother?*

An unconscious smile played at the corners of Frank's tightly compressed lips as he recalled his lanky, freckled brother working with the family's horses – the ones he loved so much. The memory of Pike smoothly running a gentle hand across the hard lines of Betsy's face, the oldest mare at home, flashed in Frank's mind as he told himself, *Pike definitely has a way with animals.*

That charisma carried over to people too, especially girls. When they were both gangly teenagers, it had frustrated Frank to no end that making girls laugh came so easily to Pike. Pike always had a story to tell, or better yet, he'd play his guitar, and on occasion he'd catch the girl's attention with his harmonica. But, wherever Pike was, the girls had flocked around him.

Chuckling a bit at his own gawkiness, Frank recalled the many times he'd stepped on his own tongue trying to talk to a girl on his own at school or after church. *At least, I beat you when it came to our studies, huh?*

A shiver rocked Frank and brought him back to bleak reality. Letting go of the past, Frank scooted up to Pike to lift his head enough so he could work his legs under his brother's shoulders. Then he tugged and squirmed and managed to get Pike against his chest. After Pike was in place, Frank wrapped his coat around them both, praying, *Please, Lord, don't take him. What'll I do if you call him home? I'd just as soon you'd take me too. Give me some strength! Please, Lord!*

Thinking out loud, Frank encouraged, "Boys, get next to us. We've got to stay warm." Shivering from the cold and their plight, Frank glanced at Ben and Tom, noting the haunted eyes, hunched backs. He knew exactly what they were feeling because he felt it too but he could do nothing more than struggle with his own demons as his fear rocketed, threatening to run wild and overwhelm him. Frank attempted to give himself some encouragement by saying, *You've got to get a hold of yourself. You've got to be strong for the boys, like Pike would.*

Even while straining to force himself to be strong, a tidal wave of terror crashed through him and he almost lost control. His mind screamed so loudly that he wasn't sure if he'd screamed out loud or not. *I can't take much more of this . . .I can't!* The screaming within caused him to squirm, but there was no escape. All that lay before the scraggly prisoners was the rest of the night and a nightmare with an uncertain ending. Frank began to wonder about what was next for his captured men. *What will happen tomorrow? Have to get though the night first.*

*

Other than the Rebel's scattered lookouts, there was little movement in the camp throughout the rest of the bleak and frigid night. The biting morning announced itself in streaking red and gold across God's ever-changing palette as the wind began to rise. The colored sky provided Frank a modicum of warmth, the gathering light lifting his spirits.

Hope we get some of that, Frank told himself as he observed the coffee being put on to boil and then smelled the bacon beginning to fry, causing his mouth to water. Next he became more aware of his aching backside, numb legs and roaring belly, as he thought again that he wanted so much to be anywhere else.

Tom and Ben rose quickly, slapping their arms and hopping around, in an attempt to get their blood moving. Frank couldn't help noting the dirty clothes and unkempt beard of the soldier who approached a few minutes later. When the Rebel got within ten feet, he angrily tossed a hunk of bread in their direction. The men watched silently, not sure what was happening as it plopped into the dirt. The soldier growled, "Eat up." Then he chuckled a bit as he pivoted on his heel and returned to a warm campfire.

Acting first, Tom scooped up the dust-covered bread, tugging it into three pieces. Tom handed one to Ben, then one to Frank.

"Thank you," Frank stuttered through frozen lips. Before eating his portion, Frank yanked a sliver of his bread and placed it into his pocket to save for Pike.

"Thank God, it's warming up," Ben offered with a grim expression, as he slapped his arms and hopped from one foot to the other.

Some time later, Frank was still clutching his unconscious brother when another Southern soldier approached.

"It's time to move, Yanks. We're bringin' ya a wagon. Put the hurt one in it."

Soon the wagon jangled its way to the prisoners as they waited in a huddle. Before it stopped, Ben and Tom assisted Frank in getting out of his frozen position and they laid Pike out on the ground. With much grunting, it took all three of them to drag Pike's broken body to the wagon and place his hulking frame in it.

As soon as Pike was in place, a voice shouted, "Get behind the wagon." Meekly, the men clustered in the area behind the rough wooden wagon and gawked about, still slapping their arms for warmth. Another soldier hopped into the seat next to the driver while several mounted soldiers trotted up to flank the prisoners.

The driver barked, "Gid' up!" Then, he slapped the reins on the backs of the blonde draft horses as the group started forward with a jangle of trace chains and creaking of leather.

Where are they taking us? Frank wondered. *Maybe Richmond?* To take his mind off his predicament, the rough trail, the lingering cold, Frank turned his attention to the Rebel soldiers nearest him and pointedly observed, *These guys look rough. Guess we are taking a toll on 'em. We've been at this for almost three years. I know Pike and I have been fighting since not long after the war started.*

Telling his parents that he and Pike were entering the war had been harder than he could have imagined. Frank recalled the night, which seemed like an eternity ago as the Wheeling family had gathered for a hearty supper of beans and cornbread.

Their father had pleaded, "Please son. Don't do it. We can't bear losing you or Pike. Please think it over."

Adamantly, Frank had shaken his head, and watched as Pike spoke up. "Sorry, Dad. We've got to fight to keep our country intact. What will happen if we don't? We couldn't live with ourselves if we didn't do our part."

Clearing his throat, appearing self-conscious, Amos then piped up to say, "I've decided to stay home and finish my seminary training."

All eyes had turned to him but no one spoke.

Quietly accepting, Frank Senior nodded his head and then he gave his other two sons one last pleading look before he diverted his eyes, saying not one more word.

The tears streaming down Frank's mother and sister's faces had hurt the most.

Frank couldn't stop the many horrible images that blazed a trail across his thoughts of what he'd encountered in the war, scenes that no eighteen-year-old had any business witnessing. But they had happened none-the-less. Frank had to shut down his mind and refocus on his problem at hand, which was his wounded brother and where the Rebs were taking them. While staring at Pike's unconscious form, his heart, unable to stop the onslaught of dread, fluttered with fear.

*

The troupe traveled several miles before Frank recognized the outskirts of the town of Richmond. Soon, they faced the long main street with its hustle and bustle. Frank couldn't help but note the many comments thrown at them as they plodded. "Damn Yankees! Pigs! Why don't you just shoot them?"

Trying to turn a deaf ear as they passed the angry eyes, Frank kept his own averted. But the angry comments only added to his discomfort and brought his ever-present fear to a boiling point.

One local man, dressed in a clean suit and highly polished boots, sat atop a striking dapple-gray gelding. For a time, he trotted alongside the wagon and glared at the prisoners. His stony silence screamed loudly of his personal hostility as hate radiated from him like heat from an iron skillet atop a blazing wood stove.

"Hey! Move on, Mister," one of the soldiers finally ordered. But before the local followed the directive, he pierced the Union soldiers with one last withering stare of unadulterated abhorrence. Then, finally, he thumped his mount with his boot and loped away.

*

Strange voices now started to drift into Pike's dreams. The order given by the soldier to the local man brought him fully awake as his eyes fluttered against the bright light. *God help me with the pain!* Pike pleaded inside as he growled and rocked and inched his way slowly to the side of the bouncing wagon. He couldn't help but want a better look, and there was only one way to get that, so he had to steel himself against the thrumming of his thigh.

His unsteady hands had finally managed to grip the sideboards after a few minutes of work, and after several attempts, he pulled himself up high enough to peer over the sides and he was quick to note, *Richmond. Should've known. I knew we were close when they caught us. Where are they taking us?*

The flooding cloud of hurt shook through Pike and fogged his brain. He set his jaw and struggled against it to give himself more time, while thinking. *Must be head-*

ed to the train station. *Only thing I can figure.* A new ripple of agony made him struggle to maintain his grip on the bouncing wagon's side but he set his will yet more firmly against it. *I've seen the station before. I know it's on this side of town.*

Now on the horizon, Pike detected the tiny speck that was to grow into the train depot. It didn't take long for it to bloom and take shape as Pike bounced along. It rose out of the dark and imposing hardwood forest like a specter. Men became visible, swarming about like so many ants at their daily chores. Pike told himself as he watched, *I see some of our boys. Must be hundreds. God, help us . . .I can't count them all.*

When they drew closer, Pike could evaluate the men who were likewise held captive, quickly noting that they were a tattered looking collection and told himself, *I guess we all look that way.* As his eyes drifted around the large encampment, he spied the many prone and frozen bodies of the dead. Pike couldn't look for long - too painful.

Pike decided then and there, *They are shipping us to a prison.* Keeping his throbbing at bay became too much as he continued to be jostled unmercifully. As his injured thigh sent another screeching shiver of pain through his core, he let go of the side of the wagon and flopped back to the wagon's floor, his mind screaming, *I can't take much more of this!*

"Bring those prisoners over here," a gray-clad soldier near the wagon ordered. "Then wait." Within minutes, the man peered over the side of the wagon and sneered as he uttered, "This is where we leave ya. Get this cripple out of the wagon."

Whispering in Pike's ear, Frank said, "Hang on," as he clutched him.

Pike was proud that he managed a tight smile while valiantly straining to assist Frank in moving out of the wagon, but he was soon croaking and huffing and he dropped against the side. "I need help. Sorry."

Lending their backs to the predicament and taking a firm hold of his legs, Tom and Ben half-carried, half-dragged him out of the wagon. Pike couldn't stifle a few moans from the onslaught of pain.

Once Pike was plopped on the ground, the group was able to drag him. But, all at once, a dark form blocked their pathway. Looking up, Pike spied a gargantuan black man. The newcomer took a step and whispered, "Git over. Lemme at him." Single-handedly, the black man took over the operation, hoisting Pike's six-foot-three frame like a sack of feed.

When the man gently set him down by a miniscule fire, a buzzard of light-headedness loomed over Pike. He did manage a breathless, "Thanks," before the man vanished.

Worry, free to race the wind, ran rampant as the men huddled around their wounded leader. Pike, too, couldn't stop his mind's wanderings. *How could this be any worse? Wish we'd been shot fighting rather than this. Wish I were home. What's going to happen to us? Okay, God, You've got to help me endure this. My men too! Give me the will to survive and the strength to heal. I feel weak. You, Lord, can lift me up and heal my wounds. Please Father, You have the power. Amen.*

Still, Pike couldn't keep his thoughts from racing away from God and peace. Seductively, his mind whirled with thoughts of this nightmare being over - permanently. He couldn't help it; death still had its appeal. Death said to him, *Just let go. Stop fighting to get well. Give up. Drift off. Just don't come back. You can go to sweet Rebecca.* Pike heard her voice immediately. "Come on, love." It was too easy, letting go. He allowed himself to drift and felt lighter all at once.

Too quickly, his soldier-side reappeared and scolded, *That's the coward's way out!*

But death wasn't to be denied that easily. It cajoled, *No, it won't matter if you die. Go on. They'll get over it.*

Reason then reappeared and said, *I promised Rebecca I'd come back and we'd get married.* That promise the night before he left to go into the war now came home to roost in his thoughts. As always, he meant to keep his word.

*

"Okay," was what Frank thought he heard from Pike. He wasn't sure, so he knelt and queried in a soft voice, "How're you doing?" Then Frank remembered the rock-hard morsel of bread in his pocket and his fingers latched onto it, then held it out.

Shakily, Pike reached for the bread.

"Take it, Brother," Frank encouraged, noting the pain-filled light in his brother's green eyes. He, too, felt sinister panic rise; deep, lurking, searching for its death grip.

Chapter 2

The whistle of the train came to Pike's ears in several haunting blasts as it chugged closer to where the prisoners were clustered. Waiting with the others, Pike could feel Frank's knees against his shoulders as he uncomfortably rested on the cold ground. The swirling pellets of sleet plinked against his frozen cheeks spinning his morale to a dangerously low level that was equal to the frigid, gray morning. From Pike's position on the ground, his only view was the sea of tightly-packed legs of the other prisoners which blocked Pike's view completely. Ben and Tom stood next to Frank as they vainly attempted to block the north wind from freezing Pike by forming a wall.

Clamping his jaw, as he had been doing for what seemed an eternity, Pike strained against the unrelenting ache and told himself over and over again, *I've got to keep Rebecca here with me*, while he lightly caressed the hair of the watch chain with his fingertips, wishing he were home. Black cinders began to rain around Pike plunking lightly on the frozen ground and on his shoulders, as the train slid and belched its way into the depot.

Wishing and struggling to see through the wall of navy-colored legs, Pike tried to ignore the drumming of his heart, but the thump-thump-thumping of it in his ribcage revealed his own truth. *When we get on this train, we're done for. Guess a lot of us aren't going to live through this. It's going to be hell. Hope I'm wrong. Bet I'm not.*

As the drumming continued blaring in his ears, images of Satan and his demonic angels danced across his mind's eye and blocked out the other sounds around him, sending him into a deep void, but the wave of terror lost its grip on Pike after a few minutes and he began to collect himself. Sighing - tilting his head to look at Frank, he barked, "I can't see! What's going on?"

Staring off in the direction of the waiting train, Frank scowled and shook his head.

Grumping internally with a few choice cuss words, Pike gave up to wait. It didn't take long before he heard orders being yipped behind him.

"Time to load up, big brother," Frank said in a light-hearted voice, one Pike knew must be for his benefit. It was a nice attempt but it fell flat in lifting his troubled spirit.

Knowing it would be some time before they would load onto the train since they were in the back of the pack, Pike had plenty of time for more worry. *Now it's time to face what's to come. God help us. God . . .please. Hope it's not as bad as I think.*

The black giant that had previously assisted Pike came to help him when it was time to load and announced, "I's Buster." Looking up from his frozen pose, Pike couldn't help but note the disfiguring line that ran from the corner of the right side of the big man's mouth to his eye, pulling the corner of his eye downward. It looked strange to Pike that the scar stood out so snow-white against the coal-black skin.

Looking Pike straight in the eye and smiling crookedly with his chocolate-colored, full lips, Buster bent down to lift Pike in one swift motion.

"I don't know how to thank you," Pike huffed as a growl of pain suddenly escaped from him, causing him to fall silent as he strained to stay conscious against the fresh onslaught of agony.

Buster plodded toward the waiting boxcar.

*

As Pike fought to deal with his misery, he watched the men come up the ramp and fill the car to near-bursting. Observing the others, he wondered, *How many are there? There's no place for them to sit. Man, they stink.* The foul body odor was not unfamiliar but his eyes stung and his troubled stomach clutched. Feeling weak and nauseated, Pike reclined against the rough wall closely packed next to five other injured prisoners as cackling laughter floated on the cold air, causing him to lift his heavy head to search for the source.

A greasy, pimply man stuck his head into the open door; a smug smile creased his face. "You kid glove boys ain't goin' to like where yer headed." The light went out of the man's eyes, to turn beady, with a defiant look. "You'll get what ya deserve!"

Pike took note of his fellow prisoners' responses. Some stared icily back while others looked away, trying to ignore him all together. As quickly as he'd appeared, the evil man slipped away, leaving the over-flowing box-car in downtrodden silence.

Suddenly, the train lurched and began to inch forward, sending the standing men swaying with it. *I need to stay awake,* Pike instructed himself. He repeated that one phrase over and over, hoping it would help as the train picked up momentum. It didn't take long for his resolve to crumble as Pike thought, *I'm so cold. This wind. . . ouch, its cutting right through me, or am I just feverish? Will I ever get warm? Will this ever end? How will I make it through?* Pike couldn't help but wonder again how this nightmare would end. Pushing the thoughts from him, he weakly wrapped his coat around himself. No longer able to hold onto consciousness, he escaped into a deep, fitful slumber.

*

Jerking, Pike's body awakened him as the train belched and hissed its way to a stop. The wall of identical legs in front of Pike, his only view, reminded Pike of where he was. *Still on this train. But where are we now?*

The never-ending waves of cold rocked Pike, unrelentingly, as the stinging of his eyes brought his attention back to the men's rotten odor of nervous sweat and human waste. The onslaught of the oppressive stink caused Pike's stomach to wrench violently. Swiping at his burning eyes with the back of his grimy hand and fighting back the nausea, Pike noted Frank standing at his left hip. Through strong eye contact, he gave his brother what support he could.

Blessedly, fresh, February air filtered into the boxcar as the door rattled back along its track, and the men began to disembark. Kneeling beside Pike, Frank said, "I'm going to see what I can find to eat. You hang in there." Frank firmly gripped Pike's shoulder and gave it a squeeze.

Only the injured were left and no one conversed. Pike glanced around and was aware of a wave of heaviness engulfing him - a heaviness that never stayed at bay for long. On the cold afternoon air, he heard soft pleadings from the gut-shot man next to him.

"God, take me now! Don't make me suffer anymore! No more, please!"

Reaching out, Pike began to scoot over to the young man, taking what little strength he had left with the effort. He puffed and let out a few grunts as the hurt ripped through him while moving. As he reached the injured soldier, Pike worked his hand across the rough floor until he touched the man's wrist. Then Pike wrapped his hand around the wrist, not strongly, but he hoped it would be enough to provide the man with some comfort.

The man thrashed a bit, moaning. "Please let me die!" he cried, over and over, but in the midst of his agony he must have realized Pike had his wrist as he in turn latched onto Pike's hand, squeezing it. The action brought swift tears to Pike's eyes as he fully realized this was all he could do.

Soon the prisoners were herded back onto the train. Rushing to his brother's side, Frank knelt beside Pike and said, "I got you something," before he handed Pike a slab of bread.

Retrieving the dry clump, Pike managed to choke it down, never letting go of the injured soldier. He whispered to Frank, "Can you do anything for him?" Frank's response was a grim shake of his head.

Knowing the soldier he gripped was dying zapped what residue of strength Pike had gathered. His morale hit rock bottom and a wave of sleep swept over him with tidal voracity. All he could do was close his eyes.

*

It was sometime the following day when Pike awoke. As his eyes readjusted to the light, Pike realized that his escape into his dream world had given him back a modicum of strength since he felt a bit clearer-headed. First, he pivoted his head, remembering the injured man next to him. The blank, staring eyes of the young man beside him told him he was finally free of all his hurt and suffering.

Pike didn't know whether to give thanks or cry. Reality was something he just couldn't comprehend anymore. The pain was too sharp - too hard.

Who-o-sh! The engine, commencing another stop, released its pent-up steam as the whistle blasted. A shaft of energy rolled through Pike as he heard from outside, "Okay, everybody off!" Now, Pike knew the worst was likely to come.

Tension replaced the energy burst as Pike realized this leg of the journey was over. At least he felt a little stronger as the fever had broken. But, what was next for them?

"Thank heaven, its warmer," Frank stated, as Pike's group waited to dismount the train.

"We've been heading south this whole time," Ben observed. It was a truth they were all aware of, but Ben seemed to need to state it anyway.

Buster could be seen working his way through the throng of men to Pike's side. Tilting his head back, Pike gaped at the scarred man. Awash with gratitude for Buster's presence, Pike said, as he moved stiffly, "I don't think you are going to have to carry me anymore. If you can just let me lean on you, I think I can walk."

"Okay," Buster replied as he lent his large hands in assisting Pike in rising to his unsteady feet. "Leans on my shoulder, there. I's goin' to hold round you's middle." Buster maintained a tight grip on Pike and waited for him to find his balance.

Blood rushed from Pike's head as his right foot kept

him upright. "Damn!" he cursed as he grappled with the fact that he was still as weak as a newborn. He fussed at himself, *Don't faint . . .don't faint . . .get a grip.* A few seconds later as his head cleared enough for him to slant his eyes at Buster, Pike announced, "Okay, I'm ready."

Since the wounded were the last to be removed from the car, Pike's view remained unhampered as he hobbled to the top of the ramp. He paused to gawk at the chaotic scene playing out before him while men milled about everywhere.   The sea of gray and navy colors swirled together like an ever-changing school of salmon. As soon as he adjusted to the sight, Pike and his band clunked down the ramp and into the masses to be swallowed up in the commotion

Leaning hard on Buster's shoulder, Pike turned his head, taking in the towering pines rising around the edge of the depot. "We've got to be in the deep south, Frank," Pike stated.

"Think you're right. You think we're going to Andersonville?"

"I've heard tell about the place," Ben blurted with a down-turned mouth before anyone else had a chance to say anything.

Pike had heard of Andersonville prison too. *Is that where we're headed?* he wondered with pure dread lacing through his heart.

*

While Pike bumped along in the wagon into which he had been loaded, Frank and the others tramped over the trail to their new fate. At first sight, the prison brought images that sank Pike's heart. While Pike strained his eyes, watching the prison come slowly into better clarity, he couldn't help but drink in every detail.

Towering above the Georgian soil stood hundreds of rough-hewn pine logs attached to one another to fashion the boundaries of the prison. Scores of Rebel soldiers milled about its exterior. Hastily-constructed houses and storage buildings, rough and unpainted, had been erected at the western edge of the complex. On the south end, the guard's light-colored tents, at least fifty or more, stood in several straight lines and contrasted with the dark forest backdrop.

As Pike gazed somberly up at the top of the prison walls, he noted the "pigeon roosts" for the first time. These regularly-set sentry posts were crudely covered and stood at thirty-foot intervals.

The wagon came to a jolting halt not far from the west wall. Knowing it was time to face his fate, Pike's pulse blared in his temples as an order came from somewhere behind him.

"Get the wounded prisoners outta them wagons."

Turning toward the voice, Pike looked at the soldier calling out the order. In amazement, he noted that the sentry couldn't have been more than sixteen or seventeen. He also noticed a man standing in front of the largest house. Dressed smartly in a captain's uniform, the man's eyes seemed to be held captive by the arrival of the new prisoners. *That must be the boss man,* Pike thought to himself as his gaze lingered, taking in the details of the captain's well-worn face.

Like a guardian angel, Buster suddenly appeared. "What would I do without you?" Pike declared to his new-found friend as he struggled to pull himself upright. Once he was hauled out of the wagon, Pike stood shakily on his right foot while Buster propped him up with his massive frame. As they began to walk, Pike's shoe on his useless left foot drug a line in the dust causing a new crop of throbbing for Pike to deal with.

Frank, Tom and Ben hovered nearby, all looking scared out of their wits, studying the scene before them and the towering prison walls. It was time to face their fate - whatever may come. Together, the new and old companions turned and slowly trudged toward the huge double gates that were swinging open to the mass of prisoners. All of the newcomers were rocked to a standstill, frozen in time, as they spied the chaos inside.

Pike drank in the narrow snippet of life that would soon be his. Inside the exterior walls, recessed about fifteen feet stood another rough pine wall that encompassed the entire sixteen acre prison. Soon, Pike would learn this was called the "dead line" because any prisoner caught crossing into this open space would be shot and there would be no second chances.

Now gawking through the second set of doors, Pike could see the squalid living conditions. What crude structures he could see were made of a mish-mash of materials, mostly tent canvas, but many other types were being used. Then, Pike couldn't help but note the men swarming about inside the prison and his mind quickly pointed out, *There's got to be thousands of them. Oh God, what have you done to me?*

The swelling roar of the crowd struck Pike like a physical slap, knocking him back into Frank. His ears couldn't decipher any one particular sound as it was too much - too loud. He screamed inside, *I can't take this. Father, take me away from here!* The crowd of men behind Pike shoved forward, pushing him and his group into the depths of their freshest and most sinister hell.

*

Sharing Pike's terror, Frank felt an icy stab clutching his stomach and bladder which threatened to let go as he gawked into the depths of Andersonville. Frank's terror-seized mind shrieked, *How can there be so many? Can it be thousands? Where will we go? How'll we live?*

After being roughly bumped from behind, forcing him forward, Frank let go of his frightful thoughts to trudge forward with the mass of prisoners. It took but a scant few seconds to trickle through the gates and enter into the unreal world - his new home. His eyes swept left, then, riveted back, noting the men and tents - filth - everywhere. A few well-used trails existed through the jigsaw puzzle of a slum, but with no rhyme or reason as they twisted this way and that, around and through the hordes of tents.

"Let's stop a minute", Pike commanded breathlessly and stood panting. "So that I can think."

Only too glad to follow Pike's directive, Frank trailed along beside Pike and Buster, feeling as lost as a Canadian goose in a tornado, hoping to find some haven within the hysteria. "What're we gonna do, Pike?" Frank squeaked.

After several tense minutes Pike said softly, weakly, as he drooped beside Buster, "Stick together." As his green eyes gaped around, all at once they lit up.

"What is it" Frank asked. "You got an idea?"

"No. Thought I saw someone I knew. Not sure though. Got to go on to see. He's sitting just beyond that clump of men standing there with the Indian-looking brute." Pike lifted his nose in the direction to look, backing up his words.

Frank had taken note of the powerful looking half-breed talking to the new prisoners, but he wasn't sure which man Pike had pointed out. "Want to head for them and see?" Frank encouraged, hope framing his words.

"Only choice we've got."

Not able to help but be concerned for Pike, Frank knew Pike still looked sickly pale, showing just what a precarious position he was in. It caused him to ask with his brotherly concern, "You up to moving, Brother? We can wait some more."

"No. We need to get going. I'll be alright."

Although Frank didn't like the pallid color of his brother's face, especially the gray lips, he noted the pre-datory-sharp gaze in Pike's eyes, showing his determination. Following Pike, the group started forward. Frank decided to stay focused on Pike to avoid thinking about the swirl of activity around them as it was the only thing he had left that he could do.

"You boys looking for a place to stay?" a deep voice growled.

Caught off guard by the question, Frank turned, as did his whole group, to see the thick-bodied, droopy-jowled, red-eyed, half-breed man blocking their path. The man's ragged followers stood in a cluster behind him, all eyes on the newcomers.

The rank stranger didn't seem put off by the lack of response as he questioned again, "Hey, you boys thick between the ears?" His dark eyes studied each of them carefully, in turn. As his black, cloudy eyes came to rest on Buster, his eyes opened wide in surprise and he stared for a few beats at the big man.

Guess he's never seen such a big, black man, Frank reasoned to himself. *Don't know why else he'd look that way.*

Pike, Tom and Ben stood quietly, taking in the man's actions as no one seemed to understand what was going on.

A mean-spirited light registered in the man's black eyes for a split second before he opened his mouth again. "Well, well, if it ain't Nigger Boy. Smack my ass. Didn't get to tell ya how much I enjoyed that night with your sweet wife."

Swinging his gaze to Buster, Frank still did not comprehend what was taking place and hoped to figure it all out, quickly.

In a flash, Buster dropped Pike into a groaning heap beside his big, worn boot. Emitting a guttural growl, Buster churned forward, arms in front of him, hands outstretched, lethal fury etched into every line of his face.

Not shrinking from Buster's charge, the stranger leapt straight at him, arms sweeping forward, slamming into Buster's trunk-like midsection with his head. The men who had been standing behind the half-breed hopped into the melee as if on cue, and the fighting spread as fast as new gossip among an old lady's sewing circle.

Riveted in his spot, Frank gaped, struggling to understand what had just happened. Why was everyone fighting? A struggling duo slammed into him from behind, knocking him off his feet, causing him to slap the ground hard. When he was able to collect himself and look for Pike again, he couldn't see him for the men swarming around were blocking his view.

I've to get him, Frank instantly realized as he broke his trance and forced his feet to move. He leapt forward but instantly lost his footing as he tripped over a man grappling with Ben on the ground, just under his feet. He slammed into the pair and fell over them. *Damn!* his mind screamed as he strained to get up and find Pike.

Flopping over the two men grappling under him,

Frank felt a kick in the shins, elbow in the belly. But, he ignored it all as he glared forward, hoping for a glimpse of Pike's red head and hoped against hope, *Let him be okay!* Soon enough he rolled to his unsteady feet and spotted Pike a short ten feet in front of him, with a man bent over his prostrate form, looking him in the face, hand holding onto his coat collar. Frank could see Pike returning the man's gaze.

God help him, Frank pleaded as he shoved forward with blind rage blazing in his heart. *I'll kill him if he's hurt him.* Coming up behind the stranger, Frank grabbed the tall man roughly by the back of the elbow and as he yanked back his fist, Pike's pain-choked voice penetrated his blind rage.

"Don't, Frank, I know him."

A hornet suddenly blasted past Frank's right side and found its mark in a stranger nearby, dropping him like a stone which caused all fighting to freeze.

The man who had been shot crumpled over from where he had been sitting on Ben's chest, pounding his face. The dead man toppled over, spraying blood, to land partially on the cold ground and still partially on Ben.

Pale and bloodied, Ben swiftly rolled the man off his legs and rose to his knees while another ringing shot pierced a man about eight feet from Frank. He, too, fell into a broken heap.

*

The searing agony of Pike's thigh made it impossible for him to focus, but the explosion of the guns pierced into his frail thoughts. Pike looked up to see Frank still holding the arm of his friend and former philosophy teacher, Professor Collin Danvil. "Let him go, Frank."

As soon as Frank released his arm, Collin turned to Pike. "Come on, son, we've gotta get out of here. Let me help you." He latched onto Pike's prostrate form and huffed as he tried to move him.

Stepping in to help his brother, Frank and Buster grabbed onto Pike. That was all that was needed to get Pike up and moving.

"This way," Danvil cried as he sprinted off through

the crowd of running bodies, showing the way.

Racked with agony, Pike began to slip away. The most difficult days of his life, the days of bleeding, little food and high fever had left him on the brink of death. And now, the fighting and gunshots were more than his body could take. *No, God. Don't take me now!* With these final pleas, the world disintegrated, setting Pike free to roam the worlds where he felt safest and where hurt did not exist.

Chapter Three

When Pike awakened several hours later, he was aware that night had taken over from the day. Even before his sight cleared from the hazy clouds that hung like clumps in his vision, he recognized his brother's voice. "Pike, can you hear me? Look at me. Can you do that?"

Unable to do more than roll his head until Frank's familiar form came into view, Pike blinked rapidly and repeatedly, working to further clear his eyesight. The first thing he noted as he looked back above him was the tent canvas. Then, he returned his gaze to his little brother's broken face, long beard and truly troubled expression.

It was easy for Pike to note the trembling of Frank's lower lip, the flooded eyes. Next, Pike became aware of Frank's warm forehead on his temple after Frank listed over to rest against the side of his head and Pike heard Frank's sigh. *Wish I could reach out to Frank. Give him comfort. Can't though. Feel frozen. Am I dead? Am I?* The movement beside Pike brought him back to reality when Ben plopped next to Frank as he could see Ben in the dim light. Feeling another person on his left, Pike rolled his head and was aware of his behemoth, dark protector.

At least if I'm dead, I'm in good company, Pike told himself. He strained to force his stiff lips to do his bidding and move but a tiny croak was all he could manage. *Am I alive . . .or dead?*

Taking over in the gap of silence, Frank brought

home to Pike that he was still among the living when his words registered, "Pike, your friend has given us a place to stay. So don't worry about us. They've got some cornbread and beans. We're going to lift you. See what we can get in you. We need to get water in you too. You'll feel better."

Together, Buster and Frank hoisted Pike. That's when Pike's old college professor came into his line of sight. Seemed like only yesterday, instead of five years, since he'd been in one of Collin Danvil's classes, discussing how life of a thousand years ago was just like the life of today-with the same wants and needs, same problems.

Danvil's curly, floppy mop of brown hair sure hadn't changed and his wry smile brought comfort to Pike where none had resided but moments before. Collin bent over Pike as he entreated, "Here now, eat some of this. But first, take a swig of water. You need that more than anything." The professor held out a battered tin cup, half-filled with cold water. He wasted no time in pressing it against Pike's cracked and raw lips and tilting it back.

Pike managed to swallow most of the cup's contents. Next, came the food and after the water had moistened the way, it went down much more easily. Pike managed to swallow a piece of cornbread and a few scoops of beans before he shook his head that he was done.

"That's all you can eat?" Frank queried, trying to encourage Pike into taking a few more bites.

"That's it," Pike struggled to say. "Too tired. Sorry." Then, his head flopped back.

Carefully, Buster and Frank lowered Pike back to let him rest against his army-issue backpack. When Pike drifted off this time, it wasn't into unconsciousness, but into a slumber filled with sweet Rebecca. With Rebecca, came the familiar comfort and welcome fire it stoked within his core.

*

Lost in one of those dreams of remembrance of Rebecca and their love, Pike could feel as well as smell the humid, cloying, living, deep-summer air of his familiar Baltimore. The heavy night wrapped around him as tightly as an infant swaddled by his protective mother, as he slipped from his family's home, out the creaky front door, with one thought - go to Rebecca - find the comfort only she could provide.

He tripped across the well-groomed lawn on his way to his other haven, the square wooden barn. As he pushed through the front, swinging doors, the familiar peace from within the confines washed over him which was brought on by the familiar scents, causing an unconscious smile to form. As always, his steps quickened.

Nickering a satiny tune of welcome, Hank, his favorite horse, shoved his bulky head over his stall's half-door, seemingly eager for Pike's company. The gelding nudged him with the end of his bristly nose and blew several short blasts of air through his nostrils, talking to Pike in his horsy tone. Then, he sniffed along Pike's cheek. Pike's hand lightly traveled the length of the gelding's nose and wandered to his flat forehead to stroke it unconsciously before he attached a lead rope to Hank's halter and took a moment to lean against the animal's warm neck, to rest, to ponder. Thoughts of what tomorrow would bring, as he was to leave and join the army and the raging civil war, flowed through his thoughts.

After saddling Hank, he led him out of the barn. The star on the buckskin's forehead shone brightly in the glow from the almost-full moon. The welcome drops of liquid light from the festive heavens would allow him to easily cover the five miles to Rebecca's family home.

As Pike swung his right leg over the saddle and searched for the stirrup with his boot toe, he silently and fervently hoped he would be able to awaken Rebecca and get her out of the house - without stirring her parents. *I've got to see her one last time. I need to tell her myself, I'm leaving. She's going to be mad as a hornet. Can't help that. Maybe she will understand, but probably not. Hope she'll wait for me to come home. Sure want to marry her . . .but can't think of that now. Got to do this.*

Got to look out for Frank. Damn this war to hell. Why did it have to happen?

"Okay, boy, let's go," Pike cued his steady mount, urging him quickly into a long ground-covering lope. Though Pike's heart was wrapped in lead at having to give up his personal dreams, he knew he had to face what came his way in the war. He also knew that joining the war was going to change his life forever - maybe for the worse. But, what could he do?

"Things don't always turn out the way we'd planned, Hank," he declared to his working horse. By saying his thoughts out loud, he hoped he would feel better about leaving Rebecca behind - but he didn't. The time in the saddle did provide him with a few minutes to wrestle with his emotions and to try to cement his resolve to face Rebecca. He took a break from his internal battle to gaze at the faraway, glowing moon, wondering for the hundredth time if anyone lived on that distant orb, a point that his class had argued in his favorite professor's class at the university - none other than Collin Danvil.

Even though the ride took twenty minutes, it wasn't long enough by far, for Pike to come to grips with the difficulties in telling Rebecca he was leaving her, maybe to never to return. When he trotted down the path to Rebecca's house, he wasted no time in tying Hank, to tip-toe to Rebecca's bedroom window and to lightly rap on it with a knuckle. After a few small taps he found himself startled when his girl appeared, smiling into his eyes, her light-brown hair cascading heavily down her back.

She nervously tucked her locks behind her ears as she asked, "What are you doing here?"

"Can you come out?" Pike whispered through the glass. He grinned his quirky, dimple-cheeked grin. "I've got to talk to you. It's important."

Rebecca nodded and instantly replied, "Give me a minute and I'll get dressed."

"Hurry, I've missed you."

"Me, too." She pivoted to disappear into the darkness of her room. It took but a few short minutes for her to reappear around the corner of the house.

Seeing his love stirred a hunger within Pike. As his eyes drank in every detail of Rebecca, the moonlight bounced from her soft, blue dress. She seemed to almost glow as she glided swiftly toward him, causing Pike's blood to hum even more. His stomach tightened as his true love closed the gap between them as it always did whenever they were together. And like always, Pike felt it difficult to breathe but he couldn't help reveling in his rising wave of youthful desire - flaming and unquenchable.

Rebecca rose on her tip-toes to brush her soft lips across his cheek. "Hop up on Hank," he whispered. "Let's go someplace where we can visit awhile."

When she found her seat in the creaky saddle, Pike swung up behind her and took advantage of the excuse to wrap his arms around her. As his chest met and pressed against her petite back, the contact caused his passions to rise. *Umm . . .sure wish I could kiss her. She looks so pretty tonight. I'm going to miss this. How can I let her go? Do I have to? . . .do I?*

Cueing Hank with a kissing sound, Pike continued to clutch Rebecca as the buckskin freely trotted forward. In less than a quarter of a mile he turned off the road, into a field, to their favorite place; a far-reaching silver-leaf maple. Pike pulled Hank back to an animated walk and when they reached the tree, stopped.

"Let's get off here," Pike huffed into his love's ear. As soon as they dismounted, Pike cleared his throat nervously several times, then held his arm out to direct Rebecca to the tree's base.

Easily, Rebecca led the way through the moon-lit grass. Together they sat under the tree's sweeping branches, to lean against the rough bark. Silence hovered over them while Pike listened to the locust's tune and fought to gather his courage. Clearing his voice with a couple of coughs, he started by saying, "You know I love you with all my heart."

"Yes." She plucked up his hand and lightly rubbed it on her cheek. Then, she placed a whisper of a kiss on its palm.

It was impossible for Pike to stop the shiver that reverberated through him. Next, the unexpected onslaught of his desire clouded his thinking so easily, it frightened him. *Get hold of yourself. You can't think about how much you want her. You've got to tell her. Go on . . .get it over with. You hear me? I said get a hold of yourself.*

Doing his best to control his passionate longings, he shakily began. "I've got to tell you something, sweet. I hope you won't hate me for it. It's something I've got to do. Tomorrow . . .I'm leaving to sign up to fight in the war.

Rebecca didn't say anything but she gasped as she dropped his hand, then blurted, "No, Pike! Don't do this to me . . to us. I can't stand the thought of losing you. We were supposed to get married in October. I've dreamed about it for so long. Don't do this to us." Her watery eyes, glowing with hurt pleaded with him. "Please," she added, then quit trying, dropping her eyes, body slumping over.

I don't want to go, Pike told himself as his own fear and desires rampaged within. *Look at her. I can see how much she loves me. How can I leave? But, how can I let Frank go without me? I can't.* Pike felt the weight of his decision pressing against him, causing the next thoughts. *I know it's what I've got to do. I can't let Frank go without me. He might get killed. He'd think I was a coward and I would be. Can't let that happen. Can I?*

Cementing his resolve before he replied, Pike said somewhat gruffly, "This is something I have to do. I can't hide while others fight in my place. Anyhow, Frank is going and I can't let him go by himself. I've got to look out for him. You have to understand. I promise I'll come back. When the war is over, we'll get married for sure. Will you wait for me?" Pike grabbed Rebecca's slack hand and gripped it, and waited, eyes locked onto her teary eyes.

A few tears trickled down her cheeks then sobs broke, waving from her as she put her head in her arms over her bent knees.

The crying weakened Pike's resolve, which threatened to crumble all together. Wanting to soften the situation, he began by soothing, "It will only be for a little while, I promise. This war is going to be over before you know it. Just hang on. Will you do that?" He planted a kiss on her wet cheek.

The sniffling continued for a time, but her tears finally eased. She hiccupped as she said, "I'll do this because I have to. Don't get killed. I couldn't stand losing you. Come back to me."

The only answer Pike could muster was a kiss - swift and passionate - sweeping down upon her. As he lost himself in the pleasure of the contact, his thoughts wandered back to his body's wants. *Feels like I'm on fire. God help me. I want her so much. Should I? Should we?*

Every fiber of Pike's being sang with his youthful lust as his cravings demanded his full attention, causing him to be aware of how unsteady he felt, his self-control slipping. As he deepened his kiss, the pair drifted from their sitting position to stretch out on the warm grass. Leaving Rebecca's mouth, Pike let his lips drift along her jaw to the tender skin of her neck, and he nuzzled her there for a moment, drinking in the scent of her skin.

She responded to his touch with soft sounds of pleasure - almost too faint to hear.

The moment of letting go presented itself. Pulling back from kissing Rebecca, Pike gazed deeply into her yearning eyes as he noted his own ragged breathing. He asked, "Do you want to stop? We've got to. I can't take any more of this. You are too beautiful." His words drifted away as he took several purifying breaths.

Flashing a fleeting, shy smile, Rebecca then averted her gaze for a second. Slowly, she raised her eyes to lock onto his. "I've dreamed of this moment. Nothing will stop us now. Not tonight." There was no more need for discussion as she planted her lush lips on his.

*

Pike awakened with a start and as his eyes fluttered he wondered. *It must be night, as black as it is. How late is it? I don't hear much.* Taking advantage of the quiet to revel in the warmth that still flushed his body from the dream that was his reality the night before he had joined the civil war, Pike rested. He welcomed the lingering heat of their shared passion. While enjoying himself, he breathed deep, cleansing his mind, remembering.

Turning his head to the right, he spied Frank snoring lightly beside him and to his left lay Buster's imposing form. A deep moan, from somewhere nearby stopped Pike's warm revelry. He lost the last scraps of joy as reality flushed his veins with its icy vengeance. For several minutes, moans and coughs, coupled with, "Help me. I'm dying," continued to come to Pike. The man's obvious pain was too much to bear.

What can I do? With as much force as he could muster, he cried out, "Someone help that man!" But, his voice came out as a tiny squeak so no one responded, and as grim as the reality was, no one could help. There was nothing Pike could do but suffer along with the man, listening to the dying, lonely soldier and wonder if his fate would soon be the same.

After some time the pleadings stopped but the moans continued for awhile longer - eventually, they ceased. Pike's stomach, which had felt twisted by the man's suffering, finally relaxed. *Why is being a soldier such a dry business? Hope he will be okay,* Pike told himself as a way to avoid what he knew was the truth of the matter - there would be no escape for the unknown soldier, nor himself.

In the welcome quiet, Pike closed his eyes and wished for five minutes of time with Rebecca. *How many nights of Rebecca's body have I missed? Since I've been gone three years, guess a lot. God, I miss her.* His own mournful moan escaped into the black night. It was a long time before sleep took over Pike's troubled mind.

*

When the first shafts of light pierced the sky to chase away the dark, Frank's eyes opened. The dread for Pike was Frank's one thought. *Please, God, don't have taken him in the night.* This prayer joined the constant procession of others Frank kept sending heavenward as he turned back to his injured brother.

Rising to a cramped sitting position since all the

men were packed like sardines, Frank quietly eased over his brother's pale face and prayed for signs of life. *Thank you, Lord!,* there was a noticeable rise and fall of Pike's chest.

The other men began to stir and Pike's eyes fluttered, then gazed into Frank's. "You okay?" Frank inquired as he strained for signs of mental clarity.

"I think I'm better," came Pike's tremulous answer.

Thrilled beyond measure to note the stronger quality of Pike's voice, Frank had his answer - Pike was going to live.

"How's he?" Buster asked in his hushed baritone.

Pike managed a grin and a nod at his newfound friend.

"Good," Buster nodded as he continued to stare.

Clearing his throat from behind Buster, Collin inquired, "You boys ready to head to the sumps?"

"Pike," Frank said, "Collin and the other three from his group are taking us out to show us around. When we get back, I'll tell you about it. I'm not sure what we'll see, but guess we've got to go. We're real lucky we ran into him. They seem like a good group."

"Sure, you go on. I'll wait here. Guess I can't keep up today."

The subtle humor wasn't lost on Frank. He grinned at his brother while his heart sang, *It's a good day, even if we are in this hellhole!*

Buster didn't move when the group crawled out of the tent. "I's stay if you's needs me to."

"No, you go. I'll be fine. Thanks though."

Frank looked back into the tent as Buster began his crawl out. "Be back soon," Frank offered as he grinned and gave Pike one last wave of his hand.

*

The familiar voice of Frank brought Pike out of his daze. As the men dribbled back under the tent, they squeezed in to find their place in the dirt. "You weren't gone long," Pike observed, eyes trained on Frank and Buster as they sat beside him.

"Who'd want to?" Frank mumbled, looking down, as

he ran a quick hand through his dirty blonde hair.

Pike couldn't miss the weary creases in Frank's forehead and around his mouth which caused him to ask, "What'd you see?"

After scooting in next to Frank, grinning down at Pike, Collin asked, "How's the patient?"

"I'm better." But he couldn't wait any longer, so he questioned again, "What's this hellhole like?"

Out tumbled Frank's words. "You should have seen it! I couldn't believe it at first. We hadn't gone more than fifty feet when we saw a man just lying on the ground - dead. Couldn't believe it. Looked like he had been gone awhile. He was stiff. Must of died in the night. Guess he had nowhere to go." Frank's words suddenly stopped. He dropped his vision and shook his head. As he was looking down he mumbled, "He wasn't the only one we saw."

Since Frank had paused from telling his story, the professor hopped into the silence, working to ease the tension. "Time to tell you fellas what you need to know. You've gotta understand a few things. Got to, if we're going to keep ourselves alive. After I do, then I'll rustle up something for us to eat. Then, I'd like to hear from this big fellow here," he indicated Buster with his head. "I need to know and you'll understand why after I explain a few things."

Pausing, Collin glanced around to make sure he had everyone's undivided attention. "First let me tell you a few things about me and my men. We were a part of the Pennsylvania 101 Unit. This man to my right is James Oldfield."

James nodded as part of the introductions. Pike looked the short-of-stature, thin man over, noting he appeared to be book-wormish, like the professor. His physique did not speak of hard work or time in the sun. James did appear older than most with deep lines in his forehead, crinkles at the corners of his eyes and a defined sag in the skin under his chin, and he was unwashed and ragged, as they all were.

"He's from Pittsburgh," Collin added. "He taught English at the University too."

"Now this is Daniel Reynolds from Farmington, Pennsylvania. The young man the professor pointed to was a stringy, scarecrow of a man.

Maybe he's a farmer, Pike mused. *Sure looks like one!*

"And the last one in the back," Collin pointed to the dark-complexioned man, "is 'Sharp Shooter' or just 'Shooter'. Been known to shoot the eye out of a turkey at one hundred and fifty yards."

Rugged and stout, the man rose and quickly made friends, shaking hands all around. "Glad to know you. And, where might you all be from?" he inquired, face open and interested.

Hopping in for the group, Frank offered the introductions and finished by saying, "We're all from the New York 12th."

With the introductions completed, Collin rose to pace in what little space he could. His spectacles were perched on the bridge of his nose reminding Pike of the many lectures he'd heard in the past, causing him to grin internally.

"Let me tell you how things work. My men were captured and brought here a couple of weeks ago. It took several grueling days by railroad to get here. When we came to the front gates, we were shocked and amazed, just as you seem to be. We didn't know what to do or how to survive. Luckily, we had most of our gear still with us. We pooled what we had and found some extra stick poles. We've stuck together and it's kept us alive."

While his pacing continued, Collin wasn't shy with gazing at each of the newcomers. A serious expression painted his face as he continued. "A stream runs through the middle of the prison. It's the main source of drinking water. Men are forced to use it, since little water is provided. But, men also use it for washing and relieving themselves near it. So don't use the creek for anything. If you do, you'll regret it. I've seen many sick men die from drinking the water. We call it 'The Bitch'. It looks good from a distance, but she'll get you for sure if you give in."

His brown eyes pierced the listeners as he added for emphasis, "I'm telling you boys, stay clear of it. If you know what's good for you."

Ben's young face pinched, he queried, "Then what do you do for water?"

"Well," Danvil said, "we catch runoff from the tent in anything we can. We use our blankets to soak up rain and wring them into our canteens. What else can we do?" He peered over his glass rims as he added, "We'll die for sure if we don't. We've been okay, so far."

Pike couldn't help but see the disturbed and fearful faces of his comrades - all but Buster. Buster appeared as calm and unflappable as ever.

Collin continued, "Noise, as I'm sure you've noticed, is another factor; smells, too. The roar of all these prisoners, and more coming in all the time, is like Niagara Falls. Any of you been there?"

The newcomers all shook their heads.

"Well, then, let me tell you. It's so loud most all the time - like now, you have to talk loud to be heard."

Breaking in, Frank asked, "Doesn't it ever get quiet?"

"It's way into the night before it ever gets close to quiet. Then, you can hear the sick ones. They moan and plead for help. I know for me, sometimes it's more than I can stand. It'll make you wish for the day to cover up the painful noises of the sick."

"Now, you've all noticed the smell. Can't do much about that other than stay upwind of the sump area."

The professor ended his lecture with some encouragement. "With everyone sticking together, we'll see if we can't ride out this terrible storm. Men die quickly out there." He backed up his words with a hitching of his thumb over his shoulder.

"We get our rations daily if they've got enough to go around. Usually it is some corn-shuck-riddled cornmeal. If they give us some sticks we make cornbread. It isn't much but we get by on it best we can. When they've got bacon or beans, we'll get that. But, it's usually pretty slim pickins."

It had hit home with Pike that he and all the others were in a precarious live-or-die situation. He had known that all along but now, it was worse than he'd originally figured. Who were the ones who would succumb and die? Only time would tell that tale.

"The prisoners die so fast," Collin continued, "that a man can spend all day helping the sick and hauling the dead out to the front gate for disposal. If you are up to the work, your time will pass more quickly. When rations are few and far between, we'll get weak quick. I don't expect that to get any better, probably worse. At least we have each other. No one lasts here long without friends."

"Something else you need to know. There is a group in here we call 'The Raiders'. These men sneak around, mostly at night, and pilfer what they want. They'll take what they want or kill you in the trying. They don't care much that we all used to fight on the same side. Be careful about getting into scrapes with them. A small injury can spell doom in here. Infections and dysentery are our number one killers."

Before continuing, the professor paused to look directly at Buster. "Let me tell you a bit about 'The Raiders'. The leader is that half-breed that jumped Buster. His name is Drisco. But, I guess Buster already knew that."

Nodding, Buster said nothing.

"Well, anyhow," Collin continued, "there are quite a few men that run with that bunch. His cousin Rufus is one. What I want to do now is turn the talking over to Buster. Let him tell us how he knows Drisco. With trouble brewing between them, we've got to know what happened with you two in the past. While he tells us his story, I'll scrape up some vittles."

Pike felt his own curiosity piqued about his new black friend. Now that he'd been filled in on life in Andersonville, he was anxious to understand how his newest friend had ended up fighting in this war and how Drisco fit into that story. "Buster, you mind telling us?" Pike jumped in to see how his friend felt.

"No. I's tell you. Lemme start from the beginning."

Chapter Four

"I never knowed there was life different than workin' on a plantation. Hard work all's I ever knowed. When I's a li'l boy they called me Jonas. My ma's a strong woman and she reared me by herself. I runs wild for my youngen years, so my ma could work all day. I loves the woods and liked to stay out of the drafty ol' shanty we was livin' in.

"I had a real good friend. Her name was Daria. We growed up together. She was a quiet girl that didn't smile much 'cept when she was with me. Since I's big for my age, I was made to work when I's still a might young. Didn't get to play with Daria much after that. But, she's always special to me. I hoped one day when we was older, we's could live together. Sometimes, da Master allowed that.

"Anyhow, one night, when I was growed up, I went out for my nightly walk. Of course. . ." A shy crooked smile grew on Buster's face. ". . .by my girl's shanty."

The men chuckled at his shyness and Pike couldn't help but chime in. A new light shone in Buster's eyes as he continued his story and Pike could easily see the spark of life radiating through Buster.

"I was startled when I see a man goin' into Daria's shanty. I's see red, I was so mad at that man. So, I burst through the front door and saw the back of the man holdin' Daria. I don't know how I got the skillet in my hand, but the next thing I knows, I hit the man in the head. It was the Masta's son, Lucas! I see he was dead.

'Girl, we's in trouble now,' I told Daria. "We gots to run. Are you ready?'

"She nodded her head and said nothin'.

"So, after I hides Lucas in the big pond, we run. We was lucky when we runs away because the first barn we slept in belonged to a widowed man that helped us get to another man that was part of a bunch called the 'Underground Railroad.' These people gots slaves safe to the North."

While Buster's eyes rested on Pike, where they seemed most comfortable, Pike grinned into the troubled eyes of the black man, hoping to encourage him.

"Here, take this," the professor directed Pike as he held out the meager fare.

"Thank you, Professor," Pike managed. "I think I'm better. This is just what I need."

"You're welcome. Glad you are coming around. How about you, Buster. Ready for some?"

Giving a slight bob of his head, Buster paused from speaking, lost in his memories. Absently, he took a bite, chewing.

Anxious to hear more, Pike encouraged, "So, Buster, keep talking, this is a good story."

Before Buster could respond, Ben piped up, "Were you and Daria happy after that?"

Pike chuckled to himself because obviously, he wasn't the only one captivated by the black man's story, which pulled up his own thoughts of Rebecca. His hand folded into the left pocket of his worn and bloody army-issue pants. As his fingers slipped around the ribbon of watch chain, Rebecca's image floated into his mind's eye. She grinned back at him. Her twinkling smile and loving eyes brought a flush of warmth as surely as if he'd just come in contact with a roaring fire. *Must be feeling better,* Pike mused.

With a well of pain displayed in his eyes, Buster swiveled to look at Ben.

Pike's stomach fluttered in response to the grief-stricken expression, chasing away his stirrings for Rebecca. He took several cleansing breathes to clear his inner tension. Suddenly, a bell clanged off behind Pike which caused him to gawk around to locate its source.

"What's that?" Tom inquired as the professor's group stirred and began to rise.

"Come on 'Shooter' directed. "It's the ration bell. Better hurry to get in line."

Frank looked to Pike, eyebrows cocked.

"You all go ahead and get in line with the rest. I'll be fine."

Wasting no more time, the group scurried off.

*

Pike scraped the bottom of his bowl of beans, noting the cupful portion. It wasn't much, but was more than breakfast which might satisfy his stomach for the time being. *Think I'm going to make it. My leg sure hurts. But, I feel better. Food must be helping. No more fever, either. I'm thankful for that.*

As Pike rested his bowl on the ground, his mind wandered to Buster and his story. Looking again at the deep scar on his face, Pike broke into the silence to urge his new brother to complete his history. "Buster, would you finish your story?"

"Yes," Frank urged. "Would you?"

Buster cleared his throat a couple of times, then the story began to roll off his tongue. "Our long trip ended in a li'l town in New York called Bear Branch. I sho thought it was a strange name for a town, but it was a purty sight for me and my tired partner. We gots to a place where there weren't no slaves. We'd found our 'North' in a place I couldn't never have conjured up. I's had a pitcher of the north as a mighty grand place. Bear Branch weren't grand, but it sho' was the end of the line for me and the girl who had come so far and so fast with me.

"We was finally free, and the day I had waited fo' my whole life finally came. I was marrying Daria.

"Mister Charles and his purty wife tol' us they would take us to town. I's wouldn't be able to ever thank them enough for the clothes and the new boots. I never had such boots. They sho shine and fit my feet like my own skin. This couple of fine folks give us some money. I never had a jingle in my pocket before. Mista Charles' wife, she was so nice when she found out we was wantin' to get hitched. She tol' the mista to get us a preacher. That's when we hopped into the wagon and went to the church.

"I's try to feel every minute, for I knowed I's never been happier. I wants to put each second away in my heart. I couldn't stop starin' at Daria in that new dress Missa Charles had give Daria. It was bright red-check, with flowers on it. I sho' never saw anyone look so purty as she did. She even had a rose in her hair, behind her ear.

"I's could tell she was excited too, by her smile and the light in her eyes. I grabbed her hand and we walked side-by-side to that ol' rundown church jus' down the road. The ol' white paint was a-peelin' off and lookin' gray, and one window was busted out. The shingles on the roof was missin' in lots a places, but it sho' looked good to me.

"I's sees a black man, who was the preacher a-waitin' outside fo us. He was a-sittin' and soaking up the sun. He sho nuff looked important in his black shirt and pants, and he had a li'l white collar around his neck with a cross hanging over the front of his buttons, so everybody could see it. His smile made us feel good cause we was mighty excited 'bout gettin' married.

"Welcome to the Lord's house. He has given us such a beautiful day for your wedding. Please come in and we'll get started. Yes, sir, He's given us much to cele-brate."

"Daria's kiss was warm and lovin' when the preach-er tol' me I could kiss the bride. I grabbed her up and lifts her way atop my head. I's throwed my head back and laughed so big and loud. I's wantin' to shout to the world that I just married me the best woman in the world. How could life get any better than this?

"Mista Charles fixed it for Daria and me to live in a li'l one-room house that was out behind the Big House the Brown's lived in. Daria was goin' to work in the house as a maid for Miz Brown. They had two youngens and needs help with the chores and them li'l ones. I was gonna work in the sawmill down by the river. It was a ways from the house, and the hours was long, but I would get paid for my work. I's couldn't wait to start. I had big dreams for us, and I's goin' to save up some money and gets a place of our own. I wanted to farm. That's alls I ever knowed - raisin' crops.

"Our one-room house weren't much. The walls had some holes, and I could feel the cool spring wind a-blowin' in. The only furniture was a table with two broke chairs but it had a fireplace. A mattress made of cotton tickin' was on the floor, too. On top was a weddin' ring quilt and two pillows, a present from the Charles. A lit candle and a basket of food was waitin' on us. The light from the candle throwed comforting shadows across the walls. I's could smell fried chicken in the basket.

"Standin' there, I says, 'Girl, we is finally home.' Then I nuzzle her warm neck and says in her ear, 'Daria, always 'member I love you. . .only you.'

"When we land atop that ol' mattress and I feelin' my wife agin' me, I hears her say, 'Jonas, I'll never forget.'

"Then I saw the love shinin' back at me in her eyes, as I lay with her on that ol' mattress." Closing his eyes, Buster paused.

As Pike watched the big man, he sensed that these savored moments from the past were soon to be overridden by the sadness that seemed to permeate Buster's massive frame.

Finally, Buster opened his misty eyes and continued. "The happiness that filled my life's cup stayed warm and full. I just had to think of my wife and everything else just didn't matter no mo'. Like the way the lumber-mill boss, Drisco, called me 'Nigger Boy', when he talks to me. I feels mad 'bout how he was always yellin' and cussin' at me, but I kept my mouth shut. I had years of that beaten into my back. I sho' could keep my temper with the likes of him.

"That man was as mean as a badger and had a foul mouth. And his cousin Rufus work there with him, too. Always lurkin' behind Drisco, makin' sure I didn't haul off and hit him when he talks so mean to me. Drisco left the other men alone and knowed better that to cuss them. He didn't cuss me whilst there was others around. He knowed better'n to talk that way with someone listenin' in. But, just as soon as I walk out the back of the mill to drag in some tree parts, he pop up behind me somewhere's just to throw as much meanness at me as he could think up.

"One time he even had a board in his hand. He's a yellin' at me and says, 'Nigger Boy', you better hurry up. You're slower than molasses in winter. Get that stack of wood and hurry that ass up to the mill.'

"That was when he hit me cross the back with that board. I's froze up for a minute, thinkin' on what to do. I wanted nothin' mo' than to turn around and take out all them years of slavery on that rank, mean, low-down skunk. I knowed Rufus, his cousin, was behind him, but he weren't that strong. They sho' didn't scare me none.

"I turn 'round to face Drisco and his low-life cousin. Both of them was dirty and shaggy looking. Their clothes hadn't been washed in a long time and they was covered with mud, dirt and sweat. I towered over Drisco, so I leans over him to come down to his level. I stares him right in the eyes and say real gentle like, 'You's ever hit me again and I sure you is gone forever.' I turn and goes back to work, jus' like nothin' ever happen.

"I sho' wish with all my heart, that I kep' my mouth shut that day. Drisco lef' me alone after that, but what I didn't know was he's plottin' against me. I thought once he lef' me alone, everything was goin' to be okay." Buster put his big hands together on his knee and bowed his head.

Although the noise of the prison yard permeated the area, Pike found himself mesmerized by Buster's story. But finally, Buster continued with a sigh. "I's been savin' my money and stopped by the general store on Bear Branch's main street on my way home from work. I's wantin' to buy Daria a cradle for the baby we had a-comin in about five months.

"It was dark when I got home. I sees the candlelight aglowin' through the window like it did for me every evenin'. I stepped through the door with a bang. All I got out of my mouth was, 'Wife, come. . . Then I feels somethin' hard hit me on the side of my head. I falls like a passin' out drunk and don't know much else for a time. How long I don't know.

"When I comes to, my feet and hands was tied with

rough feelin' rope. There was a rag in my mouth. It was gaggin' me and I's havin' trouble breathin'. I's down on my side. There, lookin' at me was that stinkin' man Drisco. His foul breath was hittin' me right in the face, but I stares right back.

"'So, Nigger Boy is finally awake.'

"The words come to me on his stinkin' breath. 'We've got a little surprise for you. I ain't going to let no nigger get away with threatening me. No, boy, you're going to pay for what you done. When I saw your purty gal, I said to Rufus that we're gonna have us some fun with her!'

"I look over at Daria and saw she was scar't. I knowed what them men was plannin' on doing and I went sick to my stomach. I fought them ropes cutting into my skin. I couldn't get them off. All's I's thinking' about was gettin' loose and keepin' the pigs off my wife. She looked so helpless asittin' in a chair with her hands tied and a rag stickin' outta her mouth.

"Both of the men looked at me and was laughin'. Drisco come over to me and kicked me in the belly. I went out for awhile. Then, he pulled out a big huntin' knife and cut me across the belly and chest. The knife slashin' me made blood run down on the floor. It was a-poolin' up under me. He took a cut at my face, right up my cheek, clean up to my eye.

"Then Drisco laughs and say, cruel-like, 'Boy, I's want you to see what's coming next. Your blood is draining out of you. You won't last long, but you're going to know what your wife looks like with another man.' Then, he kicks me one last time.

"I couldn't move cuz I'd lost so much blood, and when they grabs up my poor wife and drags her onto the wood floor, Drisco took his huntin' knife and cut her dress off real quick-like. Then, he cut the rope round her legs. Rufus was helpin' him hold her down. He had a hold of her arms and was pinnin' her down on the floor.

"Drisco stared at her naked body. 'Um. . .she sure is a mighty fine woman.' He got down on his knees and runs a hand over her breast. All at once, he bends over her and bit the nipple he had jus' had his hands on.

While his mouth was still on her breast, he run his hand down her stomach and stops as he feels the swellin' on her belly. Then, he sits up. 'What's this, boy? You got a baby coming?' the swine calls out. 'You can watch while we take care of him, too.'

"Drisco stands up and drops his overalls and says to his cousin, 'Rufus, you keep hold of her while I get me some of this gal and then you can have all of her you want.'

"I see Drisco on her, pushin' himself in her. I could hear Daria moanin' against the rag in her mouth. My mind was a-spinnin'. I began to fade away with a sickness so strong in my stomach I knowed I was fixin' to heave. I could hear Drisco laughin' as I passed out." The story seemed too much for Buster as his huge form drooped, eyes staring at the ground.

Pike felt awash with sadness for his friend and he couldn't believe what he was hearing. *I'm embarrassed of my own kind*, he thought. *What do I say?* First, Pike gazed at the others, noting their stunned silence, Ben's mouth hung open.

"Buster," Pike stammered softly, "I can't imagine how hard that was. All I can say is I am sorry."

After a pause, Frank found his voice. "Now I can understand why you hate Drisco. I'd hate him, too."

The professor added, "So now we know why you reacted the way you did. Can't say I wouldn't do the same thing."

Sensing Buster's story wasn't complete, Pike encouraged him to finish by saying, "Since we have plenty of time on our hands, would you mind telling us the rest?"

Swiping away two lone tears that dribbled from his eyes, Buster nodded his head and commenced speaking again.

"I's still sick when I come awake, but the weakness I's feelin' kep' me down. I heard voices.

"'Just lie still, now. I'm trying to sew you up. You've lost a lot of blood, son.'

"I opened my eyes and peeped 'round the room. I seen lots of books and odd-lookin' tools. I hurt like I had so many times before when I was whupped with the whip of our overseer, Drake. I went back into the cocoon I made for times like that. I's wantin' to stay there and never come out. I jus' couldn't quite remember why. It weren't until the next day that I's forced to return by a strong voice.

"'Wake up now.'

"I hears words from somewhere. I feel a shakin' in my body. So, I tryin' to get my eyes open. Somethin' in me fought my comin' awake. I knowed there was somethin' awful wrong and I's not wants to see it.

"Strong hands was holdin' me by my shoulders and jus' wouldn't quit shakin' me. I hears my own moanin' and my eyes finally pop open nuff to see who was makin' me wake up. I saw a stranger's face. He seems to be a kind man - much older than me. The hair on his head was gone way back on both sides, leavin' a peak of gray hair right in the middle. His skin was thin-lookin' and patchy with dark spots. He weren't frail, though. He looked well-fleshed and like he stayed real busy. There weren't no fat anywhere on him.

"He says to me, 'Son, you need to wake up and eat - drink some broth. You've got to try to get your strength back. You've lost so much blood. We've got to get some liquid in you so your body can make some more blood. You're going to have some pretty bad scars. I can't stop that. You're going to live, but it'll take awhile to get strong again.' His head shook, sad-like, at what he'd seen on my body.

"The thought of what happen to my wife and baby came aroarin' back to me right then and there. What I seen, hits me so hard I moanin' and starts to thrash.

"The doc says, 'Now, son, you're going to have to keep still or you're going to start bleeding again.' He shook me again, hoping to get through.

"I listens to him and gets still. My head was apoundin'. I knowed what had happened to my Daria, but I had to hear it from him. I was jus' able to whisper, 'Doc, Please tell me what happened to my wife. I sho' gots to know. Please tell me.' I's look in his eyes, pleadin' with him to tell me what I knowed in my heart and was afraid to hear.

"'Son, we should talk of these things later when you are stronger.' The doc tries to turn away and leave the room. The poor man didn't wants to tell me about what had happened.

"I grabbed him by the wrist but didn't have the strength to hold on. As my hands fall away, I's feelin' as lost as I'd ever knowed. How was I goin' on without my woman? My love for her was what give me my onliest happiness in this world. Daria was gone forever, and everythin' that mattered in my life left this earth with her.

"Daria was free of the chains of slavery when she was sent to heaven so early in her life. She knowed what it was like to have the bonds of slavery took off. At least, I give her that. My slavin' days was gone, but without the love of Daria and our life together, I had nothin'. Nothin' was left and my life was over - gone.

"'Doc, you's gots to tell me,' I pleaded to his retreatin' back.

"The man stops and looks at me before he shakes his head and lets out, 'I'm so sorry, but your wife is gone. I'll leave you alone for awhile.'

"The doc were a kind soul and he's let me stay with him whilst I's gettin' well. He tried to talk to me whilst he's takin' care of me. Mostly, I jus' stares off. I had no reason to live. I wants to die and go to heaven to see my gal and my chil'. I willed it to happen. I begs God to take me, too. Every day, I begged him.

"Then, the day come when I's well nuff to be on my own. I thought what to do, but my dull mind couldn't figure out what to do with my life. Durin' the long evenin's, the doc ties to get me to talk about the war between the states. He said most of the young men in town had signed up to fight. They was fightin' to get the states back together and, now, to free the slaves." Suddenly, Buster's eyes came alive again as he looked around at the men.

"My mind grabbed onto the notion of fightin' in the war. I sho weren't afraid to die. If'n I could help in the fight to stop the sufferin' of all my kind in the south on them plantations, I could be proud of that. Dyin' to save the ones left down south would be a blessin'. It was right then and there that I decides to see if they would let a black man into the Northern Army. I was meanin' to find out real quick-like.

"A man dressed in navy-blue uniform, who sho' looked smart, was a-sittin' at a table talkin' to the men that come to sign up for the fightin'. I stood off to the side and jus' looks at them all. I didn't see no black men, but I weren't goin' to run off. I stiffen my back and walk right up to the man with the uniform and says right out, 'I want to fight in this here war.'

"The man looks right up at me and looks kinda surprised. He jus' sit there for a minute. 'Sure would be a first to have a black man fighting. Buster, you have as much right as any man to fight in this war. I'd be right proud to have you in my division. I've never seen a 'Buster' as big as you. Let's get you to fighting.'

"When he say that, he starts laughin' till I thought he wouldn' stop. Everyone 'round me started laughin' too, 'ceptin' me. I don't know if'n I'd ever feel like laughin' again. My old life ended that day I join up with the Northern Army. Since I started this new life, I decided to keeps the name the captain gave me. Buster weren't such a bad name. I kinda like it. The name sound strong, so I stick with 'Big Buster'.

"I fought in the war for a long time before we was captured, so here I sits with you all today."

Instantly, Pike's hand reached out and gripped Buster's shoulder as Buster fell silent and they shared a moment of quiet. Pike didn't know what else he could do.

Frank uttered, "Sorry, Buster. That's a rough story."

"Yeah, it is," Tom stammered from the back of the pack.

It had taken Buster all afternoon to finish his lengthy story. The afternoon had slipped off to let the dusky night take its place.

Looking around the darkening tent, Pike felt as a lion would in a small cage as panic slipped back into his thoughts, blotting out all else. He was trapped in this prison and there was no way out! So, searching for comfort, his free hand slipped into his interior coat pocket to grasp his long-forgotten harmonica. Pulling it free, he put it to his lips and gave it a few warm-up toots, hoping to provide a diversion to the men, but more importantly - to himself.

As he warmed up his mouth blasting his harmonica, he glanced at the eager faces, noting the looks of hope he had awakened in them all - even Buster. Pike looked at 'Shooter' first and asked, "So, what do you want to hear?"

The man's smile could be heard in his voice, "What else but the 'Battle Hymn of the Republic.'" As Pike wasted no more time in beginning to play the chosen song, Frank jumped in and commenced the singing.

The voices blended together in a most pleasing fashion, even though a few of the men couldn't carry a tune, but it didn't matter because they were sharing these brief minutes of escape from their imprisonment as their hearts lifted in song. When Buster's deep, sonorous voice joined in, Pike reveled in a moment of pure joy as his heart swelled as much as a croaking bullfrog calling for a springtime mate.

When the last note of the song drifted away into the cool, night air, Ben piped up with a request. "How about 'The Old Oaken Bucket'?"

Later, after numerous songs, Pike announced with a sigh, "This is going to be the last one. What'll it be?"

Buster's deeply, commanding voice asked, "How 'bout 'Amazin' Grace.' I sho likes that one."

The rising lump in Pike throat couldn't be helped as the last refrains of the song came, which forced Pike to quit just before the final measure in order to keep from letting go. Not alone at this touching moment, Pike noticed that everyone else hushed with him - quiet prevailed.

Collin cleared his throat a couple of times and spoke into the frosty blackness. "Thank you, Pike. What a gift your music is. We'll be able to enjoy many more nights of it. The camp is quieter now and we should try to get some rest. I know we're going to feel better now that we have each other to lean on."

"Good night, big brother," Frank whispered into Pike's ear as they found their sleeping spots.

"Same to you." Pike closed his eyes. Still sore from having to lie in the wagons and on the ground for so many days, he thought he would never get to sleep from the aching in his body, much less the throbbing in his thigh.

Suddenly, an errant shiver coursed along his spine, rippling into his limbs, and ending in his fingertips. Pike prayed the fever would not return as he wrapped his coat tightly around himself. Tugging his hat forcefully over his eyes, the urge to shift to get more comfortable nagged, but in these cramped conditions, finding comfort seemed impossible. Still, he went through the motions to try to entice sleep, knowing it was a long way off. *Almost as unattainable as the uppermost peaks of the Rockies.*

As he closed his eyes, he became conscious of the moans of the sick as they floated to him on the blackness. *God help them!* Pike entreated. *God help us all.*

To take his mind off of his misery, Pike flew to find Rebecca and draw her near. But instead, his thoughts of his predicament dogged him unmercifully, so he was lost trembling in the darkness.

*

On the other side of the prison, Drisco lay heavy in thought on his blanket. *I'd better figure out some way to get rid of the 'Nigger Boy' and anyone else in his group. I'll bet he'll be looking' to get me. I'd better take care of him first. I'll find out who's in his group and get my men together. We'll show 'em who's boss around here.*

Images flashed across his mind; wicked, lustful ones, recalling the night of sheer pleasure with 'Nigger Boy's' young wife. The memories of stripping the dark-skinned girl intoxicated him with a rush of power and lust. In instant response, his loins began to throb and into his imagination crept her hard, dark nipples and melon shaped breasts, full from her pregnancy. A heady rush of libidinous adrenaline flowed freely through him and set every nerve on fire. His breaths came in shallow, rapid huffs.

Sure could use me a gal like that now, Drisco told himself as he relaxed against his sleeping roll and fixed his eyes on the roof of the dark tent to continue pondering. *Can't get my mind off that nigger gal. She's all I could'a wanted in a girl. Didn't put up enough fight but I need something like that now. Shit, now I'm all worked up.* Drisco wasted no time in slipping his hand into his open pants to run his hand along his pulsing erection.

The pleasure he found caused his to gasp and the accompanying rush of blood, pounding in his ears, shut out all other noises. After a few more strokes, he jerked his hand out of his pants and jumped up with a growl. *I've got to get me something better than my hand. That new boy Harry? . . .Harold? . . .must be about fourteen. He looks good enough to plug.*

Storming from the tent, fixing his pants as he went, Drisco cursed himself as he glared around for his skinny cousin. *Damn it! Where's Rufus? Should be on lookout. I'd better find his sorry ass first.*

Chapter Five

"Whew!" Pike gasped to Buster and Frank the following day as he plopped into the dirt under their crude shelter. "I think I overdid it." Even though the temperature wasn't more than forty-five degrees, profuse sweat trickled down his ruddy cheeks and his breaths sounded in the cool air.

"At least I know what we're up against now, "Pike continued. "I'm glad I got to see the camp. Who'd have guessed there're so many men in here? I can see the groups closest to us and spoken to some, but I never dreamed they could fit that many men in this amount of space. Now, I know why it smells so bad. Good grief."

A grim nod of his head was the only response from Frank.

Eyes downcast, Buster didn't say a word.

"Thought we'd come back too," the professor said, as he, Daniel and James trudged back under the tent. "Not much we want to see, either."

Ben, Tom and Shooter joined the clan before long. Pike easily noted the haunted expression emanating from Ben's gray eyes and his brow that was deeply furrowed. As Pike's heart rocked with sorrow for the young boy - the nagging anxiousness returned, which brought up another item to discuss. "I think it's time to decide what to do about Drisco and his bunch."

"We're going to have to be careful," Pike thought out loud. "Drisco isn't going to forget Buster is here. We all know that. Since that bunch runs wild in here, we'll have to be vigilant to keep ahead of them."

Pike drew in a deep breath, pondering the situation before he continued. "We've got to make friends here as fast as we can. Buster, you need to stay out of sight as much as you can. We'll need some time to get the support of others. While we do that, I'll work on a plan to get rid of the 'Raiders' - every last one of them. "I still can't believe they've been allowed to run roughshod over everyone in this prison."

"You're right, Pike," the professor said, jumping into the discussion as his mop of curls snaked around his face, pushed by the southern breeze, "We need to stop the 'Raiders'. The guards do nothing about their nighttime stealing forays. We're going to have to take the bull by the horns. Not sure how, but there's got to be a way. We'll put our heads together; see what we can come up with."

Breaking in with an idea, Shooter offered, "Why don't we have the men on either side of us join us tonight for singing?" First, he looked at the professor, then Pike, eyebrows lifted.

Nodding, Pike agreed. "Good idea. Watch them though. Be careful about telling them anything personal. We'll have to figure out who to trust, but it's a start."

*

That evening, Pike gazed at the scraggly group that had gathered in front of his tent. Frank, Daniel and Collin had gone to the two closest shelters and introduced themselves, and had persuaded the newcomers to join them for Pike's harmonica playing.

When all had gathered in the gloom, Pike asked Frank, "What should we start with?"

Without hesitation, Frank blurted, "How about Tramp! Tramp! Tramp!

Smiling, Pike said, "Sounds good."

As the cold night wore on, the hearty blend of voices carried far through the camp. Other men, drawn by the singing, dribbled into the group, one by one.

Still forced to brace himself against his army pack, Pike was grateful for the easing of the pain in his thigh. His energy was still low but getting back to his previous vitality wasn't going to happen under these dire conditions - no matter how many times he wished for it. *Why can't I be anywhere else?* Pike wondered as an internal sigh flowed inside and he gathered his strength to keep blowing while he also decided, *I'll play as long as I can.*

*

"So, Harold," Drisco barked at the nervous, baby-faced boy, who had hesitantly stepped through the open tent flap, "What did you find out? This had better be good." Seeing the dark bruise on the lad's hairless cheek brought back images of the previous night's fun. Drisco chuckled to himself. "Well you snivelin' shit, get to talkin'."

"I-I-I walked over to the other side of the camp, like you said. It took me a while to find the tent with the black man in it. When I did, I watched from a distance. Then I wandered over to one of his neighbors. They didn't know much, but one of them said they were going to go to their tent for music. He invited me to come along, so I went. The man that played the harmonica seems to be their leader. He's redheaded, tall, thin and has a red beard too. His name is Pike Wheeling. Got a brother with him . . .Frank, I think."

"You better not think," Drisco blasted. "You'd better know!"

Visibly jumping, Harold cowered close to the exit, staying as far from Drisco as possible as he answered, "W-e-ll, yes. His brother's name is Frank. There are several others in the group. There's nine altogether. The black man is one of them."

"Damn it all to hell. Guess we're goin' to have to be careful in pickin' them off. Maybe we can catch them by themselves, one at a time. But first, we'll steal their stuff. Then, we'll jump 'em. Maybe when I send someone out to take their things, he can cut one of their throats while he's at it." Drisco released a particularly wicked cackle as his head nodded.

Eyes rising back to Harold, Drisco spat, "Git outta here, you stupid bastard. I'll call you when I want you."

Stumbling blindly, Harold bolted out the door.

*

The early springtime sun was warm on Frank's shoulders as he led the daily procession to the ration line. He did appreciate that Pike had been going with them for the last few weeks, and for that small gift, he was grateful but it was the only thing he'd been grateful for in some time.

Feel myself getting weaker by the day. Since I had the quick step last week, can't get my strength back. My energy is gone. Hope I can make it to the line and back. To Pike's face, he flashed a toothy grin as he chugged up beside him.

"Are you feeling better today?" Pike inquired.

"Fine and dandy. Better than you."

"Hm-m-m, don't know about that."

"I am. So don't worry. Think we'll get something besides cornmeal?"

"I hope so," Buster's low voice returned before Pike could answer.

Along with Frank and Pike, Collin drug along, visiting with one of the group's new friends, Steven McFarland. At a first glance, Steven appeared pale and sickly with his white hair, translucent skin, colorless blue eyes and skinny frame. But, it was just his own genetics at work as he was albino. Steven and Collin were lost in a heavy discussion on their favorite subject-books they'd read.

Heading straight for their favorite southern private, Frank stopped in front of the grizzled, old man. After Pike had selected him as their best bet to make friends with, all in the group were extra nice to him. Pike had said that maybe they could use that friendship later on, hopefully to the 'Raiders' detriment.

When all of the group had joined Frank, Pike hollered out, since Private Dunbury was hard of hearing, "Well, if it isn't my favorite guard."

The stooped, little fellow visibly puffed up when he recognized Pike's voice, grinning from ear to ear.

Frank couldn't help returning the friendly smile.

"How are you boys this warm day?" the private asked as if he were truly interested in the reply, just before he handed Frank and Pike their scant bundle of peas, beans and sticks for their fire.

"Its sure feels good to my old bones," Pike retuned. "How 'bout you?"

Awash with relief at the sight of the extra provisions the private had slipped them, Frank thought, *maybe we'll make it yet.* All he could do was hang onto that single notion.

*

Pike could still hear the echo of the music from the evening's session of song. In the forefront of his mind were the words of one of the men's favorites, one they sang every day.

> *In the prison cell I sit*
> *Thinking, mother dear, of you. . .*

While wishing sleep would replace the words ricocheting through his mind, Pike's thoughts finally meandered to his far-away home and his parents. He stared at the tent's ragged ceiling, listening to the fabric flapping in the night wind and after a time, sleep did sneak up on him and he followed where it led.

Later, something made him jump. What, he didn't know - for a second. But, when he looked to his right as his eyes were accustomed to the dark, he detected the outline of a man leaning over his brother, working his precious pack from under his hand.

The danger flashed through Pike's consciousness. He reacted without one more thought, forgetting his bad thigh, slamming into the thief's left shoulder. Together, they toppled to the ground as Pike's big hands found and began crushing the intruder's throat. Using his large frame, Pike pinned the smaller man under him. The stranger did manage to slap at Pike's hands but having his air cut off, he lacked any strength.

The others had been roused by the battle but none

moved to help because they could see there was no need.

After several minutes the man went limp, so Pike loosened his death grip - then let him go. Panting from his exertion, Pike stared at the dead man as he rocked back on his heels, before he also slipped to the ground. Then he folded his arms around his bent knees to rest his forehead.

Collin scooted over to the dead man, then caustically remarked, "That's one of those 'Raiders'. I recognize him. Good thing you caught him before he got away. What should we do with the body?" the professor continued. "There's going to be hell to pay for this from the 'Raiders'."

"We need to take the man to the front gate at first light," Pike replied. "If we can get him there before anyone sees us, no one will be the wiser. Let's sleep until then. James and Tom can hurry the body to the west gate and leave him there with the other dead. Buster, why don't you sit up and keep watch, just in case!"

The hours drug by as Pike vainly courted sleep while his eyelids refused to rest. Finally, after an eternity, the first hint of light filtered into the tent. Pike motioned for Buster to wake the two men.

James clasped the dead man's filthy legs and Tom his forearms. Within seconds, they quietly, but hastily, passed out of view into the misty shroud of morning.

Spying something shiny on the ground, Pike reached out to lift the object. It was a knife. *Well, well, well, what have we here?*

*

The minutes became hours as Drisco's unease mounted. Pete had not returned from his assignment - stealing from Pike's group and hopefully killing one of them in the process.

Should'a been back long before now, Drisco told himself. And as the sun began to filter through the mist, Drisco's red-rimmed eyes peeked out of his tent, hoping to spot Pete and listening to his cousin's peaceful snoring added to his mounting irritation.

Ah hell, better get Rufus up. With another curse, Drisco turned back and dealt Rufus a swift kick with his boot heel.

The small man yelped, "Hey! What's up?"

"Listen, son-of-a-whore, Pete's never come back. I told him to take what he could. I gave him the knife to use on one of those men's throat. You'd better get your lazy ass out of bed and go find him."

Rufus rubbed his eyes a few times, yawned, and rolled to his knees, mumbling a bit, before crawling out of the tent.

Pacing, Drisco waited.

The sun was just peaking over the horizon, streaking red, violet and orange on the cottony clouds that banked the eastern sky as Drisco continued his wait. A strange quiet pervaded the camp and time seemed to creep as Drisco paced and talked out loud. Drisco hurried out to meet Rufus as he slipped back and asked quickly, "Well, what'd ya find?"

"I didn't get very far before I spotted two men toting Pete's body to the gate. He's dead. Those men from Pike's tent was a-carryin' him."

Drisco said through gritted teeth, "Well, they ain't gettin' away with it."

*

Pike shuffled as fast as he could across the camp with Buster after receiving the daily rations. Precious moments had been lost by making the trek, but they had no choice. If they didn't get their rations, they might soon join young Jeffrey, a neighboring friend, in his death spiral.

I do what I can, Pike thought, *to help the sick and dying, but it's not enough by a long shot. What else can I do?* Yanking back the tent flap, Pike thankfully noted Jeffery was still breathing.

"I wait fo' you outside here," Buster mumbled.

Leaning over the dying soldier, Pike placed his ear inches from Jeffery's mouth. He felt the man's breath coming in short, rapid bursts. Then, he ran a hand lightly across the boy's forehead, noting the intense heat radiating off his dry skin. *He won't last much longer. I'll stay til he passes.*

The wait was shorter than he'd estimated. When Jeffery's eyes popped open, to focus on Pike, the poor boy managed to croak out, "I'm so scared."

Washed by sadness but also rage at the plight of all the prisoners, Pike held the young Union soldier's gaze, while his mind screamed, *Why can't I save him!* Pike plucked up Jeffery's hand, hoping his squeeze would give a small measure of comfort.

Leaning over the pale youth, he whispered, "I'm here. I won't leave you. Don't be scared. God is waiting for you on the other side. I'll help you on your way. Heaven will be wonderful. Are you ready?"

Jeffery lost his voice, but nodded his head. What little strength he had flew away as his spirit left the broken form behind, eyes rolling back, body going limp.

Relieved that Jeffery was no longer suffering, Pike began to pray. *God please take Jeffery into your loving arms. Give him peace and most of all, wings. The boy deserves it! Amen.*

*

A symphony of male voices fell like soft snowflakes throughout the northwest side of Andersonville that summer evening. As the long shadows of the day collected to give way to a restless, whiningly, windy night, the men gathered to hunker around Pike, their ringleader of song.

Enraptured by the rousing tunes Pike played on his trusty harmonica, the group had grown steadily each day. Pike's newfound friends lent their voices to their heartfelt singing. It brought a rare release within the confines of the prison.

Sticky, hot days had been the norm for some time, but this night the rain clouds skittered across the evening sky, chased by a whipping wind. Pike's eyes darted to the dangerous sky as thunder clapped, followed by a slash of jagged lightning.

The last refrains of "Nearer My God To Thee" hung

in the air and straining to hold onto the last note, Pike willed it to last forever, not to ripple away into the vast darkness - but, it did.

"Well, boys," Pike shouted above the moaning wind, "we'd better get to our tents before the storm sets in. Guess we'll have to do double duty tomorrow. See you then."

Sorrow hung on Pike, as he watched the rickety men work themselves into standing positions. He was relieved to note several of the stronger ones lending hands to their weaker compatriots. *Damn this place!* Pike flung the outraged words heavenward. *Can't take much more of this. How many have to die?*

Scurrying about, James and Daniel gathered up all of their canteens and pots as they prepared to collect the rain from one edge of the canvas, which had been sewn specially for this purpose. Buster shambled through the tent to collect all the available blankets, shaking them vigorously.

Frank joined Pike and Buster momentarily to await the first drops. Over the howl of the wind, Frank shouted to his brother, "Whew, I'm thankful for the rain. We sure can use it."

Suddenly, the storm blasted them all in the face with a blessed downpour. The storm's wrath punished all in its path, but undeterred by the ferocious onslaught, each man in the group kept his assigned post and focused on capturing all the fresh water provided by the tumultuous sky.

Sending up a quick prayer of thanks for the much-needed rain, Pike faced the storm's fury, which seemed minor compared to suffering at the hands of a sadistic 'Thirst', which laughed at them all and threatened to get its claws into their parched throats with talk of heading over to 'The Bitch'. She was only too eager to do her damage.

"Steady, boys," Pike bellowed above the clamor. He could see the men briefly during the flashes of lightning. Daniel and James handed full canteens to Frank to be stacked at one end of the tent. The remaining men braced themselves against the pelting rain, holding their blankets out to soak up the fresh, God-sent liquid. When they filled all the available containers, their job was completed.

Together, they hustled back under the tent's inviting warmth to start the drying process. Shuffling, Pike located a dry spot under the tent to plop down into it. Being the last one to rest from the exertion, he gladly took his place, but a chill ran its hand over his body and invited 'Shivering' in to do its work. Even though he felt cold, as much from his weakened condition as from the water, he wanted to alleviate the demoralized silence among the men. "I can't wait to shave in the mornin'. You fellows sure look scraggly. What a sight you are. No one back home would recognize you."

A couple of half-hearted chuckles met his comments, but nothing more.

The rest of the night hours whiled away for the prisoners as few slept. Pike raced off into his well-honed fantasy world where Rebecca reigned and the horses were fat and glossy. While lost in his dream world, he fingered his watch and chain, enjoying the familiar comfort they brought.

Gratefully, Pike noted the beginning of the new day. 'Dawn's' fingers massaged her cheerful warmth back into Pike's stiffened body as the cotton-candy colors began to dot the eastern skyline. A warm breeze accompanied 'Dawn', lifting Pike's spirits even more. Promise of dryness blew across his rough cheek, kissing it ever so slightly as Pike reminded himself, *Enjoy it now, 'cause in a few hours, it's going to be hot again.*

Rejoicing in the few moments of comfort and reveling in the newly-birthed morning, Pike glanced around at the skeletal faces near him and he thought, *We've got to get out of here soon, or we're all going to fritter away.*

Chapter Six

After nearly six months of imprisonment, Frank awakened that morning after the storm, as the sun peeped over the horizon, immediately aware of his constant companion - 'Desperation'. He sensed that something ominous was coming, and it wasn't going to wait much longer.

The 'Raiders' had made several weak attempts to get at them, but to this point Drisco hadn't shown his face. As continually as Frank fretted over the 'Raiders', the hunger in his core loomed even larger and more fierce. *How much more of this can we take? Will I make it out of here alive? I'm going crazy.* Frank's eyes swept the men sitting nearby, judging how they were holding up.

Ben looked so frail and his skeletal body hardly managed to get up anymore. Everyone else reclined in silence and stared into space most of the time as the hours seemed like days.

Looking out into the haze of the morning after the storm of last night, Frank detected a number of vague figures approaching from a distance. The large stocky man in front walked with the confidence of the well-nourished. Frank's back stiffened as he recognized the long, stringy hair and brown, fleshy face of Drisco.

Buster and Pike shot up with the other men in their group, their voices a chaotic jumble of sounds.

Turning into the tent, Frank scrambled for the knife. *I've got to protect Pike . . .and Buster!* He grasped Pike's pack to then clutch the thick blade to his stomach, hands trembling. As he scooted under the flap, he spotted Buster barreling toward Drisco, Frank took in the scene playing out before him.

Buster appeared like a rabid bull, bearing down on a matador as his eyes bulged and his mouth grimaced with white teeth flashing in the morning sun.

Pike, one step behind Buster, screamed, "No, Buster! Wait." His words were lost on the man consumed with his past agonies. Behind Pike, Frank sprinted after him and the others in their group howled in hot pursuit.

Drisco met Buster head-on in a tackle. Rufus and the rest of the 'Raiders' scattered around behind their leader, searching for their victims.

Men from the surrounding tents rose to their feet to rush into the confrontation, piling onto the 'Raiders'.

Closing the distance swiftly, Frank whipped back the knife, plunging it deep into the bowels of the first unsuspecting 'Raider', and he couldn't help but stare into the man's dark eyes as the knife found its deadly mark. A low moan escaped from the man when Frank yanked out the weapon and allowed the victim to fall back, hands gripping his ripped entrails. Raising his head, again, Frank searched for his redheaded brother.

Frank spotted Pike performing a dance of death with Drisco's cousin, Rufus. They circled one another with their arms out and in Rufus's right hand, he clutched a knife, similar to the one Frank wielded. Not far from Pike, Buster and Drisco flopped around in a heap in the dirt.

Not able to focus on Buster, Frank knew he had to save his brother. His feet shot forward and sprinted across the ten yards that separated him from Pike, with a speed that surprised even himself.

Rufus must have noted Frank's approach because he stood upright to face Frank and the distraction allowed Pike to jump forward and plow into his opponent - both expelling grunts.

The resounding crack of the muzzleloader shocked Frank to a standstill. He had forgotten about the guards because his desperate life seemed so separated from outside existence. On a daily basis, the guards did little to interfere in the dog-eat-dog world of the prison. And since there was so little intervention, Frank hadn't taken the sentries into account as the melee had broken out.

The first hornet found its mark in a man with bushy, brown hair. He dropped to the rain-soaked ground and clutched his bloody, broken ankle, shrieking in pain. Instantly, Frank recognized the wounded man as Quinton, one of his closest neighbors and a friend of Steven's.

Glancing around, Frank quickly noted most of the prisoners were frozen in place, but there were others, like Buster and Drisco, who seemed unaffected by the first volley. Buster clutched Drisco by the throat.

Leaving Rufus to jump into Buster's fight, Pike screamed, "I'll kill you, you whore-master." Both fighting men craned their heads, their struggle momentarily ceased. Pike drew back his fist and brought it forward into Drisco's left eye with a hollow-sounding thump.

Another shot rang out, dropping a man, and a third shot erupted and found another live mark. Taking heed of the shots, the prisoners yipped louder than wounded coyotes as they scurried and scattered while Drisco crawled away quickly on his knees, then scrambled to his feet and bolted.

As he feared receiving a ball of his own, Frank bellowed, "Come on, boys. Let's get out of here double quick." He grabbed Pike and Buster by the arms and dragged them from the fracas until they willingly followed on their own.

Luckily, all the men from Pike's group plopped safely onto the ground under their shelter. Some were worse for wear, but all were alive.

The professor uttered, panting, "We were lucky. Hope everyone else made it out okay. I don't hear any more shooting."

Peeking out from under the shelter, Frank scanned the area for the injured, or God forbid, the dead. He stared at the three men lying in the dirt evaluating their conditions - two of them not moving. Quinton still rocked back and forth, crying like a baby, clutching his bloody, busted leg.

From the shelter, Frank strained to evaluate Quinton's ankle injury and thought, *Looks like he won't survive that wound.* But, Frank thought it best to say nothing out loud because things were bad enough at the moment.

From somewhere on top of the prison wall came a

voice.

Frank hearkened to the sound and held his breath.

"You prisoners better not do anything like that again. We'll shoot anyone else trying to start an uprising. You may remove the dead and injured. We won't shoot. Now move!"

"Frank," Pike directed instantly. "Why don't you and Collin lend a hand to the injured and the dead, if you can. I'll see if I can locate some sticks for a splint. It's probably a waste of time, but I hope not. Quinton might make it. We'll do all we can."

Pinched expression showing he was worried, Pike's troubled green eyes lingered on Frank's face, seeing something Frank did not want to admit about his own growing weakness. To top things off and adding more worry to the pot, it was obvious that the fight had taken its toll on everyone. Quietly, his voice just above a whisper, Pike asked, "Can you manage? Someone else can, if you aren't up to it, or I'll go."

"No, I'll be okay. I'll look in my pack for more rags."

A resolute smile tugged on Pike's lips, his eyes crinkled. "Okay."

As Frank plodded his first few strides toward Quinton a wave of weakness surged over him and his knees began to buckle while his head spun out of control. 'Feebleness' took charge, halting Frank in his tracks. All he could do was wait - and hope, and curse, *Damn this weakness. Am I going to die? . . . Can I survive this? Come on body, I've got work to do. Don't have time for this.* A deep, rasping groan escaped as he gritted his teeth and rocked back and forth precariously, waiting for his head to clear.

Collin stepped beside him and asked in a hushed tone, "Are you all right? You look pale."

"Come on, I'm okay," Frank snarled as he stepped forth with as much energy as he could muster. The weakness was losing its toehold on him, if only for a moment. The voice of 'Frailty' turned to a whisper, but he couldn't completely tune it out. *You are mine,* it sang. *It's only a matter of time, but you are mine.* Shaking his head again and trying to force the voice to go away, Frank continued his unstable, shambling gait to Quinton's side.

*

Pike joined Frank and Collin as they waited with Steven and another man named Samuel, who was part of Quinton's group. "Here, let's splint and wrap that leg," Pike suggested in a light tone, one he hoped would sound comforting.

The groaning from Quinton continued and intensified as Pike sliced the leg of his britches with the knife and tugged the cloth back. Quinton bawled, "No! No more. . . please!"

Shaking his head in sympathy, but knowing there was no shirking what must be done, Pike instructed the men near him, while swallowing his own dread. "Here, everybody, get a hold of him. I'm going to have to get the splint on." *Probably a waste of time, but we've got to try.*

After pulling in a breath, and with Quinton pinned under the attendant's hands, Pike placed the two sticks on both sides of the shattered, bleeding ankle.

A thick shard of tibia visibly strained against the skin and stretched it to the splitting point. The bone of the ankle was twisted at a grotesque angle and only a scrap of skin held the foot to the end of the leg.

As Pike released his gulp of air, he set his mind to his task and blocked out his dread and hesitation. With a twist of hands and firm guidance, he snapped the ankle back to its correct angle with a disgusting grinding of the bone.

Quinton screamed once and fell silent.

Luckily, he's passed out cold, Pike thought. "Frank, will you wrap this while I hold onto the sticks?"

With a grimace and frighteningly pallid color to his lips, Frank knelt next to Pike and took hold of the clump of rags, winding them around the ankle and splints several times.

Studying the wrapped ankle, Pike observed, "That's all we can do, except pray." He looked Steven in the eye and nodded firmly, then rose and shuffled away with

Collin and Frank.

The others in Pike's group, all still shaken from the morning's fray, were anxiously awaiting news of Quinton.

"How is he?" Ben was the first to ask.

Shaking his head, Pike shifted his gaze to Buster. He eyed the black man's puffy, bleeding lips and scanned for other injuries. "How's the lip?"

Buster nodded his head, eyes focused on the ground.

Pike said to himself, *I'd better find a way to do in those 'Raiders'. Drisco isn't going to rest until he kills us all. Think I'll talk to Private Dunbury about meeting with the captain, maybe he'll help us.*

*

Maybe we need to sneak up on them scumbags in the dark, Drisco pondered while he wiped the sweat off of his brow. *That way the guards won't interfere. I'll get all the boys together and we'll just creep up on 'em and wipe 'em out. I'm going to see to it that Pike and Nigger Boy gets theirs. Yes, sir! I'll see to it personally. Better not waste any more time. Tonight is the night. I'll tell the boys.*

*

"That's a good idea," Frank stated matter-of-factly to Pike as the group rested in the heavy heat of the afternoon . . .you talking to Private Dunbury."

Staring at the sky intently, noting the dark clouds forming, Pike's wandering mind floated back to respond to Frank. "I hope so. Maybe he'll speak to the captain as I asked. I hope the captain will see me on the premise of stopping any further violent outbreaks. I think he might. We'll just have to wait and hope for vindication."

"Poor boy a shuckin', its hot," Daniel carped.

Silence reigned for several minutes. Collin broke the silence, "I see clouds gathering. Looks like storm clouds to me." He rustled in his worn pack and pulled out a tattered Bible. "Who wants to hear a few passages from

Luke?"

Pike and several others made the effort to nod. "Anything would be fine," Pike offered as a distant rumble registered on his ears. He gave Frank a sideways glance.

Twisting his mouth, Frank bestowed Pike his best sardonic grin. "I think the heavens just said, 'Good going, Professor. Keep up the good work.'"

Shooter chuckled wryly. "Glad to hear we have the support upstairs."

With the storm's vague promise of relief, Pike was pleased as he gave the professor his undivided attention. As he listened to the words being recited, his heart flew home to his parents, feeling closer to them for this fraction of time.

*

Not only did it rain that night, but the water poured forth from the sky in great driving sheets. Hour upon hour, Drisco lay under his dry tent and listened to the onslaught. It didn't take long to saturate the ground, but Drisco didn't pay much attention to that. He just listened to the hypnotic pelting of the rain as it assisted him in drifting off into a pleasant slumber.

A loud crack suddenly tore through Drisco's consciousness causing him to sit bolt-upright. *Sounded like wood cracking to me,* he told himself as he shook his head, trying to force away the lingering sleepiness. *Somethin's wrong.*

Drisco looked at Rufus and found he was sound a-sleep. "Hey, cuz," Drisco hissed into his ear. "You and I need to get outside and do us a little lookin' around."

Rufus grumbled, "Oh, come on, it's raining. Let's stay in where it's dry."

"Priss pot, get up and follow me . . .now! You got that?"

Drisco vacated the tent and ventured out into the darkness and the slashing rain. He shuffled through the night with care, feeling for each slippery step. Flashes of lightening allowed him to see what was ahead, in the briefest snippets.

"Shit fire!" Rufus yipped as he trailed after Drisco.

After much work and plodding persistence, Drisco located a pile of debris at the base of the outermost pine wall of the prison. He gazed up and noted the interior wall had broken through completely under the force of the water and debris. *Yahoo! The water crashed through the prison. Now we can get out!* Drisco's mind told him as he slogged along.

The roaring 'Bitch' was higher than Drisco had ever seen her and she seemed to be in her utmost glory and rage as she crashed through the prison. With his muddy boots, Drisco felt his way along the boards, and after several minutes of slippery work, he found himself near the hole in the broken wall. With a few more minutes work, he and Rufus pushed the debris pile out of the way enough to push through the hole, plopping out, unceremoniously, on the other side.

Euphoria enveloped Drisco as his boots slid in the thick mud and he hooted, "We're free!"

Suddenly, Rufus slammed into his back, causing them both to topple into the murky water.

"Smack my ass!" Drisco spat at him as he swung around with his tight fist, hoping to make contact. "God damn your hide."

After releasing his anger, Drisco floundered. Finally, he put his soggy boot onto solid ground and began slogging forward as a deranged laugh rose from his throat, while Rufus snickered with glee behind him.

As they found the forest's edge, Drisco turned back and, with confidence no one would hear, he shouted, "See you kid glove boys!" Together, the lucky pair trotted forward, away from the prison walls as rapidly as the mud would allow. Soon they were swallowed by the pine trees of the forest.

*

The next day at noon, Pike dragged himself along as he tried to get back to his tent as quickly as he could - before he fell down. It was his only haven from the heat and stifling blanket of humidity. The sogginess of the ground didn't help the matter of the overwhelming heat.

Can't believe how many died in the flood last night! I know I can't drag one more dead body. Too tired and too gruesome. Someone else can fix the broken prison wall. I can't do one more thing.

Ummm . . .that's a sight there," Pike mumbled to the down-trodden group, all of whom sagged from the ghastly sights of the hundreds of dead. "I'm headed for a nap. How about you boys,"

All he heard in reply were a few grunts.

While waiting for sleep to find him, Pike wondered about Drisco and how his well-fed men fared in the torrents of last night. He hadn't noticed any of the 'Raiders' helping with the clean-up, nor did he see any of them among the dead.

I wonder if Private Dunbury talked to the captain, like I asked? Hope so, maybe we'll find out when we get our rations next time. Should be later today. Won't know til then.

*

Hearing a commotion outside of his tent awoke Pike some time later. As he peeked under the flap, he spied a Grayback soldier squad marching straight for his tent. Now, he couldn't keep the smirk off of his face as his blood began to pound with excitement and his mind cried, *Guess it worked! The private did what he said he'd do!* Pike said to his companions, "Guess we're going to find out today if my plan is going to work." He rose and strode out to meet the rebels.

They stopped and turned at the sight of him.

Pike followed as there was no need for instruction.

*

The rough planks of the porch sounded hollow as Pike and the soldiers clunked across the wooden surface. Standing as tall as his frail, injured leg and body would allow, he hoped he appeared confident - at least more than he felt.

Wish I could have cleaned up for this, Pike mused as

he listened to the rumblings of his stomach, feeling as hollow as an empty silo.

The soldier on his right-hand side stepped up to the unpainted door and knocked once. He announced, "Captain, we're here with Sergeant Wheeling, sir. May we enter?"

A deep, commanding voice instructed, "You may bring in the prisoner."

The first glimpse of Captain Henry Wirz stirred Pike's instincts. It wasn't so much the uniform, which was neat and in good repair, but the man himself. Sizing him up, Pike noted the clear blue-gray eyes that locked onto his own. The captain's look of curiosity and appraisal was evident.

I like him. Looks like an officer in control of himself and others. A wave of warm relief spread through Pike's bones.

"Sergeant Wheeling, I'm Captain Wirz. I've been informed that you wish to speak with me on a plan to keep the prisoners from uprising. I'm willing to listen to what you have to say. Please, tell me what you have in mind." The Captain made a sweeping motion with his hand. "You may sit in this chair by my desk."

With as strong a voice as he could muster, Pike commenced, "Thank you, sir, for seeing me. I appreciate your time. The other prisoners will appreciate it as well."

Taking in a deep breath, Pike prepared to give the most important speech of his life. "Sir, I would like to request something of you. I need your support with a problem I'm about to spell out for you. If you help me, I feel the whole prison will become involved. The prisoner's focus will stay on what I'm going to ask of you, rather than on their anger and frustration of being underfed and at war with one another."

Nodding his head, the Captain indicated to Pike to continue.

"Sir, I need to explain something first. There is a group among the prisoners who seek to steal what they want. These men run rampant throughout the prison and take what little the other prisoners have. They are called the 'Raiders' by their fellow prisoners. These are the most vile of men. They don't mind killing anyone

who gets in the way of their abuse. I can't tell you
enough that these men need to be gotten rid of."

"Sergeant," the Captain broke in, "I am fully aware
of the men's actions among you. I'm kept abreast of everything that takes place in the prison. The guards see all
of what goes on here. So, tell me what you want to do."

"Yes, sir. I'm proposing the 'Raiders' be rounded up
and put on trial for their lawlessness. The trial would be
a great diversion to the camp, and all the men who are
strong enough would want to participate, or at least
watch. I would hope that you would be part of the trial
process. It would be helpful for the men to see you sup-
porting them. You can decide how to work out the parti-
culars of the trial. I just wanted to give you the idea. I
would leave the rest to you and your experienced hands.
What do you think, sir?"

His body language did not reveal his thoughts, but
the captain's head nodded ever so slightly as his eyes
were fixed on a point in front of him. Time dragged on
for several minutes. Breaking out of his introspection,
the secessionist leader tilted his eyes back toward Pike
and allowed a smile to crinkle his eyes.

"Sergeant, what you're proposing sounds quite un-
conventional, but I like the ring of it. Give me some time
to arrange the matter. I do support the proposal. I'll
come up with a plan to put these 'Raiders' on trial. I'll
summon you when it's time to enact it. That will be all."

Captain Wirz stood up and summoned his soldier.
"Corporal."

"Thank you, sir," Pike said enthusiastically. The
prison will be a much better place without the 'Raiders'.
It will be calmer after the trial."

*

Distinct sounds of hammering drifted into the prison yard the next day and caught Pike's attention as he
sat outside his tent. *I know, sure as sin, they're building
something for the trial. Wish I could see what it is.*

The other men in his group likewise rested with him
after they'd eaten what little they'd put together.

"Do you hear that hammering?" the professor said. "What do you think those Rebs are up to?"

With a lemon-sour laugh, Frank interjected, "Hope it's something to eat. I'm about to start eatin' my shirt."

Appraising the men, Pike's eyes rested on Ben. *That boy looks extra pale today. He's not going to make it much longer. Just like Quinton, there's nothing we can do but watch him die.*

As weak as Pike had become, he was no longer able to perform his ministrations to the sick and dying because he just couldn't force his body to work for that long. Cupping his watch chain in his hand, Pike drew on its calming effect to aid him in focusing his mind on Rebecca and to share a few minutes in her loving arms. His eyes stared vacantly as he thrilled to her touch.

Breaking into his reverie, the sound of soldier's footsteps drew Pike's attention. Everyone roused around him at the sound. *Those are southern boys,* Pike noted as the sun glinted off the muzzleloaders slung across the five gray chests. *Glory be!* Pike's mind shouted. *Thank you, Lord!*

To his attentive group, he said, "Okay boys, We're going to get the 'Raiders'. I'll explain when I get back." He forced his frail form erect, then shambled out to meet the soldiers.

The man in the center of the group summoned Pike with the words, "Sergeant Wheeling, you're to come with us."

Nodding his fatigued head, Pike eased out to meet them.

*

"I want you to listen closely," Captain Wirz stated, locking his blue eyes on Pike. "This is my proposal. You're going to be in charge of orchestrating the trial. I want you to assign one man to prosecute and one man to defend the men you personally point out as the 'Raiders'. You'll also appoint a judge and a jury of twelve. You'll not be one of the people directly involved in the trial proceedings. You're in charge of deciding how everyone will participate.

"I will oversee the trial and make certain it is carried out properly. My soldiers have already constructed a platform that I will stand on during the trial. It will be used to hang the men . . .if the jury decides to convict them. The trial will be conducted behind the west gates and all of my soldiers will be observing from the pigeon roosts with their rifles pointed at the prisoners. You must stress to all watching that no threats will be tolerated. Any threatening action by the prisoners, and they will be shot on the spot. Do I make myself clear?"

"Yes, sir. When will the trial take place?"

"I want you to immediately go with the soldiers waiting for you and gather up these 'Raiders'. We will hold them in a pen outside the prison. Then, I expect you to choose your defense and prosecution and your judge and jury today. The trial will commence tomorrow at one o'clock. We'll ring the ration bell one time to gather the prisoners. Can you get everything done by tomorrow? I want to get right on the matter."

"Yes, sir! We'll be ready and waiting tomorrow at one. Thank you, sir. Everyone in the prison will be grateful."

Pike rose and strode as steadily as he could to meet the sentry. *Yeah! Today is the day Drisco and his Sunday soldiers will get what they deserve. Let me at 'em.*

*

The late afternoon breeze rippled through Pike's hair as he and the soldiers openly strode through the prison camp. All activity along their pathway immediately ceased and the watchful prisoners snapped around as deer startled by an unusual sound, watching their approach. While clearing a path for the soldiers, smiles appeared on the eager faces. It took but a few minutes for the contingent to arrive in the 'Raider's' territory.

Pike couldn't contain his cat-eating-mouse grin and released it to slice across his face, showing all his teeth. Smugly, he noted the tensing of the 'Raiders', whose uncertainty was exhibited in their expressions.

The entourage halted a few feet from the group. Pike

pointed at six men. "These six, here, are the ones you're looking for. There are two more." Pike's head began to swivel, scanning the area for the two most important 'Raiders'. "Where's Drisco and Rufus?" Pike directed the question to the nearest 'Raider'.

"Drisco and Rufus both disappeared the other night with the flood," the man blurted, glaring at Pike. "We ain't seen 'em since. We're thinking' they made their way out of the hole that was in the prison wall. The hole got fixed yesterday mornin'. Never saw their bodies, so that's all we figured."

The man smiled a tight smile, brimming with satisfaction.

What do I do now? Pike asked himself. *What's Buster going to think?*

One of the Graybacks broke the silence. "You six men are being arrested for the crimes committed against your fellow prisoners. You'll be put on trial tomorrow by a jury of your peers. Now, step away from the tent. Get in front of us." The soldier emphasized the order by pointing his muzzleloader in the direction they were to take.

The six men grudgingly took their spots in front of the squad's escort.

"Move out," the soldier shouted into the hot, hazy air.

Everyone within earshot stood, gaping at the scene, and as the contingent passed from view, a buzzing noise erupted among the prisoners.

Pike, upset by the news of Drisco and Rufus escaping, stood in place, eyes glued to the ground.

Several familiar men approached and inquired, "What's going on? Would you tell us?" More men collected like crows to a corn patch with ears open and waiting.

Lifting his gaze, Pike forced a determined smile and hoped to cover the heaviness in his heart. He stood as straight as he could in the sun-seared path and gathered his resolve to continue. It was time to prepare for the trial of the 'Raiders'.

"Now, they can pay for what they've done to us. The trial will be held tomorrow at one o'clock. All men willing and able to participate should gather by my tent on the north side of the yard in one hour. We'll work out who will be participating. We'll draw numbers for the positions. We'll only let the first two hundred men participate. We can't handle any more than that. If you aren't willing to defend the 'Raiders', please don't get in the drawing because one of the unlucky souls will have to be responsible for the defense. Thank you all, in advance, for your help with taking care of these killers. See you in one hour."

Chapter 7

Even before the sun had made its first call on the day, the towering west gates swung outward in the hazy mist the following morning. Pike's group ambled through the awakening prison yard toward the gates and Pike couldn't help but note the groan of the doors opening, urging him to move faster across the rutted ground than the mere shuffling he and the others had been performing. *Shut up, leg, and let me be for awhile.* Excitement rushed through him, setting his belly to fluttering at the thought of what was to happen this glorious day.

Pike and the others abruptly stopped when they spied a platform being hauled into the prison yard by Rebel soldiers. The imposing gallows rocked Pike to a standstill, rendering him temporarily speechless as he gawked. Then he glanced at the small band of prisoners with him, noting they all looked like a gaggle of startled guinea hens, temporarily hushed and waiting to fly. But, just as suddenly as guineas take wing, Pike found his feet once more to hobble off, the others trailed after.

When the men came abreast of the guards, they halted. Pike gaped at all the equipment the Rebels were dragging in front of the west gates. He stared at the pine platform and told himself, *That's what that hammering must have been about.*

The platform towered over his head and an arch rose above the base, extended across the whole platform and attached to both sides with massive-looking beams. A set of stairs had been attached to the back of the structure. Pike spied the cutouts in the platform base so he now knew for sure that it was a gallows. Turning to Frank, Pike spoke with a smile in his voice, "What do you think about this?" He indicated the gallows with a nod of his head.

"Looks to me like these Johnny Rebs mean business. I think they're going to let us hang these boys."

Pike swung around and shot a look at Buster, who stood directly behind him with an unusual grin displayed on his scarred face. Although Buster had taken the news of the escape of Drisco and Rufus fairly well, Pike wanted to make sure Buster was enjoying himself. "What do you think, Buster? Are those boys going to get their just desserts today?"

"Yes, sir. I's thinks they is. Sho goin' to please me to see that. I was sho hopin' Drisco and Rufus would get what they deserve, but this will sho nuff please me."

Bringing his gaze back to the procession, Pike scrutinized the scurrying guards. A couple of pairs of Rebels ushered in two long wooden benches and placed them in a row along one side of the gallows.

Are those for the jury? Pike wondered. *Looks like seating for them.* Next, he spotted desks being arranged in front of the gallows.

"Looks like they are ready to go," Collin indicated.

"Yes, it does," Frank returned.

"You all ready to rest until it's time?" Pike queried quietly.

Everyone turned and began to plod away.

*

By noontime, that late August day had turned as hot as a hen in a cook-pot, but the steamy air didn't dampen Frank's spirits nor did it seem to affect the upbeat mood of the rest of the crowd. Sitting directly behind the tables for the defense and prosecution, Frank rested next to Pike, along with their friends.

The festive temper of the masses dominated the scene before the west gates even though most of the men hovering around the trial equipment looked more like fully-clothed skeletons than real men. Even so, the hope of hanging the 'Raiders' drew all those capable of walking to the gates with a magnetic pull.

Gazing about and shading his eyes with his hand, Frank felt a giddiness welling up within him at the wonder of the moment. A laugh threatened to escape from him, and he worried that it might erupt in front of everyone and clearly exhibit just how unstable he felt these days. His stomach clutched, reminding him to keep a tight rein on his laughter. As he struggled to maintain his sliver of sanity, he thought, *Don't know if I'm not going stark-raving loony in this place. Guess my mind is fading away with the rest of me.*

Refocusing his errant thoughts, the joy of the moment flooded back to reestablish itself over those frightening ideas. *Whew, that was close. Glad to get rid of those dark notions. Today, it's all about something good and I've got to keep my mind on that. This may be the only good day in here, so, enjoy it.*

As a smartly-dressed Captain Wirz marched through the open gate, the crowd went silent. The Captain appeared wrapped in an air of total control with his smart step and rigid back. Behind him, rebel soldiers ushered the six 'Raiders' into the prison yard and held them near the gallows.

Frank noted the stiff back of the captain whose gaze remained directly in front of him, never wavering from side-to-side. The captain was flanked by a dozen soldiers, ready for any trouble. The soldiers clutched their guns across their chests as their procession cut to the platform and came to a stop directly behind the stairs. On a cue from the captain, the dozen soldiers formed a circle around the platform. The wall of protection stood unmistakably clear.

Mounting the stairs, the captain strode quickly across the platform and came to rest at its edge. Gazing about, he addressed the onlookers. "Today is one without precedent. You, who are all being held as prisoners, will carry out punishment deemed appropriate for your fellow prisoners. I am pleased to have been able to help you in this trial process. The men on trial are accused of some heinous crimes. If convicted, they will receive the punishment the jury places on them. Now let the jury, judge, prosecution, and defense please take their appointed places."

The summoned men stood and strode purposefully in the direction of the gallows then each found their seat. Apprehension, as well as anticipation, filled the air around the onlookers and participants.

Frank held his breath and listened carefully.

"Judge," the captain said, "you may begin."

Abel Stuart had been chosen for this position from the drawing that had taken place the previous day. Behind his round spectacles resided a set of dark eyes, baggy from age. Hard wrinkles creased the sides of his face and his jowls flopped loosely with skin far more wrinkled than his face, only accentuated by his loss of weight.

Frank had been surprised the day before when this man had stated he was a lawyer in his home state of Massachusetts. "One of Salem's finest," Stuart had told them. *Was it true?*

Speaking to the jury with a resonant voice, Abel commenced. "The jury must remain focused on all that takes place during the trial. It is your job to vote after both sides have presented their cases. The decision of guilt or innocence rests with you." He shifted to face the audience. "I must direct the flow of the trial and handle any conflicts between the defense and the prosecution. What I say is final . . . and the only ruling on such matters. Does everyone understand?" His eyes swept the participants to note the nods before he continued.

Abel's gaze fell on Steven, the one chosen as the prosecutor. Stuart addressed him. "You, sir, are responsible for the prosecution. We will begin with you. You will be given time to present your case. Then, the defense will be allowed time to present its side. Both sides will be allowed to make final statements. Is this clear?"

Frank observed as Steven's white-haired head gave a quick nod. Then, Frank's eyes traveled to Simon, the man chosen for the defense, and Simon nodded also, indicating he understood what was expected.

"Now that the instructions have been given," the judge continued as he glanced meaningfully into the eyes of each participant, "it is time to begin. Mr. Prosecutor, it's your show."

With self-imposed stiffness, Steven rose from his seat at the wooden table and sauntered slowly toward the jury. His gaze flitted from one man to the other as he smiled into their open and friendly faces. Standing rigidly in the blistering afternoon sun, Steven began to speak. "Today, it is my greatest pleasure to give you the many reasons that the six men standing before you should be convicted of their crimes. You all know these men well. They have been responsible for a large part of the immense suffering among us. They are the worst sort of criminals. They've stolen from us and killed men they are supposed to be protecting with their very lives. These men are traitors of the lowest sort, and you should be proud to convict them."

Frank did feel proud for Steven as he made his strong opening speech and a sense of anticipation continued to hold its grip on him.

Glancing briefly at the six prisoners, Stuart then turned back to hold eye contact with the jury. "I will now describe the crimes these men have committed. They have been responsible for taking hundreds, if not thousands, of pounds of food from their fellow prisoners. They sneak around at night and pilfer what they want. The stealing of our meager rations and water is the worst crime they have committed, for these men are responsible for adding to the suffering and countless deaths of those trapped here in Andersonville.

"Not only have they stolen our food and water, they have stolen countless other important provisions. Our tents, blankets, tools, and clothes are equally important in maintaining our continued health. Our very lives depend on them. These renegades have taken, at will, what they wanted for themselves, with no regard for the lives they were stealing from.

"They also have killed, outright, the men strong enough to try to stand in their way. I have personally seen several of the dead men that the 'Raiders' have killed with their own hands. We've all seen their handiwork. These six men deserve the sentence you give them. I ask for a guilty conviction from you, the jury. Thank you." With a bob of his shiny white hair, Steven appeared a bit rickety on his feet as he returned to his seat.

Looking paler than usual, Steven turned his attention to Simon, who briefly caught Frank's eye, and Frank gave Simon a big smile and an approving nod.

Standing up, Simon, displaying a jaw stiff with resolve and a stern look in his dark blue eyes, walked to stand before the jury. An average-looking man, thin but not emaciated, Simon wasted no time in voicing his side of the issue. "It's my job to defend the men accused of the crimes the prosecution has just described fer ya. These are the facts, as I see 'em . . . Use 'em how ya'd like to make yer decision of guilt or innocence. The men accused of stealing have been openly seen takin' other soldiers' stuff. That's a fact. But, with the terrible conditions we all live under, it's no wonder men have to turn on each other. In here, it's survival of the fittest. We have to look out fer ourselves. I'm not offering an excuse, but a reason to help in understanding the actions of these here men.

"When they were caught red-handed stealing, what other choice did they have but to defend themselves? Yes, they've kilt because of this. But, again, it was fer self-defense.

"You, in the jury, please think over the reasoning I've presented to help guide ya in deciding the guilt or innocence of these here men. Thank ya."

*

Pike waited tensely as the ballots were counted and the final results of the trial were about to be presented. Every man on the jury sat back on the bench and wore a smug expression.

Abel finally rose in the tense silence, and after he cleared his throat, he called out, "By unanimous vote, the defendants are found guilty."

The words floated over Pike as sweet as any ballad. Unable to contain his ecstasy, he leapt to his feet and slapped those around him on the back. Pike grabbed Frank in a bear-hug.

The prisoners close enough to hear the verdict, bellowed and stamped their feet and word spread through the crowd quickly until the entire throng of prisoners joined in the celebration. The noise increased to an ear-deafening level among the thousands of prisoners.

Just like Frank, Pike had been having insane, rambling thoughts. Now, he could no longer contain the babbling of his frail mind, so he let his unstable laughter flow free in the noisy clamor around him. Throwing back his head, he indulged in a series of deep belly laughs that rippled out of him, one after another. As quickly as it had started, the release of the pent-up craziness ended, and in its wake, Pike felt calmer, saner. He gazed over the gleeful prisoners, then turned to see Captain Wirz rise to his feet on the platform.

The captain's movement captured the attention of many around him. In two long strides, he stopped at the platform's edge and stared out at the wild sea of men. He raised his arm for silence. Those close enough to see his directive sank back into the dirt, giving him their full attention. Within a few minutes, all the prisoners were doing the same.

The captain shouted, "Judge, what punishment do you place on those convicted?"

Pike held his breath as his gaze traveled to Abel's face.

Slowly, Abel stood and announced distinctly, "All of these six men, convicted of their crimes, will be hung by the neck until dead."

A cheer rippled through the prison crowds.

Relief washed over Pike now that the trial was over. And now . . . and now it was time to carry out the sentence and force these men to face their Maker. Pike watched the audience, noting the predatory eyes, waiting for the next step in the process as the convicted criminals trudged toward the gallows at the prodding of the soldiers. The first three 'Raiders' trained their eyes on the ropes ahead of them while being urged to mount the stairs.

Pike wondered how it would feel to be in their shoes and facing the hangman's noose. A living, breathing terror shot up inside him, making his bladder twitch with an urgent need as his mind allowed him that reality. *If I died now, would I be proud of my life? What would God think of how I've lived the life He gave me?*

A shiver ran free as Pike pondered the truth of how much work he had really done that would make God proud of him. Those doubts, coupled with the self-imposed dread of feeling the convicts' fear of literally seeing the end of their lives, made an icy sweat break out across his back. Despite the day's sweltering heat, the thoughts chilled him to the core. Shivers shook his spine until he snapped back to the action at hand and released the darker imaginings. When the heat of the afternoon sun blasted him again he thought, *Thank You. Don't want to think of such matters just now.*

From the corner of his eye, Pike caught a glimpse of his brother and friends. He could easily see Frank gazing in silence and awe at the 'Raiders' who were now slumped over and being shoved across the last fifty feet of their lives. Buster appeared as somber as Pike had felt just a few moments before. *Wonder if he's thinking about his lost love and wishing Drisco was swinging today? Can't do much about that now. Maybe someday . . .if we ever make it out of here.*

The first convicted trio stood on the platform with the nooses swinging lightly in the breeze in front of their faces. All three stared up at the beams as they appeared unable to face the crowd.

Giving his head a slight nod, the captain provided the signal to finish the task.

All three men pulled back when the guards grasped them by the arms to urge them forward. As the nooses were lowered over their heads, the men displayed tense expressions and blank eyes. Had it not been for the dark stain Pike spotted spreading down one of the convict's pants, he would have never guessed that these men felt sorry for what they had done, or were even afraid of the next step in eternity.

*

The death messenger arrived for the second set of Raiders just as the first. They thrashed and kicked violently for several minutes. Two of the men were lucky enough to break their necks, killing them instantly as they fell through the open trap doors, but the others suffered longer.

Finally, the last Raider, holding the rapt attention of the crowd, stopped kicking.

The grizzly sight of the men's painful deaths did not dampen Pike's spirits, nor anyone else's. The prisoners leapt up to instigate a massive celebration - one that continued on through the evening and well into the night.

Pike didn't want to let go of the fleeting happiness that had been found that day, and he told himself that evening, *Better hold on to this feeling as long as you can. Don't expect any more good days in here.*

The main celebration took place around Pike's tent. Early in the evening's festivities, he had taken out his harmonica and played it for the masses - until the wee hours of the morning. All the while, he couldn't quite wipe the smirk off of his face. It seemed that the grin might cement itself into place. *So what if it does?* he thought briefly, massaging his tired jaws.

As the fresh day's light began to filter into the sky above Andersonville, Pike drank in His Creator's infinite beauty and appreciated it beyond measure. He held on to his favored fob and sent his spirit to find Rebecca. How he longed for her for a beat of his heart and then the familiar ache of that longing caused his heart to clutch. *Rebecca, where are you at this very moment? Are you staring at the sky right now, wondering where I am?*

Then a mystical presence pervaded his consciousness so strongly that it overwhelmed him. The intuition caused him to whisper in the dawn, "Rebecca, is that you?" But, just as quickly as it had come, the presence vanished, and in its place there remained the lingering emptiness that had been his constant companion for months.

*

Clasping Ben's frail hand, as Pike had done so many times in the past with others, Pike provided as much comfort as he could to the dying boy.

Ben looked up into Pike's eyes and muttered, "I'll see

you again someday," just before closing his own eyes for all eternity.

Through the tears clouding his vision, Pike whispered, "Go to be in God's glory. May He take you on His wings." The tears took over, shaking Pike's thin body in sobs until he could no longer speak, and he continued to grip the dead boy's hand for an hour or more until Buster gently guided him out of the tent for a breath of fresh air.

Once Pike's tears dried, emptiness and death still consumed his thoughts. Despair threatened to squeeze the life out of him as he asked from his hoarse whisper, "Buster, what are we going to do? We've been in here seven months now. I'm going crazy in here."

"Pike, we's goin' to get through this. We's has to. God gots a plan for you. We needs you, too. Don't give up. You's all we's got leff."

Buster's words pierced through Pike's sadness and provided him a peek at normalcy. He said to himself, *Okay, I hear you. I'll be strong.* Glancing up, he spotted Frank staring at him with worried eyes and a furrowed brow so he nodded his head, indicating he was okay.

Relief flooded Frank's face and his shoulders visibly relaxed.

Rising, Pike shuffled back to his spot to rest in the dirt once more.

*

Less than a month later, Captain Wirz faced the prisoners. In a strained voice, he announced, "You are hereby free to go."

Those words passed over Pike's ears, but they didn't register immediately. As the huge pine gates began to open, he realized he had been given his freedom. *Freedom? Freedom! Oh sweet freedom!* He couldn't help himself from looking up at the clear blue sky to appreciate it from a free man's eyes.

Tears threatened to fall from the mist clouding his vision as he pranced with the others through the towering west gates. Internally, he called out, *Thank you, Fa-*

ther, for Your tender mercies. You have seen fit to bless me and deliver me from hell. The glory is all Yours. Amen. Then, his mind screamed, *Can't believe I'm free. I'm going home!* He found himself caught up in a multitude of emotions, all swirling at once, but all of them were oh, so, sweet.

Frank's hand rested warmly on Pike's shoulder as they enjoyed the moment of release. Along with the others in their group, they shared the joy of escape from the inferno of deprivation they had been buried in for so long.

Even with Pike's wobbly and weakened legs, the other men in his group struggled to keep pace. He spotted their grins as they collectively shuffled and walked over the rough road. They were a sad-looking lot, with shaggy heads and gaunt frames, but they had survived the worst hellhole imaginable.

Pike turned his thoughts to other things, and today was about the *moment,* and this moment was about freedom. *Freedom!* It was what Pike had prayed for countless times these many, many months but now, it was happening.

A clear, crisp fall day had been chosen to take the worn and weak prisoners back to the nearby town to board a train heading north - heading home. The clanging steam engine and extensive length of empty cars waited for them like a specter from Pike's past. A shudder rolled through him from the memories of the excruciating trip to the prison camp, which stirred up past experiences of hurt and sorrow, causing him to swallow hard as he strained to quell the hateful images. A memory flashed through his mind of the dying soldier lying next to him, bandages around his bleeding stomach, drops of blood dripping on the car floor.

"Pike," Frank said, breaking into his thoughts, "we are on our way home. Are you ready?"

"Naw. Let's stay a while longer," Pike quipped. It was good to feel like poking fun at Frank. Privately, Pike thought, *Glad he started talking to help me get rid of the past.*

Hundreds of newly-freed prisoners, some silent, some talking joyously, swept Pike and Frank along in their wake. Pike's steps slowed as he reached the crest of a small hill. Halting, he felt drawn to gaze for a time at the village behind the train's cars. The urge to run down the hill and gulp a few shots of whiskey, to help celebrate the day, rushed into him, but his feet could not perform what his mind desired. So, he waited for the rest of his men to join him. He drew the clean-scented air deeply into his lungs to regain his wind.

Gathering around him, the men gawked at the tiny hamlet of the town as buzzards over a dead buffalo.

"Town looks great," Collin offered.

"Who wants a drink?" Tom asked.

There were several mumbles of 'yes,' but no one made the attempt to act on it.

Taking the lead once more, Pike proceeded toward the 'Freedom Train.' As Pike stood in front of the boxcar, a tremor of sheer terror gripped him, causing him to gulp as the door opened, looming above his head. The personal horror of the previous trip washed over him again. He forced several swallows to push down the bile rising in the back of his throat as he fussed to himself, *What's wrong with you? Remember . . you are free.*

He fingered his watch chain as he struggled to refocus his errant thoughts on his love and family. *Why can't I remember what Rebecca looks like? Why can't I see her anymore?*

Drawing in a troubled breath, Pike became conscious of Frank's hand on his arm. Letting his eyes travel to Frank's anxious face, he concentrated on his little brother's blue eyes and released the ugly wanderings of his fragile mind as a smile grew between them.

With the frightful images haunting him no more, Pike took his first step to mount the train. It came easier than he had thought possible. Buster and Frank soon leapt on board and the whole group fell into laughing heaps as Collin, Tom, Daniel, James, and Shooter joined them.

Resting, Pike couldn't help the gratitude washing over him, but exhaustion laid a heavy hand on his shoulder, pressing him to the floor. New worries clouded his mind. *Hope I can get up later. What if I can't? Maybe, if I rest my eyes for a moment, I'll feel better.* He took one last look at the men so close to his heart and he couldn't help but grin because of their happy faces. Luckily, this trip wouldn't be so closely packed and a man had room to sit and lie down when he needed to, and, boy, did he need to.

Stretching out his lanky, undernourished frame, Pike indulged in a quick nap. In his dreams, his mind flew home and it called, *Rebecca, where are you? Hope you are waiting for me. I'm almost back to your loving arms.* Deep, restful slumber captured his ramblings and erased all else.

Part II

Pike's New World

Chapter 8

Caught between dizzying euphoria at being home with his family again, and the bottomless well of sorrow due to finding an unexpectedly drastic change between him and Rebecca, Pike forced his mind to focus on the vicious pew rubbing his backbone in the front half of his father's church - The First Presbyterian of Baltimore. Squirming to get more comfortable, he ordered himself, *Listen to what Dad is saying. Don't look at her!* The futile attempt to get his thoughts off his love's pretty face, did not have any effect on his eyes. They were drawn to her as surely as metal to a magnet, never straying for more than a few seconds, lovingly drinking in every detail of her face.

You've got to get a hold of yourself. Listen! His directive was to no avail, not with Rebecca sitting a few pews in front of him. He just couldn't avoid staring at her and remembering their past.

Pike's sister, Mary, sat on one side of him, Buster on the other and Pike noted Buster appearing to be deeply studying Frank Senior's words, which extolled the virtue of steadfastness in a Christian's life.

Amos, Pike's middle brother, sat a couple of rows ahead of him, just to the left of Rebecca, with their young son, Patrick between them. Rebecca held a small bundle in her arms, and baby Hannah waved her tiny fists in the air.

Openly ogling the children, Pike's shock of finding his love married to his brother crashed across his mind again and again.

As Rebecca's son, Patrick, squirmed in his seat, Pike wondered, *Why couldn't that boy have been mine? I was supposed to marry Rebecca, not Amos, for crying out loud!* Then, Pike's emotional tide turned to more aggravated thoughts as he shouted at Rebecca in his mind,

Why Rebecca? Why didn't you wait for me? I hate the sight of you. My brother? . . .two children? You sure didn't waste any time, did you? Where's the sweet girl I dreamed of all those long years?

Unconsciously, Pike's hand traveled to his treasured chain of Rebecca's hair, as always, in his pocket. When his fingers touched her hair, shaking his head, he dropped the silky locks as if they had just seared his palm. The fob no longer held the same meaning or comfort, nor would it ever again. And with a flush of anger, he yanked his hand out of his pocket as if he had just clutched a hot branding iron.

His head swayed minutely back and forth while he struggled with his rampaging emotions. More than anything, he wanted to jump up and yell out his rage before dashing out of the church and running away from reality. Knowing his actions would reflect poorly on his father, Pike kept himself under control because he wouldn't do anything to hurt his family, especially not Frank Senior, so he forced himself to stay in his pew, and groaned.

Then Pike turned from his anger at Rebecca and aimed it at Amos. *How could you do this to me? You married my love shortly after I left to fight for our country. I still can't believe it!* The naked betrayal of his brother could not be ignored. Amos was just as guilty as Rebecca in all of this. What was he going to say to him? Pike's emotional turmoil forced him to close his eyes, briefly shutting out the sight of Amos with Rebecca and, especially, the children, as tears welled.

After a time, when he felt more in control, he turned his gaze to his imposing buddy, Buster, whose anxious stare met Pike's. As much as the smile never made it to Pike's eyes, he forced a sour one, hoping it would ease his friend's apparent worry. The scrutiny of his friend made him uncomfortable, so he averted his gaze, turning back to his father.

With his eyes now glued on Frank Senior, preaching to those before him, Pike lost the battle against stopping his internal struggles. *What am I going to do or say to Rebecca and Amos when I have to face them? All I want to do is wrap my hands around both of their throats.*

Urgh! How could they do this? Can I ever forgive them? What am I going to do with the rest of my life? Rebecca was my whole future. . . And now that's gone. What now?

His physical weakness crept its way back across the fringes of his mind and blocked his brain from further pondering as his thoughts went mushy. *Damn this frailty! When will it go away? I can't do anything.* Letting out an unconscious sigh, Pike shifted again on the uncomfortable bench, hoping for some sort of relief - from anywhere; heart, head or backside.

Reality jolted him as he became aware of the congregation rising in a rush of friendly voices and the whispering around him as they trickled out of the pews. His mind now clearer, he noticed Rebecca and her family edging their way into the aisle before him. Pike watched his young nephew, bucking like a newborn colt and seemingly filled with the glee of fresh life, happy to be released from his forced inactivity.

As Rebecca wrapped her tiny daughter more tightly in the pink cotton blanket and smiled down into the tiny face, maternal love radiated from her. Pike observed all the maternal affection and was blasted by a searing longing. The scene of bliss rendered Pike's feet motionless as his troubled heart bled anew. The blood drained from his head and left a familiar faintness in its wake which swooped down upon him and made his knees feel like buckling.

Buster reached out to grab him firmly by the elbow and prevented him from tumbling into the aisle. But, as Pike looked back he saw Amos hovering behind his wife, causing Pike to continue to gulp air as a fish on a bank.

Looking up, Rebecca glanced away from Hannah, drawn by an unseen force. Her eyes came to rest on Pike and they widened visibly as she recognized him. "Oh," she said sharply as the word escaped from her mouth.

After all these years, Pike faced his lover, and as his eyes locked with hers, he shared a brief flash of familiar ardor. Warmth plowed through his body as he reveled in the tenderness flowing from Rebecca's eyes. He couldn't help himself, but the question in his heart had been answered. *She still loves me!* His heart shouted and leapt for joy.

The tiny moment evaporated when Amos urged Rebecca to move forward. As brief as the scene had been, it created a momentary tonic for Pike's bleeding heart. *At least she loved me. Guess that part was real. But, why did she marry Amos?*

Amos and Rebecca stiffly and rapidly marched down the center aisle while Pike, Frank, and Buster trailed after. Outside, the crisp autumn air cooled Pike's flaming cheeks and the breeze helped clear his head, but anger's ember remained.

Frank Senior, stately-looking in his dark suit, stood in his customary position at the top of the steps and spoke to each member of the congregation as they vacated the church. "Thank you for your kindness. I've been working on that sermon for three years. I think I've just about gotten it right. You take care of that bad hip, Mrs. Bendleton. Yes, I'll see you next week." He guided the stooped woman down the steps to safer ground. Then his blue eyes, sparkling with vitality, turned their attention to Pike. Grasping Pike's hand, he shook it enthusiastically, showering Pike, Frank, and Buster with an open smile, permeated by his kindness. "You boys enjoy the sermon?"

"Yes, Father," Frank answered. "We did enjoy your message today, as always. Did Mother take Mary and Jane home to get lunch ready? I don't see them anywhere."

"Yes, son, the women have gone and are cooking up a mighty celebration feast. We want to let you fellows rest, but I'm afraid everyone is anxious to visit with you. The whole church wants to come over, but we've only invited a few to the house. Your mother's baked a cake. We are so excited you have made it back to us that we can't help but share some of that excitement. Hope you can put up with us today."

"Dad, it's okay with me," Frank answered quickly. "I'd enjoy seeing some of our friends. I'm hungry, anyhow. How about you, Buster? . . . Pike?"

"Fine wiff me. I's don't knowed any of these folks but I's sho could eat. I's don't mind if'n you gots company." Buster tilted his eyebrows at Pike, who had yet to respond.

With a heavy heart, Pike was as lost as a ship in a hurricane, but he managed, "Sure, it's okay with me, too." On the one hand, Pike desperately wanted to be near Rebecca, any way he could but, by the same token, he also felt that he might lose control if he were around her for even a brief moment. *And what about Amos? Maybe I can stay away from her, even at the house.* Collecting his errant emotions as best his frail body could, Pike noticed the others had turned and filtered down the steps to make their way to the waiting carriage. He trudged after them.

As he regarded his favorite team of horses, Lila and Leon, he swelled with pride. Their mahogany bay coats gleamed. The well-bred duo made a perfectly-matched team of high-stepping Morgans. Pike grinned at the patient postures of the team as the two waited for the return of their driver. The horses, even though several years older, appeared fit and healthy. The beauty of a horse never failed to provide him appreciation for God's perfect handiwork.

*

The horses' harness jangled a merry tune as the team trotted briskly toward home. The jingling and clopping brought a measure of comfort to Pike and he willed himself to focus on those everyday sounds, not on his troubled heart. He closed his eyes and rested his weary head. He could not resist an internal grin as he continued to take note of one of his favorite small pleasures of life. He had sorely missed those happy sounds during the years of fighting.

Yes, Lord, Pike thought as his mind sent his appreciation skyward, *I will listen to Your message of heaven-sent love, and take note of the wonders You give me each day.*

"Whoa!" Frank Senior called out.

As the carriage came to a rolling stop, Pike broke out of his internal reverie. He sat up and glanced over the side of the carriage, noting they were home. His eyes drank in the Wheeling home. It was a two-story house, a red-and-gray wooden structure that had been built many years before, located far from town. But, as Baltimore had spread, the town now encompassed the family acreage.

Several wagons and teams were scattered about the yard. Pike recognized some of the teams of long-time family friends. His eyes picked out the wagon that belonged to Amos as he recognized the bay-and-gray team. *Guess I can't escape. How am I going to handle this? Don't know if I'm up to it.*

"Pike," Buster said in his quiet, soothing voice, "I's think we oughtta git out."

Pike rose, forcing his body to do Buster's bidding. *You've made it through a war. What's one afternoon with Rebecca? Come on, you coward!*

Hopping down from the driver's seat and tying the team to the hitching post, Frank Senior directed, "You boys see to the horses. Rub them down good. I'll see you inside."

Together, Pike, Frank, and Buster dismounted the carriage. Frank and Pike strode to the bay beauties to begin the familiar task of removing the harness. As Frank lifted the heavy collar over Lila's patient head, he stated the obvious, "Hope you can handle being with Amos and Rebecca, Pike. I visited with Amos for a while yesterday. He's really worried about how mad you are. You think you can forgive them?"

Trying to temper his anger and hurt, Pike replied, instantly looking away, "I just don't know what to do. I leave this house to go to war and carry Rebecca's love with me. I came home, I thought to be with her, but I find her married to my brother and with two children. How am I supposed to react? I can't do anything about it, but I can't forgive and forget."

"Brother, hope you can find some way to let your anger go because Rebecca's gone and Amos is still your brother. I know it's tough, but in time, your hurt will ease."

With his face taut from his inner turmoil, Pike led the horses into the barn. Pivoting his gaze from brushing Leon's back, he leaned across the horse's withers and declared to Frank harshly, "It's almost more than I can bear . . . coming home to the loss of Rebecca. We've all lost so much in the war. Sometimes I wonder how we'll ever recover." He paused and sighed, dropping his head. Pike's voice softened when he looked up again. "Buster," he said, indicating with his head in the direction where Buster waited, "has lost so much more than I could ever imagine. So, I can't complain too much. I'll try to find a way to settle things between me and Amos. Some day . . . "

Pike tossed a pitchfork full of hay for each horse. As the team munched contentedly, he strolled with Frank through the flapping barn doors. They shut them tightly behind them.

Resting under a sycamore tree, scarlet from its fall foliage, Buster whittled on a broken hickory limb. He appeared to enjoy the warmth of the day as he was smiling.

"Buster, are you hungry?" Pike called out.

"Yes, sir. My stomach sho' is growlin'."

"I really miss the other boys around meal time," Pike declared. "I don't know what we'll do without them, especially the professor and his recitations."

"I know what you mean," Frank added. "I miss the rest of the boys, too, but I'm sure glad to be home. Let's enjoy the day that the Lord has made. 'Let us be glad in it', just like the song. We'd better join the others. I could use a spot of grub right about now." He emphasized his words by licking his lips. "Can't wait to get one of Mom's sweet-butter rolls. Come on, Buster."

*

Inside the house, the Wheeling family, along with eight of their closest friends, lined both sides of the well-used harvest table which had been laden with an array of tempting foods. They awaited in silence for Frank Senior's prayer.

From Pike's vantage point in the middle of the table he could see everyone's smiling faces with Buster and Frank on either side of him. His sisters, Mary and Jane, sat across from him with their new spouses. Mary was clearly well-advanced with pregnancy. *Being married seems to agree with them both,* Pike mused.

On the opposite side of the table near the end, next to Pike's mother, Rebecca sat. It wouldn't be difficult to avoid looking at her, but he was as drawn to her now as surely as he had been in the church.

Pike's hand twitched with the urge to dig into the mashed potatoes and corn, sitting directly in front of him. Only his years of training kept him from reaching out and grabbing what he wanted. It was hard, but Pike focused on his father's prayerful words, hoping they would be brief.

"Thank you, Father, for bringing our sons home. We can never give You enough glory for that miracle. Bless this food you have lovingly placed on our table. Thank you for the friends and family that are here with us today. Amen."

All eyes turned to Frank Senior to commence serving. He reached out and plucked up a heavy blue china plate, brimming with fried chicken. After stabbing a few choice pieces for himself, he pushed the plate on to William and his wife, Sara.

All the while, Pike continued his internal fussing as his eyes lingered on Rebecca. *Think about your rumbling stomach. Don't look at her. Don't think about her.* But he couldn't stop himself, he allowed his eyes to travel across the gleeful people on the other side of the table, to come to rest on Rebecca's perky face, and he was startled to meet her chocolate-brown eyes already gazing at him. His stomach and heart fluttered as they locked gazes and the past ignited from her eyes. Internal fire spewed forth in Pike, but, as quickly as the past had ignited, it blew itself out. The sting of hurt stomped its way into his heart, quashing the hungry feeling that had been there but a few seconds before.

Sliding his eyes away, Pike forced a quick swallow as he strained to ease the heaviness in his entrails, but to no avail. The rock that formed there appeared to be saying, "You've got to get out of here!"

"Here, Pike," Frank huffed. "Take this. It's heavy."

Grabbing the bowl of chicken, Pike stared at the plate, unsure of what to do. As the moment of confusion passed, he clumsily retrieved his fork from his linen napkin and stabbed the nearest piece, dropping it onto his plate. Head bowed, gaping stupidly at his food, he strained to appear as though he was entranced by his meal, not by his lost love.

Frank elbowed him in the side, breaking into his private thoughts.

Jerking his head upright, Pike struggled to appear as though he had been paying attention to the conversation around the table. He pushed his food around so no one would be suspicious of his not eating.

Jacob Coltrane, a writer and a round ball-of-a-man with a fuzzy halo of wren-brown hair, started the questioning. "Boys, tell us about the war. I know everyone else is dying to hear about it. Your father has told us all three of you were imprisoned in Andersonville. What was that like?"

Eyes pleading with Frank to do the talking, Pike's internal weariness rested on his shoulders with the weight of lead. He didn't feel up to telling stories.

Taking his cue, Frank began, "Well, the fighting was like nothing I could have ever dreamed up. Our first fight was in a cornfield in Virginia. When the shooting started, I was so scared, I almost wet my pants, not Pike though. He wasn't scared, not one time."

All of the eager eyes around the table stayed latched onto Frank as he spoke, but Pike's mind wandered elsewhere.

At the end of the meal, after the coffee had been served, Pike rose stiffly to go outside for a breath of fresh air. The walls around him were closing in and he hoped to take his mind off Rebecca. *Maybe if I get outside for awhile, I can think on something else. I've got to find a way to let go of all this between me and my brother and Rebecca. I know she loved me. Guess, I have that, but I want to be with her . . .and I can't*

*

As Pike stepped off the front porch, he appreciated the last few rays of sun fading from the cool day. A shiver of cold sent a shudder up his spine, drawing him to his favorite place of refuge - the barn. Shutting the door behind him, hoping for escape, he entered into the comforting world of the animals. Their familiar smells brought forth many happy memories.

Heading straight to his gelding's stall, Pike allowed Hank to press his nose against his ear and snuffle along his head, as if they hadn't been separated these last four years. Wrapping his arms around Hank's golden neck as Hank's head hung invitingly over the stall door, he rested his right cheek against the soft hair. He closed his eyes and cleared his mind, feeling his heart beat and blocking out all thoughts.

Then, speaking to the horse out of habit, he muttered, "Hank, I've missed you. Remember our last ride together? That night we went over to Rebecca's and took her on that moonlight ride. Do you remember?"

"I sure remember," Rebecca's voice quietly crooned.

Whirling around, Pike came face-to-face with Rebecca's soft, dark eyes. He wasn't sure how she had been able to sneak up on him, but now that he saw her, unbridled happiness swept over him. He couldn't help it because he still loved her, that hadn't changed, but just as quickly, anger took charge, pushing the joy aside, causing him to grimace. "What do you want?" he snarled, turning back to Hank.

Rebecca closed the distance and came too close for Pike's comfort. Due to her short stature, she had to tilt her head back to look up into Pike's face. "I wanted to talk to you alone," she whispered, her eyes lingered warmly on his.

Her gaze created a heat in the pit of his stomach that radiated throughout his body, bringing him alive. Still, he glared at her and answered her in a curt voice. "What do we have to talk about? It looks to me like it's pretty clear how things are. You're married to Amos and have two children. Hope you're happy."

Her eyes swam with unshed tears as she wheeled away from him and faced the opposite direction, her voice seemingly gone. After a few tense moments, she turned back to face him, her back straight with resolve. "I thought I was over you 'til I saw you again. I just can't deny my true feelings for you."

Letting the comment hang between, Pike didn't respond.

"I wanted to let you know how it was for me, once you were gone. The first few days after you left to go to the war were the worst ones of my life. I cried till I thought I'd go crazy. Finally, I went to visit your family, hoping that being with them would help somehow.

"When I got to your house, the only one home was Amos. He sat me down at the kitchen table and gave me a cup of coffee. We talked for hours about you until I was laughing and feeling better. I really appreciated what Amos did for me that day." She continued to stare at Pike while she spoke, her eyes pleading for understanding. "After that, Amos began making it a habit to come and visit me, and our friendship grew. He saved me from the loneliness and despair your leaving caused in my life."

"A few weeks later, I began to suspect that I was pregnant from our night together. When the morning sickness set in, I knew for sure, and panic hit me hard. I didn't know what to do. Amos was so sweet to me. I told him of my predicament and he spoke right up, offering to marry me in your place." She pinched her lips together. "Pike, I didn't know what else to do. I had no way to know if I would ever see you again. I couldn't scandalize my family. So I married Amos."

She put her head down. "I can't say I regret the decision. He's a fine man. I don't love him the way I love you. I hadn't regretted marrying him, though, until I saw you again." Her eyes, stricken with pain, gazed at Pike. "I love you so. That's never changed. I have Patrick and Hannah, now. They are my life . . . and, yes, Patrick is your son. I know all I've said today is hard for you to hear, but I had to marry Amos. Please try to find it in your heart to forgive me."

Pike felt a sense of emptiness pass through him as the story sank in. *Patrick is mine?*

Also now, he could see Rebecca's pain and the logic in her words, but his heart ached beyond comprehension at what was never to be, that could have been.

Rebecca's eyes continued to plead with him through the soft evening light. "I need to ask something else of you. I don't want you to say anything to anyone about

Patrick being yours. I don't want him to ever find out. It's best that way . . . Please find it in your heart to forgive us - especially Amos. He does love me. More than I will ever be able to love him. He's saved both me and your son." Rebecca reached out, clasped Pike's cold hand, and brought it to her cheek to rub as she had so many times in the past. "I wish things hadn't turned out this way, but God has set us on different paths. We must accept His will. Follow where it leads."

A sound welled up in Pike's throat that came out like a low growl as Rebecca brushed his hand against her cheek. So many feelings overwhelmed him at once, all too many to face. Now that he understood what had happened to Rebecca, he couldn't deny he felt responsible for the turn of events. Pity seeped into his mind. "I had no idea. Now, I know what you went through after I left was difficult. I never considered the possibility that you could have gotten pregnant." He closed his eyes for a moment to gather himself together. When he opened them again, he could see hurt and anger lingering in Rebecca's face. "I need some time to think," he offered. "I can't comprehend the fact that I am a father. Give me some time. Can we talk later?"

"That will be fine." She turned and disappeared as quietly as she had come, vanishing into the darkness.

"Did you hear that, Hank?" Pike announced to his trusty friend. "I'm a father. Not only have I lost my love, but I've lost a son while I was away. Who would have thought it?"

Pike decided to stay in the barn a while longer to mull over the events of the day, and this was by far the best place to do it. He retrieved a large wooden box and set it next to Hank's stall, and sitting, he leaned back and closed his eyes. Feeling Hank reach down to nuzzle him, he stroked the horse's muzzle and appreciated the softness and warmth he found there.

Chapter 9

Buster's even breathing formed a soothing back-drop for Pike as he lay in his toasty bed later that night, again mulling over the day's events. Now he understood the magnitude of the predicament he had left Rebecca in. Although it eased his anger, an equally painful and deep emotion took its place; an all-encompassing long-ing to be a family with Rebecca and Patrick.

Why'd You do this to me, Lord? Pike sent his ques-tion heavenward, hoping for an answer, or at least for some small relief from the pain. While waiting for the reply, he recounted many events from his life before the war. First came the night he had spent making love with Rebecca under that steamy, starry summer sky. The passion had gleamed in Rebecca's eyes as her warm arms wrapped around his shoulders. Those images kin-dled his flame of desire as he fervently wished to be the one beside Rebecca this night and sharing their love.

But as Pike lay in his bed, he realized, on some lev-el, that no matter how much he wanted to be the one to share her life, it would never be so. Misery slithered around his heart, constricting it like a twelve-foot py-thon suffocating its prey. The pressure goaded him to get up and pace the floor to find escape, but instead of rising, he willed himself to concentrate on what he should now do with his life - a life without Rebecca. He had never considered a future without her, so now he felt adrift and didn't know what direction to take.

Before the war, he had worked as a carpenter, but somehow he just didn't feel like picking up where he had left off and little about his past held appeal.

Suddenly, an urge struck Pike with the explosive-ness of a thunderbolt. *Why don't you head west? Get away from here. Do what thousands of others have been doing.* The sudden notion took hold of his thinking, sending out tendrils of possibilities, racing his heart with excitement. *Yes,* he gleefully told himself. *That's the answer. I'm going to go west to the frontier and make a new start. Just need a plan. Wonder what Frank and Buster will think about this? …. can't wait to tell them.* Ideas ricocheted through his mind, exploring every conceivable avenue. The glorious, golden West lay before him, untouched and untapped.

*

Pike roused from a deep sleep and opened his eyes. The sun's rays announced the new dawn. He didn't remember falling asleep, but the night had obviously flown away as the new day's light crept into his room. Unable to contain himself with thoughts of his new plans, he tossed back the heavy quilt and threw his legs over the side of the bed. Quickly, he slipped his feet into his socks and boots to protect them from the cold wooden floor. He gave his stiff thigh, aching as it always did in the morning, an unconscious rub.

Buster began to stir in the bed next to him.

"Good morning," Pike said cheerfully. "How're you?"

Buster's jaw wiggled as he worked to erase the sleep still plaguing him. "Mornin', Pike. I's be fine this mornin'."

"What do you think of this?" Pike said, anxious to lay out his ideas. "I've been thinking and I've been wondering. How would you like to move out west with me? I just don't feel like staying to make my life here." He didn't add, *now that Rebecca is gone.* "My future isn't here in Baltimore. Our future, if you want it, is in the vast land to the west. I want to try my hand on the frontier and see what we can make for ourselves." Pike tried to decipher his friend's blank expression. "Buster, are you with me? I'll understand if you want to stay. Don't worry about how I'll react. Just tell me what you think."

"Pike, you's and Frank is my onliest friends. I's stay wiff you, if'n you'll have me. I be's right happy to head west wiff you. I'd like a new start, too."

Unable to hold back a grin, Pike held the black

giant's eyes and nodded his head in acceptance. Pike said grinning from ear to ear, "Okay, sounds like a plan. I'm going to think about the details some. Let's get some breakfast. I smell bacon and coffee. Can't wait to get a cup. How about you?"

"Um, my mouff is a-waterin' from all them good smells."

The platter of eggs and bacon steamed in front of Pike as he waited for the prayer. At least this morning, his stomach wasn't tied up in knots as the excitement of a new start rode roughshod over his bitterness, and that made him more than ready for food.

Frank Senior said the familiar morning prayer - which was an unquestioned family tradition, one that took place every day in the Wheeling household. *A tradition that must be written in stone somewhere,* Pike thought, amused as he waited and listened.

As the "Amen" ended, Frank immediately swooped in first to stab up a couple of fried eggs. He laughed at Pike and Buster while he made them wait their turn. "Here, boys. You can have what's left. I think you might get a piece. Hope that's okay?"

As Pike started to eat, he felt only too happy to be home and enjoying a family moment again. But all too soon, he was stuffed and couldn't finish his breakfast, much to his chagrin.

His mother glanced at him uneasily when she noted he was no longer eating.

"Sorry, Mom," Pike declared when he noted her crushed face, "my stomach must have shrunk." He decided now would be a good time to tell his folks about his decision. "Dad, Mom, I want to talk to you about something." Pike gathered strength as he collected his thoughts. "I've been thinking about what I want to do now that we're home. I don't feel my future is here in Baltimore. I want to get a fresh start. To do that, I need to go somewhere new." Pike paused as he let his first comments sink in.

His father put down his fork to give him his full attention while his mother's eyes exposed her apprehension.

"I want to move west," Pike continued. "I've thought

about it, and I've heard tell that the Indian Territory is wide open. I'm going to head in that direction in the spring and Buster's going with me. I guess I'll let Frank go. I haven't made up my mind on that one yet." Pike eyed his brother to gauge his reaction.

"Pike, I can't believe you said that," Frank hurled back. "You'd better let me go."

His parents exchanged alarmed looks then Frank Senior spoke with a tight set to his jaw. "Sons, both you and your friend have been through a lot. More than we will ever be able to understand. I can only praise God for protecting you and bringing you back to us. You are all a little worse for wear, but in time you will heal and get your strength back. Your mother and I would prefer you stay here. We could ask for nothing more than for you to start families and continue your work like you used to."

Pike noticed his mother shaking her head sadly. She did not offer her thoughts.

"You boys have lost so much in the war," his father continued. "We'll support you now, any way we can. If that means letting you go west, that's what we'll do."

His mother spoke up with a catch in her voice. "Boys, I'm going to miss you so much! Please reconsider!"

"We'll miss you, too," Pike responded, "but this is something I need to do for me. We'll need time to get our strength back and save our money. We can get prepared over the winter. In the early spring, we'll head out. I'm hoping to get some land and have a farm of my own. From there, who knows? I might like to start a business, like a sawmill. I'm not sure right now, but I've got time to think about it."

After a brief silence, Frank Senior smiled, setting his jaw and offered, "Why don't we all go fishing and enjoy the day. It's going to be too cold, soon enough, to enjoy the outdoors."

"Sounds good to me, Dad," Frank replied. "I'd love it."

"After we fish," Pike said. "I need to go into town and get my hair cut." He looked intently at Frank and Buster. Teasingly, he added, "You boys should go with me. You both could stand some scissors to your heads. Your hair looks like a turkey in full strut."

"I'll feel better," Frank responded, scratching the top of his head, "when I can get rid of this mess."

Pike looked around the table. "Sounds like we've got a full day planned. Let's get started."

*

Some months later, Pike couldn't help but feel smug as he thumped up the stairs to his bedroom. He slid into his room, pulled open the top drawer of his dresser, and placed the week's wages in the bundle of money already waiting. "Yes, siree," he said out loud to himself, "I'm going to have a fine start in Indian Territory. I've got enough money now, but in another month, I'll have plenty extra for the unexpected."

While gazing at his growing funds, he heard horse hooves trotting toward the house. Hoping to spot Buster and Frank coming home from work at the steel plant, he peeked out the nearest window. A cold stab of anger and dread shook him as Amos pulled a wagon into the yard. Amos, dark-headed and lanky, hopped down from his perch in the driver's seat and tied up the horses.

Great, Pike grumbled, *now I've got to talk to him.* Grumbling out loud, he turned to wind his way downstairs to meet his brother. Tension kept a tight hold as Pike opened the front door and slipped through the opening. *What am I going to say to him? Guess I'm about to find out.* Pike put on a straight face and lifted his eyes to meet his brother's gaze.

Once more, Pike noted Amos had the most unique crystalline blue eyes, as they bore into him. Framed by dark brows, Amos's eyes pulled like magnets, causing a person to forget his other less-impressive features.

Although Amos stood close to Pike's six-foot-three-inch height and was gangly like his older brother, the similarities ended there. Amos's black hair contrasted sharply with Pike's robin-colored, red hair. Their eyes and complexions vastly differed.

"Hello, big brother," Amos began before an uncomfortable silence could settle in. "I was hoping to catch you at home. I could sure use a cup of coffee. Can we go in and have some?"

Bobbing his head and pivoting, Pike led the way into the house to the kitchen. He placed the coffeepot on the stove to heat and while pointing to the chairs with his outstretched hand, he said, "Let's sit while the coffee warms."

Amos sat to then fold his hands on the table, holding his felt hat. Taking charge, he filled the empty silence between them. "Pike, you and I haven't visited since you've come home from the war. I feel it's time for you and me to come to some sort of an understanding. So, I'm going to be honest with you, no matter how painful it is. When I finish, you can say what you want. We are still brothers, no matter what's happened. We can't go on not speaking forever."

Saying nothing, Pike waited for Amos to continue. Seeing that Amos seemed a little nervous, Pike figured his brother had probably rehearsed his speech before arriving, but still said nothing.

"Before the war, I would have never considered being close to Rebecca. You two were clearly in love. But, the days after you joined the Union Army, my life took a most unexpected turn. In fact, the day after you left, Rebecca came flying into our yard on her horse. I ran out to meet her. I wanted to see what was wrong. I could see her tear-stained face and sorrow for her took hold of me, so I spent the afternoon with her, trying to cheer her up. After that day, I felt an attraction to her, sorry to say. I wasn't sure then if I just felt responsible for her, or if it was something else. I wasn't ready to admit that it might be more than responsibility, at least not then.

"When Rebecca told me later that she was pregnant with your child, God help me, I was overjoyed at my luck. Now, I had a justifiable reason to ask her to marry me. I told myself, even then, it was just to protect her honor, but the truth was, it was because I had fallen in love with her. I hate to admit that to you. I've prayed about this and I feel God is pushing me to tell you everything. So, as hard as it is, I'm going to be brutally honest."

Pike stared at the table and even though not really wanting to hear more, he allowed his brother to finish what he had to say and didn't interrupt.

"Yes, I love Rebecca. I love her more now than back then. I can't apologize enough for what I've done to you. I know how much you have suffered in the war. Coming home to find me married to your love must have been incredibly hard . . . I'm very sorry." Amos paused briefly and shifted in his seat. "I want you to know, I will always provide for Rebecca and also for your son. I will do everything in my power to make sure she is happy, as well as the children.

"Rebecca told me she had asked you not to say anything about Patrick. We think it's best he doesn't know the truth. How you are going to deal with all of this, I don't know. I know you must be hurting."

Amos's words rekindled Pike's anger, flaring it up to a white-hot rush of emotion. His heated glare lifted from the tabletop to his brother.

Amos sat forward and spoke earnestly. "Pike, can you find it in your heart to understand? Can we get past this? I need your forgiveness. I pray some day that my big brother can forgive me." He slowly dropped back in the chair and lifted his gaze to the ceiling.

Silence hung between them as Pike reeled with so many thoughts and feelings, he didn't know where to start.

Noticing the boiling coffee, Amos rose and removed it from the stove. He took two cups from the cupboard and set them on the table, then poured the brew. Amos sat, lifted his cup, and blew across the top absently as he studied Pike.

Pike wanted to lash out at Amos and hurt him like he had been hurt, but he clamped his jaw against the rush of angry words and said nothing. He feared that, if he let go just a tiny bit, the dam would burst and the pain would flow for both of them. Pike knew that would not be good, but did he care? He wasn't sure, but for some reason he kept control of himself.

After waiting for a response, and after letting the silence go on for several minutes, Amos spoke again with a tinge of hesitation. "Pike, I have something else I want to ask of you. Rebecca and I have discussed your decision to head to the Indian Territory. She and I agree that we would like to accompany you when you go. We want to acquire land of our own."

Pike jolted straight up in his chair, a 'NO!' rising in his throat.

"Rebecca's sister, Rena; she's something else. We want to get away from the family home and especially from her. I've been saving my money. We'll be anxious to go when you're ready to leave."

Pike's mouth gaped open. *What are they thinking? No. They will not go!*

"Now, Pike, try to think it over before you give me a 'yes' or 'no' answer. We wish for a new start, just as you do. It will be much safer for all of us if we travel together."

Snapping his jaw shut with an audible click, Pike remembered his father's words on many occasions in the past - *Pike, shut your mouth before a fly gets in.*

Recovering from the initial shock wave, Pike rubbed his jaw and strained to find an answer. "I honestly don't know how I feel about what you've just told me. I'm mad as hell at you. All those months of suffering, I dreamed of coming home to Rebecca. I realize, now, that I had left her in a tough spot, but, I just wish everything had turned out differently than it has. I long for what will never be. Losing Patrick hasn't been easy, either." He took a deep breath. "I don't know how to respond to you and Rebecca wanting to go with us. Give me a few days to think it over. I'll let you know what I decide. I don't know what else to do." The sound of approaching footsteps carried to Pike's ears. "I think I hear Frank and Buster."

Before he could turn, Frank strode into the kitchen with the black man behind him. "Brother," Frank said as he spied Amos, "to what do we owe the pleasure?" Frank plopped into a chair and gazed from Amos to Pike and back as Buster sat down next to him.

"Well, Brother," Amos stated, "I came for a quick visit, hoping to catch you at home. I found Pike just lounging around, so I thought I would pester him a while. Now that you and Buster are here, we can talk. Maybe if I wait long enough, Mother will show up and fix us something to eat."

"Sorry, Amos," Frank chuckled, "Mom and Dad have a church gathering tonight in town. They won't be home until later. We boys are on our own tonight."

"Sorry to hear that," he said with a grin. "I'd better run along then. Rebecca's a might better cook than any of you fellas."

"We've gotten a lot of experience during the war at rustling up our own food," Frank offered with a smirk on his face. "But I'm sure Rebecca is a lot better to look at. Hey, look at Buster. Who would have imagined he stirs up a mighty fine biscuit?"

The men shared a healthy laugh and even Pike couldn't keep a straight face.

When the mirth died out, Amos rose from his seat and nodded. "Good night. I'll come back and visit soon, but I'll make sure Mother will be here."

*

Curious about the interaction between Amos and Pike, Frank tailed Amos out of the house.

In the yard, Amos turned and said, "I let Pike know about us wanting to go with you. Don't know what he thinks about the idea. Hopefully, you can feel him out. Let me know if he comes around. We'll go one way or the other, but I sure would rather make the trip with you."

Even though Frank and Amos were just a year apart in age, Frank had never been close to Amos. The normal brotherly jealousies that had occurred between them had followed them into adulthood, but since returning from the war, Frank's outlook on life had been altered. The appreciation for his family was much more finely-honed than ever before. So the idea of Amos and his family going with them on their travels west brought a measure of sheer joy to Frank's heart. Having both of his brothers with him in the frontier made all of their futures more secure. None of them knew what awaited in the wilds of Indian Territory, but the more of them that relocated, the better chance they had for survival.

"Brother," Frank replied firmly, "I'd be real pleased for you and your family to come west with us. I'll talk to Pike about you coming. I think I can put some pressure on him. I'll let you know when he comes around, hopefully soon."

"Okay," Amos said as he untied the team. He stepped up on the wagon and moved to the middle of the bench. "I'll be waiting to hear from you. I'm serious about going. What an adventure this will be. I'm excited. Rebecca wants a place of her own, and I mean to give it to her."

"I'm glad you want to come with us. It's time for us to get to know one another better. With all of us boys working together, no telling what we can accomplish."

Amos grinned. "I'll see you on Sunday."

Frank stepped back as Amos waved and clucked to the horses. His wagon headed down the lane toward the home of Rebecca's parents, some five miles away.

As Amos disappeared into the dusk, Frank thought about Frank Senior, who, fresh out of seminary school, traveled across the Atlantic to start his church in Baltimore many years ago. He wondered if this was where the adventuresome nature had gotten into him and his brothers - to want to travel across the vast open country to a new territory - *Maybe so.*

*

Pike's best thinking seemed to come in the solitude of the night. Not a soul stirred as he tried to make sense of his continuing troubles. His earlier talk with Amos had stirred up his hurt over losing Rebecca and caused a fresh crop of pain. *I'm going to have to get a hold of my feelings,* Pike chided himself. *I can't have Rebecca. Never again will I feel her in my arms. God help me! I don't want to let her go. I can't even think of how I've lost a son.*

Pike began to ponder the question of having Amos and his family on the trek west, and reasoned with himself, *Our trip will be slower with the kids and Rebecca in tow. Can I get past my feeling? She'll be with me every day. There won't be any escape. Part of me wishes, sure as sin, to be near her any way I can. I have to be honest about that. Don't know how smart it will be to be close to her every day. Sure would be easier if she'd stay in Bal-*

timore. *I may never get over her this way. I have to admit to myself that I love her as much as ever.*

On the other hand, Patrick is another matter. If he goes, at least I can have some time with him. I can be something of an influence in his life. Only as an uncle, but I guess it's better than nothing. Can I learn to live with that?

The pain of loss gripped his mind and heart. Anger, his constant companion, flared up like an ember in dry grass. *God, how could You do this to me? What I went through in the war wasn't enough? What have I done to deserve this? I just don't understand. Please Merciful Providence, ease my troubled mind and heart. Help me to understand. I'll work hard to hold my faith. I'll follow the path You set before me. Just show me the way.* He continued his railings at God until, slowly, temperance returned and he released his pent-up anger and a small measure of peace came over him.

The watch chain, the once treasured piece, now resided in his dresser drawer. Slipping out of bed, he retrieved the chain and watch and padding quickly across the freezing wooden floor in the dark, he perched on a chair near the window.

Heavy sheets of snow swirled in the wind outside the frosted panes. The snow possessed a furious nature as it pelted the window and accumulated along the ridge. The sheer beauty of snow, even in these intense moments, never failed to touch Pike. He rested, watching the storm's fury in stunned solitude.

As the minutes ticked away, he thumbed the chain of brown hair and after a bit, the grandfather clock in the hallway downstairs chimed the hour. Eleven rings tolled throughout the sleeping house and added to the serenity that settled over Pike. Nature's unbridled beauty captured his attention as the night slipped slowly and quietly away.

All too soon, the Westminster chimes played again on the family heirloom. No longer caught up in his troubles, Pike felt as light and calm as the fluffy snow, which had piled up several inches along the window panes. *Guess I won't be going to work tomorrow,* he told himself. He rose and dove under the warm quilt his

Grandmother Wheeling had given to him long ago.

He spoke to God again. *Lord, I'll have faith that You have Your reasons for the pain I am enduring. I know I am stronger for what has happened to me. You know what You want for me. I'll follow where You lead. If that means I have to love Rebecca and Patrick from afar, that's what I'll do. Yes, Father, I will find the strength to be near them both and allow them to make their new lives in the West. I don't know how it will all work. It'll put my faith to the test. I'll just let go and let God. What else can I do? Thank You for my eternal salvation. Amen.*

Sleep overtook him as his head found its resting place on the downy pillow. The images of Rebecca and Patrick seemed almost real as he spotted them walking toward him. Even though he couldn't quite decide if they were authentic, he smiled and held out his arms.

Chapter 10

Sunday came as it always did, with a hearty breakfast and a scurrying among the other members of the Wheeling household as all prepared to dash off to church.

"You boys got the horses hitched up yet?" Frank Senior bellowed from his bedroom, in high spirits as the time for him to go to work drew near.

"Dad, don't we always get the horses ready?" Pike quipped back to his father with a light-hearted response. "We boys will be waiting outside."

Turning to his friend, Pike asked, "Buster, you ready to brave the cold?"

Buster often gave Pike reason for pause and this moment was no exception. The brown woolen trousers and tan-colored jacket brought Buster a stylish appearance. Now, that he was clean shaven, and his flesh had filled out, the man made an even more imposing presence than before. It had been an all-day task in the many shops of Baltimore to locate a couple of sets of clothes that fit the big man.

"Get your coat, Buster," Pike urged, "and we'll get Frank so we can hurry and hitch Lila and Leon. I'll saddle Hank and ride him. That way, we won't have to hitch up the other team."

Buster peeked out the frosted windowpanes and declared, "Looks mighty cold out there."

The snow had begun melting the day before, but a few inches still remained in drifts along the sides of the house and the ground was frozen solid.

Pike appreciated that the ground was not a sloppy mess, but the ice could be slick and dangerous. Even though the wind cut like a knife, Pike happily tacked up the horses with Buster while Frank snuck in a few minutes later.

*

When his father finished his unusually-uplifting sermon about receiving God's blessings, Pike trudged along through the buzzing congregation as they gathered on the church steps. After visiting with his parents and the rotund Jacob Coltrane, Pike said goodbye to the group. "Mom, don't wait on me for lunch. I'll be back sometime in the afternoon. You all enjoy your meal."

Hopping down the stairs as gracefully as his bad leg would allow, Pike suddenly felt his feet slipping on a patch of ice. In surprise and dismay, he performed a shuffling dance as his arms flailed wildly just before he took flight off the last few steps. His jaws snapped together in an audible click when he met the hard ground. *Hope no one saw that*, flashed across his mind as he came to rest in the only mud puddle in the area, with a thud. Quickly, he turned his head to where most of the people were clustered, then he turned back and just to his left, his eyes met Patrick's wide-eyed gaze.

The boy stood quietly, eyebrows raised, eyes twinkling, bundled in his heavy coat and gloves.

Right away, Pike broke out with a smile - he just couldn't help himself.

Patrick grinned back and started to laugh. "Pike funny." He pointed with his chubby finger.

Not able to resist the merriment, Pike released an embarrassed, lopsided grin.

Rebecca stepped into view and gaped down at Pike. A smile, that she struggled to keep in check, quivered on her lips and lit up her eyes. "Why, Pike, what happened?"

"I had a little accident. That's all. Help me up."

Rebecca stuck out her small hand, covered with a woolen mitten.

Tugging himself up without much effort and taking advantage of the moment to speak to her, Pike said, "I would like to come to your parents' house and visit with you and Amos. Would you mind?"

"No, not at all," she blustered as she pulled her coat closer around her neck to clasp the collar to her throat. "We'd enjoy that. Come on. We'll get Amos and Hannah and start for home. It's still cold out here."

*

Gathered around the kitchen table at the Williams' home, Pike strained to tune out Rebecca's older sister Rena, who prattled on and on about the high price of cotton.

"I went to town yesterday. I just couldn't believe the prices of the bolts of cloth. It's double what it was a couple of months ago. I just can't understand why everything is so expensive these days. If it keeps up, we won't be able to afford to buy a thing we need." Rena had dominated the conversation from the moment the Williams family and Pike had begun the Sunday ritual of the noontime feast.

Even with the wonderful baked ham, green peas, and fresh-baked bread, exasperation settled over Pike. He focused on the food on his plate and strained to shut out Rena's ranting and railing.

Ruth, Rebecca's other sister, sat next to Rena and she seemed intent on eating, oblivious to her sister's blabbering. Rena more than made up for the quiet manners of her two younger siblings. She provided an opinion on everything and anything as long as she had a live body to talk at. She even spoke to the animals the way she spoke to people, in a never-ending stream. Pike had been told that only the goats seemed to enjoy her constant babble. One nanny goat, in particular, named Star, followed Rena everywhere, seemingly mesmerized by her. When Rena paused too long in her dialog while milking Star, the goat would butt Rena softly as a gentle reminder to keep talking. Other than Star, everyone sought cover when Rena's ponderous frame came into view.

At the lunch table, however, the family was trapped, and escape was impossible. Noticing the vacant expressions of the others as they consumed their food, Pike decided they looked like cud-chewing milk cows, staring off into space. Covertly, Pike observed his freckle-faced son throughout the meal as he tuned out Rena's droning.

Amos sat directly across from Pike, and Pike tried to ignore Amos's glare lingering on him after he had caught him glancing at Patrick.

The moment Rena took a brief pause from her complaining, Enos, the head of the family, hopped in and asked Pike, "Is it true that you, Frank, and your black friend are going to head west in the spring?"

"Yes, sir," Pike stated, back stiffening. "We're heading to Indian Territory. We're going to try our hand at farming. And, I've been thinking about possibly starting a sawmill, since I like working with wood. That is, if I can get the necessary parts shipped in."

Reaching for another slice of bread, Pike let the cat out of the bag. "Didn't Amos and Rebecca tell you they were coming, too? They want to tag along." Although he heard Enos and Amos sputtering on the food they were chewing, he didn't look up and just kept talking at a casual pace. "Guess we'll have plenty of us traveling together. It should be safer that way. I hope we can acquire a big chunk of land. We'll need lots of hands to help with the sawmill, anyhow. Should be a challenge, but I think we're up to it. Don't you, little brother?"

Trying to appear casual as he spread honey on his bread, Pike snuck a peek at Amos through what he hoped appeared to be serious eyes. A mischievous smile tugged at the corner of Pike's lips, barely able to contain a threatening ripple of laughter.

The sisters and mother all sat in a dazed silence. Rebecca held Pike's gaze, though, in that warm, familiar way she had. From her expression, she was the only one pleased with his approach on the subject.

"Amos and Rebecca," her father complained, "I'm ashamed of you for not telling us of your plans. Why can't you stay here? You can get a place of your own, if that's the problem. We'll help you build on our land. Don't just leave and run off to the wilds of who-knows-where. We may never see you again."

Rebecca began with a pleading look in her doe-like

eyes. "I'm sorry, Mother, and to you, too, Father. I've been happy here with you and our family. I wish for a place of my own . . . and a new start like Pike. Please forgive me, but Amos and I have made up our minds. I'm sorry we haven't told you sooner. We were afraid you might be upset with us."

"Hey, I want to go," Rena blurted. "What a grand idea. I've always wanted to see the frontier. Maybe now, I can find a man worthy of me. I'll bet there are some strong men there. That's just what I'm looking for. You bet. I'm in!" Her brow wrinkled and she eyed everyone at the table. "No one try to stop me. I've got plenty of money saved from my sewing. I'll get a place of my own. I'll get me a tall, handsome cowboy; maybe even an Indian. Wouldn't that be exciting? Can you imagine me with an Indian husband?"

The private laughter that had been rejoicing within Pike disintegrated. In its place came a deep-seated consternation. *Why did I open my big yap? Now, Rena's going with us. Heaven help me and everyone else.* Pike slumped in his chair and rolled his eyes. As his glance hit Amos's face, he paused to gauge Amos's reaction - a taut face, scrunched lips, and narrowed eyes. Shrugging his shoulders, Pike forced a surly grin. *Oh well, what are we going to do now?*

Throwing up his hands, Enos declared gruffly, "I guess that settles it."

Patrick took the opportunity to announce, "I want to go play!"

Rising from his seat, Pike set his napkin in his chair. "Thank you for the lovely meal. I must get home and help Father build some shelves. You all have a wonderful afternoon."

"Don't you want some coffee?" Rebecca's mother asked.

"No, thank you. I'm as full as a tick on an old bull. I enjoyed the food and the company, though." Turning away from the shocked group, Pike strode across the room to retrieve his coat and hat, which were hanging by the front door.

Amos came up beside him and offered with a smile, "Let me help you saddle Hank."

"Okay."

As they tromped across the snowy ground to the barn, both men flipped up the collars on their coats, tugged down their hats, and attempted to block the wind's blast. Safely inside the building, Amos said, "Thank you for deciding to let us go with you. It means a lot to me and to Rebecca. I can't say I'm happy about Rena tagging along." He shook his head and pensively stared out the barn window. "I'd hoped to get away from her."

Pike tried looking on the bright side. "Well, maybe she'll find a husband. We'll keep our fingers crossed." He pulled Hank out of the stall. "Amos, I'm thinking about heading out the first of March. Hopefully, the weather won't be too bad. We're going to take the train to St. Louis. From there, it will be on foot or by wagon. Think your family can make it?"

"I can't wait to get started," Amos replied, clapping his hands. "We'll be ready."

Ambling out of the barn, Pike led Hank into the overcast, frigid afternoon. As he tugged on the girth one final time, he said to his brother, "We'll need to get our train passage paid for soon. I'll let you know how much it is. Until then, take care, and tell Rebecca bye for me."

Looking up from the ground, Amos said earnestly, "We're excited about going. Thank you for finding it in your heart to let us come."

Hope I'm doing this for the right reasons, Pike thought, just before he clucked to Hank. The steady mount took his cue and lumbered off in a ground-covering lope.

*

That most momentous first of March, Pike stuffed the last shirt into his battered army pack as Buster prepared his own bundle of clothes. The words of the song Pike had played for his family the night before still echoed through his thoughts. He hummed them to himself:

Fair as a lily, joyous and free

light of the prairie home was she . . .

Pike's eyes were drawn to the window just above his bed and relief flowed through him as he noted the blue sky and clusters of vagrant gray-and-white clouds, lazily trailing after one another across the heavens. He poured out prayerful thanks to God as he paused from his packing. *How lucky could we be with this beautiful weather for the start of our journey?*

Clasping his treasured pack, Pike hefted it over his shoulder. In his right hand, he grabbed his worn guitar. He loved that old guitar. Mostly, he loved the feel of the strings under his calloused fingers. "Buster, you got your stuff together?" he questioned with a perceptible tremor in his voice.

"I's sho nuff ready. Let's git."

"Good morning, Mom," Pike offered with a cheerful grin as he pecked her on the cheek.

She removed the eggs from the heavy iron skillet as she answered with a weak smile, "Good morning to you both."

Already sitting at the table, Frank said, eyes shining, "Come on and fill your plate."

Frank Senior breezed into the kitchen and joined his sons and Buster. After he picked up his plate of bacon and eggs, he stated, "We'd better get our breakfast and get the horses hitched. The Williams should be here soon."

Relishing the warm flaky biscuits, Pike knew these might be his last home-cooked ones for a while. He heartily gulped down the rest of the food.

"Pike, I want you to take Hank with you, Frank Sr. said after clearing his throat. "He'll take care of you out there on the frontier. You'll need a good horse."

When the words sunk in, Pike paused from stuffing his mouth and a lump formed in his throat as this was a most unexpected gift, one he had never hoped to receive. After a few moments, he found his voice and spoke barely above a whisper. "Thank you, Dad. That means more to me than I can say."

Smiling, Frank Senior beamed at his oldest son with fatherly love, showing his pleasure at Pike's heart-felt response. "I'd be proud to know you're well-mounted. We'll miss you boys. Make sure you write."

"Looks like we're off to a grand start," Frank offered. "You boys ready to get the horses hitched? It's time."

*

The families clustered under the overhang of the train depot. Since the day had warmed considerably by noon, the travelers waited comfortably outside until they could board. Hugs abounded as Pike strode to the group after settling Hank and Buster in a boxcar. Pike hustled with a quick step to bid his final farewell to his family. At least, this time getting on a train didn't have the apprehension and terror associated with it like the ones taking him to and from his imprisonment in Andersonville.

"All aboard," rang out along the track.

Pike clutched his mother and she sniffled into his ear as he bent down to receive her ardent embrace. "Son, please take care of yourself and your brothers. Please write. We want to know what's happening in your life. Will you do that?"

Returning a tight squeeze, Pike replied, "Sure thing. You and Dad take care. We'll miss you and your wonderful cooking, but most of all, I love you."

Turning to his father, Pike grabbed him in a bear-hug before his father could say anything. Generally uncomfortable with public displays of affection, Frank Senior quietly accepted Pike's hug.

"I'll miss you, Dad, Pike whispered, "Thank you for Hank. You know how much that horse means to me. I love you. Maybe you and Mom can come and visit when we get settled."

"You take care of yourself," his father replied with a painful huskiness in his voice. He let go of Pike and repeated the goodbye to Frank.

As Pike turned toward the passenger car, he spotted Amos with his arm around a weeping Rebecca. The scene halted him in his tracks as he stared at Amos whispering into her ear. He hadn't thought about how hard leaving might be on everyone. Even he, who desperately wanted to get to the frontier, was sad now that the moment was upon him to leave. Pike sighed deeply and, along with the others in his miserable-looking group, trudged forward.

Rena cried openly at the entrance of the car door, so Pike hung to the rear of the passengers. He wasn't eager to have a sniffling Rena clinging to his arm.

Slowly, Amos succeeded in herding Rebecca and Patrick to the train's steps. As Amos turned to hug his mother, Pike wasted no time in striding forward to reach out and lift Patrick up in a whirl to the top of the steps. He set the giggling boy down on his feet and ruffled his wavy, dark mop of hair. "You ready to ride the train?"

"Yes, I am!" squealed the vibrant child.

"You go find Aunt Rena. I'll be right behind you."

"Okay," he replied as he dashed into the car.

Turning back, Pike caught Rebecca's tear-streaked face a few feet behind him. Smiling, Pike hoped to lift her spirits and as he held out his open hand as he noted, over Rebecca's shoulder, Amos still talking to his mother. To Rebecca, he said, "You and Hannah ready for our big train ride? Everything will be okay, I promise. Try to think about the adventure we're going to have. Here you go, let me help you. Watch your step."

"Thank you," Rebecca sniffled as she clasped Pike's hand. "I'm just a little sad. I'll be better soon." She mounted the steps and quickly disappeared into the train.

Frank boarded next.

As Amos tramped forward to enter the train, Pike asked, "Well, are you ready?"

"Guess as ready as I'll ever be," he retorted in a brusque manner, refusing to look at Pike as he stomped up the steps with a stiff back and a scowl on his face.

What's his problem? Pike wondered. He shrugged it off and took his turn to hop up the steps. Pike turned one last time and waved at his stricken parents. "Bye," he shouted. Now, there was nothing left to do but find his seat.

Scanning the car, Pike and made his way carefully to the only vacant spot he could see. *Oh no,* his mind howled when he discovered Rena would be sitting next to him. *Now, I'm stuck with her. What can I do to get out of this mess?* His eyes darted about for another seat, but to no avail. *Great! Guess I've got no choice.* Fleetingly, he thought about trying to hide, but realized that would be impossible. With a loud grumble, he stepped forward to plop into the seat next to the thick-waisted body, which sat perched on the edge of the long bench just across the aisle from Rebecca, Patrick, Amos, and Hannah.

As Pike looked the other way, he spotted Frank huddling at the end of the same bench. "Chicken!" Pike hissed, just above a whisper. "Thanks for looking out for me. Why do I have to sit next to her?"

"You first, big brother," Frank chuckled. "You're man enough, aren't you?"

"I'll remember this," Pike stated with a hint of malice coloring his tone.

Immediately, Rena commenced with her complaining. She grabbed Pike's hand in her clammy palm and complained with her strident, grating voice. "Oh, Pike, I'm so sad about leaving. I didn't think about it being so hard to say goodbye. I'm scared, too. What's going to happen to us on this trip? Do you think we'll be attacked by Indians? Could we be shot by marauding bad men? I just didn't think this through before you all talked me into coming on this horrible journey. What's going to happen to us? Are we going to have a place to live? Do we know where we're going? . . . Oh, I'm so scared."

Drawing in several lung-filling breaths, Pike attempted to keep from yelling at Rebecca's bubble-headed, plain sister. With her sweaty hand squeezing so hard, he couldn't focus on what she was rattling on about, her unending questions left him dumbfounded. But at one point, he became aware of total silence, so he glanced at Rena.

Her eyes were locked onto him, apparently waiting for an answer.

Completely at a loss as to which question she last asked, he said meekly, "I'm sorry. What did you say?"

"Well, I never!" She sniffed and shoved his hand away. Turning her cheek, she stared, back bolt-upright, out the window.

Thank you, Lord! Pike thought.

The train lurched forward, forcing the passengers to sway with it and Patrick let out a gleeful squeal.

"We're moving," Frank crowed to Pike. In a quieter voice, he asked, "How did you get Rena to shut up?"

"I don't know, but I'm thanking my lucky stars that she quit yammering."

After the first hour, Rena started belly-aching again. "Can you believe how hard these seats are? They are hurting my back. I would have never dreamed we would get so much soot on us from the coal. I'm already covered in it, and it's hot in here. Can you stand that couple's kid running up and down the aisle? Where's the water closet? I sure could stand a break." Her plump body rose. I'll be right back."

Breathing a sigh of relief as Rena swayed down the center aisle and wound her way to the back of the car where she stepped behind a polished wooden door, Pike pleaded, "Frank, change seats with me. I can't take any more of her. You've got to help me out here."

"No way am I going to switch seats with you. I'm enjoying visiting with the man beside me."

Pike let his eyes drift to the other side of the aisle. Sleeping, Hannah lay curled up on her mother's chest. Patrick stood at Amos's knee and stared out the window at the rapidly moving landscape. As Patrick turned back, Pike caught his eye and motioned with a crook of his index finger for the boy to come to him.

Grinning brightly, Patrick let a giggle slip out as he dashed across the rocking car to stand by Pike.

"You want a horsy ride?" Pike asked his son.

"Yes, sir." He placed his tiny hands on Pike's bony knees and struggled to get on top of his legs.

Taking the boy around the waist, Pike hoisted him onto his lap. He clasped Patrick by his wrists as he bounced him vigorously, all the while chanting in a singsong voice to a tune his father had taught him as a small boy. "Ride a little horsy down to town, to get some corn to feed old Bill."

Patrick's hair flapped up and down as he shook with laughter and a burst of brilliant sun radiated from his smile.

A rush of warmth shot through Pike's belly, rendering him awed by the overwhelming emotion. *This is what it feels like to be a father. What a glorious feeling!* An unfamiliar emotion, Pike could only describe it as love, but he sure wanted more. *How can I ever get enough of this?* Once again, his personal railing began. *Why did You do this to me? I want to understand why I'm being put through this torture of love from a distance. Help me, Father!*

Patrick's waves of delight broke through Pike's thoughts. The child's breaths came in short, hitching gasps as he continued his deep belly laughs.

Pike laughed, too, as tears streamed down his cheeks.

At that moment, Rena bustled through the passenger doorway. "What are you boys up to?" The fun came to an abrupt halt.

"Nuffin," snickered Patrick, after he and Pike got control of their runaway fun.

As Pike let Patrick down on the floor to return to his parents, his belly let out a growl a lion would be proud of. Pike leaned over to Frank and asked, "Hey, what has Mom sent with us in that basket?"

Chapter 11

Out of curiosity, Frank had been eyeing a young woman further in the front of the car. He just couldn't help himself any longer. So, while he chewed on his ham sandwich, he leaned over and whispered into Pike's right ear. "Hey, what do you think of the girl sitting in the front row?" When Pike pivoted his head, Frank snuck another peek.

The young woman wore a simple light-green dress, which complemented her honey-bronzed complexion. A few tendrils of jet-black hair trailed out from under her straw bonnet. Her luminous dark-brown eyes set off her face as though a light shone from within.

Maybe she's Creole, Frank told himself as he gawked at her and his eyes trailed down her small neck to take in the swell of her chest. Even though she was covered from ankles to throat, he could not help but notice her ample bust. The notion of seeing those young breasts, exposed and free, sent a flush of thrill through him.

"She's quite unusual," Pike replied, then looked quickly away.

"I think she's pretty."

Even though Pike didn't seem impressed, evidenced by the way he turned his attention to another bite of pecan pie, Frank still felt drawn toward the girl. Secretly, he glanced at her often while they finished their meal.

"I'm going to try to talk to her," he whispered into Pike's ear. "Maybe when we get off the train."

"Good luck, little brother. I can't wait to see if she takes pity on your homely mug."

Irritated by Pike's mention of his looks, Frank sat back. Even though he was the shortest of the three brothers at six-feet, his frame had filled out more fully than either Pike's or Amos's. His blonde hair wasn't thick and wavy like Pike's red hair. Instead, his straight locks tended to fall over his forehead and into his eyes. He unconsciously swept his bangs off his face as he tightened his jaw at his brother's jibe.

Besides feeling inferior to Pike in the looks department, Frank wasn't musically inclined, nor quick with a humorous story, but he didn't feel he was ugly, either.

"Just you wait and see," he barked at Pike. "She'll talk to me."

"Can't wait to see this," Pike chuckled.

"Hey, when do we get to Pittsburgh?" Rena interrupted.

"Not much farther," Pike replied.

Rena muscled into the conversation and leaned over to look at Frank. "I've always wanted to go to Pittsburgh. Don't you think it's pretty out there? I've never been out of the Baltimore area. Oh, this is so exciting." She emphasized her words with a forceful clap of her hands.

In the past, Frank had usually managed to escape from Rena. Now that he was trapped, he found it amazing how much one woman could talk. Attempting to block out her babble, he twisted his head to gaze out the nearest window. He observed thick, fluffy clouds moving across the evening western sky. Salmon pinks, deep, vibrant blues and lavenders streaked raggedly across the blazing backdrop. The countryside rolled and pitched as far as the eye could see. Thick trees covered the vast territory. Plowed fields and open grazing areas were scattered here and there. The farms had a dormant appearance, since spring planting had not yet started. That would come soon enough.

As the first buildings of the outskirts of Pittsburgh came into view, Pike turned to Frank. "You ready to see Pittsburgh?"

*

Pike and the group dribbled out of the train with their few belongings. They traveled light, waiting until they arrived in St. Louis to purchase what they needed for their start on the frontier. Picking up his army pack, Pike led the way to find a hotel.

As the unusual young woman, who had caught Frank's eye, disembarked from the train, Pike tilted his gaze to his younger brother to gauge his reaction.

In a few smart strides, Frank raced to the steps to gallantly hold out his hand to the girl. A friendly, masculine grin formed on Frank's face.

The young woman glanced at him but did not return his smile. She frowned instead, giving him a scathing look. Then, she stepped backward.

Appearing undaunted, Frank offered, "Let me help you." He beamed another smile, fit to break a woman's heart.

The lady hesitantly clasped her hand lightly over Frank's fingers and gave in. She gracefully stepped down the three stairs with her buttoned-up leather shoes. She mumbled, "Thank you," then sprinted away from Frank without as much as a backward glance.

"You sure won her over," Pike guffawed.

Still entranced by the girl, Frank did not answer. He stared after her swishing skirts.

"Hey, Frank," Amos jibed. "Get hold of yourself!"

Rebecca and Rena giggled as they watched Frank gawk at the retreating girl.

"Huh?" Frank stuttered after he tore his eyes away from the woman and gazed around. Instantly, a crimson shade rose from his neck to his face and he stammered, "I was just trying to be a gentleman."

"Yes, Brother, you were just what?" Pike teased. "Come on before you step on your tongue. Let's find a hotel."

The women continued to giggle as Amos started forward to the front of the railroad station.

After speaking to a local resident, Pike turned to his group and shared the information he had learned about where they could stay for the night. "The hotel is just a block and a half down the main street to our left. The livery is behind it. I'm going to round up Hank and Buster and meet you there in a few minutes."

As Pike wound his way to the back of the train, he spotted Hank being led on a rope by Buster. As the gelding plunked down the ramp and struck solid ground, his feet performed a jig, causing Pike to smile. The prancing horse tossed his golden head as he trotted forward with Buster to meet Pike.

Making their way through the hustle and bustle of the streets of Pittsburgh, the men and the horse wound into the alley that adjoined the hotel and led to the livery. A freshly-painted sign hung over the double wooden doors: 'Grand Hotel Livery'.

A boy, not more than twelve years old, burst from behind the livery doors. "Can I take your horse, mister?" His eager face gazed up at Pike. His sandy-colored hair hung long under the woolen cap which was perched jauntily on the crown of his head. The boy's woolen trousers, clean but worn, matched his cap perfectly.

Pike had to grin, as he wasn't used to such service. "Thank you, son. Please give him a good feed. He's gentle. Here's something for your help." Pike tossed the boy a coin. "I'll come for him early in the morning. Will you be here?"

"Oh, yes, sir," the boy replied in a high-pitched voice as he eagerly took the rope from Pike's hand. "Thank you, sir. I'll be here with my pa. We run the place." His pride rang evident in his voice.

"What's your name, son?" Pike asked.

"Cayenne, sir."

"Well, glad to meet you, Cayenne. Is that like the pepper?"

"Yes, sir. My father likes it so much he decided to name me after it."

"Okay, Cayenne. We'll see you in the morning." Pike turned to walk away.

"Uh, Pike," Buster said. "You's knowed I got to stay out here. They's not going to let me stay in that hotel."

Pike stopped. "Sorry . . . I forgot. Come on. Let's follow Cayenne. See if we can find you a place for the night."

Trotting after the small boy, the men took but a few seconds to catch up with him. Pike sang out, "Say, Cayenne. We need your help."

The boy pivoted as if he were a dressmaker's dummy on a swivel. Even though both Buster and Pike towered over him, the young fellow seemed comfortable in their presence.

"Cayenne, I forgot to ask if my groom can stay the night in the barn. He's traveling with me."

"Yes, sir, he's welcome. We have cots just for that. Come on, I'll show you. Come on, boy." Cayenne tugged the horse forward. He yelled, "Pa, we've got company."

A gravely voice echoed back. "Okay, bring 'em in."

Inside the barn, Pike happily noted the stable was roomy and completely enclosed. It was well-lit with lanterns, hung for safety.

A stooped, spindly man hobbled from the doorway and wagged his bushy head at the newcomers. His bristly eyebrows matched his salt-and-pepper beard. "Could I help you, sir?"

"Maybe so," Pike replied. "Could my groom stay here in your barn? I'd sure appreciate it. Cayenne said it would be a bit extra for him, is that right?"

"Yes, sir," the man nodded. "That's right. My name is Bass. I'll show your servant his cot. He should be right comfortable."

"That'll be fine. I'll bring him some supper."

"That won't be necessary, sir," Bass interrupted. "I can get him some food from the hotel kitchen when I get mine and my boy's."

"I'd be much obliged if you would do that." Pike handed the man another coin, then turned to Buster and said, "I'll be back to fetch you and Hank. I'll see you bright and early."

"That be fine," Buster replied just above a whisper.

"Well, you all have a good night then," Pike offered as he patted Hank one last time. Twisting on his heels, he headed out into the dark of the night.

*

Rebecca couldn't help feeling festive as she sat in her chair ready to eat her evening meal. Hannah, nestled in the crook of her arm, was sleeping. The maternal glow she felt inside burned bright as she lovingly gazed at her tiny infant.

Breaking into her silence, Rena remarked as she sat

down beside Rebecca, "Oh, how much fun this is. We never get to eat in a restaurant as wonderful as this one. Doesn't the steak that waitress is carrying look yummy? This place is top rail. Did you see our room?"

Internally, Rebecca sighed as she thought about the long night ahead of having to share a room with Rena, Patrick, and Hannah. The men had paid for cots in the communal room, so they could save money.

Since Rebecca faced the door of the dining room, she immediately caught sight of the young woman from the train. In a merry mood, Rebecca grinned and let her eyes drift to note Frank's reaction to the girl's presence.

His face perking up visibly as he spied the shapely young lady, Frank's eyes trailed her every move.

My gracious, Rebecca thought silently, measuring the large chest of the woman. *I can see why so many of the men in here are staring at her. Poor thing. She looks uncomfortable.*

Pike elbowed Frank openly and said, "She thinks you're ugly."

"Leave me be," Frank bellowed with a scowl.

After the woman found a seat by herself, with her back facing most of the customers, Rebecca noted Frank continuing to watch her. *Men!* Rebecca told herself, then focused on the steak and potatoes that the waitress now placed in front of her.

*

Early the next morning, Pike rushed into the dark street. Surprised to find it quiet and empty, he tromped his way to the livery stable and he struggled to relieve some of the kinks in his sore shoulder, which resulted from his restless night on the hard, unforgiving cot, and his aggravated thigh.

Pike mulled over the information he had been given by a man sleeping next to him. "You need to go and see Lewis Livingston," the man had said, "just a couple of miles north of St. Louis. He's got the best mules and horses around. The Hansons' have a general store on Elm Street. They are real honest and will get you outfitted."

As Pike had talked with the man, he had noticed the surliness of Amos. Amos just seemed to keep to himself, disinclined to speak to the helpful stranger.

Oh well, Pike told himself, *Guess there's nothing I can do about Amos. Don't know why he's so withdrawn. He sticks to Rebecca like glue. Maybe that's the rub; Rebecca. I guess he could be jealous of me and her, or is it me and Patrick?*

Dropping the situation with Amos, Pike grabbed the handle on the door of the livery. He moved into the warm, inviting interior and was pleased to note Cayenne brushing Hank's coat to a shine.

"Son, you're hard at it already?"

"Yes, sir, I wanted him to be ready to go. He's been fed."

The gelding peered at Pike in his usual friendly manner. As he tossed the youth another coin, he offered, "Thank you, Cayenne. Here's payment for all of your hard work."

"Mornin'," Buster offered, coming from the back room.

"Morning to you, Buster. Have a good night?"

"Sho nuff did. I's slept jus' fine."

"Good morning," Bass hailed in a hearty greeting. "Are you ready to get on your way?"

"Morning to you, Bass," Pike said. "Yes, we're ready. We'll go to Cincinnati today and then on to St. Louis. I hope the weather holds out. Thank you for seeing to Hank and Buster. We're much obliged. You and Cayenne take care."

Buster took the gelding's lead in his huge, thick-fingered hand to fulfill his role as groom.

"So long," Pike called to Bass and Cayenne as he strode out into the quiet streets and headed toward the train. The sky now possessed a multitude of colors as a new day took its place in history. "At least, it looks like good weather," Pike said, with a smile, to his companions, Buster and Hank. Pike then sent his gratitude skyward and hoped his Father would hear.

After seeing the golden steed and gigantic black man into the boxcar, Pike ambled off to locate his family and his passenger car. As he walked along the tracks, he appreciated the beauty of the train. *Are the cars new? Or is it just the fresh coat of paint?* The sharply stenciled black letters displayed *Pennsylvania-Illinois* in large, easily deciphered letters.

Being the last one in his group to board the train, Pike again was relegated to the seat next to Rena. *Just my luck*, he thought as he glided to his open spot. *I'm going to get Frank over by her, somehow.*

On Frank's opposite side, a shriveled old gentleman sat next to the window. The man talked incessantly while Frank bobbed his head and responded with an occasional, "Uh huh."

After eavesdropping on the elderly man, who was rambling on and on about his grandkids in Cincinnati, Pike couldn't help but smile to himself. Maybe sitting next to Rena wasn't the worst fate of the day. Pike listed forward to whisper in Frank's ear. "Having fun, little brother?" He let loose a couple of the chuckles.

Almost growling, Frank answered, "You be quiet and mind your own business," and continued nodding his head.

Straightening, Pike turned his attention to the rest of the group.

Smiling, eyes bright, Rena inquired, "How are you this morning, Pike? Did you sleep well? We had a long night with the kids. Hannah was fussy all night and Patrick kicked me continuously. I think I'm black and blue . . . "

Tuning out Rena, Pike raised his eyes to Rebecca, who sat on the other side of the aisle. She locked onto him, bathing him in her warm gaze, a look that never failed to lift his heart into song. He returned her smile with his characteristic grin, rolling his eyes, signifying his current plight with her sister.

She gave him a fleeting grin, one that let him know she fully empathized as she shifted a happily-sleeping Hannah in her arms. Luckily, Pike didn't have to deal with his surly brother, Amos, who was looking out the window with Patrick. Gazing around the packed car, Pike spotted the object of Frank's desire as she now sat behind them.

Pike struggled to turn a deaf ear to Rena as the day

drug on. All the while, Frank was forced to listen to the old man. Frank wore a tired, resigned expression, similar to how Pike felt.

As a last resort, Pike leaned his head against the back of the seat and pulled his new felt Stetson down over his eyes.

"Well, I never!" Rena huffed.

*

Hours later, Pike, Buster, and Hank ambled along as they stepped away from the horse's boxcar in Cincinnati. Pike's eyes struck on the dark-skinned young woman from the train.

Crying and distraught, she gaped around wildly as her head snapped back and forth, searching the crowds. Not able to stop himself, Pike came to a halt next to her and inquired, "What's the trouble, miss?"

The young lady continued to sob.

Pike shifted nervously from foot-to-foot and struggled to figure out what to say next.

Taking a tentative step toward the woman, Buster placed his huge palm on her shoulder, and tugged her about to face him. His velvety voice seemed to penetrate her fog. "Missus, what's the matter? Let's me hep you's." He gave her a gentle shake on the shoulder. "Missus, now looks at me. Now, tell ol' Buster what's the matter."

Stemming the steady flow of tears, she stuttered, "I-I-I got my b-b-bag stolen. They got my money. I don't know what I'm going to do. I lost everything!"

Buster turned to Pike with a plea for help in his coal-black eyes.

Taking his cue, Pike spoke up with what he hoped would be a soothing voice. "Miss, I'm sorry someone took all your things and your money. What can we do to help you?"

"I don't know what to do. They stole every bit of my money to travel. It was money I needed to pay my way to New Orleans. I was going there to work for a rich couple. I was going to care for their three small children, but that's not going to happen now." The tears flooded her face again.

"Now, miss," Pike soothed, "please don't cry. Let us help you. You can stay with our ladies tonight in their hotel room. We can't pay your way to New Orleans, but we can get you to St. Louis. Or you can stay with us and work with us. We can use another set of hands where we're going. Or, you can find work in St. Louis."

Swiping at her cheeks with the back of her hand, the lady paused. "I'm not sure what to do, but I wouldn't mind staying with your ladies. I watched them the last two days. They seem nice. I'd be real thankful to you for helping me. I'm not sure what the best thing is to do after that, but I'll think on it tonight."

"Well, it's settled then," Pike announced. "Let's find the rest of the group at the hotel. Come on." Pike gave Hank's lead a tug as Buster urged the woman to move forward into the flow of traffic on the dusty street. Plodding along, Pike asked, "What can we call you?"

"My name is Lyric," she said in a stronger voice. "Lyric Jones. I'm from the far north side of Baltimore in the neighborhood called 'The Falls'. Have you heard of it?"

"Of course," Pike answered, sounding impressed. "Who hasn't heard of that neighborhood? It's mighty high-falutin', isn't it?"

"Miss Lyric," Buster interjected, "my name is Buster and this here is Pike Wheeling. We's glad to meet you. We's sho will be happy to help you. Sho will. Anything you's need, just asks."

Hmmm, Pike pondered, *what is making Buster so talkative? He's usually not this open with strangers. I wonder if this lady is having the same effect on Buster as she has on Frank?*

As Buster left to enter the barn with Hank, he said, "Good night, Pike, and to you, Miss Lyric. See you's in the morning'."

Chuckling to himself at Buster's attention to Lyric, Pike continued on to the hotel with Lyric beside him. As he listened to her melodious voice, clear and vibrant with a bit of a trill, he decided that she was aptly named. He wondered if she might have a sweet singing voice, too.

*

In the dining room, Frank listened to Lyric tell her story about losing her money and about Pike saving her. A grumble flashed through his thoughts as he felt a pang of jealousy for Pike's afternoon activities with her, but the aggravation passed now as Lyric sat at Frank's table.

Frank was struck by the sweet quality of Lyric's melodic voice. *Matches her looks,* he told himself as he reached out and buttered another yeast roll. He found himself unable to contain his eagerness to get to know this woman. *What good fortune. The gods must be smiling on me today.*

"What a wonderful name you have," Rena said. "And you have such pretty light-brown skin. How old are you? Tell us about yourself."

"Well," Lyric began as her eyes shined in her softly-rounded face, "I come from a long line of slaves. My mother was born a slave on a plantation in Virginia."

Shocked at her words, Frank stopped chewing on his roll. *I would have never guessed that she was black.* Not knowing exactly how he felt about this, he watched her and listened all the more closely.

"My grandmother was born on the same plantation, and when she was a teenager, the overseer took a shine to her and started coming around. There was nothing a little slave girl could do about her master's desires. Soon afterward, my grandmother found out she was expecting a baby. That was my mama, her name is Birdie. She also grew up working on the same plantation as my grandmother. As she grew up, she had the same problem my grandma did with a son of the plantation owner. But my mama decided, after that first time that he got at her, it wasn't going to happen again. She ran away from the plantation and hid until she got to Baltimore. By that time, she knew she was expecting me.

"My mama wandered the streets, trying to find a way to feed herself. Mostly, she ate out of garbage cans. She hid behind a big house in Baltimore."

Frank found himself mesmerized by Lyric's story,

although he also found himself growing a little distant from his initial reaction to her. Chewing on another roll, Frank continued to listen as she continued.

"A groom found my mama and dragged her into the house to let the Missus talk to her. The Missus took pity on her and decided to let her stay with the family. The woman needed a new cook.

"I was born in that house. I grew up there. The Missus saw to it that I got schooling. I love to read and write. But mostly, I love to sing. I've sung my whole life. The Missus and Mister would have me sing at their parties, and I learned to cook, too. As I grew up, I helped around the house, but I'm eighteen now, so my mama thought I should see the world. She asked the family for help. The Missus had relatives in New Orleans, so they arranged to send me. I was so excited about going. Now, here I am."

"Well, Lyric," Rena said the moment Lyric paused, "what an interesting background. You have light-brown skin, but you don't look black. I don't mean to offend you. It's just an observation."

"I'm only part black," Lyric stated as if it were a trifling fact. "I can pass for white. How else could I get on the train?"

"Lyric," Pike interrupted before Rena could speak again, "We are glad to hear you like to sing. You'll be a welcome addition to our music sessions. Hope you know some gospel music."

"Oh, yes," Lyric responded enthusiastically. "I know plenty of gospel songs. I went to church every Sunday. I sang in the choir since I was ten. I love to sing, even more than I love to cook, and I do love to cook, especially cobblers and cream pies."

"Lyric," Rebecca asked, "do you like taking care of children? I would appreciate some extra hands with my two."

"Yes, I do like helping with the little ones."

As soon as the steaming plates of food arrived, everyone dug in. The silverware clacked and clanged as Rena took over the conversation again.

Frank scooped up his first mouthful of peas and drifted off into his own thoughts. *Hmmm . . .don't know if I can get serious with a black girl. What would my family think? Boy, I like the looks of her. Especially those breasts, but, guess, it will never be. Too bad. She looks good enough to eat.*

Chapter 12

"Look, look!" Patrick squealed as the train chugged over a most impressive expansive bridge, suspended across the mighty Mississippi River.

Not being able to stop himself from taking a long look through the window, Pike also watched as the water churned below and observed the few steam boats gliding under them. True to form, from what he had heard, the "Big Muddy" was as dark as milk chocolate and high on its banks. Gazing up at the sky, he cast a worried glance at the angry skyline. It possessed a wild, boiling persona with its gunmetal-gray clouds banked in a low wall on the skyline.

Hope a storm isn't coming. Still, he couldn't help being thrilled to finally arrive in St. Louis. Now, the real journey would begin. Where would it lead him?

Whispers of doubt began to rise in his mind about the future for his family and friends. Quickly, he pushed them away, leaned over, and quipped into Frank's ear, "So, you ready to put your lazy behind to work?"

"Just watch me go, Brother!"

The train eased its way into the depot.

"We're here!" Rena crowed as the engine began its clattering stop. Then she jumped up, lifting her hefty hips from the wooden bench, the one that she had complained about for the entire trip, now forgotten.

The wind blasted Pike full in the face as he stepped from the car, almost whipping his Stetson from his head. He grabbed it as he directed, "I'll see you at 'The

Mountain Man'. It's only a few blocks from the station. I need to get Hank settled first."

As Pike located and approached the black and buckskin duo, patiently waiting, he boomed out, "Solid ground again. How are you boys?"

"We's jus' fine," Buster replied with his characteristically twisted smile. "Guess we's goin' to see some weather. Smells like snow. What'd you think?"

"Think you're right," Pike said. "Hate to say it, though."

Pike turned to locate the new stable for Buster and Hank. Both men bent their heads against the bitter north wind as it ripped and tore at their clothes, cutting right through them.

While they hiked along, Buster asked in a nonchalant manner, "How's Miss Lyric doin'? She been enjoyin' the train ride?"

"She seems to be surviving. At least she hasn't run away yet, if that's what you mean." Pike chuckled at his own attempt at humor.

Buster didn't join him.

"Do I sense an interest in the young lady?"

"I jus' wants to know she's okay. Jus makin' sho, that's all."

"Hmmm, I'm not sure I believe that," Pike replied.

The trio entered into the bustling street traffic, and were forced to carefully wind their way through pedestrians and wagons. While snaking along the air began to swirl with snowflakes, urging Pike forward a little faster to get out of that mean wind.

As the wind wrestled with his felt hat and tried to yank it from his head, Pike glanced at the buildings closely lining the street's edge. Most were constructed of wooden planks, many with decorative painted fronts. Quite a few were painted in subdued shades of gray and white. Intrigued by the brick buildings sprinkled here and there, Pike took special note of one structure built with deep-red brick. Out front, a big sign displayed three-foot golden letters which read; 'Bennet Bank and Trust'.

The cold temperature seemed to intensify, slicing right through Pike. He turned his eyes to hurriedly locate their destination. Luckily, just ahead stood 'The Mountain Man Hotel', a plank-constructed, two-story structure with a long porch running across its length. Pike hustled, leading the way into the alley. Almost directly behind the hotel, stood an unpainted rough-planked barn and no sign adorned the exterior.

It must be the livery, Pike surmised as he pushed through the open door while gratitude from getting out of the cold washed over him. The dim light of the barn made it difficult to see his surroundings, but as his eyes adjusted, he called out, "Hello. Is anybody here?" His ears detected a rustling of hay somewhere off to his right.

"Can I help you, sir?" a man's squeaky voice queried. The small man looked sleepy as he stumbled into Pike's line of sight. Slight of form and short of stature, the man's dirty clothes were sprinkled with clumps of hay. A few strands stuck out of his dark, greasy hair.

Wanting to laugh out loud, Pike managed to keep it down to a small grin. "Yes, my horse and groom need lodging. Do you have room?"

"Yes, sir, we do. We'd be right proud to give them a place to stay. Let me take your horse. What a fine piece of horseflesh he is. You could get a pretty penny for him."

"No," Pike mumbled without hesitation, "he's not for sale." He slipped a hand along the horse's rough winter coat.

"I understand, sir," the little man said, reaching out to clasp Hank's lead. "He's a nice one, he is. Don't blame you one bit. Let me put him up."

"Buster, my groom, will come back this evening to sleep. We'll see you then. What's your name?"

"Willie, sir. Just call me little Willie." The diminutive frame disappeared into the dark folds of the barn.

Pike and Buster trailed out of the door and back into the frigid wind, which put a hustle in their step. "Let's find the others," Pike blustered as he hung onto the brim of his hat.

"Yes. I's ready to visit wiff Frank. I's hopes we can work some on my reading'. I's enjoyin' that. I's like to see Miss Lyric, too."

Pike wasn't fooled by the innocent-sounding statement. He smiled to himself. "Well, let's get to the hotel to see if we can round them up."

The inside of the hotel, furnished with the finest mahogany furniture Pike had ever seen, was fancier than he had expected. Several sofas and settees sat in cozy groupings throughout the spacious lobby. Directly across from the front desk, a cheerful, snapping fire blazed. Thick, colorfully-flowered rugs were scattered about the floor. On the ten-foot walls, vibrant paintings hung with colorful scenes of mountains, rivers, and trees.

Wow, Pike thought, *I like this place.*

Hanging above the river-stone mantle, the stuffed head of a huge moose resided. How that massive head and antlers managed to get hung that high remained a mystery to Pike. A full-sized, stuffed black bear stood growling in the corner. Gaping at the bear's feet, Pike spied Patrick gawking up, spellbound by the towering form.

Sneaking up quietly, Pike tiptoed behind the boy, grabbed him at the waist, and growled into his ear.

Startled, the child's eyes shot open wide. He gaped around to see who had scared him. "Uncle Pike!" he howled. "Don't do that!"

Pike and Buster hooted at his fright. Pike asked, "Do you like the bear?"

"Yes, I do," the boy replied. "He's really big!"

"Come on, Patrick," Pike directed as he held out his hand. "Let's get back over to your parents."

"Okay." He clasped Pike's hand with his tiny fingers.

*

While resting on his cot later that evening, Pike stared at an unusual man on an adjoining cot. The middle-aged man wore a set of old buckskins, adorned with plenty of fringe along the chest, as well as fringe hanging from the sleeves and his matching pants were fringed down the sides.

The man's face, coordinated with the rough leather of his clothes, appeared well-worn and creased. A canyon of deep fissures formed along his cheeks and his dusky-brown eyes and muddy-colored hair - a mixture of gray and the younger shade of brown - gave him a rugged appearance. Moccasins encased his feet. The man sat on his cot as he oiled his Winchester rifle.

Fascinated by the stranger, Pike felt compelled to speak to him. Pike nodded when the man met his gaze and offered, "How're you this evening?" Before the man could answer, Pike added, "Where'd you get those buckskins?"

The man grinned, seemingly cheered by the opportunity to visit. "My Sioux wife made this for me," he said proudly. He pointed to his shirt and pants. "She can sure tan a hide, can't she?"

"Your Sioux wife?"

"Yes, siree. You heard me right. Let me introduce myself." He rose from his cot and vigorously shook hands with Pike. "My name is Scratch Thomas."

"Pleased to meet you, Scratch."

As Scratch sat next to Pike on his cot, Frank joined them. Scratch asked, "You all friends or something?"

"We're brothers," Pike answered

"I see. Where you boys headin'?"

Pike carried the conversation. "We are wanting to get some land in the Indian Territory to do some farming. Have you ever been there?"

The man stroked his unruly beard a few times. "I've been in that direction, but I don't think I've been to the Territory. I've been through Kansas many a time on my way to the Rockies. I went to the mountains almost twenty years ago. I used to trap beaver, but that petered out. I got to be friends with the Sioux Indians in the area. I eventually moved in with them. I got me a Sioux wife and three kids by her."

"What brought you to St. Louis?" Frank inquired.

"I got a letter from the local post saying my sister had died. I'm on my way home to take care of some legal matters. She's got a half-grown son. Her husband died two years ago. I need to find out what's happened to the boy."

"Sorry to hear that," Pike offered.

"So, you boys are headed to the Indian Territory.

Have you gotten outfitted?"

Pike didn't know if Scratch was asking to be friendly or if he might have some helpful hints. He hoped the latter. "No, we just got to St. Louis on the afternoon train. Since the weather's been stiff, we've done nothing."

"Maybe I can give you some help. I don't get this way often, but I spent the afternoon down the street at the 'The Last Rose of Summer'. It's a saloon. I talked to a wagon train guide. He's been doing it the better part of ten years. He told me to get myself a new mule from a man up north of town by the name of Livingston. He would be the best man around to get you some good teams. You'll need 'em where you're headed."

Feeling relief, Pike listened intently, easily noting the former information about Livingston verified since he'd heard it before. He knew it must be reliable. "Did the man in the saloon tell you where to get supplies?"

"Yes, he did. I've been there several times myself. The best is Hanson's over on Elm Street but Brewer's on Montgomery is pretty good, too. They are the most reasonable."

"Scratch," Frank piped up, "we can't thank you enough."

"Yes," Pike agreed, "we've had little information to go on. What we have been told has been about as thin as frog's hair, if you know what I mean."

The man bobbed his head and gave them a knowing wink. "Sounds like you boys don't lack for gumption. You'll need it where you're headed. Sure will. This country is being built by fellas like you. Before long, the countryside will be settled. Hope I don't live to see it. The army is pushing my wife's people onto reservations. They've refused to do it to this point, but before long they will have to give in. It's a sad turn of events in my estimation. Good luck to you though. I'll be heading out at first light to hop a train to Louisville. I wish you good luck in your travels. Watch out for bad men in the Territory. There's not much law there."

*

Early the next morning in the dining room, Pike said

to the group, "This is my plan." Everyone had their eyes on him, except Amos, who stared at the bottom of his coffee cup as if it held the answers to all of the mysteries of the world. Pike tried to ignore Amos's continued distancing toward him but it was beginning to wear thin. "I'm going to head to the Livingstons' place to buy some mule teams and a few horses. It's about ten miles from here. It may take me the better part of the day to get there and back. I'll bring the new horses with me. That way, the men can ride back to fetch the mule teams. Is everyone agreed?" Pike's eyes drifted from face to face as he registered the nods and agreements. "What's everyone going to do while I'm gone?"

Speaking up first, Lyric chirped, "We ladies are going to stay by this warm fire and read. We may even do a little knitting."

Pike's ears rejoiced in the nectar of Lyric's trill and reminded him about hearing her sing. "Maybe we could sing this evening," he said. "How about that?"

"Well, Pike, I would enjoy that," Lyric announced with evident enthusiasm. "Hurry back."

"Yes, Pike," Rebecca added, her eyes lingering on him. "You be careful. It's so cold. I'm afraid we're going to get a bad storm."

Pike peeked at Amos with a side glance.

Amos speared him a withering, hate-filled look.

"Oh, now," Pike soothed the group, feeling a little on edge by Amos's reaction. "No one worry. No blizzards are coming our way . . . at least, I hope not."

*

"Willie!" Pike wheezed through the mind-numbing, cold morning air as he reached the barn. Each swirl of his breath condensed into a thick cloud that hung like a shield in front of his face. *Just my luck the weather would turn nasty. My luck seems to have run out. Not the first time in my life. Got to get out there and get our animals, or we'll be behind in getting on the trail.* Pike peered through the dim light, straining to make out the sound of someone rustling in the hay.

"Sir?" the sleepy voice of Willie replied as his figure

appeared from the back.

"There you are, Willie. Would you saddle Hank? I've got business I need to tend to. If you'll get his saddle and bridle, I'll get him out of his stall." Pike attached the lead rope to Hank while saying, in a crooning voice, "You ready to get out, boy?"

The shaggy gelding poked his snuffling muzzle into Pike's coat and nudged him softly. Tying the rope to the leather halter, Pike rubbed the horse's shoulder and made a half-hitch knot to tie the horse to a rail. He turned just in time to grab the saddle and blanket from Willie's small arms. After spreading out the woolen blanket, Pike heaved the creaking leather onto the horse's back. He gave the cinch one last heave, tightly tying the strap. Shortly, the snaffle bit rested in Hank's mouth.

"Thank you, Willie," Pike tossed over his shoulder as he stepped away with the horse and headed to the barn doors.

When the first blast of wind hit, the gelding humped his back and performed a jig on the tips of his front hooves.

"Okay, boy, stop so I can get on," Pike commanded as he tugged firmly on the reins and urged the horse to stand still. Jerking on the reins again, he shouted gruffly, "Whoa, Hank! Whoa!"

The horse stopped prancing and paused momentarily with his head high, eyes bright and jaw rigid. Having been inactive for several days, along with the brisk weather, the horse's energy could barely be contained.

Ignoring his mount's body language, Pike tugged his hat down on his head and inserted his boot into the stirrup. The instant his butt hit the saddle the buckskin took advantage of it and bolted, leaping sideways and jerking his head down. The reins yanked right through Pike's grip and with a free head, the gelding humped up and pitched hard.

Caught off guard by the gelding's unusual behavior, Pike slipped sideways out of the saddle. Pike frantically grabbed for the saddle horn, but his hand only grazed it before he dropped to the unforgiving ground with a teeth- rattling thump.

Disoriented, he lay on his side and took stock of his body to assess the potential damage. It didn't take long to determine that only his pride had been hurt, nothing more. He carefully returned to a sitting position, feet stretched out in front of him, and gawked around for his trusty mount. His eyes came to rest on the horse, standing fifteen feet away, patiently waiting.

Leaning against the horse's neck, Willie clutched onto the reins with his small hand covering his mouth. His shoulders wiggled up and down as he attempted to hide his mirth and even the horse looked amused with his brightly shining eyes.

Pike grumbled to himself as white-hot anger flew across his vision and clouded it briefly, pushing him into action. He shot to his feet and marched stiffly toward the pair.

Willie's laughter ceased instantly as fear replaced the amusement in his brown eyes.

Reason returned to Pike as quickly as the anger had struck and he began to see the humor in what had just transpired. A grin crossed his face and when he reached Hank's shoulder, he leaned against it and gave in to the laughter that flowed.

Willie joined in, snorting a few relief-filled chuckles.

"Okay, Hank. You think we can get it right this time? Come on, horse!" Pike laughed into the freezing wind. This time he made sure he held the reins tightly as he mounted. He forced the gelding to keep his head up so he could stay in control. Clucking once, Pike utilized the horse's energy to take off at a good lope. Hank didn't give up the fight easily. He released another good-natured buck while he rolled down the alleyway.

As Pike and Hank clomped their way through the deserted streets of St. Louis, Pike fervently wished it were warmer for his ride. Not only did he shiver from the cold, but the biting wind made it almost impossible to enjoy the view of the buildings along the streets as tears streamed from his eyes.

Once the pair had the first mile under their belt, the horse settled into a steady rhythm that ate away at the distance before them. Puffing into the wind, a crust of frost, created by the condensation of Hank's warm breath, formed on the horse's whiskers.

After a couple more miles, Pike swiped at his burning eyes to clear the tears that constantly formed from the stinging gusts of wind. While his sight was momentarily unimpeded, he took a quick glance around. On one side of the lane, a dense forest kept a silent vigil. On the other side, he detected a well-constructed log cabin with outbuildings. Smoke lazily drifted from the stone chimney.

Suddenly, the wind nipped him so hard he ducked his head, vainly wishing for a scrap of warmth. *Wow, it's cold,* he told himself as he tried to stall a shudder, but he could no longer hold the shivering at bay. It took over his being, plaguing him relentlessly.

While attempting to escape the painful cold, he released his mind to travel elsewhere. Andersonville had molded him into a master at such techniques of escape. It took but a moment to divert his consciousness to happier places. His father and mother appeared before his mind's eye, smiling their loving paternal smiles. Easily, he could see them sitting at the kitchen table near the brick fireplace, aglow with a blazing fire.

Adding to the blissful scene, Pike placed himself there in a ladder-backed chair, holding his trusty guitar. The chords of his favorite song, 'Down By The River,' strummed through his mind, reverberating throughout his body and adding its magical sounds to the tingles in his numb fingers and ears as he began to hum.

Snapping back to reality, Pike spotted several homesteads along the well-traveled road. Stinging pellets of snow plinked against his cheeks and icy bits rained on his hat. It was too late to turn back now. *I can always stay at the Livingston's place if this weather sets in,* Pike reasoned as he urged Hank onward with a couple of kissing clucks.

By the time Pike reached his destination, he was almost too numb to care about buying animals; all he could focus on was how frozen he was. He managed to guide Hank into a light trot as he came abreast several corrals containing a large mixture of work animals; mules, horses, and oxen.

The Livingston's cabin resided on the farthest point

of the property, sitting well back from the road. Smoke visibly drifted from the rock chimney. The well-worn path between the corrals, barns and outbuildings would easily direct Pike straight to the cabin's front door.

Since Hank was sweaty, Pike couldn't just tie him up and leave him in the cold wind. He feared he might colic or get pneumonia. So, Pike halted the horse by the first large barn and stiffly led him inside for protection. As he struggled to disengage his frozen limbs from the horse's back, a hearty voice rang in his frozen ears.

"Is it cold enough for ya? Can you get down?"

Pike glanced over his shoulder at the stranger covered in a knit cap and heavy coat, while he lifted his sore, frozen leg to slide it over the horse's broad rump. Luckily, his legs maintained his weight as his ice-covered boots struck solid ground. Pike groaned at the shooting pain from his soles upward.

"Here, let me take your horse," the stranger said. "Follow me if you can."

Managing a bob of his head in response, Pike shuffled through the inviting barn doors. Once out of the wind, he regained his bearings and gazed about appreciatively, quickly noting the various box stalls - all full. Even though it was probably still freezing in the barn, it seemed warm in comparison to the outside with the wind.

The stranger made short work of unsaddling Hank. "I'm Lewis Livingston. I'm guessin' you were sent here to buy some animals to head west. Am I right?" Resting his hand amiably on the gelding's withers, the man paused to gauge if Pike could speak or if he was still too frozen.

Shaking his head in an attempt to clear it, Pike locked eyes on Lewis and gave his head a firm nod, letting that be his answer.

Livingston's auburn hair stuck out from under his knitted cap, which was pulled down so far over his brow it almost covered his steely eyes. The man wasn't young, evidenced by the heavy creases lacing his leathered skin. Even though he possessed a rough exterior, Lewis's voice contained friendliness and laughter, as though he had known Pike all his life. "Let's get on up to the house," Livingston bellowed. "And get you a cup or two of coffee. Once your brain and body thaw out, we can talk about what you are looking for. Come on and follow me." And follow Pike did, as quickly as his stiff limbs would allow.

Chapter 13

Upon entering the bright, two-room cabin, Pike took full advantage of its penetrating warmth, sighing with relief. The pleasant heat radiated not only from the hearth but from the family enclosed within its well-built walls.

"Caroline, come and meet our guest," Lewis boomed, as though she weren't in the same small room.

The sturdy-looking woman dropped the clothes she had been mending, rose from her rocker and swept across the dirt floor to join her husband in the center of the room. She allowed Lewis to place his arm lovingly around her shoulders as they swung around to face Pike.

"It's nice to meet you, sir," Caroline said while she quickly studied Pike, her head cocked side-ways, sparrow-like. Her blue eyes snapped merrily, just like her husband's. "Could I ask your name, and won't you please come and sit by the fire while I heat some coffee?"

"Thank you," Pike stammered. "Let me introduce myself. I'm Pike Wheeling . . . from Baltimore. My brothers and I are moving west to homestead. You, Mr. Livingston, have been recommended to me as the man to see about buying top-notch mules and horses to get us to the Territory."

Caroline's soft heart twinkled through her gaze. A grin slanted on her pink lips. "Well, Pike, it's nice to meet you. Do come over to the fire." She held out her fleshy arm to guide him to the second rocker placed directly in front of the fire. It was obviously Lewis's chair.

"Please sit," Caroline said as she bustled over to the

hearth to place the coffeepot over the fire.

Gladly, Pike took a seat in the well-worn rocker to finish thawing out. Walking to the other chair to rest in Caroline's chair, Lewis quickly followed suit. "How long have you been travelin'?" he asked in a polite tone.

"We got on the train four days ago." Pike's head slipped back to rest while he soaked up the fire's heat.

"Can you tell me what you're lookin' for? I've been gatherin' stock all winter. Most people haven't started west yet so I've got lots of good stock to choose from."

"I'm going to need three more riding horses for some of the men in my group. One needs to be gentle enough for the ladies. I intend to start a sawmill and will need at least four good mule teams."

"I see. I've got several animals that will fill the bill. You can't have too many good animals. They're your best investment. Buy top-grade stock, that's my belief. A good mule or horse can save your life."

Pike showed his agreement with a silent nod.

"Here," Caroline said to Pike as she held out a steaming tin of coffee.

"Thank you." Pike instantly grasped the cup and blew across the top of the dark brew. Immediately, he sipped the scalding liquid, unmindful of his tongue burning. The warmth soon began to work its magic and began thawing his cold bones.

After Pike had downed several more cups of coffee and had polished off the beef stew and cornbread Caroline had served, he and Lewis bundled up to face the cold once more. Now that he was warmer, Pike felt excited about selecting his new stock.

"Let's start with the horses," Lewis stated as he hustled through the swirling snow. His voice barely carried over the wind. "The horses are in the first barn."

Pulling on his coat around his neck and hunching against the sharp gusts of blowing snow, Pike's eyes riveted on Lewis's back to aid in guiding his steps.

Lewis opened the latch to the barn and pushed the door back. As the men strode into the center aisle, Pike gazed with wonder at all the heads hanging over the stall doors. "How many head do you have?"

"Seventy, more or less." A female liver-and-white

pointer came out of nowhere to trot up to Lewis to then nose at his hand. He unceremoniously scratched her ears. "Hi, girl. How are you, huh?" The dog jumped up eagerly to rest her front paws on her owner's chest. Gladly, Lewis obliged her with another scratch.

Pike couldn't help but note the swollen teats of the nursing bitch. His eyebrows lifted as he asked, "Do you have puppies?"

"Sure do. I had a pair of fine huntin' dogs. They had pups a couple months back. I lost the papa dog a month ago. I went huntin' and he was a-runnin' ahead of me. He came upon a mountain lion. Before I could catch up, that cat had cut him bad. There was nothin' I could do for him. Damn shame. He was the finest huntin' dog I ever had."

Hearing rustling sounds, Pike looked around, spying several puppies tumbling into the aisle. Stumbling over one another, the pups wrestled and nipped each other as they drew near.

The floppy ears and loose skin of the puppies captivated Pike. He reached down and lifted up one of the females, enfolding the wiggly pup into the crook of his arm. The tiny dog began licking at his hand, then chewed on it. Pike lifted the squirming bundle up to eye level to snuggle it but the puppy grasped the end of his nose with her needle-sharp teeth. "Hey, cut that out!" Pike yelped as he laughed and pulled the pup away from his stinging nose. "Lewis, can I buy one of these, too? I've wanted a hunting dog. Couldn't hurt to have the protection, either."

Grinning, Lewis answered, "Sure. I'm only keeping' one to replace the one I lost. The others need new families. I'd be glad for you to have one. What do you think about the horses?"

"Oh, yes," Pike replied as he continued to clutch the puppy next to his warm chest. "Let's look at the horses."

Strolling down the aisle and touching several eager muzzles, Lewis declared, "I've put my best in this barn. They're all young and broke. Some better than others, but they're all healthy. They're ready to go to work. You should get you one good stallion and a couple of mares."

Setting down the pup, Pike began inspecting the

horses by checking their teeth and feeling them over with his experienced hand. Peering over one stall, he noted an unusual specimen nearly eighteen-hands tall and almost painfully leggy and lanky. The horse was bay-colored, but that wasn't what made him stand out. It was the white blanket that extended from just past his withers all the way across his refined rump. Within the white blanket were many black, oblong spots.

"What kind of horse is this?" Pike asked mystified.

Lewis strode to the stall. "That's one fine stallion. He's an Appaloosa. They come from the Indians out west. I bought him from a mountain man who recently came through here. He's hard to handle, since he's a stallion and all, but he can run all day. He's got the heart you'll be a-needin'. He'd be a fine breedin' animal.

Looking closer at the horse, Pike observed the strangely-striped hooves as well as the mottled skin around the muzzle and eyes. It gave the animal a wild look. The stallion's overall appearance and unusualness captivated him. "I like him," Pike said, cautious with his tone in order to hide his enthusiasm. "Show me some of the others."

After looking at all the horses, he chose a pair of mares rapidly. Both were well-broken and both were marked with white stockings and blazes, one being sorrel and the other black. Pike knew they would cross well with the stallion he wanted - the Appaloosa. With his mind made up on the horses, he said, "Let's look at the mules."

"We're going to have to go outside for that. I've got so many, I keep them in several corrals. Let's go."

As the pair strode into the yard, the tumbling snow greeted them and blasted them with her icy breath.

A dozen mules milled about in each corral. Most were bunched at one end munching hay. Once again, an unusual animal, a good-sized spotted mule that was standing off by himself, captured Pike's attention. A white streak ran down the mule's face and several white patches stood out on each of his sides. Pike knew a spotted mule was hard to come by. He pointed to it and asked, "What about that one?"

"That's Dunk. He's a booger. Bites, kicks, and generally gets along with no one, includin' the other mules. At least he likes his teammate. That's the one over there." Lewis pointed to an average-looking bay mule. "Those two can work circles around the other teams, if you can stand the surly one's attitude. Watch his hooves, too. He's gotten me once."

It didn't take long for Pike to choose a pair of chestnut mules and another two teams of bay mules. He couldn't help taking the spotted-mule team, too. Something about those spots intrigued him. He was also curious about how mean the mule could be, since Pike loved a challenge with animals.

When Pike told Lewis his choices, the man nodded his head and began adding up the costs. "That'll be fifty dollars a pair for the mules and thirty-five each for the horses, seventy-five for the stallion. Do you need a harness and wagons?"

Pike, silently adding up the amounts in his head, answered, "Yes, we sure do."

"We've got some good used wagons and harnesses. I can get you saddles and bridles for the horses. The total will include fifteen for each wagon, ten for each harness set, and eight for the saddles. I'll throw in the bridles and the puppy. These are fair prices, and the goin'-rate around here. That makes the total four hundred and forty-nine dollars. What do you say?"

Pike felt the prices were fair for the quality of the animals and the equipment. "You've got yourself a deal." Pike grasped Lewis's beefy hand and pumped it several times. "I'll take the horses with me. I'll need to get the men back out here to drive the wagons into to town and pick up the womenfolk. Here's your money." Pike plucked the bills from his interior coat pocket.

Lewis stuffed the money into his coat. "Here, let me help you saddle them. The stallion's name is Clash. He's a handful. He's got a big trot and lots of heart but be careful. He'll dump you if he can. The black mare is Raven and the sorrel is Gertie."

"I'm going to have to ride the stallion and lead the rest," Pike decided. "That's the only way I can manage the horses tied together. Let me get on Clash first and ride the orneryness out of him, then we'll head to town."

It took but a few minutes to saddle the animals. Pike gathered Clash's reins to vault onto the stallion's high back. With a snort and a head toss, the pair dashed sideways while Clash fought for his head. Clutching the leather of the reins as tightly as he could and straining to keep the determined horse's head up, Pike maintained control of his head. So, the horse could do no more than crow-hop.

Within five minutes, the stallion decided to take it easier and settled into a nimble trot.

"Okay," Pike puffed, breath freezing in his nose, "I'm ready for the others."

Quickly, Lewis fetched the waiting horses, which had been tied together in a line with Hank in the lead. Handing the gelding's lead rope to Pike, Lewis said, "I hope you make it back to town. If the weather sets in, just come on back here."

"Thank you, Lewis. I'll do that. I should be okay. I need to get back and get these horses put up. Thank you for everything. Thank Caroline for the hospitality." He reined Clash around and as he came about, the stallion took a swipe at Hank with his bared teeth. To save Hank, Pike jerked hard on the horse's head to intervene. The stallion's ears laid flat against his handsome skull as he let Hank know just what he thought of him.

Waving one last time, Pike and the horses plunged forward. The snow continued to fall from the ominously-gray sky while Pike sent a plea heavenward, hoping to keep the weather at bay.

The stallion fussed with the gelding as Pike maintained a brisk pace. Minute by minute, the wind picked up, blasting them harder and harder. As additional snow tumbled down from heaven's gate, the horses settled into a fast, ground-eating pace.

The bite of the wind and the pelting snow chilled Pike to the bone as he knew it would. He bent his head against the blizzard, struggling to send his mind off to his fantasy world. After what seemed like an eternity but was only a half an hour, he asked himself, *Should I turn back?* He instructed himself, "No!" Minutes later, he asked the same question, but once again, he fussed at himself to be quiet and ride on.

Not ten minutes later, Pike shook with raging chills and wished he would have listened to the subliminal question and turned back. His mind began to slow down, along with his numbing extremities. The cold became the sole focus of his thoughts.

During the next two miles, Pike dreamed about the roaring fire at 'The Mountain Man'. Shudders wracked his body as snow swirled around him in a wall of white. He could not see even three feet in front of him.

Though his speed had lessened, Clash still plowed forward. At this pace, the other horses could keep up without being taxed to their limits. The horse's panting could be heard in the biting wind.

Within the next fifteen minutes, Pike's mind began to get away from him in hallucinations. He didn't know if he was heading in the right direction, either. Everything around him was white and the ankle-deep snow forced Clash to walk as time slowed even more.

Completely numb, Pike's mind wanted to shut down with the cooling of his body. Unable to focus on any one thing, strange images splashed across his mind's eye. *Where am I?* his mind screamed. *I don't know where I'm going. What do I do?*

The horses plunged on through the bleak, dark blizzard. Their heads bent against the fury of Mother Nature and met her head on, never faltering.

Pike's delirium passed for a moment as the horse beneath him whinnied and broke through his crazy ramblings. Pike realized he was no longer moving and an instant of mental clarity struck him like a bee sting to his face. Then, the brief flicker of sanity vanished as a black cloud engulfed him. Falling, he slipped into the welcome warmth of the darkness.

*

With several flutters of his eyelids, Pike awoke. Confusion clouded his vision which caused him to shake his head to try to clear it. Not comprehending where he was, he gawked about from his spot on a dry floor. Pike could feel that his body was covered with blankets and he could see several chairs around him from which three sets of alien, worried eyes stared back. That the eyes were strangers added to his confusion, while panic clutched him by the throat and sent him into furious action. Leaping up, he swung his tight fists at the enemy.

Two men and a woman shot from their seats in surprise. The men flew into action and grabbed Pike's flailing arms. Pinning him to the ground, they held him down for several minutes while Pike babbled, yelled, and fought for his freedom. Sometime later, how much later he didn't know, Pike's cold-induced craze eased and as he relaxed he was sent back into oblivion.

This time when Pike's eyes broke open, clearer thought was there to greet him. Slowly, he gathered himself to sit upright.

"Here, drink this," a shrill, girlish voice said.

A cup of warm broth found its way into his hand. He had to focus his mind on stilling his shaky hands long enough to bring the welcome liquid to his cold lips. Pike had the presence of mind to stutter, "Tha-a-n-k-y-o-ou." After a few sips, he looked at the strangers.

"You sure gave us a scare, mister," the smaller man said. "You sure did."

"My name is Eric Stubblefield," the bigger man offered in the intervening quiet. "This is my cousin Reuben Stubblefield and his wife Karen. What might your name be?"

Glancing at the brawny, blonde-headed man, Pike offered, "My name is Pike Wheeling. Thank you for saving me. I'm much obliged. I don't remember getting here. What happened?"

"We heard a horse neigh," Eric said. "We rushed out to see what was happening and we spotted you, just before you pitched out of the saddle. As luck would have it, we were fast enough to catch you before you took a dive in the snow. That spotted stallion of yours saved your life. That's all I can tell you. We put him and the others in the barn. They're safe. What were you doing out on a day like this?"

With his brain and jaw thawed out, Pike felt up to talking. "I was at the Livingston's, getting outfitted to head to the Territory. The weather caught me on the way back to town."

Gratitude washed over him now that he had had a moment to process what had happened. Pike flung up a hasty, *Thank you, Lord!* - realizing just how lucky he had been. It was easy to discern God's hand in the day's events. "I just bought that stallion today. What a stroke of good fortune. He's a keeper!"

Pike shook his head in amazement and he told himself, *Saved by the grace of God, I'd say.* Then, he asked, "What do you folks do out here?"

Eric replied, "My cousin and his wife farm and raise a few cows. I'm visiting with them. I've spent the winter months cutting down trees in the Upper Lakes region for one of the sawmills. I've done that for so long now that I'm interested in moving to a new place. I've been thinking of the frontier myself."

The broad-shouldered man's comments stirred some ideas in Pike. A notion blossomed that Eric could be an asset to his operation, but for now, he said nothing. Instead, he began to explain what he intended to do in Indian Territory to see if this square-jawed fellow would be interested.

Tossing out the bait, Pike said, "I've been thinking about starting a sawmill operation of my own. I'm going to find land on a river. Then, I'm going to order in the necessary equipment. I'm glad I ran across your path. You can tell me exactly what to order."

Eric's eyes blazed like a lit candelabra. As they glowed, his thick torso straightened from the slump it had been resting in, showing his interest.

Before the evening finished, Pike asked, "Eric, would you like to join my band heading west?"

"Let me think on it some," Eric replied. "When you come back this way, I'll give you my decision. How does that sound?"

Grinning, Pike felt a sense of hope bloom. "Sounds fair enough to me. I would like you to come with us. Your expertise will be a great asset to our operation."

As the wicks of the candles burned low, the howling wind moaned around the cabin while cool drafts swept through the room. Pike tugged his borrowed patchwork quilt more snuggly about his shoulders as he noted Karen's slight form. She had been dozing, off and on, for a while now. Taking hold of Karen's hand, Reuben urged her up and guided her to their bed in the back of the room. "Goodnight," Reuben said as the pair shuffled away.

As he stood up and stretched like a lazy cat, Eric said, "Guess I'll turn in, too. See you in the morning. Goodnight."

"Goodnight," Pike replied as he lay in front of the radiating flames and soaked up every degree of warmth coming his way. He tugged his treasured fob and watch out of his pants so he could hold them. Listening to the soulful tune of the blizzard, Pike released his thoughts, giving his mind free rein. Gratitude and sheer amazement ran through his head, alighting his body with an internal fire.

God, what have You showered on me today? Don't know if You pushed me to buy that lion-hearted stallion, knowing he was the only thing that could save me, or that You put Your hand on Clash to lead him to the Stubblefield's door. Either way, my eternal appreciation and gratitude goes to You. Thank You for protecting me this fateful day. Also, thank You for putting me on the pathway to cross with Eric. You have blessed me in so many ways. I can never thank You enough. Know that I fully appreciate Your continued guidance in my life, in Your son's name, I pray. Amen.

As Pike lay silent, his mind took a familiar pathway to return to his past love and his son while he fingered his watch chain softly. Their images loomed before him and their loving warmth added to the other sensations he already felt. Every fiber of his being thrummed while every nerve pricked his spirit. Sleep became as elusive as a frightened quail, not that Pike cared. He had been given a wondrous gift that day - his life.

Knowing how close he had come to dying and how uplifting it was to know he would see tomorrow, seemed too important to shut out with sleep and he didn't even try. That night, Pike meant to fully experience every breath of his lungs and every beat of his heart. He knew he would have to come down from this high wave sometime, but for now, he was content with enjoying this night in the universe as a living soul.

By dawn, Pike's eyes were still open as he smiled in the dark. His life's highest wave had not yet crested but this ride was more thrilling than any he had ever had.

*

The glare from the snow nearly blinded Pike as he labored to keep his gaze out in front of him and away from the shining sea of white. The killing wind was gone, replaced by a calm landscape, bathed in the kinetic energy of the sun. The day's temperature responded and rose accordingly.

The horses had their work cut out for them as they plowed through the knee-deep snow and heavy drifts. Still grinning, Pike rode along on his wave of happiness as the horses trudged their way back to St. Louis.

What a difference a few hours could make. The virginal beauty, left by the storm, took Pike's breath away, humbling him by God's handiwork. He wondered if there was any place that could be more beautiful than these snow-laden trees and hills that lay before his eyes.

Continuing to guide the trail-savvy Clash through the treacherous mounds of snow, Pike forced his eyes to focus hard on the trail before him. He honed his ears to the sound of the horses' breath and to the crunching snow beneath their hooves as bliss continued to blanket him in its warmth.

Chapter 14

"I fold," Drisco grumped as he flipped his losing poker hand onto the table's rough surface. With a growl, he shoved his chair back, shot to his feet, and stalked away from the other three players to the nearest window. His shoulders humped in aggravation as he struggled to contain the anger welling up inside him.

Drisco strained his eyes to stare balefully out at the snow piled up just outside the front door of the '*Last Rose of Summer*'. He and Rufus had stayed in the saloon all night, playing cards, rather than braving the blizzard. Now, that it was midday, Drisco felt antsy about moving on again because he didn't like to stay in one place too long - a dangerous habit for a man such as himself.

With his eyes lingering on the shimmering snow, Drisco saw no beauty in it as it just got in his way. And beside the obstacle the snow presented, he hated to lose at cards, or at anything, for that matter. Today was no exception.

His hand itched to draw a gun on that dandy-looking fellow who had just won. The man's bowler hat, white shirt, and pressed pants irritated Drisco to no end. Compounded with the fact the man had beaten him at poker, he wanted to shoot the man right through his gullet and laugh while he expired.

As Drisco glared out the window, he contemplated ways to get his money back. The best way would be to jump the man later and take what was rightly his and if the man happened to get shot in the process, well, so much the better. A evil, malicious grin slipped across Drisco's face.

Outside, plowing through the main street, a man on a tall, lanky horse, and leading several others, struggled through the snow, alone on the street. They captured Drisco's attention and for a few minutes, he watched them slog their way closer.

Contemplatively, Drisco rubbed his chin. *That's some fine horses,* he told himself as he wondered how he might take a horse or two from that man. As his eyes locked onto the rider, coming closer and closer, something about the man rang with familiarity, especially his above-average height. When Drisco finally snatched a glimpse of the man's face underneath the brim of his hat, a thunderbolt struck.

Its that red-headed shit, Pike! Pike's light-skinned face and green eyes had been burned into his memory, never to be forgotten. Now, an even brighter flame of anger exploded through Drisco. As a result the rush of blood in his ears pounded so loudly, he didn't hear Rufus slink up behind him.

"What'cha looking' at?" Rufus inquired, gazing over his shoulder.

"Look out there," Drisco spat, pointing to the man on the horse. "It's that redheaded shit from the prison. What do ya think about that?"

Slipping forward to gawk out the window, Rufus said, "Well, hell's bells, shit fire! We're lucky whoremasters today. What do you aim to do to him? I say we shoot him and take them horses."

Nodding, Drisco said nothing as he quietly observed Pike turn by 'The Mountain Man' and ride to the back of the hotel. Drisco instinctively knew the livery must be there. "I'll think of something'," he said, mostly to himself.

Rufus chuckled a sick, snorting laugh. "I'll betcha you will."

*

Pike shouted, "Willie, come out here. I need a hand."

The man flew out of the barn as he was pulling on his coat and halted with one arm not quite in the sleeve as his eyes came to rest on the new horses. A stunned expression settled onto his narrow face. "Sir, you got you some fine horses there."

Tossing him Hank's lead rope, Pike replied with a light voice, "Thank you. Can you take Hank and the mares? I'll keep the stallion away from the girls."

Dismounting, Pike trailed into the barn after Willie and the other horses. "Thanks, Willie, I'll bring the men back as soon as the weather will permit. We'll go and retrieve the rest of my new outfit." Giving Clash one last glowing look, Pike watched the stallion gobble eagerly at the oats he had placed before him. Then, Pike ambled out the door to head to the hotel, calling out, "Bye, Willie."

"Bye, Mister Pike."

With a buoyant heart, Pike sloshed his way to the front porch of the hotel. Stomping across its wooden surface, he grasped the door handle and let himself inside. Quickly, he spotted the members of his group clustered around the roaring fire.

"Pike!" Patrick hooted. His eager greeting captured the attention of the others which brought them to their feet.

Frank and Buster raced toward Pike with relief evident on their faces. Eyes wide, Frank blurted out, "Am I glad to see you. We were worried. How did you make out in the storm?" Frank punched Pike's shoulder in a brotherly way, showing him that he was truly glad to see him.

"I's real pleased to see you's," Buster added.

"Sorry that you were worried. I was fine, just fine." Momentarily, he paused to catch his breath and pull off his gloves.

"When I was on my way back to St. Louis, the blizzard hit. I was real lucky that the new horse I was riding took me to a cabin. The people at the cabin let me stay with them. They are some nice folks and one of the men is an experienced sawmill hand. He's thinking about coming with us to the Territory."

Rena raced over and clutched Pike's hand. "Pike,

come and sit by the fire, warm yourself. Tell us all about what happened. What did you buy for us? The men went shopping yesterday and bought all our food and supplies. Come, Pike. Sit, tell us everything."

Allowing Rena to lead the way, Pike followed her to the welcome fire and sat on the nearest settee. The pink and burgundy needlepoint fabric gave a fraction as he settled himself on its surface. He drank in the sight of his family and closest friends and automatically, his eyes were drawn to Rebecca's pretty face. Noting her eyes already focused on him with a warm, open expression, he felt pleasantly surprised and excited. He had seen that look many times in the past.

Dragging his eyes away from the one he loved, Pike caught a glimmer of a hate-filled gaze from Amos's icy, blue eyes. The force behind Amos's hard eyes made Pike feel a bit guilty about the love-infused look he and Rebecca had just shared. Pike diverted his gaze to the ground for a moment to clear his confusion so he could tell his story.

*

The next day, Pike sat astride Clash as he led the men and horses out of the livery and on their way to the Livingston's place. Listening to Lyric sing the evening before had been such a delicious treat that Pike relived it again as Clash clomped along the street. *That girl sings better than the angels above.* Glancing behind him, Pike looked in the direction of Frank, who rode Hank. The trotting gelding soon caught up to the fleet-footed stallion.

Amos and Buster rode the gentler mares and kept a safe distance from the Appaloosa stallion.

"How long does it take to get to the Livingstons'?" Frank asked.

"Oh, maybe an hour or two. Depends on the mares. Don't know how hard we can push them."

"Wow!" Frank suddenly cried. "Look at that brick building. What a beauty. What do you think?"

Pike, still riding high from his near-death experience, blurted, "You're right, Brother. It's a beauty, must be a bank."

Gawking at the sights, it was easy to see that St. Louis was a large and fairly modern city. Pike enjoyed watching the variety of people. Most were dressed primly in city duds and sprinkled among them were the people more sensibly dressed for the rigors of the trail. A few mountain-men types stood out in the crowd with their buckskins and big-handled knives. One even had a fur cap on his head which caused Pike to itch to get started on the trail himself.

"Pike," Frank said as he clipped along beside the temperamental stallion, "I spoke to the owners of the general store where we bought our supplies. They told me about a settlement near the Neosho River in the north part of the Indian Territory. Sounds like what we are looking for."

"Yes, it does," Pike replied. "They told you how to get there?"

"Uh-huh."

"Good. We'll get directions again before we leave."

"Are we stopping at the Stubblefield's on the way there?" Amos asked.

Pike quickly answered. "I thought we would stop on the way back. Look, that's their cabin there." He pointed at the short log structure about a half-mile down the road. As the group trotted closer, Pike could see the two men performing their daily chores.

Swinging an axe with a practiced grace that could only be developed through hours and hours of work, Eric had large pile of wood lying at his feet. When he glanced up, Eric caught sight the riders and halted his axe in mid-air. He allowed it to drop to the ground, then ambled out to meet Pike and his crew and his cousin followed closely behind.

Waving as they approached, Pike hollered, "Hello!"

Grinning, Eric and Reuben raised their arms in return.

When Clash came to a stop, Pike asked, "Eric, hope you had time to think on coming with us. What did you decide?"

"Well," Eric stated, "it wasn't a hard decision. I'm ready to head out. You're heaven-sent as far as I can say. I'm ready. I was just waiting on you to show up. Who do you have with you?"

"I'm glad you'll go with us. This is my little brother, Frank. The big fellow next to him is Buster, and the scruffy-looking one on the end is my other brother, Amos."

The men all nodded their heads in acknowledgement.

Buster said, "I's pleased to know you."

Pike said to Eric, "If you want to get your things, we'll pick you up on the way back with the wagons. It should be about an hour or two."

"I'm ready. I'll be waiting here. I know Reuben and Karen will be glad to be rid of me, won't you, Reuben?"

"You know we've enjoyed having you here."

Eric laughed. "Thank you, little cousin." He turned back to the visitors. "I'll be anxious for your return."

*

A couple of days later, just after sunset, Frank strode excitedly down the alleyway to the livery with Pike at his side. They were just returning from the Hanson's general store.

"You're right, Frank," Pike said, "that area on the Neosho sounds like the spot to head for."

Twice now, Frank had listened to Mr. Hanson tell about the thick trees along the river. He had spoken of tall oaks, hickory trees, and the bountiful grasslands in the area. The ready supply of water from the river put the icing on the cake. Anticipation fluttered through Frank as he grew more excited about his future home because the journey would start tomorrow. Frank felt more than ready, and wondered who was more excited, him or Pike. Guess it didn't matter. A new life awaited them both in the distant untamed land of the red man. It suddenly hit Frank that everything was now in place to follow their dream.

"Let's head to the Territory," Pike hooted as he grasped the handle on the door and dragged it outward. A bounding puppy, Candy, broke through the open door and straight into Pike's arms. Scooping her up, Pike turned her over to rub her pink belly.

"You're right, brother," Frank blurted, "I'm ready to get to the wilds of the Indian Territory. Been ready. Now we can get on our way."

"We're leaving tomorrow, bright and early. Let's fetch the wagons to the Hansons' and get them loaded. Come on!" Pike moved into the dark interior of the barn to hitch up the new teams.

Frank stood, back stiff, behind Pike and gazed into Dunk's stall. With amusement, he noted the mule's threatening rump pointed at them with his left hoof cocked to strike. Frank coughed, then laughed at his brother's poor choice of mules. "Think you bought yourself a real jewel there."

Pike grumbled, easing into the stall without answering Frank's jab.

*

Drisco crouched behind a barrel of oats on the outside of the livery. He had watched the two brothers pass by on their way into the barn. Drisco had been spying on Pike and their group for the last two days as they were preparing to leave for the trail. Drisco wanted to know their plans, and he meant to follow them, pick them off, steal their horses, and use their women in the many different scenarios floating through his mind. As bloodlust filled his mind, the prickle of excitement teased his stomach and his crotch.

Drisco had overheard Pike's brother mention the Indian Territory. *So, that's where they're goin'. Just where we were headed anyhow. What luck. Doesn't matter, they're never goin' to make it!* Drisco covered his mouth and smothered the flood of laughter that threatened to break from him and instructed himself, *Get hold of yourself!*

Not wanting to give himself away, Drisco rose from his hiding place before his laughter got the best of him. Making sure that the brothers wouldn't see him, he snuck along in the dense shadows.

Down the street from the livery, Drisco observed the dandy dude who had won all of his money enter the saloon to play cards. Once the man vanished inside, Drisco slipped into his hotel room to collect Rufus from the whore he was dallying with. Cursing and bellyaching, Rufus buttoned up his pants as he followed Drisco into the cold darkness of the street.

Waiting impatiently in the alley across from the saloon, Drisco hissed into his cousin's ear. "This time, I'm getting what's mine back." Only two things mattered to Drisco now, one was to shoot that dandy fellow and retrieve his money - and hopefully some extra - and to kill Pike. That would come next. And after killing Pike, he planned to head to safety in the Indian Territory where a man like himself could easily hide from the law and stay there forever.

The welcome strains of bloodlust broke to flow through Drisco's veins. Every time, he felt so alive and powerful before a kill. It was an addiction of the worst kind, but knowing that another life was in his control always gave him a obsessive rush. And at the moment of greatest danger, just before he gave his victim a stab with his knife or a bullet from his pistol, he sought the window to their souls - to see knowledge reflected there and the terror of their impending death. Drisco could hardly stand still at the thrill that coursed through his body.

Drisco tromped up and down the alleyway, clutching the handle of the pistol that he carried in his belt. While he paced the alleyway waiting for the dandy to come out of the 'Rose', images of his daddy filtered into his thoughts.

From the time he was a small fry, he had been at his daddy's mercy. How many times had he pleaded with his daddy to stop the beating or the sodomizing? But, Drisco never got through to his daddy. Never once did his daddy stop what he had set out to do and early on, Drisco learned to shut up and do what his father wanted or suffer more. As he grew older, he learned to like what he did with his daddy.

Later, Rufus came to live with them. Now, they had a new body on which to act out their desires. At first, Rufus cried and begged for mercy, but he eventually came around to their way of thinking.

Prickling with delight, Drisco remembered that eventful, bloodthirsty day that changed his entire life. When he was fifteen, Rufus was thirteen; and after a particularly hard beating from his father, he gathered all his strength to turn it on his daddy. Rufus assisted him in holding the man down. Then, Drisco cut him up, ever so slowly, taking several days to complete the act. He started by peeling his skin off - like from an orange. Next, he cut off his fingers, toes, and finally, his balls. Groveling before them, his daddy begged for mercy, but just as his daddy did not listen to Drisco in the past, Drisco did not listen to those pleas. Drisco had learned his lessons well. Now, he ached for the power that killing brought him - that moment when he had total control over the life of another person.

Now, the blood pounded in Drisco's ears as his excitement mounted. Once again, he reveled in the rush that came with the anticipation of capturing his prey and watching him suffer.

Rufus, protecting himself from the cold, curled up in a tight ball next to the building and dozed off.

As the hours passed in waiting, Drisco's energy began to wane, but still, he would not give in and leave until he got what he wanted. To keep his mind active, he entertained himself with all the many fantasies for killing Pike and for raping Pike's women. As he strolled, he grinned, while recalling the pretty girls he had seen with the brothers and Nigger Boy. Yes, Drisco had done his homework well.

A new stab of excitement ran through him as he thought of that black behemoth. Now, he would have the opportunity to finally kill him as well as Pike and his brother. What a bonanza!

Suddenly, the dandy and his bowler hat swayed out of the saloon's front doors. Drunkenly, the man stumbled down the steps and muttered something to himself. Hanging on to the hitching post momentarily, he shuffled out into the bleak night and stumbled toward Drisco, unaware of what monster was stalking him.

Drisco crouched against the building and peeked around the corner cautiously, waiting for the right moment.

"Damn it!" The dandy uttered as he toppled in the mud, not ten yards away.

Excitedly, Drisco kicked Rufus in the ribs.

"Hey," Rufus yelped, "cut that out."

The dandy's head whipped around and he quipped, words tumbling out quickly, "Who's out there?"

Drisco could wait no longer. He clutched his pistol in his cold hand and fired, splintering wood on the saloon wall behind the dandy.

The man ducked, then raised his head with his mouth open in shock, knowing he'd been shot at.

Letting out an evil laugh, Drisco squeezed the trigger again and this bullet found its mark. Scurrying to the moaning form, Drisco flipped the man over and gazed into his fear-filled eyes. Chortling, Drisco hurriedly felt over the man's body to find the money. Pulling out the man's bursting money belt, Drisco's eyes widened with delight.

"What happened?" someone called out into the night. "Anybody hurt?"

Without looking around, Drisco took flight with Rufus into the dark alley. He heard more voices, as well as running steps, as Drisco made his way along the back of the buildings toward the livery.

"You should have used your knife, cousin," Rufus huffed.

"Shut your mouth!" Drisco spat as he smacked the man across the head. Instantly, he turned and tromped into the quiet, darkened livery behind the 'Mountain Man'.

A small form shifted in the hay.

Drisco could barely make it out, but, when he realized it was the livery man, he grabbed the man by the shirt collar and hauled him to his feet and slugged him in the stomach. A whoosh sounded from the man's lungs as he was struck. Moaning, he doubled over and dropped to his knees - wheezing.

Livid, Drisco reached down to yank the man to his feet again. "Rufus, you and this skunk get a horse saddled and make it quick." Drisco cringed at his stupidity of accidentally saying Rufus's name but before he could warn Rufus to be quiet, his cousin had the words out.

"Sure, Drisco, we'll get one saddled."

With the men in the street looking for him, Drisco didn't want to waste any more time. Now, since he'd messed up, he couldn't stay to kill Pike, but he could take Pike's grand Appaloosa. Shoving the little man back into the hay, Drisco stepped into the stallion's stall.

The horse, with ears pinned back, lunged at Drisco and knocked him down. Then the horse stepped on Drisco's leg, ripped open his pants, and tore into his skin. Hurting, Drisco crawled out of the stall on his hands and knees. Momentarily stunned, he stood and leaned outside the stall door to catch his breath and think, whining at the blood dripping from his stinging leg.

The commotion in the street grew louder.

Beginning to panic, Drisco shakily glanced into the next stall. There stood the golden gelding that was also one of Pike's horses. "You'll do," Drisco grumbled as he limped forward to clutch the spooked buckskin by the halter.

*

Pike slept fitfully, restless to start on the trail. So, as early as feasible, he dressed and slipped through the street to prepare the wagons and animals as it would take some time. Before he reached the barn, he sensed something was wrong because lights lit up the building like daylight, and boisterous voices could be heard inside and several men stood talking to Willie.

"What's happened?" Pike asked, uneasily glancing around with concern.

Willie turned with a stricken look on his face and a lone tear trickled down his cheek.

Swallowing back his apprehension, Pike asked again, "What's happened?"

One of the strangers replied. "There were two men who shot a man tonight in front of the saloon, and then they came over here and stole two horses. They've hightailed it out of town."

"Willie, did they take any of mine?" Pike shot a look toward his horses' stalls.

Willie lowered his eyes.

Pike flew to the stall with the door standing open. Hank was gone. A sharp agony wrenched his insides. "No!" Pike screamed and he turned back to Willie and the strangers, one who had a star on his chest. Consumed with rage and fear, Pike demanded, "What are you going to do about catching those men? Do you know who you're looking for?"

Raising his eyes, Willie offered, "I heard the one man, who looked Indian to me, call the other Rufus and the other one was called Drisco."

The names struck Pike with a stone-cold dread. *It couldn't be them, or could it? It had to be them. Now, they had Hank. I won't let them get away with that!* "Let's get a posse together," Pike commanded.

The man with the star nodded. "I've got several men coming and we're going after them."

"I'll get some of my men to join us," Pike replied as he stalked out into the dark, then, fear for his horse drove him to run. *God, please take care of Hank!*

Chapter 15

As Clash eased through the thick timber to descend into the deep ravine, Pike heard the horse grunt from the effort. He sensed the horse was about give out, but they *had* to keep going. Trailing after Drisco and Rufus for three days now, he, Frank, Buster, and the three men with Sheriff Braxton found themselves deep in the heart of the Ozarks.

Fuzzy from lack of rest, Pike's head nodded forward as sleep tried to overtake him. He snapped his head upright just in time to see the horse in front of him, carrying a sleeping rider, stumble and go down on his knees. The horse and man flayed violently, then slipped off of the steep incline to disappeared all together.

Rocked by shock, Pike halted, then jumped to the ground and hobbled forward as quickly as his stiffened limbs could carry him. He strained to hear sounds from the man or the horse.

Frank and Buster followed suit to gawk down the steep slope and fear radiated from their eyes.

Leaning over a boulder to see further down the slope, Pike felt relief wash over him when he spotted the horse thrashing in the brush below, but he couldn't see the man. "Let's get down there, Frank," Pike directed as he scurried to retrieve the rope from his saddle.

Carefully, the men eased downward, slithering and groping their way along the slippery, rough mountainside. The evening light was beginning to wane but shafts of sun still filtered through the treetops. Below them, the sorrel gelding screamed and flailed and his eyes brimmed white with fear.

Pike knew the horse was in a bad way by the pitiful screams. When he found his footing beside the injured beast, he discovered two broken front legs. With a heavy heart, Pike tore his attention from the suffering animal to continue scouting for its lost rider. *He's got to be here,* Pike insisted, trying to force his mind off the crippled horse.

Quietly, Frank told Pike, "I'll try to ease on down the mountain while you search in the brush around the horse. He can't be too far."

Bobbing his head, Pike placed his hand on the nearest rock and pulled himself forward and his steely eyes sharpened for any indication of the man, as he heard Frank slip on the rocks and fuss his way down the steep incline.

Soon, Frank called out in a panic-filled voice, "Pike, he's down here."

Returning through the brush to the thrashing animal, Pike spotted Frank near a large jutting boulder. From the expression on Frank's face, Pike knew the situation was dire, so Pike mouthed the words, "Is he alive?"

The single nod of Frank's head indicated an affirmative answer.

"Okay, I'm coming down." Pike resisted the urge to hurry, for he knew how dangerous the slick rocks could be. He focused his mind on carefully placing each hand and foot on firm holding. Finally, he halted beside Frank and announced, "Whew! That's steep."

The injured fellow moaned, beginning to stir as blood trickled from his head, mouth, and various cuts on his arms. His pants were torn and the lower right leg lay at an odd angle. It was easy to see the young man could not have been more than eighteen years old, at most.

Pike's stomach sank for the youth and Hank, as the loss of precious time in chasing Drisco was a tough pill to swallow. It all looked so very bleak. To this point, they'd trailed the thieves consistently for the past three days and they'd seen only hoof prints, nothing more.

The unscrupulous duo were obviously driving their mounts hard.

Instantly, fear prickled Pike as he realized Hank would be worn down, or more like near-dead. He hung his head and entreated, *God, please don't let that happen!*

The young fellow began to cry and thrash.

Forced to bring his mind back to his current situation, Pike had to get this injured man up the mountain for medical attention. *Damn my luck!*

Standing again on the edge of the cliff with the tortured horse, Pike aimed the rifle the sheriff had loaned him. He squeezed the trigger and watched the pain and suffering disappear from the horse's eyes. "Sorry, fellow," Pike whispered as he placed his hand briefly on the horse's forehead. He wasted no time in turning to begin the difficult climb back up the steep bank of the cliff, leaving the sorrel where he lay.

By this time, the day had given way to night, forcing the group to stay put and wait until daylight before heading to the nearest village, many miles behind them, for medical help. The long night and the long trip would mean the loss of precious time for the injured man, who was now unconscious, not appearing to have much time left.

Pike feared Hank didn't have much time left, either. He had to make a decision as he rested next to the warm fire with the other men around him. "Frank," Pike grumbled, "I'm not going back with you and the others. I've got to keep after these scum. I can't let them have Hank."

Grabbing him tightly by the arm, Frank made eye contact. "You need to listen to me. You're never going to be able to catch them. Not only are they faster than us, but they are better at making their way through this country. It's a damn shame they got Hank, but, we've got to let 'em go. I don't want you getting killed, and we've got to get this man back, or he may die. He might anyhow, but we've got to do what we can.

"Anyway, we need to get on the road to the Territory. We're going to need all the time we've got to get our new homes located and started. I know you know that, but keep it in mind. You've got to let Hank and Drisco go." Frank released Pike's arm and sighed. "We need you, big brother. Without you, we may not get where we need to go. You know that, right?"

Struggling within himself, Pike strained to block out Frank's words. He just couldn't accept Hank's loss, but he had heard the words, nonetheless, and even though his mind feared for Hank, some of Frank's words did hit home. He had other responsibilities and knowing that he had to let Hank go plowed up new pain that threatened to engulf him. His heart constricted as his mind cried out in anger, *No, I won't let him go. I won't! Do you hear me, Frank?* But, Rebecca's shining eyes glowed in his mind, and Patrick's giggling face was impossible to ignore. Pike realized there was no escaping the decision he was forced to make. So many others depended on him and he hung his head in acceptance. Mumbling the words from his cold lips, he said to Frank, "I'll go back with you."

Laying his large hand on Pike's shoulder, Buster looked him in the eye. "I's wants him, too, but we's got's to let him go."

Pike scrunched his face as tears stung the corners of his eyes. The frustration and grief of having to give up his treasured friend overwhelmed him. All he could do was wait and pray - again.

*

Several days later, in the early morning darkness of St. Louis, Pike set about the last chores in the barn. Today the group was heading out to find their new home. There was still much to accomplish before they got underway.

"Dang it, Dunk!" Pike fussed at the ornery mule as the mule's teeth barely missed his cheek. Grasping Dunk's bridle below the blinkers, Pike shook the mule's head and commanded, "Settle down, whoa!"

Not in the least daunted, Dunk snapped his teeth and laid his long ears against his skull.

This mule's been beaten, Pike reasoned. *That's all I can figure as to why he's so mean.* He struggled to keep from retaliating against the vicious animal while Willie strained to latch up the trace chains. "Whoa, you jug-headed mule!" Candy yelped her puppy barks and darted through the swarming legs. The mule jerked his head up to watch Pike in a wary manner, sizing up his enemy and Pike just glared back.

"That's one fine animal you got there," Amos chuckled. Ignoring the teasing, Pike continued the hitching chore. By the time the sun peeped over the eastern horizon, he was ready to announce to his eager group that it was time to leave. And he felt a tiny thrill at the prospect of getting started.

"Okay, let's get the last of our things loaded and get going," Pike said as he scooped up Candy and headed toward the prancing stallion. He stopped briefly at Amos's wagon and asked Patrick, "Would you keep Candy today?"

A big smile bloomed on the youthful face. "Sure, Uncle Pike."

*

The cheerful jangling of the mule's harness rang through the crisp morning air. Pike sat astride Clash with ambivalent feelings. On the one hand, he was thrilled to be underway. But on the other hand, he still felt the sting over the loss of Hank and the loss of his love. The deep hurt bled like a fresh wound at the thought of the loss of his friend. Also, on this moment-ous morning, not only did Pike have to accept leaving Hank out in the wilds with Drisco, but he felt it was time to walk away from the demons that still plagued him from the war as well as release his love for Rebecca.

As he clomped along, he turned his attention to the last four years and their lingering effect on him. The pain of the war had left its mark, molding him into the man that now sat on the trotting stallion. Gone was the silly clown-of-a-boy he used to be. All the pain he had suffered helped to mold him into a man that knew how to appreciate each day, and to treasure those he loved and through that pain, God had become a stronger force in his thoughts and in his actions. He could always lean on Him.

With each step through the cool, damp morning, as Pike listened to the jingling chains, a new calm settled over him and he felt only this moment for what it was - glorious. Everything he had learned and experienced came together at this moment, assisting him in acquiring a well-deserved second wind and with it a lessening of his deep hurts. A strong surge of energy flooded his being, making it easier for him to breathe. As he defiantly shook off the hurt from his past and turned to face his future with all of its promises, he blocked out all negative thoughts and pain and instead, gave unending thanks to the one who deserved it. *Thank You, Father. To You, I give the glory of the day and gratitude for my life. Please watch over Hank, because I can't.* To those traveling with him, Pike shouted, "Keep 'em moving. We're on our way."

Clash suddenly bowed his back, bolted sideways with stiff legs, and strained to get his head down. Totally focused, Pike hung on to keep the feisty stallion's head high, knowing he would be launched through the air if the horse got his way. "Dang it!" Pike huffed as he gained control of the horse. Centering himself in his saddle once more, Pike angrily shoved his hat back into place.

Frank, trotting nearby on Raven, laughed hilariously. "You're going to get left on the trail somewhere with that one. I'll lay a bet on it."

With the horse under control, Pike couldn't help joining in the teasing. "You may be right. I'll have to be wary when I ride him, sure will." Secretly, Pike found himself pleased by the horse's escapades. He loved a challenge and it would be fun to match wits with this horse.

That evening, after the tents had been pitched for the night and the ladies and the animals were settled in, Pike rested near the fire's welcome warmth with the other men. He idly watched Candy as she twitched in her sleep. All his muscles ached, especially his bad leg. He looked over at the man next to him and casually asked, "How're you doing, Eric?"

Eric's deep masculine voice filtered through the

darkness. "Just fine and dandy. I enjoyed the day. I've seen enough trees and hills for one day, though. Hope we get to see something else soon."

Adding his two cents worth, Frank said, "I know what you mean. Trees are plenty thick around here." He gazed over toward the women. "Come on. I see supper's about ready. I'm starved."

After dinner, Pike noticed Buster standing close to Lyric.

"Good night, Miz Lyric," Buster said as the young woman tripped her way to the tent.

Lyric paused briefly, flashing her pretty teeth. "Goodnight to you. I'll see you in the morning." She disappeared into the tent.

"Looks to me like someone is in love," Pike teased. "Or should I say, struck dumb by love?"

Buster stared at the tent for a few moments, then ambled away from the fire. He stretched his long form out on a few blankets.

Leaning over, Pike whispered to Frank, "Think it's going to work out for those two?"

"I hope so."

Looking around the campfire, Pike addressed the others. "You boys ready to turn in?"

Eric and Amos lifted their eyes from their discussion on their common interest of metal-working. Eric smiled, stretched, and replied, "I could use some sleep."

*

The afternoon had warmed considerably for a day so early in spring. Pike gave thanks to his Father for the dry roads and the toughened mules and horses, which helped the group to make better time than at the beginning of the journey.

As Pike jaunted along ahead of the procession, he heard a thunderous crack. Bringing his horse to a stop, he turned to see Rena's lead wagon lurch to the right as she rolled across a hump in the road. A wheel on the back came off, bringing the wagon to a halt with a thump. The sudden movement frightened the bay mules and yanked them sideways and one of them reared.

Rena shouted, "Easy! Whoa!"

Pike and Frank spurred their horses into a flurry, covering the ground between them and the wagon. Pike leapt down to grasp a mule by the bridle.

Frank gazed at the wheel and shook his head.

"Okay," Pike commanded the rest of the traveling party. "Let's unhitch here for the night. We'll let Amos and Eric work on the wheel. Nothing else we can do. Move the wagons to that grassy area."

The clan parked the wagons and unleashed the animals to graze on the new shoots of grass. Once the necessary chores were performed, Pike grabbed a small chopping axe to collect a load of wood for the cooking fire as he secretly wanted some time alone to think.

Managing to slip off unnoticed by Patrick or Candy, he vanished into the trees. Drawing in a cleansing breath of the forest-scented air, he strolled through the budding trees in appreciation of the new plant buds covering the forest floor. The fresh life around him infused him with similar, life-giving energy, making him burst at the seams. He felt like running and jumping but his bad leg protested, so he contented himself with trotting along.

Pike happened on a small creek, swollen from the spring runoff and winding through the trees. At its edge, he peered into its clear, inviting water, then knelt down to scoop up a mouthful when he heard a scream.

"Please, someone help me! Help me!" A feminine voice cried from Pike's left, behind the next stand of trees.

Dashing to the lady's aid, Pike burst past a budding sumac bush to see Rebecca frozen in place with her hand over her mouth. A wooden basket swung from her arm as her eyes locked on the ground in front of her.

Following her line of sight, Pike spotted a tightly-coiled diamondback rattler, at least six feet long, coiled threateningly. *I've got to save her,* he thought as he flew toward the snake. Yanking the hatchet from his belt, he aimed for the viper's head.

As the snake moved, the hatchet missed its mark and struck the neck, slicing through the thick body. The serpent had enough time, though, to plunge its two front fangs into Pike's boot. At the sight, Pike sucked in an audible lung-full of air.

Gasping in small breaths next to him, Rebecca held her hand on her heart.

The snake's head remained latched onto his boot. First, Pike wiggled his toes to determine if any damage had been done. Luckily, none of his toes had been pierced. He plucked the snake's head from his high leather boot to toss it aside. Turning to Rebecca, he softly inquired, "Are you okay?"

With wide, frightened eyes, she stammered, "I-I-I w-a-s s-o-o scared. Thank you, thank you so much." In the afternoon light he couldn't help but note how young and vulnerable she looked.

Not able to help himself, Pike became consumed with a familiar sharp longing for his love, or was it that he didn't want to stop those thoughts? Either way, his actions were dictated by his undying love for the trembling woman in front of him. His long legs brought him to her side in a second and his hands reached out and clasped her tiny waist just before he lifted her from the ground and brought her to his chest.

Apparently not startled by his actions, Rebecca threw her arms around his neck, clinging fiercely. Fire ignited between them as their lips sought each other and pressed tightly. Together they reveled in the not-forgotten heat of their passion and love.

Blocking out everything else, Pike took pleasure in her pliant lips and her soft body, conforming against his hard one with every nuance, hill, and valley exposed. Their kiss deepened until the never-ending well of passion exploded into a blazing inferno. All rational thought vanished from Pike's mind. The only thing existing now was the love he still shared with this woman.

Pike groaned inwardly as he was blasted by the full weight of his desire. Now, he realized just how hard it had been to deny his true feelings for this woman who responded to his desire head-on.

"Mommy! Where are you?" Patrick's little voice carried through the trees.

Shocked back into the moment by their son's voice, Pike allowed Rebecca's body to slide down his chest until she stood on her own feet. Quickly, he took a step backward, just in time to see Patrick bounce into view, dragging Lyric with him. Candy's wiggly body rushed to meet Pike with a whine and a jump. The fire still blazed in Pike's heart as he struggled to regain his composure while red colored Rebecca's cheeks.

Rebecca flashed Patrick a weak smile and as she cleared her throat a couple of times, then spoke shakily. "You found us."

Lyric immediately spotted the carcass of the mangled snake and gasped. "Oh, my. What happened?"

"I was lucky this day," Rebecca spoke up. "When I came to get water, I almost stepped on that big rattler. I froze when I saw it and called for help. Luckily, Pike heard me. He rushed over to kill that awful snake. I'm so grateful."

Once again, Pike noted the flushed face of his love and hoped her explanation was believable. His heart still thrummed from the passion and from the fear of their almost having been caught. What could have happened if they hadn't been interrupted?

*

The next day, drawing near Springfield, Pike plodded toward the top of a hill where the party would rest for the night. Tired and sore, his screaming muscles took over, averting his mind from recalling the pleasurable tryst with Rebecca. Getting to the top of the hill became his only focus, releasing him from his fantasy and his hurting body.

When the rest of the group mounted the knoll, they all stopped to begin the preparations for the night. As soon as the animals were unhitched, Pike snatched Patrick and hefted him onto the stallion's saddle to head for town. "Easy, boy," Pike soothed as he lifted himself onto the horse's back. To Patrick, he said, "Think you can hold on tight if I make the horse go fast? Would you like that?"

"I'm ready, Uncle Pike," Patrick said eagerly.

After nudging Clash, the stallion picked up the right lead, loping off at a smooth gait.

"This is great," Patrick yelled. "Let's go faster!"

Only too happy to oblige, Pike bumped the stallion one more time. The horse stretched his God-given form to quicken his stride. The ground below the riders flew by so fast that Patrick remained speechless. Quickly, the town rose on the horizon, forcing Pike to slow down. "Easy, boy." The horse instantly slowed to a trot, bouncing the riders along the streets of Springfield.

Gawking at the town, Pike noted people milling around on the streets. As he drank in the sights of the densely-packed buildings, most having been constructed of rough planks or logs, he thought, *Let's see. There's a bank. There's a café' and hotel. There it is, Hucklee's General Store.*

From the time Pike had been a small boy, general stores and all of their stacks of goodies had fascinated him. That thrill seemed to have followed him into adulthood. He reveled briefly in the rush of anticipation at the sight of the store.

After the pair had dismounted, Pike peered through the glass window in the front of the store. The vast assortment of displayed items instantly captured his attention. Bolts of colorful fabric, along with a couple of matching hats, were displayed in the window, A white feather stuck out of the brim of one hat. He passed over those items without much interest. A new shiny revolver, resting in its case, caught his eye.

Guns had never been a big part of Pike's life, not until the war. Those years had provided him with the skill to utilize these deadly tools. When he had returned home to his civilized life, he had not picked up a gun until he had chased Drisco. The dastardly deeds of his archenemy brought the realization to Pike that he had better get himself well-armed for life on the frontier.

Although the group had purchased several rifles and shotguns before leaving St. Louis, they did not have a revolver. Admiring the six-shooter, Pike thought to himself, *Hmmm . . .it might be good for me to pick up a pistol like that. It won't hurt to ask about it.* "Patrick, let's go in and do some shopping."

Inside the cramped, cluttered interior, Pike gazed about, trying to take in all the sundries the store had on display. Tools caught his eye, just as the guns had. He ambled over to the well-forged axe-heads, tongs, and anvils to feel their cool, smooth surfaces. *I wish I were as good with these as Amos and Eric are,* Pike mused.

"How are you two fellows doing this fine afternoon?" a spectacled man said as he stepped up next to Pike. "What can I help you with today?" Average-sized, the man wore a well-pressed shirt, tucked into dark woolen trousers and cinched with a wide leather belt. His slicked-back hair pronounced the tiny round spectacles perched high on the bridge of his hawkish nose. Standing straight, he possessed a professional air. Retrieving a stick of peppermint candy from his pocket, he bent his head toward Patrick and asked, "Would you like one of these?"

The small boy seemed unable to decide what to do first - pop the candy in his mouth or say thank you. Patrick froze, his brain working on a response.

The man chuckled and rumpled Patrick's thick mop. "My, what a fine youngster you've got there. He's going to be a big one like yourself."

"Say 'Thank you,' Patrick."

The boy mumbled, "Thank you."

"Well, you're quite welcome, young fellow," the man replied. His jolly, hazel eyes turned to Pike. "Where are you from?"

"We're from Baltimore. I'm with a good-sized group making our way to the Indian Territory. We aim to settle there. I want to start a logging business and do some farming. I need supplies for the trip. What can you tell me about the Territory?"

"First, let me introduce myself. I'm Ferris Hucklebee. I own the store. I've been here a good ten years. The Cherokee and Shawnee Indians come up here a couple of times a year from the Territory to do some trading. They've got the best woven blankets and baskets around. I get a good price for their products. If you can get your hands on their molasses, grab it up. It's the best in the country."

Nodding his head, Pike glanced around. Quietly, he said, "I saw the gun in the window. I'm thinking I might need one of those where I'm headed. Can I look at it?"

"Sure. Let me fetch it for you. You're right, that area has lots of outlaws running wild. You're going to need some protection." Ferris pattered along the cramped aisles to retrieve the gleaming revolver. As he carefully held it out to Pike, he said, "Here, hold it and see how you like it."

Eagerly, Pike took the hefty metal piece into his hands and the weight surprised him. With his long fingers wrapped around the cool metal, images from the war flashed into his thoughts. He pushed them away and inquired further, "What can you tell me about it?"

"That is one fine gun. It is made by the Colt Company. It's called a Colt .45 revolver. It shoots these big bullets here." Hucklebee fingered a couple of brass bullets from the display. "That should stop just about anything in its tracks. It can be shot six times without reloading. You just have to pull the hammer back between each bullet."

Pike tested the gun at arm's length. He liked the way it felt in his hands - heavy, imposing, and giving him a sense of power. He also liked the silver-dollar shine. "I'll take it, plus a couple of boxes of bullets."

Laying the revolver on the counter, Pike collected the other items the group needed. He picked out nails and several pieces of metal for horseshoes and he also purchased several axes and a long-bladed, cross-cut saw. Lastly, he restocked the group's dwindling food supply.

"We'll be back bright and early," Pike stated, "to load our purchases. Then, we'll be on our way. I'll take the gun with me now, if that's okay?"

"Here, take it." Ferris gladly handed over Pike's new revolver. "You'll need to oil it like a rifle, but it should give you years of good service. I'll see you first thing in the morning." The owner stuck out his smooth hand to Pike.

Pike clasped the hand and pumped vigorously. Picking up Patrick, who sucked happily on his candy, Pike stepped outside and hoisted Patrick into the saddle. Over his shoulder, he hailed the storekeeper, "See you in the morning."

Chapter 16

With each passing day, the wagons chipped away at the road before them. While journeying south and west from Springfield, Pike noticed that the landscape took on a different theme. The forests and hills blended into softer, rolling mounds, sprinkled thickly with various types of oaks and other species. Resplendent dogwood and redbuds burst with pink and white blossoms along the trail.

Another long, upward slope soon faced the clan. The mules gamely leaned into their collars to drag the wagons and Pike listened to Clash puffing in exertion as the horse strode toward the hill's crest. His eyes detected a hint of something glowing through the tree limbs. *Is that the river?* Pike thought and signaled to the other drivers to halt, giving the mules a break.

Frank trotted up next to him. "Look, I see the river. Are we finally here?"

Excitement stole into Pike's mind as he replied, "Looks that way, brother. Looks like we're here." He hollered to the group. "Come on, everyone. We're here! Let's find a spot to build our cabins." The babble of animated voices rose in Pike's ear with pleasure and he grinned.

"Gid up, mules," Rena shouted, leading the way on the last part of the journey.

Trotting ahead, Pike and Frank rested by the water's edge while waiting for the wagons to catch up. Pike turned to Frank and said, "What a great spot. Look at all the grass. It goes as far as I can see to the east. Look over at the river. It's thick with oak trees. They're good-sized ones, too. What do you think?"

Before he answered, Amos and Buster strolled up. Rena scrambled down from her wagon and scurried to the cluster of men where she wedged herself in. "What did you all decide?" she boomed. "Looks like a great spot to me. Are we stopping?"

"Yes, if everyone agrees," Pike responded. "This looks like just the place for our new homes. It has everything we're looking for. We can camp here tonight. Tomorrow we'll scout the area to see what's around." Feeling ecstatic, Pike took in the sight of the men and their enthusiastic smiles. "Let's get the mules and horses rubbed down and out to graze. Eric, how's Dunk doing? You think he's settled down enough to turn out with the others?"

Rubbing his dimpled chin, Eric replied, "He's a mean old cuss, but it's worth a try. He's not tried to kick me in a couple of days." Eric began to snicker. "He seems to be a might tired. Maybe we've worked the mean off him, for at least a day or two. It's worth a try."

Whistling "Old Dan Tucker," Pike hobbled Clash and rubbed down his sweaty back with a handful of dead winter grass. He slipped an appreciative hand along the horse's neck and swiped off a fistful of long winter hair then let it fly away on the late-afternoon breeze. The image of the stallion with a slick summer coat danced across his mind's eye as he scraped his way along the lengthy neck.

The horse lifted his nose momentarily for a pat, then went back to snatching all the new grass he could find.

A puppy's bark captured Pike's attention and he pivoted away from the contented moments with his horse. Hank's image nagged at his consciousness and wiped away the light-heartedness he had been enjoying. A frown creased his brow, but the furry puppy hopped up and down, begging for attention, diverting Pike from his pain. Twisting, squirming and whining, Candy coiled about his ankles.

Lifting her up, Pike gave her a few strokes and shuffled toward the others. Buster performed Pike's usual chore of helping Amos pound in tent stakes so Pike was at a loss for what to do.

Rebecca's dark, pony-tailed head poked around from the back of her wagon. Lugging out some blankets, she tugged at her load.

Springing forward, Pike lent his able hands.

Rebecca beamed him a winning smile.

Noting the enthusiastic grin, Pike's heart took flight. "Here, let me help you."

"Why, thank you. That would be just great. Let me grab some more things, since you've got the blankets." Rebecca disappeared into the depths of the wagon, then reappeared in a flash, carrying a coffeepot and Hannah's small crib.

Offering her a further hand, Pike guided Rebecca to the camp. The pair tripped along together, heading toward Lyric who busied herself with constructing the evening fire by using dried grass and a few sticks.

As they approached, Lyric called out, "Pike, I feel like singing. Would you play for us tonight? Let's celebrate. I'll whip us up something tasty for dessert."

"I can't think of anything I would like more, Miss Lyric. I'll make sure my guitar is warmed up and ready when we're through eating your special supper. I know my stomach is rumbling. I'm going to sneak off and see if I can get some birds or a couple of rabbits to cook. How does that sound?" Noting the happy nods of Lyric and Rebecca, Pike scampered off with Candy to collect his shotgun and ammunition.

As soon as Pike slipped into the woods, a melodious song struck his ears. The birds had burst forth with spring life and they twittered, cheeped and trilled out their glee in the rebirth of the forest. While Pike and Candy wormed their way through the newly-budding trees, Pike craned his head to study the splendor of the natural world.

Just a few feet in front of him, a cardinal's familiar song fell on his appreciative ears. Pike reached out with his hand to rest against a redbud tree as the tiny bird's tune captivated him and reverberated in his ears, a sense of well-being engulfing him. His voracious appetite for enjoying life's simple pleasures took control.

Candy rustled playfully through the dry leaves with

her nose sniffing the ground.

"Come on, Candy," Pike commanded his wandering pup. "Let's search for a scent trail."

Bounding forward, Candy's exuberance showed in her bounce and lolling tongue. She trotted out in front of Pike as he wandered across the edge of the tree line and traversed the vast field of grass ahead of them.

I can't believe that pup. Look at her go. Candy plastered her young snout to the ground with her tail stiff in the air as she utilized her instinct to sniff out birds.

Heart ballooning, Pike watched as Candy did what came naturally, albeit earlier than most. He placed his gun in the crook of his arm and readied it for the birds Candy could flush out. Within moments, Pike detected a distinctive fluttering of wings. He shifted his gun, aimed at the darting quail, and pulled the trigger.

Whoom! The bird dropped from the air.

Turning his attention to Candy, Pike hoped she wouldn't be cowering from the loud noise. "Oh, no!" he fussed out loud when he didn't see the puppy. *Guess, I'd better go and look for her. Must be hiding someplace.* As he strode forward, a movement captured his attention and he hesitated and turned.

Trotting along with her head held high, the liver-and-white pup gripped a fluffy bundle in her tiny mouth. Prancing along to display the pride in her treasure, Candy's dark-brown eyes gleamed.

Kneeling down, Pike encouraged the pup to come to him. He held out his hand and crooned, "Come here, Candy. Good girl! Come here." Candy's talents stunned Pike as he had never seen a puppy perform so well at such an early age. Pride swelled within him, forming a lump in his throat. Candy romped around his knees as she showed off her newfound skill. She was not quite ready to part with her prize as she twisted from side to side in obvious glee.

After much praise and playful teasing, Pike grasped the quail and said firmly, "Drop the bird." Tugging gently, he encouraged the dog to give it up. After she spit out a few errant feathers, she trotted off in search of more.

Placing the warm quail into a leather pouch, Pike wasted no time in catching up with the pup. His wait was short before he had to take aim on another quail. It took the pair little time to fill Pike's leather pouch and shirt.

Tired, Pike ambled back through the woods and returned to the camp. He beamed with joy from the afternoon's experiences, all of which seemed nothing more than pure gifts from heaven.

"Uncle Pike!" Patrick's merry voice rang out. "What are those?"

"Those are called 'quail'. You want to help me clean them?"

Patrick replied with an instant nod. Together, they drifted to the other side of the camp to clean the birds.

Drawing the birds from the inside of his shirt, Pike placed them on the ground. Retrieving his knife, he hefted a tiny gray and black body into his palm. "What we'll do is just breast them. Those breasts will be might tasty once they roast over a fire."

"Hey, whatcha got there?" Frank asked, as he and Eric joined the working pair.

"I shot a whole covey of quail. You want to help me breast them?"

"Sure, let me fetch my knife."

"Eric," Pike asked, "do you want to help me with this little chore?" Pike eyed the brawny fellow from the corner of his eye as he slipped the knife tip through the bird's feathers and exterior skin to prepare to slice out the breast. Once Pike freed the first one, he handed the bloody clump to Patrick. "Now you can pull off the feathers."

Patrick gawked at the feathery mass and with a sickly pale look on his little face, he said, "Here, take it. I don't want it!" He dropped the breast into Pike's hand and dashed away.

Pike rolled out a hearty chuckle as he said to Eric, "Think you can handle it?"

Nodding, Eric snorted a laugh.

*

Rebecca silently enjoyed the pleasure of the delicious meal. It pleased her to see the contented looks on the faces of the men.

"Wow, I never knew quail were so tasty," Frank exclaimed as he chomped into another crispy-roasted breast.

"I think you are right," Pike replied.

Rebecca caught Pike ogling the dried apple cobbler, as yet untouched, so she rose to serve it all around.

When the meal was over, Pike rubbed his stomach and announced, "Thank you, ladies, that was delicious." Rebecca helped Lyric finish up the dishes while she watched Hannah lying in the crib.

"Pike, we's sure could use some music this night", Buster said. "Sho could. I's like a song or two."

Rena's imposing bulk neared Pike as she said, "We could all use some music. I feel like dancing. How about you, Eric? Would you dance with me?"

Over the journey, Rebecca had noticed Rena's growing interest in the lumberjack, so she wasn't surprised by her sister's bold question. Rena had never been shy or quiet. She blurted out whatever ran through her thoughts and this was another example of it.

Looking like a deer trapped by a pack of circling wolves, Eric's head snapped up. He gawked about for a way to escape and after a long pause, he replied, "No, Rena. I don't dance. Maybe someone else would dance with you. Sorry, I have two blocks for feet." He gaped around at the other men, seeming to be asking for their help.

Hopping into the uncomfortable silence, Pike said, "Let me grab my guitar, I'll play. Lyric and Buster, you two need to get over here and prepare to sing till you can't sing anymore."

Lyric picked her way around the fire to rest beside the brawny black man. Her white teeth glowed in the firelight.

As Rebecca wiped the last of the dinner dishes, Rena skulked away from the fire to shuffle beside her. Hannah looked sleepy on a blanket nearby.

"Humph!" Rena grumbled in a whisper, as she crumpled onto the grassy ground.

Taking note of Rena's rosy cheeks, Rebecca had to repress a smile at her sister's predicament. When she caught hold of herself, Rebecca said, "I guess he can't dance. That's all. I'm sure it has nothing to do with you. Maybe one of the others will dance with you. Frank can dance. I've seen him. Let me finish these plates and we'll get over to the music. Maybe I can get Amos to dance, too. He's not much on it, but maybe we can get him into the evening's fun." After rinsing the last plate, Rebecca quickly swished it with a rag, then she carried a sleeping Hannah to the tent.

Pulling Rena along, Rebecca sat down next to the fire to join in the songs. As she slipped in next to her husband, she added her soprano voice, melding with the others to the tune of "Let's All Gather by the River."

*

While resting next to Amos with thighs touching, Rebecca wished to be sitting next to Pike. The desire harbored itself in the pit of her stomach and drew her cheating eyes to Pike's long, freckled face with its strong chin and high cheekbones. Completely captivated by her former lover, the familiar need arose within her and squelched all other thoughts.

She remembered well their one night of passion. Her virginal body had experienced ecstasy for the first time which now seemed so long ago. Pike had lovingly ignited a fire that she had not known existed, in her body and in her loins. She drew in a deep breath as she reveled now in the heat of her response.

Something about Pike, especially when he strummed that guitar so expertly, sent tingles through her body. He had captured her heart and there was no escape.

She enjoyed listening to her true love play and yearned for him. His broad shoulders, moving under his shirt, brought back the image of his naked back and chest. The fringe of red hair, matted across his chest, and hidden by just those five buttons, swirled into her mind and increased her desire causing her to shift uncomfortably next to Amos.

Her eyes wandered to Amos's serious expression as he belted out the song. Guilt quickly replaced the lust that had crept into Rebecca's mind and she sighed inwardly and sat in silence.

The next tune had an upbeat tempo. Rebecca leaned over to Amos and asked sweetly, "Would you like to dance? Rena wants to. If you'll dance with me, maybe Frank will dance with her. Her pride is stinging a bit from Eric's rebuff. You know, as well as I do, that she is sweet on him. Maybe this will take her mind off it. Would you mind terribly?"

Amos tilted his head back and pushed his hat to his crown. His serious expression grew deeper and his eyebrows furrowed as he lifted his striking blue eyes skyward.

Deciding to help him make a decision, Rebecca feathered a kiss across the top of his ear and then stood. As she rose she clasped Amos by his warm hand and tugged gently, urging him up.

The kiss seemed to work because Amos allowed himself to be hauled to his feet without protest. "Come on, Frank," Rebecca directed. "Let's dance. Come on, Rena. Would you dance with Frank?" She clasped her husband by the waist and shoulder to guide him into their first hesitant steps together.

Amos suddenly gave in, took over, and led Rebecca around, twirling her to the lively music.

Even though Frank hesitated a bit, Rena jumped up to face him and they began to swirl to the music, too.

Rebecca smiled, pleased to see Rena momentarily distracted from her rejection by Eric.

*

With the first fingers of light, Rebecca slipped from underneath her husband's protective arm. Their night of lovemaking slipped into her thoughts, and though they lacked the dizzying heights of passion she had shared with Pike, her moments with Amos were warm, if not tender. The love she experienced with her husband would never bring her the fulfillment she would have claimed with Pike, but she would have to content herself with what she had. In her heart, Rebecca knew she had no choice. This was the way it had to be, no matter what. She had her children to think about.

Tiptoeing out of her tent, Rebecca spotted Lyric who had slept outside and was now up and about, poking at the fire's embers. Lyric's curly hair hung loose and long. Rebecca sidled up to her newfound friend and cordially said, "Good morning. You want to stir up some biscuits? I'll fry some bacon and get the coffee on to boil. I could sure use a cup. Did you enjoy last night?"

A look of barely-repressed pleasure came over Lyric's features and she glowed with happiness. "Oh, Rebecca, I had so much fun. I really have come to love everyone. I feel you are all like my family. I hope to make my home with you - forever. I've grown fond of Buster. Pike's told me about what happened to him in the past and I feel so sorry for him. I can see what a good man he is. I think I love him. He even kissed me last night when everyone else was sleeping." She covered her mouth, but she couldn't stop the giggle that leaked out.

"I'm so happy for you. Do you think he'll ask you to marry him?"

"I hope so. I would love to settle down with him. I know how much he thinks of Mr. Pike. He would do just about anything for him. I'm sure he's going to want to stay close. I want to stay close to you, too."

Rebecca reached out and squeezed Lyric, then returned to the sizzling bacon in the skillet. As she breathed in the aroma of the frying pork, she said with a devilish grin, "That should get them up. I pray Buster will ask you to marry. We can raise our kids together."

"I would love that," Lyric answered with a hint of tears in her voice.

"Mama," a childish voice called out from the tent.

Shushing her noisy child, Rebecca hoped to keep him from waking the whole camp, but it was too late. Hannah began her morning wails to be quickly hushed by Amos.

Soon Rena and Pike sat near the fire and watched the women, both eyeing the biscuits hungrily. It didn't take long for the biscuits to disappear and for the men to ready themselves to head out to begin scouting the new land. Today they would decide where to put their new homes and then see about leasing them from the

Cherokees. It was a momentous day.

Patrick dashed up to Pike and pleaded, "Can I go with you, Uncle Pike?"

"I'm sorry. I can't take you with me today. I've got to ride hard. But, when I get back, I'll take you for a ride. How would that be?"

Patrick's face turned red and pitiful as a few tears slipped from his green eyes as he hung his head.

Rebecca stepped in and drew her son away.

Buster volunteered to stay behind with the ladies.

With teasing in his voice, Pike said, "So you want to stay near your sweetheart? When are you two getting married?" He guffawed at his own humor.

Buster announced, "I's thinking' on askin' her this day, yes, it be a good day for that." He just smiled when Pike's jaw dropped open.

After snapping his mouth shut, Pike stuck out his hand. "Well, that'll be just fine by me. Hope she says yes." Pike pumped the big man's hand a few times, slapped him on the shoulder, and called out to Frank. "You need to get moving. You're as slow as molasses this morning."

"Okay," Frank whined. "I'm ready."

Chapter 17

"Whoa, you mangy horse," growled Drisco as he cruelly jerked Pike's gelding to a halt. After he dismounted with Rufus and their two new friends, Drisco tied the horse to a branch. The second gelding, the bay that had started on the trip with the buckskin, had died within the first week. Even though Drisco took out his resentment toward Pike on Pike's horse, he couldn't argue that the horse had endurance. He smiled as he looked at the dirty, worn animal. Then, he headed toward the simple log structure with the other three men.

Glancing about the dim interior of the windowless room, Drisco's mind drank it in, registering its bleakness. Still, they were finally safe within Indian Territory.

"You boys got you a fine place here," Drisco praised the two newest members of his secret brotherhood. *Only the poor saps didn't know it yet,* Drisco thought, snickering to himself. Only he knew what was in store for them. They were going to steal what he wanted, rape who he captured, and help him find Pike and his group. No matter how long it took, he would keep up his search. He aimed to rip out Pike's entrails and leave him for the buzzards. Evil notions played through his mind about what he would do with the others in Pike's group. The women held his greatest interest. A chuckle started to rise, threatening to expose his dementedness, but he managed to squelch it, at least for the moment. He had more important issues at hand, and that was getting these unsuspecting thieves, who owned the cabin, under his control and that wouldn't be hard.

Locating a crude chair by the fireplace, Drisco

watched the little man, Titus, expertly strike a fire. Titus limped with a twisted right leg and an equally twisted spine. Silas, tall and skinny, hadn't much backbone. He could easily be pushed around. A grin crossed Drisco's face. *How lucky am I,* he thought as a chuckle slipped out, one he hardly noticed.

*

"Patrick, where are you?" Rebecca hollered with clear exasperation. Patrick had been playing along the river's edge as she and Rena washed the mountain of dirty clothes, then he disappeared. *Maybe he went back to the wagons to be with Buster and Lyric. Those two seemed mighty close when we left. Where is that boy?* wondered Rebecca as she stomped through the heavily-dewed grass, holding her skirt in her hand.

As she cleared the tree line, she spotted Lyric waving and smiling at her. Rebecca waved back and decided to go ahead and tromp all the way into camp to check on Hannah, who had been left in Lyric's charge. As she drew closer, Patrick's bubbling, childish voice seemed to be speaking to Lyric and Buster who stood next to him, staring at Patrick's hands.

"What are you all looking at?" Rebecca inquired as she joined the small group.

The boy gleamed with pride as a smile broke out on his face. In his tiny hands dangled a wet bullfrog. Its thin back legs hung limply. Patrick sparkled. "Isn't he pretty?"

"Why, yes," Lyric praised, "he sure is. And so big, too. Why don't you go and play with him over by your sister. Show her, she might like him."

"Okay," the boy replied eagerly as he dashed off. Candy followed. Hannah squealed and began to crawl toward the pup to clasp one of her floppy ears. Patrick held out the frog for his sister. Unimpressed, she continued to tug on Candy's ear.

The adults snickered openly at the sweet scene. Rebecca turned to the couple as she noted their handholding and smug expressions. "So what are you two looking so proud about? You both look like the cat who ate the canary."

Lyric blushed. "Why, Buster just asked me to marry him. I said yes, of course."

Almost shouting, Rebecca replied, "I'm so happy for you! What great news. I can't wait to tell Rena." She threw her arms around Lyric's shoulders and squeezed her for all she was worth. Rebecca clasped Buster around the waist and hugged him, too. "When do you want to get married? Since Amos is a preacher, he can perform your ceremony. That is, if you want him to."

"We's be right proud for Amos to marry us," Buster said. "Sho would."

Lyric nodded her head, and seemingly overcome by her emotions, tears trickled down her cheeks and dripped unheeded onto her dress.

"It's settled, then," Rebecca said. "Let's tell Rena. Can't wait to spread the happy news. If you'll keep your eye on the kids, I'll go and find her."

Lyric bobbed her head.

Rebecca, heart near-bursting, trotted back toward the river.

*

A few hours later, the men trickled back into camp. Pike felt new energy flow through him at the prospect of finally starting to break ground for their new homes. He had a lot on his mind, trying to map out all the details.

As everyone settled down with a bowl of stew, Rena started peppering the men with questions. "Okay, tell us what you found. I've got to know. Is the town very far off? Are there others settled around here? Did you find enough land for us? Come on, tell us."

Pike stepped in. "I think you're going to be pleased to hear that we've found all the land we're going to need. Amos and Eric scouted the area to the north for several miles and found one neighbor. We all saw plenty of grasslands and thick timber. I went to the south with Frank. We found a great parcel of land that runs along the river and starts about a half-mile from here. We'll have plenty of water. Later on, we can dig some wells, but for now, the river will be enough.

"There are several creeks crossing the land. They can provide water, also. We even found a couple of ponds. We'll have enough land for everyone to make a sizable claim. Then, we can start building the cabins. We'll begin with one for Amos and his family. Then, we can make one nearby for Rena and Lyric."

"Excuse me, Pike," Rebecca interjected. "I have a bit of news I would like to share with you and everyone else." She glanced at Lyric's blushing face. "Lyric and Buster are engaged. They want Amos to marry them as soon as it can be arranged."

"Congratulations!" Pike crowed as he bee-lined it to the smiling couple. Sticking out his hand, he beamed his pleasure for his huge friend. As Buster grasped Pike's hand, they shared a knowing look.

Turning to Lyric, Pike gave her a bear-hug, sweeping her off her feet. "I'm so happy for you," Pike whispered into her ear. "Buster's had it rough. I never thought he would get over losing his first wife, but you've brought him back to life. Take care of him, he's a great man."

Ignoring the buzzing crowd, Pike stated loudly, "Well, after we get Amos's cabin built, we'll get one started for you two and the little ones you'll have. Thank You, Lord, for our many blessings!"

As everyone quieted down, Pike went back to discussing the group's plans. "Since Rena is going to want to be near Rebecca and Amos, I thought they could utilize the largest cleared section of land we saw today. It's only about half a mile south of here. We can put her up in a cabin close to them, or not real close. That's up to her." He looked at Rena and received a silent nod, then continued. "Eric has picked out his piece, about fifty acres, next to their land. It has more woods on it, but Eric doesn't seem to mind the prospect of doing some clearing. We can put Buster and Lyric next to Eric. There's another good fifty acres of grass and trees along the river.

"I thought we should stay close to the Neosho so there won't be any lack of water. Frank is going to put his cabin next to mine, and we're going to share the next hundred acres or so. Amos's piece has a natural spring on it.

"Amos and Rebecca, if you'll follow me when we're finished eating, we can pick out the place for your cabin. Eric and the rest of the men can put their axes to good use this afternoon. Does that sound okay to everyone?"

Amos spoke up first. "Rebecca and I are ready, but shouldn't we get the other tents put up now, since we're going to need more permanent shelter while we build the cabins? Which do you want to do first?"

Rubbing his stubbly chin, Pike pondered for a moment. "Well, that is a good point. Buster and Frank, would you put the other tents up? Then, you can come and help cut down a few trees. We may have to take it slow for a while. Most of us are not used to chopping and cutting all day. I'm sure we'll be mighty sore for a time."

Rebecca looked at Lyric. "Do you mind keeping the baby?"

"No, I'd be happy to. She can help me start cooking a pot of beans and making some cornbread."

"Thank you," Rebecca replied as she turned to loop her arm through her husband's.

"Don't forget to bring several axes," Pike sang out to Eric as he gathered up his tools. "We'll bring a mule team tomorrow to drag the trees."

*

The brisk spring wind did not let up, moaning louder and louder as the day warmed. Pike felt beads of sweat break across his back, but even so, he enjoyed the rays of the sun.

Perching on the side of a hill with Rebecca and Amos, he evaluated the virgin land that swept below. The river glowed through breaks in the trees. Before them lay a wide, grassy field that spread across about forty acres, bounded by an oak forest on both sides.

"What do you think about this?" Pike inquired of the couple as they gazed upon their new home-site. "Over to the south," he said, indicating with his finger, "is a spring that's just inside the timberline. You may want to build your house close to it. Rena can build her cabin close to yours, or she can go down into the field and build hers closer to the river. She can decide that. And the first chance we get, we'll go and lease the land we pick out, and it will be ours." Pike craned his head to gauge Amos's reaction, feeling proud at the prospect of having his land. "Well, brother, tell me what you think."

Surprisingly, Amos replied cheerfully. "It looks to me like you've chosen well. Why don't we build our cabin over about fifty yards from the tree line. There's a dogwood tree sitting off by itself. Can we build the cabin by it?"

"Sure. We'll start on it today. Hope we can get one up for you quickly. We're going to need to put in a garden pretty soon. We'll put someone on the duty of plowing up a spot. We aren't going to have time to put one in for each group. Isn't Rena good with plants?"

"Yes, she is," Rebecca interjected. "I know quite a bit about gardening, myself. I can hoe with the best of them. Buster'll be good with a plow. Should we ask him to start? Do you think there will be seeds over in the community you found on the other side of the river?"

"I'm going to find out in the next couple of days. I hope Clash can swim."

Amos asked quietly, "Do you want someone to go with you?"

Shaking his head, Pike replied, "I think it will be easier for just one of us to go. We've got a lot of work ahead of us. I'll be able to hurry. We have bean and corn seed, but I'd like to find some others if I can. It's the right time to get the garden in. It'll have to be a priority."

Eric marched up the hill to join in the conversation. "Are we ready?" he inquired.

"Yes," Pike replied over his shoulder as a desire to tease itched at his brain. "Amos picked out his cabin spot. We're ready to chop down some trees. I think I'll watch you from under that big maple tree over there. Maybe take a nap. Call me when it's time for supper." Pike nonchalantly sauntered off without looking back. He chuckled to himself and waited for a response and he was not disappointed.

"Whoa!" Eric shouted. "No one is getting out of the fun this afternoon. Grab your axe. I'll show you how it's done."

Pike turned and laughed out loud.

Rebecca giggled.

As usual, Amos didn't respond and no glimmer of a smile crossed his solemn face.

For his first victim, Pike selected a massive post oak. He swung his axe back, then drew it forward with as much force as he possessed. The axe head bit deep and the sound rolled over him, sending a pleasant shiver along his spine. He loved that sound as wood gave way to a tool. Nothing smelled better or sounded sweeter than wood being bent to his will.

Images of his future sawmill chased through his mind. He had pictured that sawmill on more and more occasions as the group had neared the end of their journey. Now, it plagued him, nonstop, as bad as those pesky weevils and lice had in prison. He was becoming eaten up with wood and the promises it held for his future in this untamed land, becoming his one dream.

After several minutes of uneven chopping, Pike's arms screamed for a break. Sweat trickled into his eyes, stinging them. He swiped them with the hanky he kept in his pocket.

Suddenly, he heard the groaning and snapping of a tree as it gave up its bid to stay upright. The massive expanse shook the ground as the tree crashed to its death. Pike turned his head to see who got the first tree down. It was Eric, of course.

Eric beamed at him, and then at Amos, as the delight of beating them shone on his face.

Amos and Pike rested the tips of their axes on the ground and glowered back.

"Come on, you two," Eric jabbed. "I'm going to have two trees down before you even get half of your spindly trees cut." He let out a brawny laugh, swung his axe back, then let it bite into his second tree.

This goaded Pike into action. He clamped down his jaw, swung back his axe clumsily, and whacked at his tree again.

Amos heaved a sigh, then resumed his hesitant strokes at his own tree, only one-quarter cut so far.

"Timber!" Eric gleefully announced as Pike and

Amos once again paused to gape at the falling tree.

Being behind stirred Pike's anger, so he turned back and savagely whacked at his tree to whittle the trunk to a breaking point. Within the next minute, he proudly stepped back as the tree cracked. "Timber!" he shouted as another one-hundred-year-old tree crashed to the earth. "Okay, little brother, you ever getting that tree down?" Pike hoped for a light-hearted response.

Silence followed as Amos took another break.

"Come on, you weakling," Pike teased further. "You're as soft as a girl."

Across the clearing, Amos rested a hand on the nearest tree. His azure-blue eyes zeroed in on Pike. Anger hardened them to steel as fire flew at his brother.

Startled by the anger, Pike chastised himself. *I should have never opened my big mouth!*

Then, suddenly, the anger melted from Amos's eyes. In its place, a grin formed. The smile didn't quite make his eyes, but it was a smile, nonetheless.

Relieved, Pike said, "I was just kidding."

"I know," Amos quipped. Stiffly, with his back straight, he turned back to work.

Soon, Frank and Buster joined the tree-chopping party. Relieved to have fresh workers, Pike decided it was time to begin stripping the branches from some of the downed trees. "Whew," he huffed as the newcomers got within earshot. "Glad to see you boys made it. You can get started chopping down a few more trees while Amos and I clean the branches off the ones we've got done. Watch Eric, he knows what he's doing."

Buster clutched an axe and scrambled away.

Standing behind Pike, Frank asked in a quiet voice, "What's wrong with Amos? He looks grim as death."

Shaking his head as he yanked off another branch, Pike replied, "I don't know, wish he'd get over it though. Guess he's still mad at me, or jealous over Rebecca or something. Not sure what it is."

Nodding, Frank picked up Pike's axe and strode off to find a tree.

"How do you all feel?" Pike asked the subdued group as they wandered back to camp that evening. "I feel like I've been kicked by Dunk." He received a few grunts from the men.

Eric strode purposefully, with a spring in his step. The others dragged themselves along.

Mind racing ahead to the next day's tasks, Pike said, "We'll need to bring the rip-saw tomorrow. That way, we can start shaping the logs." He stiffly reached out and slapped Buster on the shoulder. "You're pretty handy with that axe. Aren't you sore?"

Turning to look at Pike, he replied, "No, sir. I's not sore. I's a might tired, that's all."

"Lucky you," Pike grumbled, as he rubbed his aching arms and noted the blisters littering his hands and fingers.

Arriving at camp, Pike washed and collected his plate of food. Famished, he sat by the fire to eat.

Buster lingered near Lyric. She seemed more important to him than food. He hadn't yet picked up his plate.

Sopping up his plate with a scrap of cornbread, Pike started speaking. "Tomorrow, I need to head over to the town to see about getting some seeds. Buster, would you take one of the mule teams and, after Rena picks out a spot for the garden, would you plow up an acre? Well, make it two.

"The rest of you men can get back to work on those trees. When I get back from town, I'll help, too. Let's see how much we can get done tomorrow. I hope to be able to start on the cabin for Buster and Lyric in a week or so. When we get their cabin completed, I thought we could celebrate and get them hitched. They can start off in their new home. We don't have many luxuries here, but we'll do what we can. Is everyone agreeable?"

A few grunts and nodding heads passed around the group.

"Once we get the cabins almost done, I'm going to head back to St. Louis so I can order the sawmill parts. Now, that we've gotten here, I can see there will be plenty of trees available to start a sawmill. I need to make that trip so I can get the parts here before winter sets in."

*

As soon as enough light peeped through the darkness the next day, Pike climbed out of his bedroll. Now, he was sleeping inside a tent, which was much more comfortable than the open outdoors. There had been a soft rain tapping lightly on the canvas during the night which helped him find sleep.

As soon as Pike slipped on his pants and jacket, he eased out to find coffee. Every muscle screamed in protest as he stumbled forth on his rigid legs. Unconsciously, he rubbed his bad leg a time or two, hobbling stiffly toward the inviting fire.

"Rebecca," Pike whispered, "what are you doing up so early?" He couldn't help but note how becoming she looked this early in the morning as she stood near her tent.

She brimmed with life, like the bursting fields around them. Her hair, pulled back into a ponytail, set off her delicate, well-chiseled features. The perky yellow dress added a hint of sunshine to Pike's achy morning.

As always, Rebecca's face picked him up. Pike wished for the millionth time that she was still his. He just couldn't let go of his love for her.

"Well, I am ready to get up and start a new day so we can get everyone fed and off to work on our cabin. I'm so excited, I couldn't sleep. I just love our new home site. It is so pretty here. It's so different from where we grew up, isn't it?" She beamed as she spoke.

Not thinking clearly, Pike reached out and grasped her tiny hand. "I'm so glad you like it here."

When their eyes met, she caught her breath.

The pent-up passion took but a few seconds to become unleashed in Pike's loins. Tugging her to him, he wrapped his arms around her, bent his head, and planted her with a warm kiss. Sharing the familiar sensation was sweet and tender, but when his lips begged for deeper, more passionate kissing, his consciousness returned.

"I'm sorry," he stuttered as he stumbled back. "I shouldn't have done that. What was I thinking? I guess I wasn't, was I?" Averting his guilty eyes from her flushed face, he added, "Please, forgive me."

"Oh, Pike," Rebecca began in a rush, "I don't know

what came over me. I'm sorry, too. I wish things between us had happened differently, but they didn't. We can't go back now. We've got to be more careful." She turned back to the coffee that boiled nearby and poured Pike a cup.

Bolting down the coffee and slice of bread Rebecca served him, Pike hurrying to escape the quiet discomfort that had settled between them. Pike collected his gear and sprinted off to find his stallion.

Giving Clash's cinch one final tug, the flash of lust from kissing Rebecca returned to plague him. Pike struggled to turn his thoughts to something else, but the heat of passion still rushed through his veins. *What am I going to do? I need to get away from her. Hope we can get their cabin built soon. I could use a break from seeing her with Amos.*

Speaking to Clash, Pike said, "Are you ready?" With a practiced motion, he swung up into the saddle and readied himself for the bouncy ride to come. He managed to keep a tight rein on the mount and he wasn't disappointed when the stallion made a strong attempt to bow his back and buck. Forcing the horse's head up, Pike won another round.

As the horse responded to Pike's leg cues and galloped through the morning, Pike's fire-like desire diminished. To further take his mind off his personal wants and hurts, he studied the sky and noted the overcast grayness. A cool breeze whipped at his hat but he was glad, as always, to be riding this fine horse.

Chapter 18

Dark, glassy water rolled past Pike as he sat atop Clash, dejectedly gazing at the river. The horse bent his head to sip at the cool water while Pike struggled with what he now faced. The Neosho River, at least one hundred feet across, swirled past at an alarming rate. A shudder snaked up Pike's spine as he imagined how the icy water would feel. Guess, I can't avoid this chilly experience. It's the only way across.

Pike steeled his determination to follow through with the crossing. "There's no way around it, Clash," Pike announced in a gruff manner into the morning wind. "So, wait here a minute and then we'll get to it." Dismounting, Pike gave Clash one tug on the reins to tell him to stand still. Removing his clothes in the chilly breeze, he stuffed them into his coat and rolled them up. He tied them to the top of the saddle, hoping to keep them dry.

"Come on," Pike directed the horse. Wearing only his Stetson, he slid one bare foot into the river's edge. The bite of the freezing water made him hesitate. Sucking in his breath from the shock of another step, Pike fought the urge to turn around and go back to camp. Following like a lamb, Clash stepped right into the water and gave Pike a nudge with his nose.

"I'm going," Pike fussed over his shoulder as he made the commitment to slip into the murky water. He began to swim, churning alongside Clash through the biting liquid. Long before he made the other shore,

Pike's legs began to feel as though they were no longer attached. *Lord, help me make it!*

When his toe bumped the muddy bottom on the opposite bank, Pike felt ecstatic with relief. He stood on the bottom and trudged through the mud to reach the inviting shore.

"Lord, help me, it's cold!" he blurted as he clumsily redressed. His trembling limbs moved numbly, as though they were still under water. Only a hot cup of coffee would warm him up now and that's all he could think about. Rebecca had long since been forgotten.

A short time later, Pike approached the village which consisted of a smattering of small businesses and houses. He spotted the general store, a log-cabin building that displayed the name *The Pettit's Sundries.*

Pike halted the horse at the crude hitching rail in front of the structure. After tying the reins to the rail, he strode to the door, clasped the handle, and yanked it open. The door shut behind him with a loud bang as his eyes swept the dark interior. Then, he remembered the early hour. "Oh, no," he coughed, feeling guilty. *It can't be more than seven o'clock. I forgot how early it is. Should I leave?* He called out hesitantly, "Hello."

"How are you this fine morning?" said a smiling man, as he stepped through the open door at the rear of the room. Just shy of six feet, with a rotund belly, the man came forward and lifted a hand cordially to Pike.

Pike said, "I'm Pike, Pike Wheeling. Just moved in across the river. Hope you can help me. I need supplies." He guessed the man to be thirty-something. His black hair, dark skin and round, smooth face fascinated Pike.

The man's thick jowls moved loosely as he talked. "Hi, there, I'm Stoney Pettit. I'm the store owner. Sir, if you don't mind my saying, you look pert-near froze. Come on back to our stove and warm up. My wife, Dora, has coffee on. Looks like you could use a cup; come on." Stoney held the back door open for Pike to enter.

In the adjacent room, a startled young woman with long, black hair stopped scrubbing dishes to glance at her husband. Her eyes and face asked what was happening.

"Dear, this is Mister Pike . . . Wheeling, didn't you

say?"

"Yes. It's Pike Wheeling, ma'am. It's a pleasure to meet you." He nodded his head in an affable way as he gritted his teeth to still the shivering of his body.

"Well, Mr. Pike, I'm Dora Pettit. You've met my husband, Stoney. We're pleased to meet you, but please, come and sit by the stove, warm up here. I'll pour you a cup of coffee. It's still hot." She grabbed a tin cup, filled it full with the fragrant brew and pushed the cup into Pike's shaky hands.

Pike gulped it quickly as he drew a chair from the plank table. He quickly moved it as close to the stove as he could stand without singeing himself. The warmth was so welcome, Pike wanted to sigh out loud. He quickly downed the first cup of coffee and asked his hostess for another.

Ready and waiting, she poured.

"Thank you for the fire and the coffee."

Smiling, Dora asked, "Mr. Wheeling, where did you come from?"

"From across the river. We're settling there. I came this morning, hoping to get some supplies."

Stoney broke in. "You came to the right place. We try to keep stocked as best we can. This is Indian land, and me and my wife are both part-Cherokee. Our parents were forced off their land in Tennessee and were herded here many years ago. I grew up in this area. After I married Dora, we opened the store. There's not much else around here. It's beginning to grow, hopefully more now that the war is over.

"Since this area is growing, there's more need for supplies than ever. I have a hard time keeping my stock in. Most supplies come out of Joplin. That's a pretty good ride from here."

Pike carefully noted everything Stoney told him. "Do you think this area could use a sawmill? I've been thinking about starting one."

"Why, yes! This whole territory is in great need of lumber. As quick as it's growing, we could sure use ready building supplies. The Cherokee and Shawnee are farming and working livestock. They need lots of fence posts."

"Great! Looks like I'm going to get started on that before too much longer but my main concern for today is getting our garden in."

"How many are there of you?" Dora asked.

"There's five men, three women, and two youngens."

"Oh, that's wonderful," Dora exclaimed as her eyes lit up her whole face. "I could sure use some other women for company around here."

"That river out there poses a bit of a problem," Pike grumbled. "I don't think we can cross that very often. You have to swim it, and it's real cold to do that now. Maybe when it warms up, or when we can float a wagon across, it will be easier."

"You're right," Dora replied with a sigh. "The Neosho is difficult to get across. We're going to have to work on that. It makes it so hard for people to get over here."

"Are you warm enough now," Stoney asked, "to get started with your shopping?"

Nodding his head, Pike thanked Dora for the hospitality and followed Stoney into the other room. He ogled the well-stacked goodies that swarmed throughout the thirty-foot square room. He also let his eyes drift along the log walls, noticing how well they were constructed and chinked. Then, Pike thought about the garden. "What do you have in seeds? We need to get right on our planting."

"Luckily, we got a stock of seeds last month. Come over here." Stoney moved to a corner of the room where a small shelf contained various small packets. "Go ahead and pick out what you'll be needing. I've got some onion and potato starts outside. I've even got a few fruit trees."

"Thanks, Stoney, I'll start with these seeds. I can't take much with me on this trip."

With a knowing nod of his dark head, Stoney wandered off to commence his daily work.

Pike plucked up the seed packets and began thumbing through them. *Let's see. Oh, there's some green beans, black-eyed peas, lima beans, carrots, radishes, cucumbers, okra. Here's some squash and sweet potatoes. I'll need several of these larger wheat packs. That's probably all I can carry.* "Stoney, where'd you say the rest of the starts are?"

"Come this way. I'll show you." Tramping out the front door, Stoney headed around the side to the back of the building.

Pike noted several small trees with their roots wrapped in burlap. Knowing it would be difficult to get them back across the river, he still couldn't resist. "What are those trees?"

"This is a peach tree, and here's an apple. This one's a plum."

"I'll take one of the peach and one of the apple. I can lash one of each onto the saddle horn. I need potato starts and a bunch of onions, too. That should do it. That's probably more than I can carry."

Stoney chuckled as he scooped up the requested items and put them in a gunnysack.

After settling the bill, Pike promised to come back as soon as possible then rushed out of the store. Pressure to get back to work urged him to hurry. Lashing the tiny trees to the saddle horn, he led Clash out of town and headed for the dreaded river.

Just as cold after the second swim, he redressed and cursed out loud, "Crim-in-ently." Anxious to get back to camp, he retrieved the seeds from under his hat then nudged the stallion into a brisk trot. *Hope they've got some coffee on.*

*

Lyric pressed a coffee mug into Pike's hands as he slipped stiffly from the soggy saddle. Candy came running. Rebecca, Lyric, and Patrick clustered around Pike to help him with his packages.

"Why, Pike," Rebecca sang out as she looked at the saplings, "what do you have on your saddle?"

"I thought we could use a couple of fruit trees. There's a peach and an apple. Do you think you could plant them?"

Pleasure bloomed on her youthful face. "Oh, how wonderful, Pike. I can't wait to make some peach preserves." She clapped her hands, then began to pick at the knots holding the trees to the saddle.

After eating his last mouthful of beans, Pike joined the tree-felling team while Buster continued the plowing. Pleasantly surprised at the men's progress, Pike studied the first logs that had been arranged for the cabin's exterior. He praised Eric, "Looks to me like you've gotten quite a bit done. How do you like using Dunk and Don? Are they good at log-pulling?"

Grinning, Eric replied, "I've been impressed with those two. I can get them to travel in a straight line with little effort. They put those logs just where I want them. What a Godsend they are. Dunk is still a mean old cuss, but I've grown fond of him. He's a working machine, and Don keeps right up with him."

"Glad to hear it. Sometimes, I've doubted my decision on buying those two, but now I'm glad I did. Can't wait to watch them work."

"Well, let's get right to it," Eric stated. "We've got several trees down. I just need to whack off a few more limbs. Then, we need to get them pulled over to the cabin. Amos is squaring them off. Grab up a hatchet and help me." Eric latched on to a small chopping-axe and strode in the direction of the forest.

Hacking away at the spindly branches of a downed hickory tree with Eric, Pike warmed up quickly in the cold breeze. Pike was developing a better rhythm and now got more out of each cut of the blade.

When they had most of the limbs lopped off, Eric said, "I'm going to go and fetch the mules. Then, you can see how well they work, wait, I see one more branch I need to get on my side. Let me roll it over." The burly fellow, with one hand, shoved the tree over and balanced the trunk on his knee. He hefted the axe back to let it fly.

Pike briefly turned his attention across the way to Amos, who was molding a log.

Eric let out a painful grunt.

Head whipping back, Pike spotted the hatchet tip buried deeply into Eric's upper thigh, just above the knee. Pike's mouth dropped open at the grisly sight.

Eric stared at it, too, frozen by the shock.

"Put the tree down, Eric!" Pike shouted as if Eric were far away. Gawking at the blade, Pike's mind swirled, unsure of what to do. He let his instincts rule, which kept him from yanking out the nasty blade. More quietly, he said, "Eric, let's get you on the ground. Don't touch the hatchet. We're going to get you back to camp. So don't move!" Pike guided the stunned man to the ground and raced to find Frank. He caught Amos's attention. "Amos! Get over here quick! Frank, where are you?" Pike's panicky voice carried through the forest. "Come here, now!"

Amos dropped the molding and dashed toward Eric. While Frank came running through the trees, Amos knelt beside Eric and gaped at the hatchet sticking out of his leg. Blood coursed from the wound, soaking Eric's dark pants. Eric's rosy coloring faded to a sickening shade of gray.

When Frank arrived, Pike barked out some orders. "Frank, you come with me. We need to grab the mules and head to camp. I think it'll be best to bring Eric back in a wagon. Amos, take off your shirt and wrap it around the leg. Use your belt as a tourniquet, make it tight. Come on, Frank, you grab Don." As the events began to sink in, Pike's worry reached a fever-pitch.

Dunk moved forward in Pike's hand without turning his rump and kicking. *Thank You, Lord,* Pike tossed to the blue sky above. "Thank you, Dunk! We've got to hurry. Eric's in bad shape." Pike kept up his stream of conversation with the mule as he untied him and turned for the camp. Dunk willingly obliged the request to trot.

As Pike galloped with Frank into view of the camp, he saw Rebecca rise from her cooking and turn in their direction and her hand flew over her heart. She and Rena suddenly bolted toward them, meeting them at the edge of camp.

"What's wrong?" Rena shouted.

"Eric's been hurt," Pike replied without slowing down. "We've got to bring him back in a wagon."

The ladies, holding onto each other, moved out of the way so the men could pass. As the mules were being hitched to the wagon, Rena hopped into the back, then gripped the sideboards with both hands.

Jumping into the driver's seat, Pike commanded "Gid up." As the wagon lurched, rumbling over the rough ground, the mule team pushed forward with their work-hardened shoulders and their ears flat against their necks.

Even though Pike worried that the wagon might break a wheel on the rocks, he couldn't slow down. Every second counted, and God-given luck was on his side. Within minutes, he reached Eric's side. Leaping from the wagon, Pike flopped to the ground on his knees by Eric's bloody form.

Rena got off the wagon and stood to the side.

Barely opening his glassy eyes, Eric's breathing came fast and deep.

"We're going to need to carry him to the wagon," Pike instructed Frank and Amos. "We can't waste any more time. He's lost a lot of blood." As he quickly clasped Eric behind the shoulders, the injured man slipped into unconsciousness. "Okay, he's out. Let's hurry."

With audible grunts, the men hefted the heavy burden and strained their way to the wagon. As the injured man was laid gently in the back, Rena hopped in to roost next to him.

As Eric was removed from the wagon, Pike was aware of Rena hovering near like a hummingbird around a coneflower.

"What's going on?" Patrick yelled. "Can I see?"

Yelping, Candy hopped around in the background.

Barking instructions, Pike huffed, "Rebecca, do you have a bottle of whiskey close by? We're going to need it. Hurry! Here, let's set him over near the fire on a blanket. I need rags!"

Without direction, Rena knelt beside Eric clutching her sewing kit. *God, give me strength!* She fervently prayed as she looked at Pike, her face a river of torment.

Nodding, Pike hoped to give her some support.

Then, she clasped Pike's hand. "You've got to pull the hatchet out of his leg. Once you get it out, I'm going to wipe the wound and see if I can sew it up. It's the only thing we can do." Glancing around at the others, she directed, "Everyone else just pray!"

Gathering himself, Pike grasped the handle of the hatchet, his fingers hesitant. Then, he said a quick prayer to ask God to send him the strength he would need. Focusing his mind on the task, he closed his eyes and knew the only thing left to do was yank out the metal. Now familiar with removing hatchets from trees, he opened his eyes and steadied his hands. Allowing his body to follow the practiced motion, he tugged back on the handle and yanked up with all his might and the metal slid from the bone.

Eric moaned as the blade came free.

Tossing the hatchet aside, Pike's worry continued as Eric's blood flowed. Quietly he asked Rebecca, "Do you have the whiskey? We need to clean the wound.

Pale from shock at the ghastly sight, Rebecca shoved the glass bottle at her sister to hastily retreat from the scene. Popping the cork, Rena liberally doused the bleeding gash. Wiping the wound with a rag, she asked briskly, "Who can help me hold back the skin?"

"I'll do it," Amos replied. He edged close to Eric and slowly stretched back the bloody skin.

Evaluating the open wound, Rena chose a medium-sized needle. Shaking visibly, she poked the thread through the eye, then poured whiskey liberally over her hands, wiping them on a clean cloth. "Okay," she said nervously, "I'm going to sew him up. Amos and Pike, can you steady Eric while Amos holds back the skin? Frank, I need you to wipe the blood away so I can see."

Nodding, Frank grabbed up a clean rag, then gave a swipe to clear away the blood.

While Pike sent up avid prayers as he held Eric still, he admired Rena's courage under these drastic conditions.

Rena eased the tip of the needle into the red tissue and tugged the thread through, pulling it tight. Alternating with Frank's swipes, she finally completed her task. She rocked back on her heels and sighed audibly.

"Good work, sis," Rebecca praised. "You were great. You've saved his life. I know I couldn't have done that." She patted Rena's shoulder before walking back to her kids, who were waiting with Lyric.

"Why can't I see?" Patrick whined. He broke from Lyric's hand and rushed to Rena's side. "What happened, Aunt Rena? Lyric wouldn't let me watch."

"Eric got hurt and I had to fix him up. That's all."

She smiled to comfort the boy. "Come and give me a hug."

Thankful for the help from Rena and his brothers, Pike knew the worst wasn't yet over for Eric. "We need to move him to the tent," he said. "Come on, let's get him settled."

*

A cool cloth pressed against Eric's fevered brow as Rebecca watched Rena minister to him. "I think he's going to be okay," Rebecca stated matter-of-factly, hoping to ease the worry she saw in her sister's eyes. "I know what he's come to mean to you."

Rena nodded her head but her eyes never strayed from Eric's face. She took the damp rag and wiped Eric's arms.

Suddenly, Eric's eyes fluttered open. He stared straight into Rena's eyes while confusion crossed his face. "What happened to me?"

Softly, Rena spoke, "You cut yourself with a hatchet. Do you remember?"

Eric glanced around. "I . . . I think so."

Rebecca noted the man's white face and stiff jaw. Suspecting he hurt a great deal, she held out a bottle of laudanum to Rena.

Rena clasped the bottle and instructed Eric as though he were a child. "Here, take a couple of swigs of this. It will ease your pain."

Taking it eagerly, Eric swallowed several mouthfuls. Handing it back to her, he flipped off the blanket to look at his leg. "Who did that? I don't remember a thing!"

"Well, it's a good thing you don't," Rena stated bluntly. "It wouldn't have been pleasant at all. I sewed it up. You should be as good as new in a few weeks. We'll keep it dry and change the bandages every day. That should take care of it." Humming, Rena went back to rubbing his arms and legs with the cooling rag.

Smiling to herself, Rebecca noted a new light of acceptance in Eric's face, or could it be interest? She sure hoped so. As she slipped out of the tent to leave them alone, she heard Eric's voice whisper to Rena, "Thank you for what you done. I could've died."

*

Because of Eric's injury, the progress on the cabins slowed considerably. But, Pike kept the men working steadily. They managed to erect the exterior walls within a few days. Amos busied himself making the wood shakes to put on the roof. The glass for the windows would have to be ordered, and the sooner the better.

In camp, Pike noticed that Rena seemed more subdued these days. He wondered if it might not have something to do with Eric. Pike decided to find out Eric's take on it. Slipping into the tent, he updated Eric on the cabin's progress. "You should see Buster. He can chop down a tree almost as fast as you can. He keeps us busy. The walls should be completed today." Spotting the far-off look in Eric's eyes, Pike proceeded with his plan to goad the injured man a bit to test his theory. "Hey, looks to me like you're somewhere else. Are you thinking about the north woods, or are you mooning over a girl?"

Eric blustered and stuttered. "I'm sorry, Pike. What did you say? Something about Buster?"

Tossing back his head, Pike hooted, "Boy, you look to me like you're in love. Could it be Rena that's got you daydreaming?"

Eric started to bluster again, then stopped. "Well, I am grateful to her, but that's as far as it goes!"

"Uh huh, just what I figured; it's love." Pike hopped up before Eric could protest further and went out the way he had come with a grin on his face.

*

Several days later, Pike gazed at the first cabin with pride. The chinking had dried and Amos's family, along with Rena, had moved in. The camp had been set closer to the cabin for the convenience of the women in preparing food for the men. The next log home, for Buster and Lyric, had begun.

Strengthened daily by the persistent work, Pike no

longer ached from the effort of felling trees and moving logs. Filled with energy, he felt like dancing and singing in the evenings now.

While resting his guitar between songs one night, Pike said to the group, "I'm going back to the store tomorrow and see about getting the things we need for the cabins, or at least getting them on order. Amos, you want to go with me so you can pick out what you need?"

Amos eagerly nodded his head.

"Okay, we'll start out first thing in the morning. Hey, Buster and Lyric, are you ready to get hitched? We sure could use a good excuse for a big spread and some music." Pike turned with the others, staring at the sheepish-looking couple.

"He'd better be," Lyric replied, "because he's getting married just as soon as our cabin is ready."

A grinning Buster didn't reply.

With an innocent look, Pike turned his attention on Eric. "So, Eric, are you ready to get hitched when Buster and Lyric do? How about you, Rena? Should we get two cabins ready?"

Wearing a confused expression and working his jaw a few times, Eric stammered, "W-e-l-l . . . " He peered at the sky.

Rena turned a deep shade of crimson and surprisingly, she had been rendered mute, for once in her life.

"I'll take that as a no," Pike snickered. He strummed the strings once more. The familiar chords from "Rock of Ages" drifted from the strings and laughter twittered among the others as they began to sing.

Chapter 19

"Looks like these leather boots aren't going to last much longer," Pike grumped as he tugged one well-worn boot onto his foot the following morning. He noticed Candy listening to him intently, her puppy face alight with a toothy grin. She rubbed herself against his ankles as he wished the gnawing desire for sleep would vanish. *Oh well, it's time to get started.* "Come on, girl." Candy stayed glued to his heels as he exited the tent.

"Mornin', Pike," Lyric uttered quietly as she stoked the embers from last night's fire.

Bobbing his head in response, Pike filled a waiting tin cup. "Where's Amos?"

"He's out rounding up a set of mules."

As Pike sipped at his first cup of the day, enjoying it, he thought, *Sure hope we can get that wagon across. River's pretty high. Hope those mules can swim.*

Leading his favorite pair of chestnut mules, Amos came ambling through the half-light of the new day. Tying the mules to the hitching rope, he placed the heavy collars on their rounded shoulders. The mules seemed steady and quiet, willingly sticking their heads through the leather collars. After the collars were in place, the harness came next. With the harness buckled and the trace chains tied off, Amos plodded over to Pike and sat down. After a hearty plate of beans and bread, the brothers rose to hitch the team.

"See you girls later," Pike sang out as they left

Now that it was time to face the dreaded river, Pike

wondered, *Is Amos going to freeze when we cross? How're the mules going to behave?* Uneasiness fluttered up his spine as he focused his thoughts on the happy jingles from the harness as they pulled away from camp. At least he was driving, which helped him feel a bit more in control.

Reaching the river's edge, the mules dropped their noses to sniff and drink the water. Pike allowed them time to look, then he nudged them with the reins to plow on in. The mules stiffened but they didn't move. They just stood and stared at the water.

Pike slapped them harder with the reins then clucked, hoping to get some forward movement. One of the mules, raising his head, cocked his red ear back at Pike. He pierced Pike with a glare of aggravation.

"Is there a problem?" Amos's calm voice gigged.

"No!" Pike replied, a little bit too quickly.

"Could've fooled me," Amos said as he nonchalantly gazed downriver.

Bet he's laughing at me, Pike fussed as he jolted the long lines with several more vigorous slaps. The mules took a few short, hesitant steps, but the water came only to the tops of their hooves. Their eyes rolled back in their high-held heads and even though Pike didn't like using the whip, he felt he didn't have a choice.

Crack!

The mules shot forward as the whip found its mark on the rump of one of them. The frightened animal burst forward, dragging his partner with him. The swirling water closed over their backs as they swam.

Pike and Amos gripped the sides of the wagon. It suddenly tilted sideways as the current churned around it.

Luckily, there were no mishaps. The sturdy animals breasted the current and hauled their burden to the other side.

Guiding the wagon through the town's only street, Pike thought, *It sure looks different. Maybe it's because there's more people moving around, or it may be that I'm not so frozen this time.*

The sad-looking saloon, with a hole-riddled roof and missing side boards, heralded its name, 'Black Jack

Oak', on a dilapidated sign that hung loose from a broken chain. One log structure contained a sign with the words: 'Miami Sheriff's Office'. The heavy bars on the window indicated to Pike that this was the town jail. *Hmmm*, Pike thought to himself, *I wonder who the Sheriff is around here?*

Reaching the front of the Pettit's store, Pike halted the mules. The familiar flush of anticipation at seeing all the stacks of goodies in the general store coursed through Pike as he and Amos stepped from the wagon.

"Come on, Brother." Glancing through the uncovered windows, Pike noticed the cheery morning sun streaming through the panes. He could see all the wares clearly. Then, he threw open the door and led the way into the store.

Amos silently followed.

In the back of the store, Pike noticed several people clustered around the big pot-bellied stove. All their heads craned to see the newcomers. Pike made out Dora and Stoney in the dim interior.

"How are you this fine morning?" Stoney said, with a friendly face. Stoney motioned to Pike to join their huddle as Dora sashayed out to meet them. She asked with beaming eyes, "Did you bring the ladies?"

"No, not this time, since it's the first time we've crossed with the wagon and all."

Dora's face fell in disappointment.

Pike quickly added, "But, I know they'd love to come over here and meet you. It'll have to wait a while, though."

Nodding her head with reluctant acceptance, Dora led the men to the group of expectant faces.

A young boy, not more than twelve, wandered aimlessly about the interior of the store as he touched objects and made unusual noises.

Once in Baltimore, Pike had seen a boy who had acted in a similar way. Pike tensed, knowing there was something wrong with the boy. He didn't know how to handle such situations. So, he turned his eyes back to the group of adults and smiled at the strangers.

Stoney made the introductions. "Everyone, this is the new fellow I spoke of. His name is Pike Wheeling."

To introduce his brother, Pike offered, "And this is my brother, Amos."

Standing, Stoney shook Amos's hand. "Here, let me introduce everyone. This lady here is Maude Cullen and this is her mother, Ivy."

The two brown-skinned women definitely looked related, with the same cheekbones and strong chins. Both had round, plain faces and black hair woven into long braids. Each was a little over five feet tall, plump, and small-breasted. Their friendly manner demonstrated their seeming ease with strangers.

Ivy spoke first. "Maude lives with me and my husband. We don't live far from town. It's about a mile and a half west of here, just down the road. We're the local midwives. My daughter handles most of the birthing now. I'm getting slow and down in my back. I help her out, now and then."

Maude indicated the young boy, still wandering around the room. "That's my boy, Benny."

Stoney's gruff voice broke the silence. "This tall fellow here is the sheriff for these parts. His name is Lincoln Edwards. He lives close to town. We all grew up in this area and have known one another for years."

Nodding, Amos said, "Good to know you."

Pike rested his eyes on the young sheriff. The man's alert brown eyes radiated calm and control. The long whiskers of his dark beard jiggled as he spoke, adding to his charm.

"I live about a half-mile south of Miami," Sheriff Edwards stated. "You can't miss our place. I've got a big, old mimosa tree in my front yard. It's got to be two feet thick in the trunk. Biggest one I've ever seen. I have a two-room cabin. My wife Belle and I have three boys and one girl. They keep my wife busy. In the fall and winter, she comes to town and we let her help the local kids with their schooling. It's the only formal schooling we've got around here. Sometimes there's upwards of twenty kids in her class."

Feeling comfortable in the man's presence, Pike decided he liked the sheriff. A question popped into his mind. "Do you have a church here?"

The sheriff responded, "We had a Baptist preacher

who lived here and had a church built by his home a couple of blocks from here. He and his wife took sick and died a couple winters back. We haven't had another preacher since."

"Amos here," Pike quickly offered, "is a seminary-schooled minister. He's Presbyterian. Hope no one minds that, but he would probably be happy to help out with a church. Isn't that right, little brother?" Pike devilishly grinned at Amos.

Before Amos had time to speak, Pike continued. "That river out there poses a problem, though. I think I'll see about making a raft for crossing it. How does that sound?"

"That would be great," Dora said with enthusiasm. "We sure need something like that. Maybe we can find someone to work it taking the raft back and forth. Make some money for the town."

"So, Amos," Stoney said with interest, "you're a minister?"

Amos replied somewhat rigidly. "Yes, I have studied several years. I'm going to farm my land, but would be happy to help with a church. My father is a minister back in our hometown of Baltimore. I've missed going to church since we've started this journey."

Bobbing his head, Stoney said, "That would be great if you would, but I should ask what you fellows need today?"

Whipping out his list, Pike started counting off his items. "We need more nails and seed corn. We need to put in another acre of corn to feed the animals this winter. I need another hoe and more ammunition for the rifles. We need some salt pork, beans, coffee, sugar, and lard. We need beds and bar-stock. I want to order four stoves and some windows for the cabins. That should do it. Is that everything, Amos?"

Amos had sidled away to look at the items in the store. "Rebecca asked for some thread and cloth so she can get Rena started on a wedding dress for Lyric. I'll pick some out."

"Do you know what size windows you need?" Dora asked Pike. "I can get your beds ordered, but I need to know the size of the windows."

"Yes, I need windows to be thirty inches square. I need eight of them. We'll probably make the doors. We may order some nicer ones later on."

Maude piped up. "We've got chickens that we raise. We've got lots of chicks right now. Come on by the house and we'll send you home with some. I'll give you eggs, too."

"Oh, we'd sure like that," Pike responded, "especially the ladies."

Maude collected Benny and strolled with Ivy toward the front door. "We'll get on home and catch you some, and put them in a sack"

"Well, I'd better get back to work," Sheriff Edwards said as he shuffled to leave. "Got to check on Pumpkin. He got wallpapered last night and he's sleeping it off. Guess ya'll heard him shootin' his pistol last night. Got liquored up and decided to hunt himself up a turkey." Lincoln shook his head sadly and looked at Pike. "He lost his wife and twins in childbirth a year ago. We all feel sorry for him, but we can't seem to help him."

When everyone had left, Pike asked the question that was plaguing him. "What's wrong with Maude's boy, Benny?"

Dora nodded her head as if she had expected such a question. "Well, I can't really say for sure. No one understands his odd behavior. Ever since he was tiny, he just never developed the ability to speak. He likes to stay mostly to himself. Maude makes him follow along with her when she works. She keeps up the hope that someday he'll get better. She hasn't given up on him yet but he's not getting better as far as I can tell." Dora sighed with concern. "I feel so sorry for Maude. It's been hard on her."

Now that Pike understood, he felt sorry for the young woman, too. *How would I feel if I had a son like that?* He felt an icy stab of fear before he tossed the thought aside to continue his shopping. "Don't forget to give me a sack full of candy. Make it peppermint. I like those almost as much as Patrick does. Right, Amos?"

Without answering, Amos wandered back from his own shopping. He had selected a couple of bolts of blue and yellow gingham cloth.

The brothers spent a few minutes getting familiar with the stock that Stoney had carried in for them. Then they walked outside to take a look at the farming equipment.

"We need to get one of these sickle mowers to cut the corn," Pike said to his quiet brother.

Amos ran an appreciative hand over the surface of the mower's seat. "We sure do. We could put up a lot more if we got one."

"We'll plan on getting one before harvest time." The fruit trees caught Pike's attention. *Got to get a plum tree this time,* he told himself. After selecting a sapling, he turned to Stoney. "Add this tree to our bill."

A little later, sweat began to roll down Pike's back as he and Amos loaded the last of the goodies in the wagon. To Pike's amazement, Amos hopped up into the driver's seat and grabbed the mule's reins. "Stoney," Pike asked, as he slipped beside Amos, "how do we get to Maude's house?"

"Just follow the road out of town about a mile. It's the first place on the right. It has two small cabins on the property and a good-sized barn. Maude's dad farms and should have in his crops by now. They have a wood rail around the front yard. You can't miss it."

"Thanks, Stoney," Pike said, waving to the man. "We'll see you when our order comes in."

Accustomed to Amos's silence, Pike tilted his hat over his eyes and took advantage of the time to rest as they headed toward Maude's. Pike's hearing honed in on the jangle of the trace chains and enjoyed the lift of his spirits. Momentarily, he thought of his parents and wondered how they were doing. *I'm going to have to write to them soon,* he chided himself, *and let them know we are okay.* All too quickly, the wagon bounced its way over the road.

Amos pulled the team to a stop and Pike tipped his worn hat back to gaze at the homestead. The baying of coonhounds rolled across the yard as a pair of blue ticks romped in the wagon's direction. "Look at that, Amos. Guess they're all bluff." Pike guffawed. "Those tails are a-waggin' to beat the band." Quickly, he hopped from his perch and mixed with the sniffing hounds. From the corner of his eye, he spied Benny.

The thin, dark-headed boy rested in the shade of an elm and watched Pike in return.

Pike lifted his hand in a small wave and smiled in the boy's direction.

"Hi, there," came Maude's strong voice from behind Pike.

Pike pivoted to observe her as she strode across the grass, toting two sacks in her hands.

"There you are, Maude," Pike called. "I hoped you would come and save me from these vicious hounds of yours. I was afraid they might eat me."

Her merry eyes returned his lightheartedness. "They're a couple of mean hombres. You can see why we keep them. They're great protection. Won't let anyone near the house. They'll eat your legs clean off, they will." She giggled and handed Pike a wiggling burlap sack. "Here you go. I've got a dozen chicks in each sack. Take these and I'll go and get you those eggs. We're run over with them this time of year."

"Thank you," Pike replied as he gently grasped the sacks and put them in the wagon.

Returning with another sack held close to her small breasts, Maude had one hand protectively on the bottom. She grinned. "This should get a cake or two baked."

"What do I owe you?"

"Please, take the chicks as a welcoming gift to you and your family. I can keep you in eggs, and they're five cents a dozen. I hope you can get home without breaking any."

"We appreciate the gift. We'd like to have you and your family out to dinner." Pike stepped up onto his seat. "Would that be okay?"

Maude hesitated. "Why, yes, that would be wonderful. Can't say we ever get an offer like that."

"We'd be pleased to have you over. Would you give this to Benny?" Pike withdrew a peppermint stick and handed it to her.

"He'll love this," she said with a soft voice. "Thank you."

*

Facing the rushing river, Amos eased the mules into the edge of the water and allowed them to rest before beginning the swim.

"You want me to drive them across?" Pike asked in a teasing way.

Amos tensed and set his jaw. "No," he gruffed, staring across the Neosho. "I am capable enough."

"Okay. You let me know if I can help in any way." *Wish he'd tell me what was bothering him. I hate having to guess.*

Amos brought the long lines down sharply onto the resting mule's rumps. After the first slap, the mules eased themselves into the cold water. Luckily, they did not resist this go round.

Pleased with the team's response, Pike watched as they began to churn toward the opposite shore. Suddenly, Pike spotted something coming down the river. He sharpened his eyes. *Oh, no!* "Amos, you'd better look out. There's a tree in the river and it's going to hit us. I know you don't like to swim, so you'd better get those mules turned around."

Swiveling his head, Amos gaped in disbelief at the huge tree with a profusion of roots bearing down on them. He froze, unable to move a muscle to prevent the catastrophe.

Here we go, Pike thought.

The tree struck the side of the wagon with a thud, blasting a jolt through the wagon and knocking it sideways. Both men flew from the seat.

Breaking the water's surface, Pike anxiously glanced around for Amos. He was relieved to see him clinging to the side of the wagon's wheel as the mules got their bearings and kept the wagon afloat. "Meet you on the other side," Pike called as he began the numbing chore of swimming the rest of the way across the river.

Waiting on Amos, the stiff breeze chilling him to the bone in his wet clothes, Pike yipped from the shore, "Thanks a lot. Sure needed a bath."

The wagon finally rolled up on the bank behind the mules. Pike checked the supplies and made sure everything was intact. He climbed into his seat and trembled from the cold. "Hurry up, Brother, let's get a move on."

Chapter 20

Less than two weeks later, now early May, Pike watched his family buzzing with excitement in preparation for the wedding.

"Glad you could make it," Pike bellowed to Stoney, Dora, Maude, and Benny as they strode into the merry crowd. "Hope you got across the river okay."

"Sure did," Stoney replied. "We borrowed a canoe from a friend. I just had to make two trips."

"Good," Pike chuckled. "We're getting ready to get started with the wedding. After it's over, we're going to eat. Hope you're hungry."

"I'm so hungry," Maude responded in her attractive navy dress, "my stomach is growling like a mountain lion."

Dora sounded almost giddy as she said, "We brought some baked beans and presents for the happy couple. We're just dying to meet everyone." She looked beguiling in her pink frock. Like Maude, she had her dark hair pulled back into a tight bun under her sunbonnet.

Pike found the two women pleasing to look at, as outgoing as they were. "Might I say that you ladies look lovely?" They smiled as he led them to the crowd and introduced them to his clan. Pike observed Rebecca and Rena buzz around Dora and Maude as surely as a bumblebee buzzed around grandma's zinnias.

Stoney joined the men, who were discussing farm implements.

Shortly, Amos stepped in front of the group to begin the ceremony. "If everyone is ready," he called over the babble, "we can get started. Lyric, Buster, Pike, and Re-becca, would you please come forward so we can begin?"

As best man, Pike took a firm hold of Buster and guided him to stand in front of Amos. Buster wore his brown suit, the one he had bought in Baltimore. Buster stood proudly, towering over everyone.

Rebecca and Lyric trailed quietly behind. Lyric held a lovely smile on her face, her dark eyes shining in the dazzling noontime sun. She wore the pretty yellow ging-ham dress that Rena had spent hours making for this special occasion. It fit her busty figure well and in her dainty hands, she gripped a bouquet of fresh crimson roses from a wild bush that bloomed nearby. Black-eyed Susans added a coordinated yellow to the cluster of flowers.

With his Bible open, Amos stood solemnly in a mi-nisterial pose and allowed time for everyone to take their spots.

As the ceremony ended, Pike yelled out, "Congratu-lations!" He slapped Buster on the back with his broad hand. Pike then turned to Lyric and asked, "May I kiss the bride?"

Lyric glowed as she bent forward to accept his bro-therly smack on her cheek.

"My turn," Frank said as he sidled into the mix to follow his brother's peck with one of his own.

"Let's eat," Rebecca said, smiling brightly. She stood next to the blankets that had been spread artfully with tasty treats, cooked just for the occasion.

Taking it all in, Pike saw so much delicious-looking food he didn't know where to begin. His eyes drank in the ham, rice, beans, and boiled eggs. Loaves of bread and several cakes topped off the feast. Remembering his manners, Pike said politely, "Please, Maude, you first."

She clasped Benny's hand and led him to the front of the line.

Patrick lingered near Benny with a confused expres-sion on his face.

Pike bent over and directed into Patrick's ear, "Pa-trick, Benny has a problem. It's like a sickness. You need to be nice to him. He can't help the way he is. Lat-er, you can show him Candy. He likes dogs."

Still appearing confused, Patrick stared at Benny. "Okay, I'll try to get him to play with me. Can I get something to eat now?"

Guiding the boy, who was now so close to his heart, Pike assisted Patrick in filling his plate. "Don't forget to eat everything on your plate before you get dessert."

"Okay."

As the day wore on, Pike picked up his guitar and called out to the blissful couple. "Get that pretty wife of yours, Buster, and have the first dance." His fingers strummed the first chords of a waltz.

All eyes trailed the happy couple as they swung around and around, gazing into each other's eyes. The evening passed joyously with many dances and songs and more eating. Eventually, the sun began to set.

"Guess we'd better hightail it home now," Maude remarked. "It's going to get dark soon and we need to get across the river." As the two ladies turned and walked away, Maude waved over her shoulder and shouted, "Bye, now!"

Lyric smiled and cooed, "Thank you."

While the others dove into another piece of cake and sipped coffee, Pike asked, "The cabin about ready?"

Rebecca grinned and clapped her hands together. "Oh, it's so nice. I hope, Lyric and Buster, that you'll be happy there. We've been working on it for weeks."

Pike stood up. "Well, then, are you ready to see your new home?"

Also rising, Lyric took Buster's hand as Buster said, "You know we are. We's can't wait."

"Okay," Rebecca chirped. "Give me a minute to get everything ready." She hurried to the honeymoon cabin. After several minutes, she opened the door and waved for everyone to join her.

Holding Lyric's hand, Buster led the way. The rest of the clan trailed behind. Gathering up Lyric, as custom dictated, Buster carried his bride over the threshold. She broke out in a fit of nervous giggles and after they passed into the cabin, the rest of the eager crowd pushed into the small one-room structure.

Pike noted the room was aglow with several tall candles, radiating warm light over the cabin's interior. The couple's bedrolls were open on the floor. A blue and white wedding-ring quilt, a present from Rena, had been spread lovingly across the top of the bedrolls.

The plank table that Eric had been hard at work on for the past few weeks, sat in one corner with a pair of sturdy straight-backed chairs. Collections of wildflowers had been sprinkled about the interior. Their sweet scents and bright colors added a comforting touch to the room.

Gasping, Lyric placed her hand over her heart. A lone tear dribbled from her eye and traced a wet line along her delicate cheek. "Thank you all, so much. I would have never guessed you could do so much for us in so little time. I love you all."

As hugs passed around, Pike broke the silence. "I think it's time to leave these two alone." He pumped Buster's hand and gave Lyric one more hug. "You both deserve all the happiness this world can provide. Squeeze it for all you're worth, and now, enjoy yourselves." He beamed a wolfish grin at Buster and turned to shoo everyone out of the cabin.

The others chuckled with him as they departed.

*

Now that Buster and Lyric were settled into their new cabin, Frank and Pike took time to fashion a good-sized raft for the river crossings. On their successful initial trip across the water with the raft, they decided to head over to Pettit's store.

The store's wooden door stood open in the late May afternoon to let in plenty of light and fresh air. Pike led the way into the dim interior. He stopped and gazed around to drink in all the contents displayed in the store.

Gawking about, Frank stood behind him.

"Why, Pike," Dora's friendly voice called, "how are you this afternoon? It's getting a bit warm out there, isn't it? Feels muggy, too. Think it might rain? We could use it. Who do you have with you?"

Pike responded with an upbeat manner. "I brought Frank with me today. We're looking for a place to cool off. Thought we would come for a visit. Hope you don't mind some company."

"Hello, Frank," Dora said in an appraising way. "I enjoyed dancing with you at the party last week."

Frank's eyes twinkled with the memory. "I enjoyed getting to swing you around, too. We came to tell you the raft is finished. Have you found someone to man it?"

"Yes, the Avery boy is trying to find a job. He said he'd do it."

The men moved forward to find a chair and as they plunked into a seat, Pike spoke. "That raft is going to be a godsend for us. We can get over here so much easier now and pick up what we need. When do you think the windows will get here, and the beds?"

"We're looking for them on the next shipment from Joplin. Should be this week. We're expecting the windows and mattresses. I'll let you know right away, now that we can get to your side. How does that sound?"

"Sounds great," Frank interjected.

Pike tilted his chair back to lean against the log wall. "The windows will help us out a lot with the mosquitoes we're starting to have in the evenings. I'm going back to St. Louis as soon as I can, so I can get the equipment ordered for my sawmill. I plan on having it up and running next spring. It'll take me a couple of weeks to get there and then several more to return. So, I need to do it before it gets too much hotter."

"We'll be so glad for it," Dora said enthusiastically. "The whole countryside is trying to fence off their land and build new homes and businesses." She paused for a moment. "How would you like a drink of water?"

Eagerly, Pike replied, "Yes, thank you."

*

Later at the camp, during the evening meal, Pike asked Eric, "How's your cabin coming?"

Eric shoveled a scoop of boiled new potatoes, fresh from the garden, onto his plate. "We've got the walls about half-way up. Now that my leg is about healed, and Buster isn't working in the garden as much, we're getting quite a bit done. Shouldn't be too much longer before we can start on yours."

Swallowing a mouthful of tasty hot beans, Pike said, "I think I'm going to head back to St. Louis and get the sawmill equipment ordered. Why don't you work on some pens for the animals and maybe a barn or two while I'm gone? My cabin can wait, Frank's, too."

"We can do that. How long you think you'll be gone?"

I'm guessing around a month. It could be longer. I hope not. I've got too much to do around here."

I know you need to get that done," Eric said. "Now is as good a time as any. You can be back just in time for the really hot weather. Then, you can help with the last two cabins."

"I'm sure looking forward to that," Pike teased. Getting into the mood, he decided to tease some more. "So, when is the wedding?"

Eric's face turned a deep shade of red. "Hmmm? What did you say? I thought you said something?"

"Okay, okay, I get it." Pike chuckled as he bent his head to clean his plate of the remaining scraps.

Pike reclined on his bedroll, staring hard at the tent ceiling. Sleep seemed as elusive as a spooked white-tail that night. The canvas gently flapped in the never-ceasing wind of his new home. Frank's snoring didn't help matters.

That wasn't the sole cause of his sleeplessness. He meant to leave in the morning for St. Louis and his excitement had flickered and ignited when he had lain down to sleep. Images of log-cutting and lumber-sawing played through his thoughts, keeping his mind busy.

After a time, his mind wandered to Hank. The horse was never far from his consciousness and almost always prancing around the subliminal part of his mind. Pike wondered where Hank was this night, at this very moment. *God let him be okay.* Pike hoped against hope his Father would help his horse, wherever the gelding was - if he were still alive.

Then, Pike allowed his thoughts to drift to more pleasant ones - Rebecca and her pliant young body. The fire, always latent within, burst forth to flood his veins with a pleasant tingling heat. Recounting those sweet, tender moments on that sultry summer night, his young passions stirred to a near-fever pitch. Under the old silver-leafed maple, Rebecca had let go and given all that she had to give him and his heart bled anew for what would never be.

Stroking his watch chain, he couldn't help but yearn for more. He was a virile, youthful man. Why shouldn't he have that sort of love and lustful release in his life? Why did God deny him these things? *Lord, I still don't understand why I have to endure this kind of pain. I want to be with Rebecca. Could You please take that desire away? It eats me up sometimes.*

*

Slowly, the night slipped by, and as the sun began its daily ritual of laying its fingered streaks across the land, emblazoning the sky with magical colors, Pike rose to get on the road to St. Louis. *The sooner the better,* he surmised. *I can get away from this daily agony and Rebecca's pretty face.* Yes, maybe he could escape for a while and he sure was ready to try. He eased out of the tent and away from Frank's snoring.

Pike noted the heap of glowing orange embers that remained of the fire from the night before. Feeling out of sorts, he plopped on a log to stare hypnotically at the embers and poke at them with a stick. *Guess it is the lack of sleep, or is it Rebecca?* It didn't matter, he grumbled, he just wanted to yell his left-over anger at the morning sky. *Get control of yourself!*

Pushing around the glowing coals, Pike wished away the tiredness from his body as he realized, *I still love her. I can't seem to let go of that.* Again, he tried to accept what he knew had to be, and even though he understood the truth, he didn't feel any better. If anything, he felt more like stomping about and throwing things. *What am I going to do?* Looking up, he spotted a feminine figure move toward him.

Slipping out of the predawn darkness of the trees, Rebecca strode across the grass. She stepped into the fire's weak light and sat next to Pike. In a voice contained by a whisper, she said, "Goodness, I never expected to see anyone else this early. What's up?"

Pike glanced at the object of his affection - the main cause of his sleepless night. In as nonchalant a manner as possible, he replied, "I need to get on the road. I decided to get up and around. Would you do something for me? Could you keep an eye on Candy while I'm gone?"

"I will. Patrick keeps her busy most of the time. I just have to keep her away from my shoes." She giggled, then beamed a familiar smile at him.

Pike couldn't help but edge a bit closer to her to share some warmth, even though he knew he shouldn't. After a few moments, he slipped his arm around her tiny shoulders in what he told himself was just a friendly way. After pulling her to him and shaking her a few times, he said, "I will miss you and, especially, that great food. My cooking is sure lacking. I may starve to death on this trip. I may have to eat Clash. Sure would miss that horse."

"Poor Pike. If you have to eat Clash, would you keep his hide and make me a coat? It would be so pretty." She threw her head back.

Pike caught the glimmer of her warm, brown eyes. The merriment he had been feeling grew rapidly into something more as they shared a knowing look. The longings from the night whispered across Pike's mind, telling him that what he was about to do was somehow okay. He shut out thoughts of his brother and how Amos was now the husband of Rebecca, the husband Pike wished to be. He desperately sought out Rebecca's mouth and planted his hungry lips on hers.

Rebecca did nothing to stop him but gave up her mouth to his searching lips and tongue.

Letting the glory of his passion shine, Pike kissed her for several minutes. Growing bolder, his busy lips traveled along Rebecca's jaw-line. He feathered her with soft kisses there and then made a trail to the sweet nook of the neck that he loved so much.

"I have to tell you something," Rebecca whispered with a voice racked with emotion. "It's something important."

Not able tear himself away from her lovely neck, Pike kissed on. Slowly, her words began to register. His brain sent out a signal of worry, causing a lead weight to fall in his stomach. Not wanting the stolen moment of pleasure to end, he began to move back to Rebecca's mouth and hoped to silence her words.

Placing a firm hand on his chest, Rebecca gave him no further chance to ignore her.

With his lips inches from her face, Pike found his voice and asked, "What is it, my love?"

"Pike," Rebecca's tear-filled voice wavered. "I'm going to have a baby. It's due in January."

The words splashed like a bucket of ice water over his head. They flushed the heat from his veins. Nothing else could have struck home harder than Rebecca's pregnancy. Images of Amos and Rebecca together, sharing their bodies as Pike wished to do, whirled through his mind and brought with them pain and the reality of his plight. He had been forced to give up Rebecca. With a tight jaw, Pike let her go and turned away.

"Pike," Rebecca urged, "you've got to get on with your life. As much as I love you, I've got to get on with mine. Please, let me."

The panic and fury of having to face his demons over Rebecca and all she meant to him, exploded. "Why didn't you wait for me? I came back, didn't I? Just like I said I would. You were too weak to wait. If you'd been strong enough, we'd be together now. You could be carrying my baby, not Amos's. The sight of you makes me sick. Don't worry. What just happened will never happen again. You can count on that! And one last thing, I don't know why I ever wasted my time on a girl like you. I thought we had something. I guess I was wrong."

Ignoring Rebecca's shattered face, he stomped away and refused to give her time to reply. In an angry fog, he grabbed up his gear and tromped off from the camp to find his horse. Only then did he fully realize that what he had just flung at Rebecca had been unfair and unjustified. But, his hurt overpowered his mouth and it shocked him to realize just how much need he had to hurt her. Reason didn't play a part - only pain. His primeval urge had blind-sided him. Its control still raged within, causing him to clomp through the morning with muttering and cursing.

Picking up on Pike's foul mood, Clash jerked back, trying to hop away on his hobbled legs.

Clutching his halter, Pike slung his words. "Hold still!"

A shiver rippled across the Appaloosa's side and he continued to hop and strain to get away from Pike's touch.

Registering the horse's fear, Pike slowed his angry energy down and spoke in a soothing voice. "Easy, Clash. It's okay. I'm not going to hurt you." Pike trailed his calloused hand to caress the horse's smooth muzzle. "I'm sorry, boy. I'm just upset this morning. Can you forgive me?"

The horse visibly relaxed, snuffling along Pike's cheek in response.

Taking advantage of the moment, Pike rested his flushed face against the warm, furry head to collect his thoughts. The anger still raged, but drawing in a deep breath of horse, Pike forced himself to gain better control of his emotions. Concentrating on the tasks at hand, he bridled Clash, then saddled him. He carefully tied his belongings behind the saddle. Flinging his boot over the horse's white rump, he gathered the reins. As always, the stallion took that moment to hop away and hump his back.

Focusing his mind on staying aboard, Pike welcomed the break from his anger and he gave Clash one good thump with his heel to urge the horse to move forward, not upward. Luckily, the horse obeyed his cue and slung his head high to let his legs fly.

The blustery morning played a tune across Pike's ears as he rode along and covered the first few miles rapidly. Once the stallion began to slow, Pike's mind took its cue to ease down a few notches as clear thought returned.

Regret from the morning's encounter nagged at Pike. Sadness over his actions settled on his shoulders and caused his head to droop. He felt like turning Clash around and going back to face Rebecca. He should say he was sorry but the shame of his actions seemed insurmountable. Realizing he was being a coward didn't stop him. He couldn't find the strength to go back.

Maybe when I get back I can apologize, Pike reasoned, knowing it was a justification for his cowardice.

He took a deep breath and sat up straighter in the saddle, momentarily shutting out the thoughts of the past. "Hope you're ready for a long trip, Clash. It's just you and me now."

*

After long days of riding, Pike began to notice the first buildings on the outskirts of St. Louis.

"Clash," Pike said to his trusty horse, "do you think I'll ever get Rebecca out of my heart?" The miles had provided Pike many hours to process his feelings. He'd had many a talk on the subject with his heavenly Father, as well as with his mount. Pike had pleaded with God to release him from his desire for Rebecca and now all he could do was hope God had listened.

Pike's heart lifted as he rode into town. Outside 'The Mountain Man', he drew his leggy mount to a stop. He called out to the grubby attendant whom he had grown fond of during his previous stay. "Willie? Are you in there?"

Dismounting Clash, Pike brought his boot down to rest in the dirt and his bad leg protested loudly. Used to turning a deaf ear to this type of painful talk from his leg, Pike didn't stop and give into it. Instead, one stiff step became two and then three and finally, both his legs worked with fewer protests.

While his eyes adjusted to the barn's interior, Pike listened for Willie. Finally realizing that Willie was nowhere about, he decided to take care of Clash himself. He led Clash into an empty stall and removed the saddle and bridle. As Pike dished up a sizable portion of oats and hay, the Appaloosa eagerly dipped his head into his feed and began to munch contentedly.

Pike grabbed his pack and strolled down the alleyway to the hotel. Now that the journey was over, his step felt lighter, while a carefree smile broke on his face.

An unfamiliar clerk stood behind the hotel desk. "Yes, sir? How can I help you today?"

"I need a room for one night, maybe two. I would like

one in the communal space, if you have it."

"Yes, I believe we have one more. Can you write your name in the register?"

As Pike scribbled his name on the indicated line, a voice from the past struck his ear.

"Well, if it isn't Pike Wheeling. Who would have thought?"

Shooting around, Pike scanned the room for the familiar voice from his past. When he spotted his favorite teacher, his heart leapt with joy. "Professor Collin Danvil!"

The man's curly hair flopped about his head as it always had and the eyes still brimmed with merriment. The outstretched hand met Pike's, next came the hug.

"I never thought I'd see you again," Pike boomed with a glee-filled voice. "What a surprise. What are you doing here?" Pike drew back and grinned elatedly at his friend.

Collin chuckled. "When I got home from the war, I just wasn't the same. I went back to teaching at the university, but my heart wasn't in it. My mother passed away recently, so I decided to come west and start a new life with my new wife."

"You have a wife?" Pike said incredulously. Hoping to pick her out of the crowd, he looked around the room.

"Let me introduce you. She's right over here by the fire."

A black-haired woman turned toward them and dropped her needlepoint. She eyed Pike as she rose to join the professor. Her black hair and severely-arched black brows contrasted sharply with her pale white skin and set off her gray eyes. A smattering of soft dark hair over her upper lip suggested a moustache. Were it not for her awkward smile, her thin lips and pointed nose would have given Pike the impression of being overly caustic. The tightly-drawn hair, pulled back from her face, didn't help either. Her plump frame, over a rather short body, waddled forward to greet him.

"It's so nice to meet you," Pike said. "I never would have thought the professor here would ever find anyone who could put up with him long enough to get married. He reads too much to get out. How did you meet?"

The woman's back stiffened. Her eyes narrowed and grew hard, and the thin lips pursed. Obviously, she wasn't pleased by his jibe at the professor. Rather than say what appeared to be on her mind, she replied stiffly, "I was a student at the university. I took one of Collin's classes."

"That's great!" Pike laughed, hoping to gloss over her aggravated demeanor. Cordially, he said, "I forgot my manners. My name is Pike Wheeling. Collin and I were in Andersonville prison together. It's very nice to meet you." Pike felt it appropriate to bow slightly, as he hoped to neutralize his earlier *faux pas* in gigging her and her husband.

"Pike, this is Effie," Collin said pleasantly.

Pike returned the woman's forced smile.

The professor changed the subject. "What are you doing out here? I thought you'd be in Baltimore. What made you decide to come all the way out west? Why don't you come and sit down with us on the settee and tell us about it?"

"Sure, let's move over there." Pike trailed after the couple to rest on the red velvet sofa. He started right in. "I was like you. I just couldn't seem to settle back into my former life. I had an itch to explore. I brought my brothers and several others with me. We've moved to Indian Territory. We got there about two months ago. Now, that we're settled in and have bought our land, I came back to St. Louis to order the equipment I need for a sawmill. I'm planning on starting one as soon as I can get it set up."

"Well, I can't tell you how happy I am to have run into you," Collin said. "It must be the hand of fate. I would love to hear more about where you are living. We may be interested in heading in that direction. Let's talk it over at supper. What do you say?" With his warm, open eyes, Collin gazed at Pike over the rim of his spectacles. "I sure have missed you and your harmonica, but I'm starved right now. Would you like to get settled and then meet us here in about fifteen minutes?"

"That sounds great. We can talk over old times, that is, if Effie doesn't mind."

Effie didn't reply. She maintained her distant manner with narrowed eyes and a scowl on her forehead.

"It's settled then," Collin said as he slapped Pike on the back. "We'll see you in a few minutes."

Pike nodded and went to find his room. Despite Effie's attitude, he decided he was going to have a good time.

Part III

Pike's Return

Chapter 21

The incessant, howling wind infuriated fifteen-year-old Callie Starr that warm June morning as the wagon bounced along. "I've got to get something to tie my hair back if I'm going to be able to see," she complained out loud as she gripped the reins of the sorrel and bay team. The steadily rising dust made it more and more difficult to guide the team. Angrily shoving her hair out of her eyes, she glanced at her older sister.

Irene, smaller, older and daintier than Callie, sat perched next to her, engrossed in a book. Seemingly unruffled by the wind, Irene lurched mindlessly with the wagon as it bumped over the road.

Callie's father Claude and her eighteen-year-old brother, Kyle, rode just ahead on horseback.

As Callie guided the horses, she felt comforted that they were finally returning home to the farm as she hated the trips to Joplin, where she had to put up with her younger cousin, Jenny. Callie grimaced inwardly at the thought of that mean-tempered girl. She and Irene would never let their father Claude know how little they enjoyed spending time with their cousin. He looked forward to the visits with his brother so much.

Since her mom had died of malaria several years before, Callie did her best to ease her father's suffering. They all suffered but she could see that his pain was the deepest and the loss still shone in his haunted eyes.

Callie cherished being with her father and her love for him knew no bounds. Being a tomboy at heart, she reveled in learning the tasks of farm work from him. It suited her better than the more girlish activities her mother had vainly tried to teach her. Working in the fields with Claude and Kyle made her life worthwhile.

As a tiny child, Callie had never liked playing with the dolls her mother had made for her. She would intentionally misplace them, preferring to go back to making mud pies when her mother wasn't looking.

Gazelle, her half-Cherokee mother, would scold when she caught her messing up her dresses. "Callie, you have to stay clean. I swear, I don't know what I'm going to do with you. Look at yourself!"

The sadness of those moments waved through her now as Callie recalled them. Her true nature had led her astray, even then. She had loved chasing frogs by the creek near her house and would even enjoy it still, if she had time for such diversions, but there was too much work to be done around their farm.

The longing to see her mother ate at her mind and heart. When she missed her mother, as she did now, she wished she had been a better daughter and tears misted her vision. Roughly, she swiped at them with her dusty sleeve as she clucked to the horses.

Since their mother's death, Irene had taken over being the woman of the household and had become an accomplished cook. Callie contributed to the supper table, too, but not through cooking. She could outshoot her brother and father any day of the week. Subsequently, she had developed a passion for hunting which kept their table blessed from her time in the woods.

Struggling to deal with the continual cloud of melancholy that hung over Claude, Callie knew in her heart that he wished to be in heaven with Gazelle, but he had the children to see to, which he did as well as his broken spirit would allow.

With Claude's grief, the family's forty acres of farmland had lost its appeal for him. Just keeping up with the fields of corn and oats was almost too much for Callie and Kyle who tried so valiantly to keep all of their heads above water. For the last two years Callie had, whole-heartedly, lent herself to these never-ending chores.

Claude came abreast of the wagon on his gray mount and asked Callie, "What do we have to eat?"

Irene quickly jumped into the conversation. "I've got

some deer steaks left over from this morning and some bread. How does that sound?"

Nodding and grinning, Claude looked up and motioned for Kyle to join them by the wagon. "It's time for lunch. Why don't we eat in this patch of trees so we can get out of the hot sun for a while? Kyle, why don't you gather up some wood? I'll take care of the horses. Callie, do you want me to help you unharness?"

"Yes, please," Callie replied, as she returned her father's loving smile, one that displayed to her how much she meant to him. She reined the team to the grassy shoulder under the trees and welcomed the shade as she fussed to herself, *I bet my skin is burned. I can feel it. Guess I need to rustle up my bonnet. Drats, hate those things. Where did I leave mine?*

The unhitching and unharnessing took several minutes. When Callie and Claude finished, they plopped down onto the cool summer grass and waited for their food. Kyle located a spot next to Claude.

*

Drisco spotted the wagon as it stopped along the border of the forest. He instructed his practiced trio of renegades to prepare themselves. "When I say go, you all fan out and sink behind that there dead tree."

The bandits had rehearsed these situations dozens of times over the past several months. And each time they had been successful in surprising their intended victims and taking exactly what they wanted. Stealing, raping and killing had become the way of life for Silas, Titus and Rufus.

This life was nothing new for Drisco but each time he waited to make his move on his victims, the thrill got sweeter. It was what he lived for, his sole purpose in being.

Watching the tall girl with the long, brown hair sitting next to her father, Drisco's heart reverberated in his ears. Adrenaline shot him as high as any opiate he had ever taken as his favorite moment was at hand. A malevolent grin seeped onto his face because he liked the looks of the two girls, both the tall one and the smaller one. He briefly contemplated bending one of them over and.........

No, he had to force that out of his mind for the moment as he gave himself some instructions, *Ya got to keep yer mind on what yer doin'*. Sensing the time was right, he gave his men the nod to move forward.

*

Callie perked up as the horses, startled by something in the dark folds of the forest, suddenly threw up their heads. "Father!" she screamed as she spotted four men carrying rifles, crawling behind a fallen log to disappear.

Got to get my rifle, her mind screeched as Callie sprinted toward the wagon. She heard the first shot ring out as she vaulted over top of the wagon's sideboard. Then, she dropped onto the rough boards with a thump and grunted from the pain. Carried by fear, she wasted no time with more thought of her pain as she wrapped her hands around the barrel of her well-used rifle. She placed the stock into her shoulder and screwed up her courage and prayed that her family was safe and that no one had been shot. For emphasis she gave one plea out loud, "Father in Heaven, please help us!"

In one flowing motion, Callie rose from her hiding place, swung the end of the rifle toward one of the standing men and squeezed off a bullet. Proudly, she watched as her intended victim fell to the ground like a heavy stone.

Immediately, Callie felt a searing pain rip through her right shoulder. The shock hit her before she heard the report from the gun. A black void clouded her vision and her body catapulted forward. Barely conscious of it, she fell into a deep, black well – *falling, falling, falling* and she never felt the impact.

*

Over a week on the road now, Pike was headed home atop Clash and happily humming to himself while Collin and Effie rode behind him in their new Studebaker wagon.

Scanning the horizon, Pike noted the undulating hills, tall lush grasses, and trees clustered about. A gust of wind whipped at his Stetson, causing him to grab it and shove it back into place as he drank deeply of the ripe breeze, reveling in its bouquet. It held a distinct essence of life and moist earth.

Rubbing his aching thigh vigorously several times, Pike grumbled inwardly as he mused, *I can't wait to get back to and rest this leg of mine. Would like some of Lyric's apple cobbler, too.* The notion of the tasty treat made his mouth water. Pike might have even stretched it enough to say that he missed Rena.

Jaunting along, his mind kept up its steady procession of contemplation, *We should be home in a couple more days. Can't wait to get my sawmill parts. I'm glad they'll be shipped to Joplin. That'll save me a lot of time. We can get them back in one trip. Sure hope so.*

Glancing over his shoulder, Pike watched Collin and Effie bumping along as he continued thinking, *Glad Effie has loosened up and seems to like me better than she did at first. It would be tough if she didn't.*

Suddenly, a gunshot rang out.

Yanking his horse to a halt, Pike motioned to Collin to stop the wagon. Pike focused on the horizon, trying to gauge the direction and distance of the gun's echo since there were no settlements or homesteaders in this area. Whoever was up ahead had to be up to no good. Uneasiness filled him as he groped into his bag and withdrew his shiny Colt and laid it against his trousers. To survive on this wild land, a person had to ready for anything.

"You stay here," Pike directed of Collin. "I'm going ahead to investigate." After talking to Collin, Pike thumped Clash and together they made a beeline toward the forest in front of them.

*

Drisco's world had gone a little haywire. Titus had managed to get off a shot, dropping the older man, but just as quickly, an unexpected shot had been fired at them. Drisco heard Titus scream and watched him grip his middle as he dropped into a moaning heap. Drisco couldn't believe that it was the tall girl responsible for the shot as he cursed and drew his pistol, letting a bullet fly to take care of that little annoyance. When he saw the girl plummet to the ground, a giddy feeling overtook him.

"Come on, boys, we've got 'em covered," Drisco announced, as he urged his men to fan out in front of him. He noted Titus, holding his wound, crawling back to the horses.

A tall, handsome boy and a pretty girl with dark hair and dark eyes gaped at them from the grass as they approached. The youths wore the beaten look of prey, the one that captured prey wear just before being devoured. Chuckling, Drisco felt bolder.

Drisco had seen that look more times than he could count. Their fear brought on a heady confidence and feeling of domination. "Put your hands in the air," he hissed.

The dark-headed girl quickly followed his order. The boy took longer.

Leering at the kids, Drisco savored their apprehension. "Well, well. What have we here?" He said, as he grabbed the girl by her small breast and squeezed it hard, lifting her to her feet. Tears drenched her face as Drisco shouted into her watery eyes, "Good enough to eat." Then, he licked his lips and reveled in his power and thought to himself, *What could be better than this? Nothin', that's for sure.* He savored this moment and he didn't want it to end, but he had to act.

The girl held her hand to her tanned throat and visibly shivered.

"Okay, boy," Drisco ordered, "time to get up." He motioned for Silas and Rufus to drag the boy to the wagon.

Rufus grabbed the frightened boy and shoved him forward.

The boy lost his footing and fell to the ground, and tears formed in his eyes.

The men hooted while Rufus bent over him and growled, "Boy, you'd better move your ass over to that there wagon. I mean now."

"Silas," Drisco said, "Go and find some rope."

The tall, beanpole man, stalked over to the wagon and began to rifle through the contents. Quickly, he withdrew a rope. Holding up the rope for all to see, he laughed a deep-throated laugh as he walked back to begin his task of tying up the boy, eyes ablaze from a fire within.

"Please don't," Kyle cried, as Silas came to his crumpled form and kicked him several times.

That was music to Drisco's ears and like a tonic to his insides. He unleashed his desires to run on a free rein, and a smile curled his lips.

"Don't do this to me," Kyle tried once again as several tears dripped from his chin.

"Shut up," Silas commanded, as he made his last hitch with the rope and rose to stare down at him.

Drisco bent low to the girl and cooed, "You are a pretty one, too. Can't wait to try you out." Then, he swiped at the drool, dripping from the corner of his trembling, eager lips. Not thinking, he wiped it on his pants.

*

God what's happened to me, Callie wondered as she felt herself begin to stir and she heard her own moan. Without much more effort, her eyes flickered open. Confused at finding herself on the ground staring up at the fluffy clouds above, she strained to move. The wild burning in her shoulder blistered her arm and shafted her stomach, causing her to want to curl into a ball - and cry.

As her eyesight cleared, she became aware of two ragged boots standing in the grass a few feet from her nose. She froze in place as her eyes glanced up at a pock-faced, light-skinned Indian. A wicked smirk crossed his lips as he observed her and his evil, malicious eyes razored a shank of fear racing through her bones. That face caused fear in her like she'd never known and a scream formed in her head.

Remembering the rifle shots and the need to protect herself and her family, her fear gave way to a more familiar feeling of raw, savage anger. Its swelling tide erupted out of her in a primal growl as she clenched her fists to rise and attack but a wave of pain rocketed through her body and threatened to turn her into mush. A grimace formed on her face. A grunt slipped out as she dropped back to the ground.

Her display of courage seemed to rock the man back on his heels and his brows lifted in surprise. He stepped forward, grabbed her by the arm, to savagely drag her over the ground.

Moaning, Callie tried to catch her breath as her body burned and scraped along the grass, her eyes blurred - the world began to spin. The man finally let her arm go, tumbling her to the ground with a hideous laugh. To compound her problems, his stench turned her stomach while she briefly caught sight of Irene, trembling beside her, as she flopped in the grass. Mind-numbing pain was all she was aware of as blackness fogged her head. Callie could hear the half-breed talking, but she couldn't make out what he was saying.

As her mind cleared again and the fog lifted, Callie opened her eyes and gaped around as quickly as she could. She hefted herself slightly on her good elbow to see what was going on.

Callie could easily spot silent tears flowing down Irene's pallid face as Irene kept her frightened eyes attentive to the evil man, her face a ghostly shade of white. Callie could see Kyle had been tied to the wagon. Kyle's eyes looked hollow with terror and two filthy men stood near him, laughing.

Looking back to the man nearest her, Callie watched her attacker pace the ground in front of her as she noted his disturbed eyes moving from prize to prize with a hungry, predatory gleam.

Where is father? Callie wondered, as a shudder of fear coursed up her spine but the shafting pain in her arm and shoulder kept her focus elsewhere - on the mind-blowing pain and the wonder of what horror was next. *Am I going to throw up? Please, God, help me hang on. I think I'm going to pass out again.* A ripple of light-headedness almost forced her to topple back to the grass as her mind screeched, *No! I've got to stay awake. I've got to help them,* her mind screamed. *Where is fa-*

ther? I can't let that foul-smelling heathen win. He's not going to get away with it, not if I can help it.

A fear-filled urge struck with the force of a charging bull causing Callie to let loose her true thoughts, *I want my daddy!* The tears struck hard and she bit her lip to keep her vision clear.

Her captor suddenly bent down and let his hand caress her legs and he hiked up her dress a small bit.

Filled with disgust, Callie puckered her mouth and spit into his eye and glared at him, thinking about what she could do next.

Astonished, the man fell back, then as his eyes shrunk into a hard line, he said, ever so slowly, "Listen, you side-windin' bitch."

An explosion burst in Callie's head as the man slapped her hard across the cheek.

"You're going to pay for that with your hide. And I'm just the man to do it!" He jumped up and started to unbuckle his belt and he laughed giddily with a crazed gleam in his eyes as he began talking again, "You and I are goin' to have fun. Ever been with a *man*, girlie? Um-hmmm, I'm goin' to plug you; make you scream, I am." He began to loosen the button on his trousers. "Then, I'm goin' to start cutting' you up real slow-like." He let out a demented laugh before he said, "Then, you're goin' to scream some more."

Trying to shut out what the man had said, Callie was aware how much her face burned and she could taste blood on her lip. As another rush of blackness swarmed into her thoughts, she struggled to hang onto consciousness.

Without warning, the evil man swung toward Kyle, lifted his pistol, and let a bullet fly.

Horror flashed through Callie's heart as a hole formed on Kyle's forehead and his body slumped against the ropes.

"Why'd you do that?" one of the men asked in an annoyed tone. "We could've had a little fun with him."

"We don't need him. We've got the girls now." The half-breed brayed like a crazed mule and turned back to Callie.

Unable to endure the anguish of her brother's hideous death, Callie let go of the light and raced into the arms of the comforting darkness.

Chapter 22

Still wary and holding on tightly to the Colt, Pike trotted with Clash along the road about a half-mile or more from where he had left Collin and his wife. As he listened alertly to the sounds around him, another shot echoed across the hills, this one much closer.

His shoulders tensed as a sense of dread continued to plague him. Pike bumped his horse and sent him into a headlong gallop toward the area of the shot's report and he prayed.

From a distance, Pike spotted a distant outline of a wagon and a group of ragged men clustered in front. "Easy, Clash", Pike directed his mount so they could cautiously wind their way through the trees to sneak up on them from behind. As he drew as close as he dared with the horse, he dismounted and flipped the reins over the nearest branch, then turned to hide behind the next tree.

Holding his pistol in his hand, he moved stealthily into the cover of the forest, moving from bush to tree. His years on the battlefield had developed him into a master at slipping undetected through the trees and brush. He called on those skills now as a strange foreboding ate at him and he continued to pray that it would be unfounded. Inching forward, he held his breath.

Voices drifted through the trees. The distinctive cackle of a madman echoed close by. "Now, you'll get what you deserve, you side-windin' bitch."

Instantly on full alert, Pike dashed across an open space to dive behind another tree. Close to the scene now, he peeked ever so slowly around the trunk and let one eye drink in the horrific drama being played out before him.

One man lay in a heap. Another hung limply against the side of the wagon where he'd been tied. Three gruff-looking men shifted around a petite, frightened girl as she sat stiffly on the grass. Next to her, another girl with a bloody shoulder was sprawled out on the ground. The second girl didn't move, so Pike couldn't tell if she was alive or dead.

The three men posed a problem but the odds were not insurmountable. Pike had faced worse conditions in the past. So, slowly, he raised the loaded Colt, rested it in the crook of his arm and took careful aim at the tall, skinny man who stood closest to him. He carefully squeezed the trigger while holding his breath. The report deafened his ears but his eyes stayed on the target.

The man toppled back, then fell down as blood splashed across his chest.

The other two men raced for the trees.

Pike briefly caught sight of them as they hightailed it to safety. A pang of rage engulfed him as recognition dawned, *It's Drisco and his cousin! God help me.*

Bolting from his spot, Pike frantically dashed after the fleeing renegades. He caught sight of them again just as they galloped away into the deeper part of the forest, leading two other mounts, one a distinctive buckkin carrying a man slumped over the saddle horn. There was his horse. "Hank!" Pike screamed, running after them. "Hank!"

Too soon, the thick timber swallowed the men and horses. As he knew his horse was lost again, Pike sagged against a tree and stared after them while a stab of grief burned a hole in his heart. He clenched his empty fist and pounded it against his leg as he vowed to himself, *I'll find him. I won't let Drisco escape this time. I'm going after him.*

Turning with a snapping of his head, Pike loped back the way he had come while he raged inside and this anger was lit from within by just the sight of Drisco. Pike knew no bounds on his hate for the man. But, Pike had to temper his anger to concentrate on the chore of investigating the damage Drisco had caused. *At least Hank is alive,* he told himself. *I'll get him back, I just know it!*

As Pike found his way back to the people left from the day's drama, he noted the dark-haired girl, sitting on the grass, was clasping her arms around her body and staring into space. The girl on the ground began to stir. Blood soaked the shoulder and chest of her blue cotton dress as Pike saw her eyes blink as she fought to focus them.

Kneeling beside her, Pike touched her arm and asked, "Miss, are you okay? You've been shot. Are you hurting?"

The girl's eyes swiveled in the direction of his voice. She opened her mouth, but nothing came out. Her jaws moved several more times before she began to function. "I-I-I'm o-o-kay," she stuttered.

"Here, lie back," Pike directed. "I'm going to tend to the other girl. Is she your sister?" The girl barely nodded as Pike guided her gently back to the ground. "Everything is going to be okay. Just close your eyes for a minute. Rest."

The young girl closed her eyes and quickly faded.

Pike turned to the other girl, the smaller one dressed in red. As he appraised her condition, he was pleased to note that she did not appear to be wounded, but her eyes told a different tale.

She stared at the body of the dead boy. Her pasty white face contorted as tears gushed silently from her dark eyes.

Sitting close to her, Pike asked, "Are you injured, Miss?"

The girl didn't respond.

Not knowing what to do, he said in a soothing voice, "I know what's happened here has been rough. If you'll rest here a moment, I'll go and tend to the dead. It'll be better for you both if you don't have to look at them anymore. I'll be back as soon as I finish." Pike started to rise.

The girl's hand shot out with viper-like speed and clasped him by the wrist. Her eyes grew wild as she desperately wailed, "Don't leave me! I'm scared."

Startled, Pike hesitated. Scanning the pitiful girl's face, he rested back onto the grass and pulled her to him. Holding her head against his chest, he rocked her back and forth, attempting to quiet her. Concern for the injured girl gnawed at him as he felt the urgent need to get back to her quickly.

The sound of the trace chains of Collin's new wagon flooded Pike with relief. He watched his friends break through the edge of the trees.

Collin's eyes spotted the nasty scene and he yelled, "Git up there!" causing the team to lope forward. Within running distance, Collin halted the horses and hopped from his perch and breathlessly asked, "What happened here?" Effie followed close behind, holding her skirts high.

"I came upon some men attacking this family," Pike said, still holding the girl. "I got one of them. The others ran off." He decided it wasn't time to mention Drisco and Rufus to Collin.

The professor and Effie fixed their eyes on the grisly scene.

"Effie," Pike brusquely directed, "will you sit with this young lady? What's your name, dear?"

She managed to speak through her sniffles. "Irene. My sister is Callie."

"Irene, this is Effie and she's going to help you while I tend to your injured sister. Is that okay?"

Irene's head nodded.

Rushing, Pike and the professor dropped beside Callie's unconscious body. First, Pike ran a hand over her to look for other injuries. Seeing none, he said to Collin, "Let's pick her up and bring her to their wagon. We can put her in there and cover her up. I'm going to find something to clean the wound."

With as much care as possible, the pair picked up the unconscious girl and toted her to the wagon. They wrapped her body with several quilts in hopes of keeping her warm. Pike went through the family's belongings to locate something to clean and dress the wound. He certainly was no expert but his years in treating gunshot wounds during the war had left him some knowledge to draw on.

A little later, Pike rested on his heels as he observed his completed work in cleaning and covering the wound. He stared at the young girl's pale face and thought, *Hope that holds. Those poor girls! They've lost their family. How will they ever recover? I guess I can't think about that now. Need to get after Drisco, but how can I with this injured girl? She needs help first, and there are other things to do first.* Standing up, Pike directed, "Collin, let's get the dead buried."

They started with the older man's body by lifting him between them and carrying him out of sight.

"I need to tell you something," Pike whispered to Collin as they put the body behind some trees. "You remember Drisco and Rufus?"

Collin's eyes widened in interest. "My feelings for them are better imagined than described."

"Well, they were among the men that attacked this family and laid the father and son low. Drisco stole my horse back in St Louis. I really want to go after him but we need to get this girl back to my place, or she might not make it. I can't stand the thought of letting him go again. What should I do?"

"Pike, if I knew where to take the girls, I would do it. I'd like to see Drisco get his due, just like you, but we are lost out here without you. I imagine those girls would like you to catch those killers, too, but the wounded girl should come first. That would be my advice."

Shaking his head, eyes downcast, Pike said, "The thought of it makes me sick. I've trailed them once before and couldn't catch them. Now, that I know they are in the area, maybe I can locate them." He gritted his teeth and said through a tight jaw, "Someday, they'll get caught. I just hope I'm the one to do it. Meanwhile, we'll have to stay on the lookout for them. We never know when they may pop up again."

Collin put a firm hand on Pike's shoulder and said, "Pike, let's get this task completed."

"Yes, you're right." Pike turned and headed back to

the wagons. "We need to get the family buried and then get that injured one back to the group. I hope she can hold on that long, it's one more day to my place. Let's not bother with the other dead man. Leave him lie. The buzzards can have him."

Collin nodded his head.

*

Hours later, Pike stacked the last of the rocks on the two graves. Saying a brief prayer, he turned to check on Callie in the wagon and instantly noted, *She's as white as angels' wings.*

Amazingly, her hazel eyes opened and looked up at him.

"How are you doing?" Pike asked.

She gave a tremulous smile.

"You are one strong young lady," Pike praised and smiled. "I think you're going to be just fine." He patted her soothingly on the leg. "Can you stand the motion of the wagon? We need to get you back to my family's place. It's another day's ride from here. You can rest there and get better medical attention."

Callie gave him a shaky nod.

"I'm going to need Irene to drive. Can you handle this alone?

"I can make it," she croaked in an anguished voice. "I don't want to stay here another minute." Then, her eyes turned hard and her body tensed. "Did I kill the man I shot? I hope so."

Raising his eyebrows, Pike responded in surprise. "So, you shot one of them? I killed the one here. I only saw three others when they ran off. One did seem injured."

"Well," Callie continued, relaxing back a little, "I shot one just before I got shot. I just wondered what happened to him."

"Sorry, I'm not sure. He must have rode off with the others."

The pallid girl nodded her head and stared off into space.

Impressed with the pluckiness of this child, Pike

studied her for a moment. She had gumption, that's for sure. He had never known a woman, much less a girl, that could shoot well enough to hit a man, especially under duress. *She's a warrior*, he told himself, then said to her, "You are a tough young lady. Just hang on. We're going to get going and put some distance between us and this awful tragedy. If it gets to be too much, just shout out. I'll check on you often, okay?" Her forlorn look formed a knot in his throat. But, he didn't have time for that. His main concern was getting her back so she could begin to mend.

Pike turned to Effie. The severity of her features had seemed to soften under the circumstances. "Would you please sit with Callie and holler if she can't take any more of the bumping?"

"Certainly," she said, lifting her skirts to step into the wagon.

Mounting Clash, Pike gave the signal to head out. He glanced at the grave sites and marked the location in his mind because he wanted to be able to bring the girls back here when they felt up to it. Trotting forward, Clash bounced Pike across the rough ground.

Scanning the horizon, Pike's heavy heart plagued him as he continued to worry about the young girls and how they would cope with this terrible event and the losses they had suffered. He also thought of Hank being hauled off behind Drisco. *When would things ever be right?*

*

Sitting restlessly in the hard chair, Drisco grumbled and gazed into the fire. The day had given way to night, and it was black outside.

Rufus sat at the table, nipping from a whiskey bottle.

Listening to the moans of Titus on the bed in the back of the room, Drisco felt vexed. *Damn his hide! He should have been smarter and not got shot. What a waste that sissy is.* He had spent hours training that bumbling idiot. Now, he had lost both of his new men. It would just be him and Rufus again. *Oh well, at least we have a cabin.*

Drisco looked at Rufus, then barked, "Shoot that man and drag his mangy hide outside. I can't stand the sight of him anymore."

"You don't want to let him suffer a while longer? That gut wound will get him afore long."

Rubbing his chin, Drisco mulled over his cousin's idea. *Maybe he was right. Let the idiot suffer.* With a chuckle, he growled, "Yeah, let him suffer. He deserves it." He rose from his chair. "I'm goin' to bed." Drisco flopped down on the tiny rack that served as his bed and fell asleep.

*

I hope I can stand this, Callie cried to herself as she swayed and bounced with the wagon. *God, please help me!* she silently shouted, as she rigorously attempted to keep her mind diverted from the racking pain that marched from her wounded shoulder deep into her core.

More than her shoulder hurt. Her father and brother were gone. How could she ever endure that pain? All she wanted to do was to curl up into a fetal position and die as her mind asked, *Lord, why did you do this to me? You've left me one sister. That's all I've got in the world. How can I go on? I want my daddy!* Wailing and reeling under her mind's onslaught, a fresh crop of tears ran down her cheeks and slid under her chin.

Effie squeezed Callie's hand intermittently. "There, there, dear. We'll take care of you. You need to lie back and rest."

All at once, Callie's mind began to seize up and coherent thought faded away. Shivers engulfed her and racked her whole being in seemingly never-ending waves.

Clucking like a mother hen, Effie pulled the quilt over Callie's shoulders and observed, "You must be getting feverish." The woman picked up a book and opened it and asked, "How about something to listen to? How about Psalms?"

Blankly, Callie stared at nothing.

Leading the two wagons along the trail, Pike put

more distance between them and the atrocities of the day. Tension still held him in its grasp, squeezing his innards. The pressure he felt from the need to get the wounded girl home lay heavily on his mind. Swinging back several times during the afternoon, Pike checked on Callie, noting her unresponsiveness, though sleeping at times.

As the rays of the setting sun began to flicker through the trees and send shafts of golden light across his face, Pike circled back to Collin and said, "Let's find some water before we stop."

"How's the girl doing?" the professor asked, face unreadable. "Is she making it?"

"Well, she's pretty weak but I think she's going to get past this, at least past the shoulder wound. She needs time to heal and rest. Food will do her the most good."

Collin perked up. "There's some water up ahead. Look." He pointed to the right.

"You're right. There's a creek. I'll go and tell Irene. Poor kid looks ready to drop. We'll follow you." Pike wheeled his stallion about and came abreast of the wagon. "How are you holding up?"

Irene's tear-stained face stared at Pike as her haunted eyes said everything. Tears flowed once again. Then, she put her hand to her face and sobbed openly, shoulders heaving with her hitching breaths.

Grasping the girl's shoulder, Pike hoped to give her some strength. His voice came out in a whisper as he told her, "We're stopping for the night. Can you take your team over behind Collin's wagon?"

Able to get control of her emotions, Irene tugged the lines to follow Collin. Her weary team dropped their heads when their hooves were finally allowed to stop and didn't move another muscle.

Jumping off Clash's back, Pike clasped Irene's waist to swing her down from her bench - before she toppled over. Then, he set her on a soft patch of grass and told her, "You rest here and I'll be back as soon as I can." Irene settled back quietly onto the grass.

Pike met Effie on the way to Collin's wagon and inquired, "How is Callie?"

"The poor thing is suffering so. Her shoulder and her heart are about to tear her in two but she's holding her own. Don't know how."

"Would you mind fixing them something to eat? They're going to need their strength, especially Callie. She's lost a lot of blood."

Nodding, Effie walked away, her black skirts swishing as the last rays of the sun slid on the horizon.

Peeking in at Callie, Pike did feel some relief to see her sleeping, giving him time to perform his own tasks about the camp. First, he removed a tent from Collin's wagon and started pounding in the stakes. Then, Collin joined him to help finish the job.

Together, the two men carefully carried Callie to the tent and tucked her in for the night and Pike spread a cover over her.

She moaned softly as her hazel eyes fluttered open, locking onto Pike's face and her thin frame visibly shivered.

"Don't give up, Callie," Pike whispered.

The professor said in a quiet tone, "I'm going to help Effie and see to Irene," before he slipped from the tent.

Sitting closer to Callie, Pike's mind drifted to images from the past, images similar to this in Andersonville. This time, though, his patient happened to be a female. Still, months of ministering to the prison's sick and dying guided his voice. "Callie, what a strong girl you are. I know your father is proud of you. He and your brother are looking down from their place by God's side this very night and are sending their love. You've got a lot more years ahead of you. Don't worry about a thing. We're here to take care of you. You have a home with us for as long as you and Irene want."

Several tears dribbled from Callie's grief-riddled eyes but she returned Pike's gaze with a message that was clear. She nodded her head that she understood before she closed her eyes and continued to quiver under the quilt.

Pike felt her forehead and noted heat radiating from her brow. *I hope this doesn't mean she's getting infected.* "Callie, I'm going to go and check on your supper and I'll be right back. Are you thirsty?"

"Yes," she croaked, barely above a whisper.

"Okay," Pike said, as he rose.

The others had gathered around the fire's edge for light and warmth.

"Effie, can I get some food for Callie?"

"I'll get you a plate." She scooped out some rice and gravy, then reached for a couple of leftover biscuits from breakfast. She filled a cup with water.

I hope she's hungrier than I am, Pike told himself on his way back to the tent. While feeding Callie a spoonful of rice, he couldn't help but think, *She's a plucky one.* Quietly, Pike took note of the light freckles dusting the bridge of her nose and even more lightly, sprinkling across her full cheeks. He also noted her sharply chiseled nose and high cheekbones and thought, *Her eyes are hazel but look almost golden.* Strands of her long, brown hair fell in her face which she pushed back with her hand.

Pike pressed her to eat as much food as she could stand.

She swallowed another mouthful of water, then shook her head, resisting more.

Praising her warmly, Pike soothed, "That's fine. You think you can sleep now?"

"Yes," she said weakly.

"Rest, then. Your sister will be here shortly."

When Pike returned to the fire, everyone had finished their supper. Effie had a plate fixed for him on the side. "Thanks, Effie." Even though he didn't have an appetite, he scooped up the plate and doggedly chomped a biscuit.

Irene, with vacant eyes, stared into the crackling fire.

The professor shifted toward Pike. "You think Callie is going to be okay?"

Still chewing the stale bread, Pike nodded his head.

"Would you mind if Effie and I turn in? I think we're all beat."

"I'll watch the girls and make sure they're okay tonight. Get some sleep. If I need you, I'll come and get you."

Collin took Effie by the elbow and led her into the

dark.

"Were you on a trip?" Pike inquired as he shuffled to Irene's side, hoping to draw her out of her stupor.

Her eyes drifted from the fire to gaze at him. They appeared dark and bottomless, like charcoal pools. "Yes, we were on our way back from Joplin. We live not far from here." Her shoulders seemed to relax, and her eyes softened. "Do you have land where you live?"

"Yes, we do. My brothers, family and friends have just moved out to this area and we have quite a bit of land we're going to farm. I'm also starting a sawmill. I'm on my way back from St. Louis from ordering the parts."

Irene's gaze remained steady and, for a moment, she appeared to be well under control. Then, tears clouded her eyes once more. "Why did they have to die? I've lost my mother, and now my brother and father. I've only got Callie left. Why did the Lord see fit to do this to us? Did we somehow deserve it?" She broke into sobs and covered her face with her hands.

How do I comfort someone in this kind of pain? It looked pretty bleak, his lips froze. He took her small form into his arms and drew her to his chest.

After a time, the girl quieted. "Thank you," she mumbled.

Pike continued to hold her and became aware of the warmth they were sharing. The young woman's body felt soft against his. Her dark-brown hair sweetly tickled his cheek. Pike began to feel stirrings within himself and he decided they felt good - too good. His old longing reared its ugly head to snarl at him once again. Rebecca's lovely face floated into his mind. *Damn it!* He shouted in his head. *You've got to get rid of Rebecca, once and for all. Do you hear me?*

The girl shifted in his arms.

Refocusing his thoughts, he realized his response was natural. *Yes, she is pretty and, yes, I feel the need to protect her. That's why I'm feeling this attraction.*

The justification satisfied him for the moment. Then, his mind flitted to a notion that was new to him. Maybe, this girl could be the one he could go on with and God may have brought her across his path for that purpose - only time would tell.

Releasing Irene's small frame, Pike looked at her. "You need to get some rest. It's been a horrible day. One you need to put a close on. Why don't you get yourself into a blanket and sleep?" Pike awkwardly stood up. "Here, let me help you." He guided her up.

"Thank you." She rose gracefully and brushed the clinging grass from her red skirt, then headed for the tent. As Irene flipped back the flap, she turned her head and gave a hint of a smile over her shoulder. "Thank you for your kindness today. We would be dead now if it hadn't been for you. I can't thank you enough." She disappeared into the tent.

Pike felt a full-grown boyish grin slice across his face as pride found its way into his thinking. The stress of the day melted away as he truly felt as though he had been useful and it brought a glow to his heart.

Guess I'd better get to sleep myself, he mused, as he strode back to the fire's glowing remains. Pike stretched his long frame out on his old army blanket - a reminder from his past.

Releasing his mind, it flew where it wanted. Images, past and present, flashed through his brain. Thoughts of the war burst into his memory, bringing with them the grim reality of the brevity of life. He had learned that lesson well as he had watched friend after friend die on the battlefield, or in that stinking hellhole of a prison. It didn't matter where they had died; they all were gone from this earth.

Contemplating the war, his mind lighted on the twisted face of Drisco as a cold fury filled his thoughts. The marks against Drisco were adding up, first Buster, then the prisoners, then Hank, and now other victims. Clenching his fists, Pike sat up, unable to quell the itch that made him want to jump on his horse and seek his revenge. He wanted nothing any more than to catch that miserable renegade and make him suffer. His eyes blazed as he stared out into the night. If only he had shot Drisco instead of the other man. How could he have let him get away so easily?

Gathering himself, he shut his eyes to calm his racing heart. He knew he couldn't walk away from the others who needed him now. Resigned to his fate, he unwillingly plopped back down on the blanket.

After a time, his internal ramblings turned to more glorious moments from his past, especially as he recalled the night Clash had saved his life. Pike had survived a close brush with death and a shiver slipped up his spine now. Pulling out his watch chain, he fingered it with love and gratitude. It spurred his overwhelming desire to live to the fullest each second he had been granted on this earth. *How can I do that? Live life more fully?*

In the silence of the darkness, under the starlit sky, he heard an answer from within himself: *Get on with your life. Find a wife and have some kids.*

Chuckling to himself, he spoke a new prayer. *Okay, Lord, I hear You. I'll do my best to follow the path You have put me on. But, can You provide a woman I can love and have a family with? And, could it be soon? Is it Irene? Hope You can let me in on Your plans. I'd appreciate it.*

Closing his eyes, Pike drifted into slumber. Lucid dreams - pleasant dreams of a home and children - floated into his mind. Pike felt a woman's presence, felt her snuggled to his chest. She looked up and smiled lovingly at him, but he couldn't quite make out her face.

Chapter 23

How much longer? Callie wondered as the interminable bouncing of the wagon jostled her. The morning seemed never-ending and her shoulder throbbed, worsening as the day progressed. At least the sun warmed her body and kept the shivering at bay.

Pike, riding the big stallion, appeared beside the wagon. "Are you ready for a break? We can stop and let your shoulder rest. I know you must be aching pretty badly by now. I know firsthand. I was shot through the leg in the war."

Irritable from the pain, Callie nodded a quick response.

"I'm ready to stop," Irene said over her shoulder. "Just tell us when."

Callie caught the spark in her sister's eye every time the lanky man rode near.

"Fine," Pike responded. "I'll tell the Danvils to find a spot."

Callie continued to lie back in her family's wagon. She struggled valiantly not to moan out loud.

Soon the wagon slowed and stopped on a grassy knoll. Everyone began preparations for their noontime break. Gripping her throbbing arm, Callie slowly eased out of the wagon and found a place, away from the activity, to sit on the grass.

As Irene drew near with a plate of leftovers, Callie shook her head and looked away. Her stomach still felt too queasy from the haunting pain.

"Callie," Irene said, pleading. "You need to eat something. It's the only way to keep up your strength."

"Could I have some water?" she asked as she continued to stare at the ground. She was in no mood to hassle with her sister and she hoped, by giving her something to do, she might leave her alone.

"Sure, I'll fetch you some. Please, try to eat this." Irene set the plate next to Callie.

Pike sauntered across the grass to sit beside Callie as she grumpily noted his concerned expression.

"Is the pain bad?" he inquired. "I know it must be. I almost died when I got shot. I had to ride a train in the cold for three days when it happened. Never knew a person could hurt that much."

Callie wished everyone would leave her alone but that didn't appear it would happen. Even though she didn't feel like responding, she thought she should at least look at the man while he talked. It was only polite.

"My brother took the best care of me he could," Pike continued, "but we were prisoners of war and we got little food or water. I lost a lot of blood. I could barely hold my head up most of those three days. I must have been unconscious a good part of it. I don't remember much. When we got to Georgia, I was doing a little better. Since then, I've healed up pretty well. I'm almost good as new.

"I'm telling you this so you can know how much I can relate to your struggles. I really feel for you. I want you to keep in mind that you can make it through all this and be just fine later. You'll mend sooner than you think." Pike reached out a warm hand and placed it on her shoulder. "Now, you need to eat, then take a nap. We can wait here for a while. It's only a couple more hours to get to my home. We've got plenty of time. So, we can wait until you are hurting less."

As his emerald eyes bored into hers with a touching compassion, Callie felt compelled to answer. "Thank you. I'm feeling better now. Can you hand me that biscuit? Maybe I'll feel better when I can shut my eyes for a while." She nibbled at the dry food as Pike rose and walked away.

*

As Pike crested the last hill that afforded him a glimpse of the Neosho, he luxuriated in the sight and the joy at being so close to home. He remembered the first day he had arrived on this point with his group in tow. It brought back blessed memories.

Pike shifted in the saddle. The humidity, accentuated by the unusual lack of breeze, felt clammy against his skin. The cool water, not far away, looked enticing.

"This must be the place," Collin's jolly voice boomed as he pulled his team to a halt next to Clash.

"You got that right. We're here." Pike lifted his arm to point at the grassland. "This is where my land starts. I don't have a cabin built yet but that's the first thing I'm going to do when I can. We'll need to start on one for you and Effie first. Maybe this afternoon we can locate your land and a spot to put your home. How does that sound?"

"I can't wait. This is a magnificent-looking countryside. Looks ripe for the plow. I've always wanted to try my hand at farming. I hope we'll like it."

"You may want to work at the sawmill," Pike stated in a friendly way. "That may be more to your liking. I know I'll have a lot of work there. But for now, we need to get moving and get Callie settled. She's hanging on by sheer determination right now." As Pike decided to give Clash his head and take the last bit of road at a gallop, he shouted, "I'm going to go ahead and let everyone know we're here. Come to the first cabin. You can't miss it."

The last bit of his journey exploded past him as the wind whistled in his ears. The stallion beneath him churned with his ears pinned against his head. The pair soon slid to an athletic stop outside Buster's new cabin. As Pike vaulted to the ground, the door burst open and Lyric bolted out.

Buster trotted out of the new barn with a twisted grin on his scarred face. "I's worry about you's," he bellowed. "It's took you awhile to come back. We's scared you's got hurt or worse."

"You're right about that," Lyric added with her trilling voice. "Did something happen?"

Pike couldn't repress a smile. "I ran into an old friend of ours in St. Louis, Buster. Can you believe it? I bumped into Professor Danvil at the hotel. He's married. They followed me here. They're coming behind me." Pike turned his head in the direction of the wagon that had just burst into view.

Shocked, Buster's face gaped at the distant vision.

Lyric, quick as ever, added, "I see two wagons, Pike. Did you pick up someone else?"

Pike's smile disappeared.

"Is something wrong?" she prodded.

"I saved a couple of young ladies from some outlaws on the trail. The men laid their father and brother out before I got there. One of the girls is shot through the shoulder. She needs rest and tending to. Would you mind if they stay here?"

"Why, Pike, you know that would be fine. The poor dears. I hope they're going to be okay. Luckily, we've gotten our bed since you were gone. That raft has really helped us get our supplies. You'll be surprised by what we've gotten accomplished." Lyric shaded her eyes with a hand and watched the approaching wagons.

Deciding it was best to let everyone know about Drisco being in the area, Pike said, "Buster, you need to hear this, too. Drisco and a band of traitors were responsible for the ambush on the girl's family."

Buster's mouth turned down and a cross between fear and anger rose in his eyes.

"I couldn't believe it when I saw him again," Pike rambled on. "But he's in the area now, I'm sure of it. We all must be ever-vigilant. He may get another one of us. It's too late to chase him now. Don't know what else to do except stay on our toes. Maybe I'll tell Sheriff Edwards. He'll need to know Drisco's in the area."

*

In late July, sweat soaked Pike's shirt and made it stick to his straining back muscles. The sweltering summer heat had already begun accumulating by late morning. The dry ground was starting to crack.

Pike's eyes rested on the log he now smoothed with

his broad-axe. It was his job to square it so it would fit snugly with the others that formed his outer cabin walls.

Pike and Frank worked alone. All the others were performing tasks at their own places. There was so much to do and no one had much free time. *Oh, well,* Pike told himself, *I've been enjoying the time alone with Frank. We don't get this opportunity very often.* He swung his axe one last time to chink off the last piece of wood.

Glancing up, Pike spotted a figure moving in his direction. Irritation slipped up on him faster than a coonhound on a scent trail as Irene's form came into view. *That girl has pestered me till I can't stand her. I know she liked me by the way she moons over me. I know I saved her and all, but she rambles on so when she talks. It's never anything that's interesting. I sure would like her to find someone else to latch onto.* To Frank, Pike said gruffly, "Here comes Irene. She's got lunch, looks like, anyway."

"I'm glad for a break," Frank sighed. "I think I'll go and unhitch the team. They need a break, too. I don't think we'll need 'em this afternoon. I'm so hot I can't think about food yet. I might run and jump in the river. Cool off."

"Okay, little brother," Pike said as he grumbled and turned back to the approaching form of Irene. *I've got to put an end to this school-girl crush. Got to do something, but not hurt her too badly at the same time.*

Irene's face proudly displayed a sappy grin as she closed in on her prey.

Pike politely waved and waited, mulling over what to do.

"Are you hungry?"

"I'm too hot to eat, thank you. If you will set it over there, I'll eat it later when I've had time to cool off."

Irene gloated. "I put some of your favorite peach cobbler in there. That should tempt you." She set the two pails in the shade and looked up expectantly at Pike.

Pike hoped that, if he didn't talk to her, she would go away and he could rest in peace.

Irene strode to a large hunk of wood that he had stripped and sat down. Tucking her skirts in around her ankles, she started talking. "So, are you looking forward to the wedding this evening?"

Pressing his lips together, Pike kept silent. He gazed over a log as though he were busy.

She tried again. "Are you? It should be so much fun. Dancing and music and, of course, getting to see Eric and Rena tie the knot. Do you ever think about getting married?" Her innocent-looking eyes stayed on Pike's sweaty face.

Giving in with a small sigh, Pike found a grassy spot under a sweet gum tree and sat down. He allowed his eyes to follow a fast-flying kestrel. Its black head and steady eye locked onto a bird and quickly captured the sparrow. When the bird disappeared into the next stand of trees, Pike realized how much he felt like prey himself. "Yes, I am. I know that Eric and Rena are ready to get married. It took a while for Eric to accept Rena but they should be happy together." The second those words were out he wished he could retract them. *Now, I've gone and done it. She'll never give up now.*

The glow in her eyes reflected sustenance for her cause. "Will you dance with me tonight? I sure would like that."

Ignoring her, Pike looked away, hoping she would take the hint. From the corner of his eye, he could see her eyes still boring into him and forcing him to respond. "I'll have to play music for everyone else. I don't get the chance to dance, sorry."

A flash of annoyance flew into Irene's face.

Pike gave her what he hoped was a consoling substitute. "Frank would love to dance with you. He's light on his feet." He changed the subject - fast. "How is your sister today? It's been almost a month now."

"She's doing better," Irene sniffed. "I sure wish you'd dance with me. It would mean so much to me. I really like you, Pike. I want to be with you more than what I have been."

Taken back by her forwardness, he was shocked into silence. His mind whirled about for a response. *How in the world do I get out of this one? I should put an end to this foolishness, once and for all.* He gazed across the clearing.

Frank came plodding toward them.

Relieved, Pike escaped from answering her. "Hurry up," he yelled. "Lunch is getting cold."

"I guess I'll be going," Irene grumbled, her mouth pouting.

Nodding, Pike rose to help her off the log. Putting a hand on her elbow, he said, "Thank you for the lunch, Irene. I'll see you tonight at Eric's cabin. It should be a good spread and a lot of fun. Everyone will be there. Half the town, I hear. They're making quite a bit of money from the raft we built. Billy, the boy who runs the raft, seems to be doing a good job. He's about your age, should be there tonight. Maybe he'll dance with you. I'll see you later." Pike turned to Frank, who had settled by one of the pails and had already plucked out its contents.

"Thanks for the lunch, Irene," Frank said, as she stiffly turned and stomped off. He looked at Pike. "Something wrong with her?"

"It may have been something I said," Pike responded around his first mouthful. "She seems to have a crush on me. I don't feel the same way, that's all."

"She's a nice girl, talks a lot. Don't know her well, but maybe you should give her a chance. She might grow on you."

Pike reached out and punched Frank hard on the arm. "Thanks for the sage advice, *little brother*. Why don't you take up with her?"

"Well, I just might. You'd better watch out. I may snatch her from you."

"Please do, I could only be so lucky."

*

The music floated through the gusty evening air as Pike played a song at the end of the wedding. The constant breeze kept the humidity from resting too heavily on him and the merry crowd. As soon as the nuptials for Eric and Rena ended, the boisterous group was ready to start the feast.

Scattered about under the shade trees, well-stocked plank tables sat ready and waiting. The townsfolk had done themselves proud to bring so much food; no one would go hungry this night.

Amos placed his newly-made, wrought-iron pot rack next to the other presents as he got in line to fill his plate.

While Pike observed his brother and the others, he enjoyed watching Rena run her hand appreciatively over the iron rack. It brought back thoughts of his parents and the letter he had posted to them in St. Louis.

Dear Mom and Dad,

I wanted to let you know that we have made our way to our new home in the Indian Territory. This land is so different from what we are used to. The wind never ceases. It blows sometimes more like a gale. There are plenty of trees for my new sawmill. I am in St Louis now, ordering my parts for it. They should be sent to Joplin in another sixty days.

We have plenty of land and are proud lessees. I should tell you our group has grown since we left. We picked up a young lady on the train ride who had her money stolen. She has since married Buster. Can you believe it? He's married and happy, now, I'm glad to report.

We also found another man in St. Louis named Eric. He is experienced in the logging business. He's tough and large, so he's quite an asset to this endeavor. He has taken a shine to Rena. I think wedding bells are in the air.

A town sits just across the river from where we have settled and we can get mail there.

We have quite a few new neighbors and have come through our journey healthy and strong. Please don't worry about us because we are all fine. Your grandchildren are growing and Hannah is crawling. Rebecca is pregnant again. The new baby is due in January.

Frank has been working hard and sends his love. Amos is going to start preaching at the church in the town of Miami, across the river, as soon as we can get everything finished on the land. I hope you are pleased to know he will be continuing God's work here. He should make a great preacher, just like you, dad. I sure miss your sermons, and, Mom, I miss those great meals. But, mostly, I just miss you both. Maybe you can come out in the spring and visit. Hope this letter finds you well.

I will write again soon, and I send you these thoughts from our Lord:

"But, I trust in your unfailing love;
My heart rejoices in your salvation.
I will sing to the Lord,
For He has been good to me." Psalms 14

I love you both. Please write and tell us what is happening at home.
Your loving son,
Pike

*

Playing his faithful guitar, Pike watched the couples fly about through the night. He glanced over his shoulder at Pumpkin, furiously working the bowstrings on his fiddle. Pumpkin's whiskered face and blood-shot eyes moved up and down to the current song, "The Virginia Reel." All available adults whirled and swayed to the lively tune. The stuffy air hadn't stopped anyone from participating in this night of celebration.

Pike couldn't stop his eyes from wandering through the couples until he had located Rebecca's happy face. He loved to watch her dance but a familiar wave of guilt crept over him. He had never apologized to her for his unkind words because he had never felt the time was right. After returning from St. Louis, he had avoided her as much as possible and she seemed to be doing the same.

Tonight, though, the strains of Pike's longing slipped out of his carefully locked box. The pain of loss speared his soul and he hoped no one would notice his eyes as they trailed Rebecca and Amos, laughing and dancing together.

Amos seemed more lively than ever, and with the detection of the first swelling of Rebecca's abdomen, the pregnancy could not be denied. A resplendent light shown in her eyes.

All these thoughts thrust Pike into the hand of melancholy. *I know I should be happy this evening - but, I'm not. I've got to get over this. Need to latch onto the nearest girl and run off and get married. I'd be a lot happier with someone to share my life with and my bed. I want children that I can call my own. If I had a few, maybe I could get focused on something other than Rebecca and Patrick.*

Pike continued to finger his guitar's stings without needing to think about how to play. *I need a plan. Should get out there and pick a new bride. Men do it all the time. I don't have to love someone to get married. It's about having comfort and a family. It's the only way the Lord is going to condone my being with a woman in an intimate way. I sure would like that, too.*

Pumpkin bent over Pike as the song ended and declared, "How about a break? I could sure use a glorious old drink." Though sober to this point, Pumpkin fished a flask out of his shirt pocket, gave a devilish chuckle and winked at Pike. "How about a nip for what ails you? You look like somethin' our cat drags in from the barn - wet and limp." He took one long swig and then pressed the flask to Pike's chest.

Pike willingly reached out and took the offered bottle. Although it was out of character for him, his low morale dictated his actions. He imbibed a small mouthful and forced it down his throat and then he coughed from the burn of the raw alcohol.

As the night waned, and people began to wander off into the dark to locate their beds and wagons, Pumpkin and Pike found themselves besotted. Since Pike had never been a drinker, he became drunk quickly. Swaying unsteadily on his feet, he struggled to get his thick, stubborn fingers to strum the strings.

Only the last of the couples and the single men were left as they passed around a bottle and their raucous laughter and noisy conversations were being emitted from the perimeter of the low-burning fires.

Darn these hands and eyes, Pike fussed while his body felt numb and his knees wanted to buckle. Just as he was about to topple over, a pair of feminine arms wrapped themselves about his waist and clutched him close.

"Oh, Pike, here," the familiar voice said. "Let me help you."

Pike bent his head toward the lady and squinted into the most beautiful eyes he had ever seen - Irene's. His words slurred as he spoke, "We-l-l-ll . . . just the wo-o-o-man I wa-a-nted to see. You look so-o-o pretty tonight, Irene. You're ju-u-ust the prett-i-i-iest thing I ever saw."

"Come on now," she soothed as she struggled to guide his tall form forward into the darkness. "That's it. Take another step."

Leaning against her, Pike inched his way in the direction she tugged. Where they were going, he wasn't sure. Not that he cared. He just hung on.

She guided his movements to an old oak tree. "Here, sit down," she commanded. "That's it." She sat, too, and pulled him to lean against her.

Pike's befuddled brain raced wildly. He was consumed by boldness and daring with the prettiest girl in the world. "You're s-s-such a pretty thing. Why-y-y don't you give me a ki-i-i-ss." Clasping Irene by the arm, he yanked her to him and planted his lips onto hers. Pike smacked her soundly and arousal urged within him to voraciously meld his lips with her pliant, accepting mouth.

Irene slipped her delicate arms about Pike's neck and pressed against his chest.

Happy to oblige, Pike squeezed her lithe body to his and let his hands roam up and down her back. He clumsily worked at the row of buttons on the back of her dress. His fumbling fingers ripped one off. "Damn!" he cursed quietly as the button fell and his hands went back to tearing at the other buttons with a new vengeance.

Suddenly, his head began to whirl and he blinked his eyes to try to focus but the cold rush coursing through his bloodstream forced his hands to drop before he lurched forward as everything went black.

*

"Damn!" Irene screeched, as she realized her plan

had now been thwarted. Nothing was going to come of all those sweet kisses. She gently pushed Pike off her and let his body drop to the ground. "Why'd you have to pass out, Pike, just when things were getting started? I thought for sure I had you this time. We'd make love and then you'd have to marry me. Now what will I do?" She sat up with her hands around her knees and set her mind on figuring out an alternate plan.

Suddenly, she began to smile. She quickly pulled his shirt out of his trousers and unbuttoned them, and while undoing the pants, she smiled maliciously. Standing, she gave the scene one last look of appraisal. Satisfied, she crept away and left Pike to sleep off his stupor.

Traveling back to her tent, she muttered to herself, "When Pike wakes up and finds himself partially dressed, he'll have to believe me when I tell him we made love. He'll just have to. I know he'll marry me then." A self-satisfied chuckle slipped out of her mouth as she drew back the tent flap and dropped it behind her.

Callie roused from her deep sleep and asked in a groggy voice, "How was it?"

"It was just grand!" Irene crooned.

Chapter 24

The warm morning breeze was the first thing Pike became aware of, just before his eyes forced themselves open. Instantly, he squinted at the intense morning light while his head felt as though a mule had kicked him. *Man! What happened to me?* Struggling, he began the monumental task of trying to sit upright in the grass. His mouth tasted as though he had eaten horse manure the night before. Now, sitting up, his head throbbed while his stomach protested violently and he leaned over to retch.

Shakily, he swiped his stubble-encrusted chin. *So, this is what a hangover is like.* His pounding head forced him to lean his head back against the tree trunk and shut his eyes to block out the hateful light. He fumed at himself for being so stupid. "I won't ever do that again!"

Wondering what time it was, he thought, *Sure could use a drink of water.* Again, he opened his eyes and gazed down at himself, noting he was partially undressed. Appalled, his fingers fumbled at tucking in his shirt and buttoning his pants.

"So, dear, how are you this morning?" Irene's overly-pleasant voice grated.

The vibrations of the voice renewed fresh waves of pain, pounding against his skull. He placed his hand on his forehead. "Ooow."

"Tsk, tsk," Irene clucked, as she sidled over to Pike's side. "When I got up this morning, I couldn't find you in the field. I am surprised to find you still here. I was almost bursting when I awoke, wanting to see you again. After last night, I need to share more moments with you like the ones we had under this tree. I know now that you love me."

Panic prickled through Pike at Irene's words. "What are you talking about? What happened last night? I'm afraid I don't remember it well, hope I wasn't too forward." Through his smarting eyes, he searched her face for answers.

She beamed proudly, like a lioness dragging up a zebra for her mate. "Well, Pike, I should be offended that you don't remember all those lovely kisses last night, and so much more." Suddenly, she grabbed his hand and rubbed it against her rosy cheek.

The gesture hit home. It was the same way Rebecca used to touch him in order to soften him a bit. Rifling through his alcohol-riddled memory banks, he strained to figure out just what *had* happened last night. *I guess I do remember kissing her.*

"What else happened, Irene?"

"Well, Pike . . . we made love last night. We took our clothes off and touched each other everywhere. You were so sweet to me. It was the most special night of my life. I'm a woman now." She smiled at him. "When are we getting married?"

Pike pushed her hand away. "Uh-uh... well, uh." He shook his head to clear his vision and caused a new shower of pain to course through his skull and his stomach threatened once more. *I know I've been melancholy about not having someone in my life, but I sure wish I could remember what we did.* If he had used this girl, then he regretted his actions, but he just wasn't sure that it had taken place.

Clutching his stomach, Pike wanted to hide from this day and curl up somewhere to sleep. But, with Irene sitting next to him, he couldn't ignore the situation. "Irene, I don't know what to tell you. I want to apologize for my actions last night, if they were out of line. It was not my intention to strip you of your clothes and your virginity. I can't apologize enough for what I've done to you."

"Oh, Pike, how can you say those things to me - the

woman you love? I'm offended. We shared the most special night of my life and you want to ruin it with 'I'm sorry'? I can't believe you just said that to me." Her face puckered, promising a show of tears. She sniffed loudly. "I love you. I could be carrying your child. I thought you loved me, too!" She choked those words out as the sobbing began.

I'm terrible! The notion urged Pike to fix things. He reached out and put his arms around her shoulders and pulled her to his chest, then, said softly into her hair, "I'm sorry. I didn't mean to hurt you. You are a special girl and I do mean to marry you. We'll get married soon. I don't want you to worry about being pregnant. Everything will be okay. I promise. Now, will you stop crying?"

She nestled in his arms, her sobs still shaking her body.

Why did I say I'd marry her? Maybe he liked her more than he thought. Pike knew he couldn't have her pregnant with his child and be unmarried. He looked at her pretty face and thought he could do worse, and maybe she would grow on him. *Be a man and do the right thing. She's just what you've been looking for. So, go on and get married. There's nothing else you can do about what has happened already. Now smile, and act like you mean it.*

"Irene, will you be my wife?"

The tears dried up instantly. Her voice came out remarkably strong. "Oh, yes, I will be your wife. Nothing would make me happier." She threw her arms around his neck and placed her lips on his foul-smelling mouth to smack him loudly. She leaned back and gazed up with hunger etched in her eyes, looking as though she owned the world.

Pike could not find the energy to return her excitement. Instead, he suggested, "Let's go and find something to eat." He hoped against hope that he would feel better after he put something in his churning stomach. His world looked bleak at the moment.

Jumping up, Irene dragged Pike by his hand and hauled him to his unsteady feet. She kept a tight hold as they ambled to the fires where the ladies were hard at work fixing breakfast for the many wedding guests that had camped out the night before. The coffeepots were making the rounds.

Maude and Benny sat at a table with Sheriff Edwards and his wife. The sheriff's children and Patrick raced up and down the aisles between the tables. Candy yapped at their heels. Callie rested by the fire in a chair and sipped her morning brew.

Pike scouted the crowd. Luckily, Frank was nowhere to be seen. Embarrassed over his betrothal, he didn't know how to broach the subject, especially with his brother, who deep-down knew Pike didn't love Irene.

Hearing the voices of happy children lifted Pike's troubled heart a trifle. He tried not to focus on the fact that he would soon be forced to announce his engagement.

*

Rebecca, scrambling a huge skillet of eggs, looked up in time to see Pike and Irene approaching. They were holding hands! A premonition rocked her back and forced a clipped smile as they passed. She boomed, "Why, Pike, I see you and Irene have gotten close. Does this mean something? Hmmm? Do you have something to tell us?" She averted her eyes, not able to gaze at him any longer as she scrambled her eggs with a vengeance.

Everyone in the vicinity suddenly got quiet.

Pike appeared sheepish, seemingly reluctant to speak. He weakly managed to stammer, "Uh, yes, I guess I do have something to say. Irene and I are getting married. I don't know when exactly, but pretty soon, I guess." Lifting his head a bit higher, he faced the crowd of well-wishers with his best smile.

Everyone shouted their congratulations, and some slapped him on the back. "We're so happy for you."

Rebecca saw Maude move next to Pike.

"Let God be with you all of your married days," Maude said laying a gentle hand on his shoulder. "His hand will guide you and show you both how to make each other happy. I hope I will be there for your children's births. You are marrying a fine lady. Be happy - you deserve it."

Pike hugged Maude in response,

Rebecca fumed. *She is a young girl, or hadn't you noticed, Mr. Pike Wheeling. I can't believe you are doing this!* As she poured the eggs into the skillet, she wondered, *Why in the world should I care what he does?*

*

Several weeks later, Pike, Frank, Buster, and the Professor slaved away in the blistering sun as they formed the newest cabin. This one would be Frank's home and it was being built close to Pike's, which now housed Irene and Callie, while Pike's cabin was also getting a room addition for Callie.

Amos and Eric spent the day digging springhouses for each family to store the food they would harvest from the garden. The women continued to keep hard at work picking, cleaning, canning and cooking food from the bounteous garden.

Pike's stomach growled as he shaped logs for the room addition onto his cabin. Although the smell of the wood provided some comfort and the work provided some diversion, Pike could not escape the knowledge that his wedding was rapidly approaching - just two weeks away.

During the past weeks, since his engagement, Pike vacillated between being ready to start the next chapter in his life and a deep-seated fear that he was about to do something horribly wrong. Damn his conscience! Why couldn't he be excited about finally getting what he had been asking God for all this time? He wanted to feel happy, but he didn't.

Pike straightened up and stopped his task. *What was I thinking, getting involved with a girl like Irene? She's not what I call 'mature'. She gets mad at the drop of a hat. All I did was jokingly call her a 'bit of fluff', since she's so short. She only comes up to my chest, for crying out loud. I thought she would think that was cute. Boy, was I wrong. She let me have it with that sharp-edged tongue of hers. Wields it like a spear. Maybe she's just nervous. I know I've been on edge lately. I've been short with everyone.* He shook his head. *This marriage will never be like the one I'd have had with Rebecca.*

Remorse for getting talked into this marriage never strayed far from his thoughts for long. *Should I talk to Frank about this? He knows I don't like Irene that much. No, guess that wouldn't be a good idea. If Irene found out about how I felt, there would be hell to pay. I'll keep my doubts to myself. What else can I do?*

Frowning at the ground, Pike rested on the prickly bark of the oak log he had been shaping. He set his axe on the ground. *Things could be a whole lot worse,* he chided himself. *I have a chance at a new life, one that I came close to losing in a blizzard not so long ago. Remember that? I can't let time get away from me. It's too precious and short. God only gives us a brief visit to this world. I need to utilize it to the fullest. Why shouldn't I have a wife and kids? Why shouldn't I grab that chance? I must appreciate the fact that the Lord decided to give me a wife and a second chance. My life is only what I make of it. So, I've got to make this work and enjoy it. You hear me talking to you, boy?* Momentarily, the regret for his actions subsided and relief took over in its place. Or was it resignation? He wasn't sure.

To take his mind off the problem, he thought about Hank and wondered if he would ever see him again. He wondered if Drisco was still out there and still alive. Looking up to scan the property, Pike spied two ladies in the far distance. They carried lunch pails in his direction.

"Fellas," Pike bellowed as he stood up, "it's lunch time."

"Whew, it's hot out here," Frank huffed, as he swiped his dripping brow with a piece of cloth.

*

Callie decided to help Irene bring the lunch to the men. Almost fully healed, she had gotten involved in the day-to-day activities to help in any way she could. Her natural aversion to cooking and sewing didn't seem to be a problem. She more than made up for it in other ways, like cleaning dishes and working in the garden. She also spent many an hour hunting an abundance of game to keep fresh meat on the menu.

While strolling with her sister, a conflict raged in her mind over the marriage between Irene and Pike. On the one hand, she felt happy for her sister, but, on the other, something unpleasant nagged at her. She couldn't put her finger on it.

Since the day that Pike had rescued them, Callie had developed a deep affection for him; not only had he saved her life, but he had so many attractive qualities that impacted her on many levels. If the truth be known, she adored him. Pike never failed to make her laugh and feel light-hearted. With eagerness, she looked forward to each morning as they shared a cup of coffee and discussed the day's schedule.

In the evenings, Pike would tell her many exciting stories from his past. He talked about the war and the battles he had fought in. Sometimes Callie imagined herself fighting in the war; an idea that intrigued her.

Callie loved Pike's stallion, Clash. When she had time, she would take him a carrot or a piece of bread. Now, when Clash spotted her, he would trot forward and snuffle against her chest and hands and look for the treat she hid behind her back or in her pocket. She hoped that, someday, Pike would let her ride that magnificent animal.

As she walked along with Irene, a sadness came over her to think about how much she liked doing the things that men did. Her mother would have been disappointed in how she had turned out. *I'm a failure as a woman,* she thought.

"I can't wait to put on my wedding dress," Irene said enthusiastically, yanking Callie out of her internal musings. "Rena's about got it finished. It's so pretty with all its pink and white lace. I'm going to look so good. Pike's eyes are going to pop out of his head, I just know it. What do you think we'll get for presents?" Not getting a response, Irene said with a caustic edge, "Callie? Are you listening?"

"What?" Callie stuttered. "Did you say something? I'm sorry. Say it again. I'll listen this time."

Irene sniffed and spoke with a stiff back. "I asked what kind of presents you think Pike and I'll get."

"Oh, well, let me think, maybe you'll get a coffee grinder. You know how Pike loves his coffee."

"Hmmm, I'm hoping for some fine plates and tea-cups. Wouldn't they be pretty sitting on a fine china cabinet?"

"Well, yes," Callie said, as she tried to follow along with Irene's way of thinking but found it difficult. "Don't you think that would be a bit impractical?"

"Why, Callie? Why don't you think I deserve something as nice as a few pretty china plates? Don't you think Pike would want to give me everything I want? He should. He's going to be my husband."

"I guess so," Callie replied in what she hoped sounded like an agreeable tone. She didn't want to fuss, but all the while, she thought, *I wonder if Pike knows what he's getting into? My sister is a bit spoiled and she is going to expect so much. She wants pretty things that will keep her happy for a little while. It won't last long. Then, she'll want something else. I'm glad it will be his chore, not mine.*

Thinking about Pike dredged up her constant ache inside over her feelings for him, but she couldn't stop herself. His grinning, freckled face, those long legs, and his guitar playing - pleasant images frolicked across her mind and made her smile at the winning grin he gave her inside her head. The notion of stealing a kiss from that stubbly, oh-so-masculine face thrilled her senses. But, quickly, she realized the futility of such thinking and scolded herself. *Callie, you can't be in love with your sister's husband! You've got to stop thinking about him.*

As they crested the last small hill that sloped down to the workers, Callie spotted Pike's flaming hair, shining in the sun. Her eyes lingered on him as she headed straight to his side with a bucket. Smiling at his sunburned, peeling face, she let her feelings of love flow silently. *At least, no one knows what I am thinking.*

*

The day before his nuptials, Pike burst through the open door of the Pettit's shop and stopped to let his eyes adjust to the dim light. "Is anybody here?"

"Come on in," Stoney clamored over a mix of other voices. "We're back here."

Pike glanced at the stacks of dry goods and fingered a few tools as he ambled along the center aisle. The trip across the river had been a welcome diversion to help take his mind off his wedding. He screwed his face up in a mask of happiness to appear calm and lighthearted as he exchanged greetings with the familiar faces clustered near an open window in the back. Pike waved congenially at Maude and her mother, Ivy, and nodded to Sheriff Edwards.

The local pig farmer, Bob Nickols, rested in a chair with his muddy boots propped on a sack of beans. A fly buzzed lazily around his bald head. The odor emanating from his unkempt form was unmistakable.

"You're just the man I need to see," Pike announced to Bob.

Bob swatted at the fly several times. "Pike, you must be wantin' some of my fine hogs. I've got several litters."

Pike struggled to appear as though he didn't smell the offensive odor. "You're right; I'm needing a half-grown hog so we can roast it for the wedding. I also need a couple of small ones to rear up and slaughter this winter."

"I've got just what you need. Got several, in fact. When do you want to come and get 'em?"

"I brought the wagon and a couple of crates. I'll come by your house before I go back to my place. Is that okay with you?"

"Sure 'nuff. I'll skedaddle on home and round up four hogs and get 'em in a pen. I'll be a-waitin' on you. I'm looking forward to seeing you get hitched. I'll bring my missus, if that's okay?"

Pike worked at a smile to hide his gloom. "I'll be glad for your family to come, bring your son."

Shuffling from his seat, Bob told the group, "We'll see the rest of you about sundown tomorrow night. Hopefully, this heat will break soon."

"It feels like it's going to rain," Dora interjected. "I can smell it in the air." As Bob walked away, she turned to Pike. "Pike, how is everyone? How is Rena doing with Eric? Still happy?" Rena had become one of Dora's best friends. Sometimes, they got together and quilted in the mornings, visiting for hours. Collin's wife Effie joined them when she could.

"Are any of the ladies with child?" Maude inquired politely.

"Rena told us today at breakfast that she's expecting. I guess it's due in April or May."

"Oh, that's just wonderful," Dora gushed. "I can't wait to see her. I'll fuss at her good because she hasn't told me. What about Lyric?"

"No, she hasn't said anything about expecting. I know Buster wants a child right away. Lord willing, it will happen for them soon. You can keep them in your prayers."

"Speaking of prayers," Stoney butted in, "when is that brother of yours gonna start putting on a local Sunday service? I've had a couple of boys cleanin' up and repairin' the old church. It's ready. We sure would appreciate it if he'd get us started again. Maybe we can even have Sunday school and some church gatherings. That would be a blessing for everyone here. Think you could play for us?"

"Sure, that's fine with me. If Pumpkin isn't laid up with a hangover, he can help me at the service. But, we won't count on him. I'll discuss it with Amos. He should be about ready. Maybe we can have it this Sunday?"

"Won't you be on your honeymoon?" Stoney asked with a lifted eyebrow. "You'll want a couple of days with your new bride alone. You goin' somewhere?"

"No," Pike replied, with a heavy voice. "We're staying put, so we'll be able to come on Sunday. Let me talk to Amos. How does ten in the morning sound to get it underway? We need a good church service. I've missed not having one, since my dad is a minister. We never missed going to church when I was growing up. We all need time with the Lord."

"I'm so looking forward to having a church again," Maude announced to the group. "Aren't you, Ma?"

"Why, yes," Ivy replied. "I've missed getting to sing and be with everyone. We all need time to worship, feeds the soul."

"I forgot to ask you, Sheriff," Pike said. "Have you

ever heard if those hoodlums Drisco and Rufus have been jailed anywhere?"

Shaking his head, Lincoln said, "I've still got those wanted posters, but I've not heard about them being captured. By the way, the kids in town are going to need schooling in a couple of months, when the crops are in. Do you think the professor would mind doing some of the teaching? I know my kids need their three R's. I don't want them to grow up ignorant. We can start collecting money at church to buy some books and supplies for them. Maybe we can raise enough money from the town to pay him as a teacher. We've got to do something or I'm going to have to send my kids to one of the missions. I'd rather they stay home. I need to keep an eye on my oldest boy Pete. I have to watch him all the time. He needs something to keep him busy and out of trouble."

Encouraged by the sheriff's request, Pike replied, "You're right, Lincoln. The kids need schooling and the professor is just the man for the job. There's nothing he can't teach. I've been working with him these last couple of months. He's a close friend and a great person, but he's not much of a laborer. Bless him, he tries hard, but it's just not something that he'll ever excel at. He may get by as a farmer, but he's going to need an extra source of income."

"Okay," Stoney added, eyes twinkling, "sounds like we've got a lot to work toward. See what Amos says, and we'll go from there. Sure you don't want to wait a week? Take a little time with your love?" Stoney blazed him a knowing smile.

Pike caught his meaning and deflected it. "No, like I said, I'm ready to get a church service started again. This Sunday is as good as any."

"You're right about that in one way," Stoney grinned devilishly. "You may be busy going after your sawmill parts next week, since my supplier sent word they've arrived."

"You mean to tell me, I've been here all this time and you just now thought to tell me? Some friend you are!" Pike screwed up his mouth, attempting to appear mad but he failed. The new information sent a thrill of energy through him. He wanted to scamper out of the store, hightail it home, gather up the boys, and race to Joplin. He knew that wouldn't be the right thing to do, but the urge was there just the same. Instead, he decided he had better get back to business. "I need to get a few things before I go. I need to see about getting that sickle mower, too."

"Sure," Stoney said. "What else do you need?"

"I need some of that wonderful local molasses and I need to pick out something for a wedding present. I've already gotten our beds. Eric has made me some of the other things we need but what would a new bride like?" Pike gazed at Dora and hoped she might get in on this little project.

She hopped from her seat. "I've got a couple of items. I've got a mirror and brush set. All ladies want that. I've got fancy combs for her hair. I've also got a set of lace curtains. She might like this drying rack to put her herbs on. Any of those sound like what you had in mind?"

Pike thought they all sounded like good gifts. After mulling it over, he replied, "Well, they all could work. I'll take the comb set and a tea kettle. She should like that, don't you think?"

"Oh, yes, Pike" Maude praised. "All brides need a kettle. I'm bringing her a set of sheets my mom and I made."

"I'll bring her the hair combs," Dora added.

Pike grinned. "Thanks, everyone. She'll be happy. We'll see you tomorrow. I need to get on back and discuss all of this with everyone. I also need to get to Joplin as soon as I can and get my parts hauled back here."

"Don't forget them hogs," Stoney hollered as Pike rushed out the front door of the store.

"I won't."

Chapter 25

Standing next to Irene during Pike's wedding cere-mony, Callie grappled with her feelings. As much as she had tried to accept Pike and Irene becoming man and wife over these last several weeks, to this point she had been unsuccessful. Her longing to be the one with Pike haunted her thoughts and her heart.

Tuning out Amos's biblical words, Callie tried to reason with herself. *I know how much I have come to love and respect Pike. I have to keep in mind that he is now married. Nothing will change. He will still be my best friend. I can still talk and hunt with him, do chores with him, even ride the horses with him. It will be the same as always.*

The recent memory of Pike allowing Callie to ride Clash pushed into her consciousness. What a thrill that had been. Never was there a finer horse put on this earth. They had streaked across the countryside with Pike mounted on Raven, next to her. Never in her life had she felt so free. Never in her life had she been so in tune with another human being.

Those precious moments provided Callie with a memory to always treasure. For the first time, she had shared intimacy with a man. It was different than her worship of her father. She didn't understand the feeling she had experienced for Pike as she raced with Clash across the valley but she knew deep in the recesses of her heart that the moment was special. The new feelings it aroused made her long for more.

Amos's voice seeped through her ponderings.

Remembering that she was standing beside her sister, Callie groaned inwardly and labored to stand tall. The sinking feeling she had carried around with her these past days had settled deeply and disturbingly. Callie dared not look at Pike but her eyes glanced sideways to see her sister. Irene looked so small in Pike's shadow as her eyes and smile brimmed with happiness.

Don't begrudge Irene her happiness. Look at yourself. You are just a jealous little girl. Grow up! You have your whole life ahead of you. Of course, that's thanks to Pike, but don't cloud the issue here, Missy. Keep your mind on their happiness. Are you listening to me? Now, when this is over, say something supportive to Irene and Pike. Let go of all of these girlish feelings; time to grow up.

*

Feeling sweat on his face from the midday sun, Pike gazed down at Irene next to him as the nuptials were about to end. He had heard the words that Amos extolled about honoring and keeping each other until death parted us, and he'd heard those words before, but this time they meant more to him. Truth be told, they shook him to his core. *What am I going to do now? Why in the world did I let myself get captured into this marriage? I should have been much stronger than I was. See what happens when you let yourself become weak and get drunk. I knew better! Now, I'm forced to take responsibility for my actions. Until death do us part? Cri-min-ent-ly!*

Eyebrows knitted in concern, Amos cleared his throat and stared at Pike expectantly.

"I do?" Pike stuttered, hoping against hope that was the correct answer.

Amos's face lost its questioning expression and he continued to speak. "I now pronounce you husband and wife. You may kiss the bride."

Pike took his cue and pivoted toward his new wife, he clasped her by the shoulders, bent low and planted a swift, if not chaste, peck on her wet lips.

Irene's lips remained scrunched and her eyes remained shut and as she seemed to realize the kiss was over, her eyes fluttered opened and her puckered lips gave way to aggravation.

Avoiding the glare in her eyes, Pike turned to begin greeting the well-wishers.

"Do I get to kiss the bride?" Frank asked.

*

Being true to her word to congratulate Pike and Irene, Callie sidled up to Pike as soon as the ceremony ended. As she faced him, something in her froze. Her errant notions of wanting him rendered her silent and while she didn't know to do or say, she gaped at Pike.

Pike didn't seem to pick up on her odd behavior. He directed, "Give your brother-in-law a hug." As he opened his arms to pull her to him, he whispered in her ear, "Thank you for being such a good friend." He let her go and moved on to the next person in line.

Callie stepped out of the way and her heart thumped from being so close to him as shame washed over her.

"What are you doing over here?" Maude's pleasant voice questioned. "The ceremony was beautiful, don't you think?" She gazed at Callie expectantly.

"Yes, it was," Callie responded with a stutter, looking away from Maude.

"Can I ask you a favor?" Maude queried as she moved to look directly into Callie's eyes. "I've been meaning to see if you would help me learn to shoot? You're so good at it. Do you think you could teach me?"

Callie studied Maude's earnest face. *I could do that. I've never had a close friend. Well, other than Pike, but he certainly isn't a girl. Maybe this will help my loneliness.* "Sure, Maude, that would be fun." A lightness and eagerness had come to her voice. "Why don't we start tomorrow after church? It would be a great way to spend the afternoon."

"Do you mind if I bring Benny?"

"No," Callie instantly responded. "Please, bring him." The truth was, Callie felt drawn to the boy.

"It's settled then." Maude smiled delightedly. "I'll see

you after church.

"Okay. Are you hungry? I'll bet they're about ready to eat."

*

The evening drug by slowly for Pike, and while he felt numb over the day's activities, he forced down the food on his plate. Although it looked delicious, to him it seemed tasteless.

Occasionally, Irene would slip her moist hand into his palm and give it a squeeze. Pike would turn to her and flash his best smile. *I've got to throw myself into this marriage now,* he repeated internally, over and over.

When the feast was complete, Pike jumped up to start the music and escape his misery for a while. Pumpkin had brought his fiddle and Otis Ross had his banjo. The trio would be able to make all the music they wanted, and more. Pike picked up his guitar.

Irene grabbed his arm. "Where do you think you're going, Mister?" she scolded, as she stamped her foot several times for emphasis.

Feeling as guilty as a thief caught in the act, Pike froze as he clutched his instrument.

"You have to dance with me this evening," she complained, with a smoldering look in her eyes.

"Uh . . . I need to play with the musicians this evening, so we can have a great dance. I thought that'd be okay with you."

"I can't believe you even want to play that dumb guitar and not dance with your new bride, I can't." She stomped her foot again.

"Well, I'm sorry, Irene. Guess I didn't think. How about this? Could I dance with you for the first dance, and then play?"

Sniffing loudly, she responded sharply, "Men! Just the idea of you playing all evening while I stand by on the sidelines makes me so mad I could spit. But, I guess I have no choice, do I?"

"Now, sugar, I'll dance with you during the evening. I promise. Everyone'll want to dance with you anyhow. Do we have a deal?"

Her red lips pouting, Irene replied with exaspera-tion, "What choice do I have? Go ahead and play, but you had better not ignore me all night, Pike Wheeling!"

"I promise," Pike pledged, then bolted for the comfort of his well-worn guitar and the calming songs it pro-vided. His calloused hands tuned up the strings and lightened his mood. "Okay, boys, could you play the 'Sweetheart Waltz' for me and my new bride? We're going to dance."

Both men nodded their heads.

"See you back here when it's over," Pike said, as he set his guitar down and slipped away to locate his wife.

His wife? Sounded funny in his own head.

*

In early autumn, crunching through the dead leaves under a canopy of multi-colored trees, Callie moved with her rifle as noiselessly as she could from one tree to the next. She slipped behind a large oak and peeked around the dark trunk. Her eyes lit on the rack of the monster buck she had spotted from her perch on a large sandstone rock earlier that morning.

The rock had provided her with a grand view of the meadow. When the day's first hint of light had glinted off the ivory crown of glory over the buck's head, Callie's breath had caught in her throat. From a distance, she couldn't determine the exact size of the deer's antlers but judging from the width, it was the biggest rack she had ever seen.

Now, as she watched from the oak, the deer slipped once more into the safety of the trees. Buck fever took hold of her as she told herself, *I've got to catch that boy.*

In her moccasins and pants, Callie dashed after him by sticking to the field's edge. It didn't take her long to pick up his trail. She gracefully slinked through the dark forest as the sun peeped over the treetops and pro-vided her more light. *If I get him, I hope I can get back to Pike's cabin. I'm going to have to get a horse. Maybe the mules will be there. I bet Pike's got them out dragging trees. Hope not.*

Since Pike had been to Joplin and collected his

sawmill parts, the men had been busy constructing the platform for the circular saw. Once they got the steam engine up and running, they delved into the woods to commence felling sections of timber. According to Pike's plan, that work would occupy them through the winter and into the spring. As soon as spring arrived, the collected trees would be floated down the Neosho to the sawmill to begin the first round of lumber production - an event highly anticipated by the whole community.

Without the presence of the men, Callie found herself feeling lonely. She spent time with Maude and Benny on Sundays after church, but that wasn't enough. Irene had been moody since she began the first stages of her pregnancy.

Unlike Pike, Callie had not been able to escape Irene's sharp tongue by working at the sawmill. Instead, Callie had gladly accepted the chores around the farm to get out of the cabin. Feeding the horses and hauling water highlighted her day. She spent countless hours grooming and riding the horses, especially Clash. The mares were beginning to show their pregnancies, as was Rebecca. Now that the weather had turned nippy, Rebecca's belly was beginning to slow her down, so she didn't get out much to visit.

Frank spent a lot of time at Pike's cabin and ate every meal with them. Callie had developed a friendship with Frank and looked forward to his visits every evening. Frank sometimes joined Callie in the early mornings to lend a hand at hauling the water for the horses and she listened to his idle chatter while they worked.

Callie had detected more than a brotherly interest from him, but to this point, she had not encouraged him. Her heart still belonged to his oldest brother. Living in such close proximity to Pike kept her inner-fire kindled for that redheaded man but, she refused to let it show, at least, she hoped it didn't.

The evenings with Pike weren't as much fun as they had been before he had gotten married. He seemed much more subdued most of the time. Callie wondered what kept him so unhappy. Her guess was Irene, since she wore on them all.

There he is, Callie thought as she caught a glimpse

of the antlers deep into the woods. Quickly, she ducked back behind the rough bark to collect herself. *What am I going to do now? He looks like he's about forty feet from me.*

She put one hand on the long-bladed knife that was attached to her belt. Her father had given her the knife for Christmas and it gave her comfort and encouragement as she was prepared to make the kill.

Callie's face slowly inched its way from behind the tree and with one eye exposed, she made an instant mental note of the deer's stance. She calculated the distance to then sink behind her cover. Momentarily, she took a deep breath. Then, she wheeled from her position, knelt on her right knee, and brought the rifle to her cheek. She squeezed the trigger. The report echoed through the crisp autumn morning and rang in Callie's ear.

Having learned from previous mistakes, she stemmed the urge to jump up and find her prey. She slumped back against the tree and waited. The rough bark bit into her back and she shifted and closed her eyes. Setting her internal clock for twenty minutes, she gave the buck plenty of time to lie down and breathe his last breath.

When the time was up, she prowled through the trees to find him. The idea of her grand prize waiting for her and the excitement of shooting him left her feeling shaky.

"Wow, what a beauty he is!" she exclaimed as she hefted the dead stag's antlers and pivoted them from side to side. "Let's see - there's twelve points! I can't believe it. I've never seen one this big. He's a brute. Hope Pike is proud of me when he sees it. I'm taking it home for sure. Not going to leave this one's head in the woods. No, siree, I'll clean the skull and hang it on the barn."

Callie withdrew her wide-bladed hunting knife from its sheath. Spreading the legs of the buck, she sliced the abdominal wall, pulled out the warm, slick organs, and dropped them on the ground. When the guts were removed, she whipped out a scrap of cloth to wipe the blade and her blood-stained hands.

Standing up, she puffed into the cold air. "Now, it's

time to fetch a horse or wagon. Guess I'd better get to jogging. Can't wait to see the look on Pike's face when he sees this one."

*

Callie spent most of the morning dragging the deer to Pike's cabin with a hastily-made travois she attached to Gertie's back. She hung the carcass in a tree to continue the skinning process. Wiping her hands on a clean cloth, she completed the task just as Pike and Frank returned to the cabin for lunch.

Pike's eyes popped when he spotted the deer, and Frank's mouth gaped open. The huge rack could not be overlooked.

Gleefully, Callie watched.

Pike stood beside the carcass to count the points. "Wow! Callie! What a deer! Where did you get this bugger?"

Bursting with pride, Callie replied, "I got him a couple of miles from here. I knew he was big but I didn't know just how big until I shot him. He should feed us for a while."

"I'd say so," Frank stated with an awe-filled voice. "I can't wait to have a few of those tenderloin steaks."

"Me, too," Pike added. "I love liver and onions, though. After lunch, I'll help you finish cutting him up and we can get everyone some meat. How does that sound?"

Callie grinned, basking in her brief glory.

"Come on, sis," Frank said, breaking up the moment. "Let's eat. I'm starved."

*

The biting north wind stung Pike's bare skin. Sounds of axes and saws rang out around him. He paused to wipe his sweaty brow and glance at the deep, wintry forest, left skeletal from fallen leaves. His hand ached from the morning's exertion of chipping away at the towering tree in front of him. *Just a little more,* he instructed himself as he caught his ragged breath.

Realizing his exhaustion, he hunted out a dry spot on a rock jutting up from the soggy soil. Taking his perch, he relaxed his weary muscles as he ran his hand over the bristles of his recently-grown red beard.

"How about a drink?" Callie's voice called to him.

Pike smiled at the sight of his sister-in-law. He found comfort in the strong features of her well-chiseled face and her hazel eyes always warmed his heart.

"Here, take this," she said, handing him a tin of water. "Looks like you can use it. Even if it is cold enough to freeze your nose shut." A light giggle slipped from Callie's mouth.

The sunny, teasing atmosphere that perpetually existed between Pike and this tall girl was like a salve to his troubled heart. The tough sixteen-year-old grew nearer and dearer to him with each passing week. Just how much she had come to mean to him, he couldn't fully accept. If he did, how could he continue to live with her in his own cabin?

The life with Irene had not been what he had expected. And, if he gave in to the longings he quite often had for Callie, he would do something that he knew to be very wrong. He couldn't do that because God would not approve, nor could he live with himself if he did something that wrong.

The months of personal turmoil, striving to carve out a peaceful existence with Callie's sister, had been frustrating at best and gut-wrenching at worst. The frequent squabbles over small things kept his life in constant upheaval. Pike had never expected married life to be as hard as it was. Since his parents had never fought, and since he didn't see the other couples arguing, he had no examples on how to work through the daily confrontations with his young bride. For escape, he stayed in the woods and kept himself occupied by felling, trimming, and dragging the rapidly growing number of downed trees. The strife of his own life and his mounting desire for Callie, kept him torn inside, giving him much aggravation to work out in his time in the woods.

*

One early morning when Pike and Frank had been readying themselves to leave for the woods, Callie had raced to the door and grabbed her coat and hat. Pike had known exactly what she was doing - she yearned to be with them. He had noted her desire, and it pleased him. Catching her sidelong glance, he had said nothing to deter her. Instead, he had responded, "She's going to make one fine 'bucker', isn't she, Frank?" He had tossed the comment out casually but internally he reveled in the knowledge he would have Callie with him all day. Pike appreciated this rare gem of a girl and never thought twice about her doing a man's work.

At the time, Frank had appeared uncertain about what was transpiring, but, to his credit, he let it go. "Yes, brother, she'll make a fine 'bucker'. I wouldn't mind getting some help stripping those trees so Buster and the mules can drag them off. Callie, are you up to it? It's the roughest job in the forest."

Callie clapped her hands. "Oh, yes, thank you. You won't be sorry. I'll do my share. Let's go. I'm ready. I'd rather be in the forest than anywhere."

Grinning, Pike said, "You two go and get the wagon. I'll catch up to you in a minute."

Callie didn't have to be told twice. She slung open the door and pranced out into the yard with Frank on her heels.

Pike ambled back to Irene, who was rocking by the stove and knitting yet another baby blanket.

"You want me to help you clean up breakfast, sugar?"

"No, I'll do it," Irene responded, never looking up.

Shuffling his feet, Pike twisted his wool-knitted cap in his hand. He didn't know what to do or say. "Well, we'll see you for supper. We've got plenty of food to get us through. Will you be okay until then?"

Irene gave a slight nod.

Now, that he had been released, Pike bent to peck Irene lightly on her right cheek. "Bye." He turned on his heels and nearly bolted through the door.

Once it shut behind him, he felt the constrictions within him ease. Guilt instantly took its place. *How do I make her happy?* Sighing, Pike refocused his thoughts on his new passion - lumber. It fulfilled him as his marriage never would.

*

These recollections passed over him as he and Callie shared a quiet drink of water and rested on the rock.

She spoke up in a conversational tone. "Did you see those bald eagles circling this morning?"

A ripping, snapping sound brought Pike's head up. One more forest giant had lost its battle to stay erect. Amos and Eric took no mercy on the wooden monument with their two-man, cross-cut saw. One-by-one, the trees toppled, crashing to the ground. Each time, the sound gave Pike a surge of pure delight. Time and repetition did not dull the thrill of hearing his lumber stock expand.

Moments after the tree crashed to the ground, Eric, Frank, and Amos joined Pike and Callie to partake of the refreshing water.

"Did you finish the tree we were working on, Frank?" Callie asked.

"Whew," Frank uttered, sitting on the edge of the rock. "Yes, I did get the last few branches off. Buster and I got it on the skids and he took off with it. He should be back in a few minutes. Thanks for the help. You've gotten real handy with that hatchet. I think you're faster than I am. It took me longer to do my side."

Callie visibly puffed up under Frank's praise.

*

Callie wanted nothing more than to have the men accept her efforts by matching their labor. These last few weeks had almost killed her but she would never let it show. The last thing she wanted was for Pike to be disappointed in her. *I'll break my back before I let him down,* she instructed herself for the hundredth time during these long weeks of toughening herself to the hacking and chopping of the downed trees. Grinning back at Frank, she said, "You're welcome. Need some more?"

"No, thanks, I've had plenty."

"How many board feet do you think we've got, Pike?" Eric inquired.

Listening to the conversation, Callie gloried in being a part of the work that would establish Pike's mill. While she felt completely at home in this masculine endeavor, she still felt like a failure as a woman. She knew she used the woods to escape the parts of her life that she didn't like and couldn't deal with. During her time with the men, performing their work, she experienced a sense of her true self. *What will I ever do if I can't work like this and have to do women's work?* She shifted uncomfortably at the thought as she glanced around at the men so close to her heart.

Callie caught Pike's eye and a flash of thrill swept through her when he returned her smile, leaving her tingling and breathless.

Unexpectedly, Candy shot onto Callie's lap and wet Callie's cheek with her slobbery tongue. Almost full-grown, the dog was a lapful.

The joyful hound never failed to lighten Callie's mood. She chuckled as she stroked Candy's head and shared another smile with Pike. "Girl," she inquired of the wriggly dog, "Are you ready to hunt a few Christmas turkeys?"

Candy answered with another lick to her cheek.

Chapter 26

Peeling another potato, Callie reveled in the distinctive smell of baking turkey, which wafted past her nose in the cozy, warm cabin. "When is everyone coming over?" she inquired, with a bright smile to Irene.

"The group should be here before too much longer," Irene said, not bothering to look up as she stirred a huge pot of chicken and dumplings, Callie's favorite dish. Several grown chicks had been sacrificed for the pot.

The cabin door burst open and brought a welcome breath of fresh air.

"Something sure smells good," Frank boomed out.

Pike followed him in. "Yum! That smells delicious." He hung up his coat, then snatched a pinch of a pecan pie crust. "I sure do love this flannel shirt you gave me, sis." Then, Pike scooped up a battered tin cup to fill with boiling coffee.

"Glad you like it," Callie replied, sneaking a peek at Pike in his shirt. Green was her favorite color and it looked great on him, bringing out the red in his beard. When she had spotted it in the Pettit's store, she couldn't resist getting it for him for Christmas. For Irene, she had selected a beautiful hand-woven basket made by Maude, a highly-skilled Cherokee basket-weaver. Maude had been teaching Callie how to weave but it would be some time before her skills would be honed to be anywhere near as good as Maude's.

Pike's gift to Callie, an impressive hunting knife, had

thrilled her beyond words. The knife's deer-antler handle had been hand-carved with a buck in flight. The significance of the gift had not been lost on her. It was the most precious gift she had ever received and she would treasure it forever.

"The barn is set up and should be warm," Pike commented, sipping his coffee. "We've got two fires built to chase off the cold."

"Think we've got enough seats for everybody?" Callie asked, picking up another raw potato.

"Frank and I have it all arranged. I told everyone to bring chairs. The eating tables are all set up and waiting."

"Is Rebecca coming?" Irene inquired.

Frank piped up. "Amos told me yesterday that she had been tired but, since she's not due for a few more weeks, he said they'd be here."

"Maude told me at church," Callie interjected, "that she and the Pettits were coming for sure. I imagine Benny will be with them." Callie heard a knock on the door, but before she could get up, the door blew open.

Buster ducked his head as he entered, and stated, "We's here. How's you all?"

Lyric snuggled beside him, as they entered the cabin. She exemplified the purest of love and contentment to Callie as the honeymoon glow never left Lyric's cheeks. Lyric and Buster belted out, "Jingle bells, jingle bells, jingle all the way."

Callie joined them, along with the others.

"We's put the mules over to Frank's barn," Buster said as soon as the song ended.

Lyric walked over to Irene. "I left my pies and rolls out in the barn. Pike sure has it decorated up real nice with the cedar wreaths and pinecones on the tables. It looks so festive. I'm starving. Are we going to eat soon?"

"As soon as everyone else gets here, we'll get right to the food," Irene replied, with a somber smile. "I'm starved, too. Can't seem to get enough to eat these days."

A distinctive grin beamed on Lyric's face as she turned to the others and blushed.

Callie knew something was up and she didn't have

to wait long to find out.

"Buster and I are expecting, too! I'm not far along, but I know I'm going to have a baby. I was beginning to think it wasn't going to happen for us but it was a great Christmas present. Almost as good as the rocker Buster made for me."

Callie grabbed the woman and hugged her affectionately. "That's just wonderful."

Lyric was Callie's favorite among their own group of ladies. She seemed the most accepting and was so easy to talk to. The news thrilled Callie for her good friend.

Pike slapped Buster's thick shoulder. "That's great news! Merry Christmas to you."

While the others added their congratulations, Eric and Rena burst in the front door.

"Merry Christmas, everyone," Rena shouted, her reddened face joining the others in the crowd. "Amos, Rebecca, and the kids are waiting in the barn. All of our goodies for the feast are out there. Rebecca is reheating the turkey. By the way, Callie, thanks for the big tom. What a beard he had. You've done such a good job hunting, we haven't had to butcher a hog yet."

Rena stopped talking and tromped through the crowd with two mason jars of a red-looking substance.

"Here, Irene, I brought you a couple of jars of wild grape jelly. I've got some apricot jam for the rolls. Merry Christmas"

"Thank you, Rena," Irene gushed, with uncharacteristic enthusiasm. "I'm much obliged. We've had some of that great local Cherokee molasses, but no jelly. We'll sure enjoy some of this."

From the back of the room, Pike said, "Let's carry all of this stuff out to the barn so we can eat. I can't wait. Let's go."

The women artfully arranged the food as the tide of people swept into the spacious barn. The jaunty, gay chatter added to Callie's joyous mood.

"Patrick!" Pike belted out as soon as the youngster came into view. As the child ran to him, Pike scooped him up. "Merry Christmas. I've got something for you."

Callie enjoyed watching Pike's obvious love for the child.

Pike pulled out a leather ball and displayed it proudly on his outstretched palm.

The wide-eyed boy latched onto the ball and squeezed it with enthusiasm. He squealed, "Oh, boy. Thanks, Uncle Pike."

A different squealing came from near Pike's feet, where Hannah gripped his pants with her chubby hands. Bending low, Pike hefted Hannah into his other arm and snuggled her close and her protests ceased immediately.

"I've got you a present, too, when I can get to it."

"It's ready," Rena yelled over the noisy crowd.

The conversations died down as the hungry group traipsed to their seats.

Callie rested next to Pike. On his other side, sat Irene in her usual solemn mood.

*

Pike cleared his throat and rose, with a stiff back. He gazed at all the eager faces that gazed up at him. A wave of emotion filled him before his words tumbled forth. "Merry Christmas to everyone. We have much to be thankful for. We've all come to this new land, uncertain of what it would have in store for us. We only have God and one another to thank for all the blessings that have been bestowed upon us. Not only have we been able to get our homes established and our larders full, but we have been able to become an active church family, thanks to Amos." He glanced at his dark-haired brother, who had a slight smile on his face. "He sure can preach the 'Word', and, we are blessed with the professor and Effie to instruct our children. We want for nothing. Many of our ladies are expecting, including Lyric. Congratulations to them. Professor, we aim to keep you busy."

Laughter rippled through the crowd.

Pike chuckled with them, then became serious again. "Let's not forget the One responsible for our bounty. Bow your heads, please. Father, today is the day we celebrate Your son's birth and, ultimately, His death and our salvation. You led us to this wild, untamed land. We gladly followed Your lead. We all want to thank You with every ounce of our strength for the many blessings You have given us. We can never give You enough praise for the beauty You bring to our lives. We will continue to follow where You lead us. Also, thanks for the food, lovingly prepared for us to share. In Your Son's name we pray. Amen!"

"Amen!" rang out from the crowd in support of Pike's heartfelt words.

As Pike began to sit down, he noticed Rebecca's pale face. He froze in place as she expelled a loud gasp and clutched her distended mid-section.

Amos put his hand on her. "Rebecca, is it the baby?"

She nodded her head vigorously.

Silence filled the barn and along with everyone else, Pike gaped at Rebecca.

*

Callie watched curiously, sensing the fear running through the group. She didn't know what she should do.

Maude shoved her chair back and hurried to Rebecca's side. She placed her hand softly on the top of Rebecca's shoulder. "How far apart are your contractions?"

"They've been coming every few minutes all morning, but until now, my water hadn't broken. Now that it has, my contractions are coming one on top of another." She groaned and gripped her belly again.

Patting her on the shoulder, Maude soothed, "Okay, dear, we need to get you to bed." She turned to Irene and Callie. "Can we put Rebecca in your bed?"

"Sure," Callie responded, noticing Irene sitting in shock. "You can put her in Irene's and Pike's bed. Give me a minute and I'll round up a couple of sheets or blankets to put down before you take her into the house. Is that okay?"

"That would be wonderful."

Callie sprinted out of the barn and raced through the cold wind to the cabin. She tossed back the bed covers, spread out an extra woolen blanket, and prayed that would be enough protection. It was the best she could do.

The front door of the cabin banged open with the wind. Maude guided Rebecca toward the bedroom, while Amos, Pike, and Rena trailed behind.

"Now, I'm going to put Rebecca in bed," Maude said to the group over her shoulder. "When she's settled, you can take turns sitting with her. Everyone wait here."

Callie stood with the men and watched Rebecca double over with the next contraction and she worried about the pain Rebecca was experiencing.

Glancing at Callie, Pike said, "You want to help me bring a little food from the barn for everyone? I hate to see it go to waste. We might as well get our fill while we wait. It may be a while before she has the baby."

Callie tried to suppress a smile at Pike's concern. "Sure, Pike. Let me help you. We're all hungry."

A little later, as Callie enjoyed a bowl of chicken and dumplings, Maude took a vacant seat at the table and announced, "Rebecca is coming right along. She does want someone to sit with her. I told her one of you would be right in."

"I'll take my plate and share it with her," Rena offered.

"It would be fine for you to take a plate in but it will be better for Rebecca to not have anything on her stomach."

Nodding, Rena rose with her heaping plate of food and disappeared into the other room.

"We're so glad you're here, Maude," Pike expressed with a tone of gratitude. "We couldn't have asked for it to turn out any better."

"I'm happy I'm here, too. Now, we can sit together. She's coming along fine but it may be a while before she's ready to have the baby. This pumpkin pie is so good. Oh, I hope Benny is okay."

"I asked Lyric to watch out for him," Callie said. "He's following Patrick around and playing with Candy. You don't need to worry."

Rena bustled back through the open door with her empty plate. "Rebecca is having some strong contractions but she's not complaining." She set her plate down and returned to Rebecca's side.

Callie, hoping to lighten the mood and bring the

Christmas spirit back, asked, "Why don't we sing? Pike, would you play? How about 'Oh, Little Town of Bethlehem?'"

"Let me grab my guitar. Is everybody ready?"

As the first notes rang from his strings, Callie and Maude stood, draping their arms around each other and belting out the first words. Amos and Pike joined in, lending their voices to the uplifting carol.

Drifting in from the other room, Rena's shrill voice screamed over the music.

*

Rebecca cried out in pain. *God, help me! I can't take anymore of this,* as she fought to maintain some control but it had been a losing battle. Her groans and moans increased with the frequent waves of pain. This was her third time at giving birth but she didn't remember it being this difficult with the last two times.

Amos stood at her side with sweat running down his face and she could feel him squeeze her hand.

Maude's voice coached her through another ghastly contraction. "Okay, dear, I know it hurts like the dickens, but you've got to push now. It's time."

Collecting her remaining strength, Rebecca bore down. The painful pressure from deep within her mounted and she felt the baby move with the contraction.

Maude gasped lightly. "Rebecca," she said in a calm voice, "there is a bit of a problem. The baby is coming out backwards. Now, listen. Everything is going to be fine, but we're going to have to get this baby out fast. So, when I say push, you have to push for all you're worth. Tell me when you are ready."

"Here comes another one," she groaned, in a voice that sounded far off in the distance.

"Okay, dear, push with all you've got! Rena! Stand next to me and get ready to cut the cord."

Rebecca sucked in a lungful of air. She felt Amos give her hand a tighter squeeze. She groaned again as she bore down with her dwindling strength.

"That's great," Maude praised. "She's coming! Don't

let up!"

Finally, the pain stopped and Rebecca dropped back on the bed in relief. She couldn't see the baby but she knew that Maude and Rena were cutting the cord and releasing the baby from her body.

"Rena," Maude said. "Take the baby. Clean her up and rub her real good. Make sure she's breathing well. I need to get this placenta out as quick as I can. Rebecca is hemorrhaging."

As Rebecca watched Rena clutch her new infant in a blanket and sweep out of the room, Maude's words registered. She felt rivulets of wetness flowing from her.

"You've got a daughter," Maude announced officially.

Rebecca glanced into Amos's concerned eyes and knew she must be in trouble. What Maude had said was a potentially dangerous situation. Amos's tight hold gave her support as she tried to remain calm.

"Rebecca," Maude began. "You've got to listen to me. We must stop this bleeding. The only way to do that is get the placenta out. I know you don't want to hear this but you've got to push as hard as you can. Stay strong for just a few minutes more. As soon as a contraction hits, push."

"Here it comes," Rebecca groaned as she felt the cramping from within.

"Push!" Maude coached brusquely.

Bearing down again with all her might, Rebecca tried to focus her mind on her task. She knew her life depended on it, but for some reason, she felt as though she were slipping over the edge, falling into a bottomless well. As she fell into the vast depths, sounds came from a distance.

"Amos, talk to her!"

She knew the voice must be Maude's but it came from far off.

Her husband's familiar voice spoke soft words, rousing her and stirring feelings within. "Come on," he crooned. "Push! Push! You have to push - please don't leave me."

Rebecca felt something give way within. A sweeping wave of relief washed over her being, as the placenta whooshed out of her. She relaxed back into the bed and was struck by how glad she was to have her husband helping her in a time like this. She wouldn't have it any other way.

"Rena," Maude said, "I'm going to need some rags. Can you fetch me some?"

"Sure. Let me grab what I can find."

Shortly, Rena hustled back into the room.

"Thank you, Rena." Maude applied pressure between Rebecca's legs. "We've got it under control now. I'm going to check on your daughter, rest now."

Following her directive, Rebecca closed her eyes. *Yes, I have a new daughter!* She opened her eyes, hoping to get a glimpse of her as Maude reentered the room.

"Here she is!" Maude proudly declared as she held the pink, shriveled infant out for Rebecca and Amos to inspect.

Unconditional love blossomed instantly in Rebecca's heart and her tears went unheeded. She glanced at Amos and noticed his eyes looked suspiciously damp. Gathering her new baby to her chest, Rebecca heard Maude's question.

"What are you going to name her? She's such a beautiful girl."

Rebecca looked with soft eyes at her child. "If it's all right with Amos, I'd like to call her Hope, Christmas Hope.

"That's one fine name," Amos said, eyes beaming.

"What a pretty name for a pretty baby," Maude cooed. "I love my job!"

*

Three months later, well before dawn, Pike glanced at Irene as he tossed and turned in bed. *At least she's sleeping.* This was the big day, the day that he would see those trees floating down the river to the mill. *Hopefully, we can cut a few of them, too. I'm so excited!*

The water was going to be cold but he couldn't wait. *Starting today, my lumber business is getting under way. Only the Lord knows how this is going to turn out but thank You, Father, for getting me this far.*

After tossing several more times, Pike's mind and

body flowed with too much energy to stay in bed, so he rose to a sitting position and let his legs dangle over the bed's edge. The quilt's warmth beckoned to him but he turned a deaf ear to pulling the covers back over his head. Instead, he hopped onto the frigid dirt floor and felt around in the darkness for the clothes he had laid out the previous evening. He quickly dressed, tugging his boots on last. Quietly, he tiptoed out of the bedroom and shut the door.

When Pike entered the adjoining room, he noticed Callie's empty cot. A whiff of fresh-brewed coffee floated to his nose. "Callie?" he whispered. He spied her shoving a few sticks of wood into the stove.

She lit a lantern, enabling him to see her better, even in its weak light. His eyes drank in her tall, slender frame, dressed in black pants and a red-plaid flannel shirt. Her hair hung in a single, long braid. A few loose locks hung over her temples, emphasizing the strong features on her attractive face. *She looks great,* Pike thought. The urge struck him to grab her and plant her lips with a most tender kiss. The tidal wave of emotion threatened to leak from his eyes. *God, how I want her. It's that pure and simple.*

Pike had accepted the fact of his love for her quite a while back. To this point, he had chosen to not act upon it. He was a married man. *Think about Irene and the baby. They're your fist concern.* No, he would never commit adultery, nor would he hurt this special girl in any way.

Until she spoke, he didn't realize that he was staring at her.

"Morning, Pike. Are you excited, too? I can't wait to see those logs floating down the river. What a sight that will be! I haven't slept a wink."

She's like no other girl I've ever known. Pike struggled to quench his flaming desire. Luckily, he could refocus on the excitement of this most momentous day. Beaming a boyish grin, he basked in Callie's shining beauty. "Let's grab a cup of coffee, then we can go hitch Dunk and Don. I'm ready and chomping at the bit to get those logs flowing down the river. We've got the logjam built by the pond to hold them by the sawmill. Everything is ready to go." Pike softened his voice, "I'm glad you're going to be there today." The words came out huskier than he had planned.

Callie smiled, eyes shining, and declared, "I wouldn't miss it for the world. You deserve everything great you're getting. This is only the start." Without warning, Callie tossed her gangly arms around Pike's neck and gave him a quick hug. She was so tall that her cheek reached the top of his shoulder. She released him and stepped back to the warmth of the stove.

Shocked by the realization of her height, Pike asked, "Callie, how tall are you? You look like you're around six feet. I swear you're still growing."

Callie blushed pink as she stared briefly at the ground. She seemed embarrassed by her impulsive act. "I don't know. I hope I stop growing soon. I'm taller than most boys. No one is going to want a girl so tall. Guess I won't attract anyone wearing pants like this anyhow, will I?" She snickered.

"Don't worry about finding a man. You are the pick of the litter, and don't you forget it." The notion of her being with someone else pained him but he meant what he had said.

She blushed a deeper shade of crimson.

Pike lifted his scalding cup of coffee and took a sip. "Let's get out of here. I can't wait any longer."

"I'll fetch my coat."

*

Callie stood on the bank with Frank and Buster and watched Eric and Pike, both bare-chested, move over the bobbing logs. Her breath turned to a light mist as she clutched her arms across her chest to keep warm.

Looking like a cat trying to keep its feet dry as he hopped from one log to another, Eric wound his way to the opposite side of the mossy trees, wedged together in one large mass on the river. An extra large tree gave him pause as it bucked, threatening to toss him into the frigid water, but Eric scrambled to balance himself. When he secured his footing, he stepped to the next tree and continued on his way. Clasped in his left hand was a five-foot metal pole.

Pike, less experienced, struggled behind Eric with his own pole. Callie smiled at Pike's seeming courage as he hustled to match the burly man's efforts.

"How far are we going?" Eric shouted.

"It's about a mile," Pike responded.

Eric placed his pole against the log next to him and shoved hard, loosening it from the bunch. He gigged Pike, "You still up to doing this?"

"Can't wait."

Enjoying seeing the men teasing each other, Callie stomped her feet to warm them up as she waited for the action to begin.

Pike placed his pole against a tree and heaved for all he was worth. His chosen log moved out slowly and caught the river's current. "Okay, you on shore. Go to work!"

Callie joined Frank and Buster in putting their poles to the logs along the bank to guide them, one by one, into the current. The bobbing mass of fallen trees began to move.

As Buster shoved hard on the last log, he gave a friendly wave to the pair riding the trees downstream. "I bet that's freezin'," he stated to Callie.

She observed, with some apprehension, the bare-chested men drifting further down the river. "How many times do you think they'll get dunked?" she asked.

"Pike tol' me they has a bet goin' as to who'll hit the water the least."

Callie spotted Pike wobbling on a tree. "Oh, no!"

His log bucked, shooting him up and into the dark water.

Frank laughed loudly when Pike took his dive.

Tensely, Callie waited. As Pike's head broke the surface, she exclaimed, "Whew!" She watched pensively to make sure he got up on another log. She sighed when he stood up again.

Frank turned from the river as the men vanished. "Time to get to the mill."

Callie and Buster followed him to the wagon. From her seat, she strained to see the logs and the men in the river. She caught a few glimpses of Pike through the thick trees before the wagon turned off. *What will I do if something happens to him?* She bit her lip and prayed.

A little later, the wagon rolled next to the sawmill. "Whoa, boys," Frank instructed the mules.

Hopping down from the wagon, Callie trotted after the men.

"Callie, grab your pole," Frank ordered. "Buster, are you ready? Amos and the professor should be waiting for us at the pond. They may already be out in the river. We'd better get down there and give them a hand to get that jam directed into the holding pond. Come on, we'd better hurry."

Latching onto her pole, Callie ran with the others to the river. *Hope they make it okay.* A lump caught in her throat and her fear threatened to turn into panic as she lifted her eyes toward the river and strained to see Pike and Eric or the floating mass of trees. She caught sight of a movement. There was Pike, standing upright on a log. Her tilted world righted once more, and she sighed out loud.

"Is you okay, sis?" Buster asked.

She liked how the men took to calling her 'Little Sis' after Pike had started referring to her that way as a joke. She glanced over her shoulder and grinned up at the dark-skinned man she had grown to love and respect. "I'm just fine. I was just worried about them. I can see they're okay, now."

"Buster," Frank said. "You and I need to get on that river to help guide the logs into the holding pond. Callie, you stay by the pond's neck and guide the trees in when they get close - holler if you get any bottlenecks you can't handle." He smiled teasingly and added, "And I'll come and rescue you."

Her back stiffened. "Hmph! I think I can handle my job just fine without you, Frank."

"Just offering, sis," Frank mocked, as he and Buster stripped off their shirts and shoes.

"Is it cold?" Callie asked, teasing him back.

Both responded with pained expressions, their eyes glaring at the frigid water. The sun had finally made its appearance and provided welcome light, making the water appear less intimidating. But the cold breeze blowing across the men's bare backs seemed to give them pause.

Suddenly, Buster jumped from the bank with his pole in his hand and disappeared in the icy liquid. When he bobbed to the surface, whipping the water out of his eyes, he called out between tight teeth, "Hey, is you's comin' in or not? You's a chicken?"

Frank frowned at him, then made a headlong dash into the river.

Hardly able to stand the thrill as she removed her boots and rolled up her pant legs, Callie took a deep breath, then she waded knee-deep into the shocking water with her pole poised to prod the floating timber.

They began the relaying of the trees into the lagoon.

Eric and Pike skipped over the floating logs and dashed to the sawmill to start the steam engine and warm up their cold bodies. The others, including Callie, bent their backs to get the trees into the holding pond as quickly as possible.

When the last tree found its new home, the blue-lipped workers scrambled from the freezing water, latched onto their dry clothes and made a beeline to the fire that was snapping and crackling at the nearby engine.

Ignoring the cold, Callie hustled to set out two pots of coffee near the fire. She spread out the food for lunch.

"What a ride that was," Pike exclaimed. "What did you think, Eric?"

"That was as much fun as I ever remember." Eric's voice radiated enthusiasm. "I hope it's a little warmer when we float the next bunch, though. Sis, is that coffee hot yet? Sure could use a cup."

"Coming right up."

"Thanks, sis," Pike said softly as he took the scalding brew from her.

Before long, they were into the second pot.

*

Pike, thrilled to see the successful completion of the first phase of getting his business underway, went to retrieve Dunk and Don. He brought them around to drag the logs out of the water. Callie assisted Buster in attaching the chains to the first tree, while the other men waited around the circular saw.

Hands on hips, Pike stood on top of the platform and took in this momentous moment. Every nerve in his body came alive and tingled. *Look at that girl go,* Pike told himself as his gaze lingered on Callie's maturing body. *Look how she handles those chains. Like she'd done it her whole life.*

Callie's cheerful beauty lightened his workload every day. Sharing his triumphs and sweat with her, side by side, brought Pike satisfaction beyond measure. His mind and spirit skyrocketed to unknown heights of raw delight. It even surpassed his survival of the blizzard.

Reason called to him - a whisper he could not ignore. *You'd better be careful.* But, his eyes stayed on the young, tireless woman, giving everything she had to fulfill his dream. *I know nothing can ever come from the feelings I have for her. I'm married and have a child on the way. Not only is she my sister-in-law but she's only sixteen. Well, at least I can work near her and treasure my time with her. Soon enough, she'll be drawing beaus.*

"Git up, there," Buster sang out to the spotted mule and its teammate and moved them into place.

Frank stood at Callie's side to add his strong hands to chaining the bulky tree. They grinned and laughed at one another as they worked.

Taking in the happy exchange between his favorite brother and the woman he secretly loved, Pike felt so many jumbled emotions, all warring within him. *Urgh!* A tide of hurtful jealousy swept over him, threatening to yank him under like riptides along the coast. *I can't allow my feelings to show. Frank deserves happiness, probably more than I do. I should be excited about the lumber business finally getting underway, not mourning after another girl. I went through all that with Rebecca. When is it going to stop?* Still, anger flooded him and he felt a frown crease his forehead as he continued to watch Frank and Callie. He couldn't help himself.

When the chaining job was completed, Pike watched the first tree being wrenched upward toward the mill. A renewed thrill passed through him and he let his concentration on Callie fade.

As the tree clanged its way up to the sawmill deck, Eric and Amos stepped forward, latched onto the tree and unhooked the chains to roll the log into the concave cradle of the circular saw. It crashed into place, sending a tremor through the platform.

Pike grabbed the handle to engage the saw and as the blade whined into life, the high-pitched whirring rang in his ears. A big grin crossed his face while his body shuddered. *This is it.* He set the depth for the cut and inched the tree section forward with care.

Flakes of sawdust shot into the air as the teeth bit into the fresh wood. The first plank fell from the tree.

Pike jumped up for joy and he hopped around the platform and shouted, "Glory be!"

The others joined him in shouting and congratulating each other with slaps on the back.

Pike's eyes drifted to Callie's fresh face. They lingered on her hazel eyes.

Callie returned his stare, her eyes reflecting his pleasure.

Pike looked away first. *You'll never have these strong feelings for Irene.* A fresh slice of regret, to eat and digest, was again served on his plate. Nothing could come of the feelings for the young lady he carried deep within his heart but the sorrow seemed too much to bear.

Chapter 27

With the onset of spring, Callie rose at dawn to rustle up breakfast for the ever-increasing population of their group. Now, that the sawmill was up and running, men began to trickle into the area to find work. Irene, whose belly protruded, could no longer handle the job of cooking and cleaning, so the breakfast meal fell to Callie. She did her best but still found it distasteful. Lyric helped with lunch and supper while Callie worked at the mill.

Cracking another egg into a large bowl, Callie stirred vigorously in the quiet cabin before the workers arrived.

"Good morning," Pike whispered, as he tiptoed into the room, his eyes still puffy from sleep.

Callie couldn't squelch the inner glow she felt radiate from her heart. This was her favorite time of day, the time she could share with Pike alone. "How did Irene sleep?" she asked as her heart fluttered and pounded in her ears.

Pike reached over her shoulder to pick up the pot of coffee. "She was restless, poor thing." He moved away from Callie and rested at the kitchen table, then sipped thoughtfully at his cup, appearing half-awake.

"Lyric told me yesterday," Callie babbled, that Rena and little Herman were up at the sawmill. I'm sorry I missed them. I hear the baby is growing. She said Rena stopped by to show him off here, too. Lyric was the only one around." She poured the eggs into the hot skillet. Over the sizzling crackles, she said to Pike, "Sorry I got hung up at the Pettit's yesterday and didn't get back to work. I did enjoy getting to visit with Dora."

"You needed a little feminine conversation," Pike offered, with an amused smile.

A rap at the front door turned Callie's attention to the group of men quietly slipping in. Frank brought with him the three new hands - Bear, Graham, and Clay.

"Looks like you got them up early," Callie observed, with a giggle.

"We were hungry," Frank stated as he poured himself a cup of coffee, while the new workers settled in at the table and looked expectantly at Callie.

With the arrival of good weather, projects that needed attention abounded on every farm, and this put the men of Pike's original group under pressure in dividing their time between the sawmill and their own chores. The new hands had helped immensely.

Callie glanced briefly at the men while she finished stirring the eggs. They were all of Indian heritage with dark skin and she guessed them all to be in their twenties. But, aside from this - and their being single - they were as different from one another as night to day.

Scraping the eggs into a bowl, Callie put it on the table. Retrieving a set of cups, she passed one to each of the men and began the rounds of pouring.

Bear Waite was not quite as tall as Pike, but more than made up for two of Pike in bulk. Thick stubs of arms stuck out from his barrel chest and his bullish, quarrelsome nature got him into brawls with the other workers. Bear had proven himself to be a hard worker and an asset to Pike's operation but he seemed offended by having to work with a woman, by the scowls he was constantly throwing Callie's way.

When Callie worked with Bear loading lumber, she was quick to notice his hateful stares and because of that, the man made her uncomfortable. She appreciated the fact that Pike often relegated Bear to work on the farm and assisted in making lumber deliveries. At present, Bear had been put to work doing the digging of post holes around Pike's property so the horses could have grazing paddocks. With these diversions for Bear, Callie didn't have to deal with him as much.

Graham Howard, a spindly young man not much older than Callie, came from an impoverished background. He had lost his family recently. His father had been killed in an accident and his mother and sister had died in the previous year's flu epidemic. Callie found his blue eyes unusual for his dark face. Painfully thin, he was doubly cursed with a pimply, plain face and his knobby Adam's apple, which didn't help his looks. Despite his somberness, no one could complain about his work ethic. The boy stayed on task better than anyone else.

Callie's eyes passed over Clay Crane as she picked up his cup. *Dumb as a stump,* were the words that had popped into her mind the moment she had first seen him a few weeks before and her assessment hadn't changed. A few years older than Bear, Clay had been a drifter of mixed Cherokee descent, but he sported long, stringy blonde hair with colorless gray eyes and a thick, bushy beard. Callie had been grateful when Pike insisted the man bathe and wash his clothes. Pike had even provided the poor fellow with several sets of overalls.

Callie didn't miss the adoring look Clay always gave Pike. She knew that Pike had to keep Clay under someone else's direction while at the sawmill. It wasn't that Clay wouldn't work, he just couldn't remember what he was supposed to be doing from one moment to the next. Luckily, Graham had been good in leading Clay through their daily hauling and stacking chores.

After pouring each man a second cup of coffee, Callie sat down to start her own breakfast. "Pike, I'll be out at the mill as soon as I get things cleaned up here."

Pike put down his cup and hesitated before he spoke. "Callie, would you mind staying home with Irene? I think she needs someone to stay with her and to be able to fetch help quickly. Lyric will be here to help with the cooking, but since Lyric lost her baby recently, I'd be afraid to ask her to ride Clash, if need be. Working around here seems to ease her depression but she's not healed yet."

Feeling a sharp sting from having to stay at home and listen to Irene whine, Callie mulled it over as she stuffed the eggs into her mouth. Finally, she relented, for Pike's sake. "You're right. I'll stay here with Irene."

"Thank you, sis. Bear, you can finish putting in the fence posts for the pasture you've been working on. The rest of you fellows, we need to get to sawing logs." He stood up and tromped across the room for his coat and the men followed him out of the cabin.

*

Callie, sitting back, falling into her unhappy void, unsure what to do next, thought, *I hope Bear doesn't work too close to the cabin. That man gives me the willies. I don't trust him any farther than I could throw him and that isn't far.*

"Everybody gone?" Irene asked, her hair and clothing disheveled as she waddled from the bedroom. A frown shadowed her puffy face as she huffed, "Glad to have those men gone. I don't like any of those new ones. Look at the mess they left. They think all we have to do is clean up after them."

Sighing out loud, Callie rose from her seat and tried to stem the desperate urge to fly after the men. She picked up a heavy plate and soothed, "Don't worry, Irene, I'll clean up everything. I'm going to stay with you. You just sit by the stove and finish your knitting. I'll bring you a cup of tea. How does that sound?"

"That sounds nice." Irene silently shuffled to her favorite rocker and sat down. "Whew! I can't wait to get this baby out. I could hardly sleep last night. I'm worn to a frazzle."

Callie hummed while she fixed the cup of tea to tune out her sister's complaining, but it didn't help. As Callie set the plate and cup beside her sister, Irene didn't even open her eyes. Callie gave her some instructions, "Here, eat something. You'll feel better." Turning to the stack of dishes, Callie decided to do the outside chores first. "I'll be back in a flash. I'm going to go and check on the new foal and Raven. Then, I'll come back and clean up. Eat while I'm gone. You hear me?"

"Okay, I hear you."

Eagerness enveloped Callie as she tied back her

sun-streaked brown hair to face the gusty, late, spring wind. A smile tugged at her lips as the picture of the new colt skittered through her mind. She could think of nothing else. Tossing open the door, she pranced across the grassy yard with as much exuberance as that new-born colt. She looked around briefly to see where Bear might be but he didn't appear in her vision.

Catching the light scent of lavender and mint, she stopped at the herb garden. Native grass had crept into the tilled soil and threatened to overtake the tender new herb plants. *I'll never get all of this grass out,* she thought as she bent to tug at it. Pulling with all her body weight, she tried to force a handful of roots to let go.

The whinny of a hungry horse brought Callie's head up. "I'm coming!" she responded. She turned on her heels and hustled to the horses, still locked in their stalls. "Here I am."

All the eager heads bobbed over their stall doors. Several snickered and a low mooing sound came from the back stall.

"Yes, Meg, I know you are hungry. It won't be long now. That baby will be here before you know it."

Meg had come from her family's farm. Several months earlier, Pike had taken her and Irene back to their home to pick up their personal things before renting the farm to their uncle. Callie had been pleased to be able to bring back her pet cow.

Peeking over Raven's stall, Callie gawked at the newest addition to the herd. Only a couple days old, the fuzzy black foal nursed with vigor. "Raven, how is that baby of yours?" Her pride burst as she took in the white blanket and black coat of the baby horse. She could watch him all day but remembered she needed to get back to the cabin for Irene.

"Come on, Raven, let's take that baby outside." Slipping a halter on the gentle mare, Callie coaxed the mother and foal out of their stall and into one of the newly-fenced pastures. As she shut the gate, she scanned the fields again for Bear. *Hmmm, wonder where that man is?*

Callie watched Raven and the colt trot away, then

turned back to the barn and a deep thumping sound caused her to tense - she stopped. The hairs on the back of her neck rose and prickled up over her scalp. "Bear? Is that you?"

Body odor assaulted her nose before his hulking mass came out of the shadows. "I've been waiting for you."

"What do you want?" Callie hissed, hoping to stave off his menacing intentions. "You'd better stay clear of me or Pike will have your dirty hide."

Undaunted by her threat, Bear leered at her without moving. A rapacious, hungry expression filled his eyes as they traveled up and down her body.

Callie felt naked, and though she stood a good inch taller than Bear, his bulky physique could easily over-power her. Her eyes darted about with the hope of locating a weapon. She spied a hammer not far away on the ground and a shovel leaning against the wall. Leaping to the side, she bolted for the hammer.

Bear's hand grabbed her arm and jerked her back unmercifully and he tossed her to the side. Pain shot through her shoulder as she landed in the dirt. Callie scrambled clumsily to get her footing, while Bear threw himself on her prostrate form, then pinned her beneath him. His strong thighs gripped her tightly while he rose up enough to turn her over. His lust-crazed eyes stared openly at her face as he stretched himself over her long frame.

She gasped to catch her breath from the weight of his body. Her heart pounded in her chest while bile threatened, rising from her stomach.

Holding her wrists in his meaty hands, he smirked. "Not so tough now are you, whore?" Bear spat into her face. "I've been waiting for this day. I'm going to show you where your place is and it's under a man, not working next to him. You aren't going to tell me what to do again."

Callie bucked feebly as she collected her strength to attempt an escape. *You've got to fight him! Don't let him do this to you.* She kept her lips clamped against the scream in her throat. She would die rather than grovel or plead with the likes of him. In desperation, she ejected a wad of spittle from her mouth and hit her mark on Bear's cheek.

The man paused and a deep, mirthless laugh rose from his throat. A wet leer formed on his thick lips as he continued to mold his body to hers. Another scream pressed against Callie's throat as Bear's groin began to grind against her pelvis. Even with their clothes on, his male hardness dug into her soft flesh. She tried to wriggle away from him but could not move.

Bear forced both of her wrists into his left hand, then trailed his right hand over her breast as he lapped wetly at her throat. Through his ragged breathing, he stammered, "I'm going to give it to you good."

Callie shrank at his fetid breath.

"Get ready, 'cause you're never going to forget this, babe." His hands began to tear at her clothes as his desire overcame him.

Thrashing under his weight, Callie loosened an arm and grabbed for anything she could clutch on the floor. Bear muttered vile words into her ear as his free hand traveled along her breasts.

The bodice of her dress gave way as Callie's fingertips brushed cold, hard metal. *The hammer!* She awkwardly shifted it and clamped onto the wooden shaft. Getting a solid grip, she wielded it at her attacker, aiming for his head.

The tool connected with Bear's ear with a thud. He let out a yell and rolled off Callie, hand to his injured head.

Sitting up and drawing back her work-hardened arm, she launched the hammer at Bear's beefy head again. It hit with a muffled thump, like a melon being broken open.

Bear's eyes rolled back in his head and he sank into an unconscious heap.

"Who hurt who, babe?" Callie spat.

The man didn't move as blood trickled from his wound.

Feeling weak and sick, Callie sat back with her knees to her chest. Her arms wrapped around her legs tightly and her breaths came in short gasps, while her body began to tremble.

"Callie!" Irene's voice screamed from the cabin.

Callie gaped up and tried to gather her wits.

"Callie," sounded the frightened voice again. "Help me!"

Getting to her feet, she dusted herself off. She fumbled with her torn dress and held it together in the front. *I can't let Irene see this,* she told herself as she looked at Bear's limp body and then hurried off to meet Irene before her sister reached the barn.

Irene stood near the cabin with a pinched look radiating from her face and panic shinning from her dark eyes.

"What's wrong, Irene? Is it the baby?"

"Oh, Callie, I've been having terrible pains and water just gushed out of me." She grabbed Callie's arm. "Help me, Callie. I'm so scared."

Holding Irene tightly by her small shoulders, Callie twisted her around and directed her back into the cabin. "How exciting, Irene. The baby is coming. Let's get you back into bed. Then, I'll go and fetch Maude. She'll take good care of you. She's the best, now relax. Just think about the baby." She helped Irene into bed and soothed, "Now isn't that better?"

"Yes, Callie, I feel much better now that you're here." Irene relaxed her shoulders and shut her eyes slightly. "Ow!" she screeched, opening her eyes again. "There's another one. I can't stand the pain. Am I going to die?"

"Irene, don't fret so. I know you're going to be fine but I can't keep you company. I've got to go and find Maude. I need to get Lyric over here, too. She'll stay with you while I'm gone. Can you wait long enough for me to get Lyric over here? Just think about the baby. I'm going to grab Clash and make a dash to get everyone here. Once I get Maude, I'll find Pike. Now, I'm going to go." Callie patted Irene's shoulder and turned to leave.

"Hurry, Callie. I don't know how I can stand this."

"You're tough, sis. I'll be back before you know it."

Lacking courage to look in the direction of Bear's body still lying in a heap, Callie saddled Clash and headed toward Lyric's cabin.

As she raced up to Lyric's door, she yelled, "Lyric, are you there?"

Lyric stepped outside with a startled expression. "Callie, what's the problem?"

"It's Irene. The baby's coming. Can you run over to sit with her while I go get Maude?"

"Sure. Hurry, now, and don't worry."

"I'll be back soon." Callie wheeled the Appaloosa around and gave the horse his head. The wind tugged at her hair. A distant rumble caused her to crane her neck to the west, noting the horizon looked blackish-green causing a sinking feeling to explode in her stomach. *I've got to get Maude back here before the storm sets in. With my luck today, I might not make it. Got to try.* "Come on, Clash! Hurry!"

At the river's edge, Callie scanned the opposite bank for Billy. She waved vigorously, trying to get his attention as he milled about on the other side. Finally, he spotted her and waved back.

Feeling the pressure of the growing storm and fretting about the lost time in getting back to Irene, Callie jumped on board the raft and helped Billy pull it across the rough waters. As the raft reached the opposite bank, a howling wind began to whip the water into whitecaps.

"I'll be back as quick as I can with Maude," Callie called to Billy, as she jumped on the horse and turned toward town. "Wait here for us."

Thunder echoed over the trees as Callie raced through town to Maude's place, knowing the storm was closer now.

Chapter 28

As Callie turned up the road, she spotted Maude closing the barn door.

The woman carried a basket in her hand. Maude's eyes widened at the sight of the horse. "Callie, what's wrong?" she belted over the wind.

Callie pulled back to keep control over the horse, nervous from the weather. "We've got to hurry. Irene's baby is coming."

"Looks like a bad storm is heading this way. Hope we can get to her before it breaks. I'll grab my things. Do you want me to ride with you?"

Callie nodded. "It'll be faster if you do. Get your bag, let's ride."

Moments later, Callie offered Maude a hand and helped her settle onto the saddle behind her. She set Clash off into a long lope.

As they passed through town, Dora stood in front of her store and yelled, "I saw you go by. Is it Irene?"

"Yes," Callie shouted back, slowing the horse.

"You be careful! I think I see the makings of a twister. Look there!"

Callie stared at the horizon, growing black and ominous. Sickly, green clouds churned with a menacing tail, dipping and twisting, trying to touch the ground. "We've got to get to Irene," Callie screamed as she bumped the horse. Clash shot forward, jolting her back into Maude.

"Think we can make it?" Maude shouted into Callie's ear. "I think we may be in trouble. Should we wait for it to pass?"

"We can't!"

They raced to the river. The whitecaps splashed against the shore and tossed the raft on its swells. Billy had disappeared.

"We're on our own," Callie announced, as she led the way to the raft

"God, watch over Your children this day," Maude uttered in a shaky voice, as she stepped onto the raft.

"Help me pull!" Callie blurted, feeling her panic grow with the storm's fury.

*

Pike glanced up from his work of stacking lumber. His eyes noted the ugly western sky. A deep fear surged within him. *I haven't seen a sky as green as that since that storm in prison. I have to get home to check on Callie and Irene.*

Bouncing into action, Pike hollered, "Boys!", to get everyone's attention. "Looks like we're in for it. A storm is coming our way. It's too late to get us all back to the cabin. I'm going to try on my horse. You men head for the lunch shed and hide out. I need to hurry."

Trotting off to get Gertie, Pike felt dismayed as he monitored the troubled sky. The wind whipped in his face. *I hope the girls are alright. That looks rough.*

The trees began to bend from side to side as he halted next to Gertie's shoulder. Laying a soothing hand on the horse's neck, he tried to calm her. "Easy, hold on there. Be still, so I can get on."

Once untied, Gertie raced around in a nervous circle.

Pike chased after her, pulling on her reins and gaping west, he was rocked to a standstill. A twister's tail lowered to the ground from the boiling bank of black and gray clouds. Terror swept through him, freezing him in place on the hard dirt. *I've never seen something like that. Don't know what to do.*

The monster cloud widened and continued to birth the twister tail and as the tail flicked, then licked the ground, the tornado struck with the full brunt of its rage. An expanding cloud of dust and debris rose up to join the fury.

Gertie pulled hard at the reins.

Pike's mind unlocked. *I've got to get the girls somewhere safe.* Dread wrapped his heart with a vise-like hold and his breathing quickened, as he mounted Gertie and urged the mare forward.

The horse gave in to its instinctual flight response and Pike took advantage of it. They galloped away as the thunder boomed above. Even though Pike's boots were not in the stirrups, he stuck to the saddle and gripped the sides of the horse with his legs.

Gertie's hooves pounded the road leading back to his cabin while Pike's heart hammered in his chest. *Hope I can make it!*

Gusts of wind, bending the trees lower and lower, rose around him as a whistle came shrieking through the trees and surged in intensity.

What is that sound? Pike wondered as terror gripped him tighter. It came from behind him and drowned out the moaning wind. He clutched the horse and peeked over his shoulder. *God, help me!*

Several hundred yards behind him came the grinding vacuum, roaring like a locomotive, screaming out its fury. Objects began to rain from the sky. A broken branch scraped Pike's cheek and grazed his right shoulder.

It's coming too fast. I'm not going to make it. Callie's vibrant face flashed into his mind and as always, he loved to see her flushed with excitement. Other images swirled before him; Patrick chasing Candy, a kiss from Rebecca, Frank kneeling over his gunshot body, Amos preaching at the pulpit, Hank's golden form racing across an open field. The faces merged and melded into each other. The final image was unclear - a baby, but he couldn't see the face.

His mind raced as he felt himself suddenly lifted into the sucking monster. *Please let me know my child, Lord.*

*

The raft bucked wildly as Callie strained to hold on to Clash's bridle to calm him but he could no longer keep his footing. His thrashing caused the raft to tilt deeply to one side.

"We've got to jump off!" Callie shouted to Maude. "If we don't jump, Clash may kill us. Go!" Callie dove into the churning river. Stroking the water with all her might, she broke the surface. She spotted Maude in the water nearby, then began to swim for shore. The dress twisted around her legs and made her movements difficult, but she kept swimming.

Callie found her footing just as the twister's shrill scream struck her ears. She turned to see the monstrous beast, less than a mile away, sucking up trees as it headed in her direction.

Maude clutched her arm and yanked her forward. "Come on!"

Pushed by the wind, Callie dashed through the wet grass and hoped for a miracle to save them. She remembered the hollow along the river bank. It formed a protected, tunnel-like area that had been created by a flood. "This way," she shrieked at Maude.

Finding her way against the shrieking winds, Callie crawled into the hole and called on God to save them. Maude scurried in behind her. They clung to each other as the wind blasted them harder. It sucked at them, threatening to yank them out into the storm.

The shrieks of the tornado deafened Callie's ears. She tightened her grip around Maude and held her breath.

As quickly as the tornado had erupted, it passed over, leaving a morbid quiet in its wake. The winds still whipped but the fury had calmed to no more than slashing rain, washing from the sky.

Callie opened her eyes and noted her ears still rang. She peeked at Maude, sitting stiffly beside her. Callie wasn't sure she wanted to venture out because she didn't yet trust the storm was finished.

Slowly, mechanically, both of them stirred.

On hands and knees, Callie led the way over the wet sand to look out the opening to the tunnel, noting the land had been stripped. Many of trees lay about, twisted from the ground by the roots and tossed haphazardly over each other. Other plant material added to the debris. A plow had been sucked up from somewhere and was now deposited on the riverbank, looking quite out of place.

Scanning the area for Clash, Callie saw no sign of him. Worry about Irene prodded her to ignore the wind and the pouring rain. "Come on, Maude, we've got to hurry. I hope Irene and Lyric are alright."

Suddenly remembering her earlier ordeal with Bear, she added silently, *Hope Bear got sucked up by the tornado. That's just what he deserves. I may have killed him with the hammer, but I don't know. He could still be alive.* Leaving the hole behind, Callie and Maude crawled over the soaked trees, sloshed through the mushy debris and jogged along the clearings.

"You okay, Maude?" Callie asked, as she climbed over another fallen, slick tree trunk.

"I'm fine."

On the last clear stretch, Callie and Maude began to run. Callie dreaded what she might find over the next hillcrest where she would look down on Pike's land. Her heart hammered in her chest as water poured down her face. She threw her sopping hair out of her eyes.

Maude gripped Callie's hand as they reached the top of the hill. They stopped, both sucking in air as water drenched their faces.

The deadly twister had come straight across the homestead. A barren swath of exposed ground showed exactly where the beast had passed. Even the grass had been ripped from the soil. The tornado had traveled just north of the barn, which was now a heap of logs. The main body of the cabin still stood erect but part of the roof was missing.

"Oh no, Maude," Callie whispered. Taking off at a run, she shouted, "Hurry." Her feet flew down the slope, slapping the wet ground. "Lyric! Irene!" she screamed, racing through the lopsided front door. Her eyes glanced around the first room as she noticed the flipped furniture and rain pouring through part of the ceiling.

"We're in here!" Lyric shouted from the small bedroom.

Then came a scream.

"That must be Irene," Callie said to Maude as they made their way around the chaos in the room.

The bedroom had been fairly unscathed. Only an upended chair and some wet spots on the floor gave evidence of the storm. A kerosene lamp glowed beside the table. A pot of wildflowers, serene and colorful, looked out of place next to the lamp.

Lyric rushed to Callie and threw her arms around her. "The tornado was coming. I didn't know what to do, Irene couldn't get up. The baby was crowning so we couldn't even get to the springhouse."

Squeezing Lyric's hand, Callie soothed, "You're both okay. You made it through just fine."

Another scream rent the air. "Callie! Callie!" Irene cried. "Help me, I'm dying."

Callie grabbed Irene's hand and felt her own stab of fear at the look in Irene's crazed eyes.

Maude examined her. "Irene, dear," she said firmly. "You've got to get hold of yourself and listen to me. The baby is coming with its head and face in the wrong position. I need to get its face down. Do you hear me? You've got to focus on me."

"Listen to Maude, Irene," Callie coaxed. She squeezed Irene's hand. With a dry cloth from the nightstand, Callie wiped Irene's sweaty brow.

Irene looked up at her sister. "I thought we were going to die in the storm." As another contraction ripped through her, she let out a scream.

"Bear down, Irene," Maude instructed. "Wish I hadn't lost my bag," she mumbled to herself. "I'm going to try to put pressure on the head."

While Irene struggled with the birthing process, Callie thought, *This is the second worst day of my life.*

"Here we go," Maude said, sounding relieved. "Sometimes it just takes a while for the baby to right itself. Okay, Irene, now this is it. Can you hear me?"

"Irene, can you hear us?" Callie asked, close to her sister's ear.

Irene's head turned to look at Maude and her eyes focused.

Maude started again. "Okay, the baby's ready. Don't

quit now. It's time to push. In a very short time, you'll meet your new son or daughter."

With an almost imperceptible nod of her head, Irene acknowledged Maude's words. As the contraction hit her, she screwed up her face and bore down.

"Irene, keep it up," Maude said sharply, "it's coming." After several long seconds, Maude announced, "Irene and Pike have a daughter!"

Letting loose a long sigh, Irene relaxed into her pillow and even though she looked tired, her face beamed.

"You did it, sister," Callie praised, as she mopped Irene's face once more.

Shortly, Maude handed the dry, pink baby girl to her mother. The women smiled and hugged.

Well, at least there is one bright spot in this horrible day, Callie thought. She glanced over at Lyric, who stood on the other side of the bed. Lyric stared at the infant with a tear trickling down her cheek.

Leaving Irene's side, Callie placed a comforting arm around Lyric's shoulder. She guided her away from the bedroom. Crossing over the wet part of the cabin, Callie straightened out a rocker and placed Lyric in it. "I know you're feeling sad," Callie whispered to Lyric. "I feel so bad for you."

Lyric sniffled and wiped her tears. "Thank you, Callie. It does still hurt to have lost my baby. I don't understand why I had to lose it. It's just so unfair."

"You're right, Lyric," Callie agreed. "It's very unfair. Sometimes we can't understand the 'whys'. We just have to accept God's will. There will be more chances for a baby. I know it. You'll be pregnant again real soon. You just need a little time to heal, that's all."

Lyric seemed to want to shake off her pain. "What are we going to do now? We need to find out if everyone else survived the storm. I also need to talk to you about the barn." Lyric swallowed once and looked Callie in the eye. "When I knew the storm was coming, I raced out to the barn to let the animals out, hoping they could take care of themselves. When I got there, I found Bear on the floor and bleeding from the head. I couldn't drag him out. I had to leave him. I feel just terrible. I see the barn was destroyed. I'm afraid he has been killed."

Feeling the pang of Bear's attack, Callie debated about telling Lyric the truth. She threw her arms around Lyric's shoulders. "I'll go and check on him. But, first, I've got to tell you something." Easing back, she summarized the morning's events.

"Oh, Callie," Lyric said in shock. "How could he do that to you?"

"I don't know what was wrong with that man but don't worry about him. I'll go and see if I can find him in the rubble. Please don't tell anyone what happened. They've got enough to worry about."

"Don't worry. I won't say a thing. Why don't you go and see about him? I'll start cleaning up in here. Then we'll look for the others. I'm worried about them, especially Buster."

Suddenly, Callie thought about Pike. She was worried, too, but she didn't want to linger on that fear just yet. "I'm grateful you let the animals out, Lyric. I hope they made it." She turned and took off through the crooked door.

As Callie sloshed through the mud toward the barn, she was grateful that the rain had stopped. Puddles of water abounded and droplets fell from every remaining structure. The sun, with all its shimmering glory, suddenly burst through the clouds and brought light to the devastation.

Callie glanced around, noting that in the herb garden many plants had been broken and beaten down, but the ones that remained would thrive again. Frank's cabin was completely gone and all the trees in the tornado's path had been broken, twisted, and stripped of most of their limbs.

Just ahead, the barn lay in rubble. Callie inched toward the pile of logs, hardly able to grasp what she was seeing. *What are we going to do? How will Pike and Frank cope with the damage? There's so much of it.*

Feet stumbling forward, Callie directed her body to the task at hand - locating Bear. She peeked through the gaps in the heavy logs but she couldn't see anything.

Climbing the logs, she paused intermittently to search for Bear's body through the spaces in the pile. *I wonder if he could still be alive? Did I kill him?*

She spotted a shoe, then a pants leg. *There he is,* she thought as she carefully climbed higher to get a better view. With the light of the sun filtering through the cracks, she caught sight of Bear's head and twisted neck pinned under a log. "He's gone," she whispered, feeling a sense of relief. Her work done, she scrambled down the pile.

As Callie's foot stepped onto the soggy soil once again, the sound of hoof-beats brought her head up. She gazed across the clearing. "Clash! You made it!" Her tears stung at the sight of the muddy animal. She took off at a dead run to meet the Appaloosa and as she threw both arms around Clash's neck, she released her pent-up emotions. The dam broke within her and the sobs wracked her body.

Clash stood uncharacteristically still and he seemed to enjoy the comforting presence of Callie as much as she enjoyed the relief he provided. He rested his head over her shoulder and let her tears stain his sleek coat.

As Callie's sniffles lessened, she drew back and took hold of his reins. "Clash, looks like the barn is gone. Hope you don't mind staying outside for a while." She led the horse toward the broken cabin.

There is so much to do. Pike is going to be devastated. Pike! Where in God's name was he? Let him be safe. With a new spurt of energy, she poked her head into the cabin door and yelled to Lyric, "I'm going to go and find the men." She kept Pike's name to herself, even though he was her main concern.

"Try to find Buster," Lyric hollered back.

Callie leapt onto Clash and headed for the sawmill.

Clash thundered over the path as Callie worried about Pike. *What will I do if Pike's been killed?* Her stomach clenched and tears stung her eyes.

Off to her right, she caught a glimpse of something red. "Whoa!" she yelled to her mount. Reining him in, she slowly guided him toward the red mass. *Oh, no! It's Gertie.* The sorrel mare lay prone on the ground. Even from a distance, Callie could see that the mare was not breathing.

Fear gripped her as she sat frozen on the saddle and the day's atrocities weighed heavily on her shoulders.

She wanted to turn and run. *I don't want to know if Pike was on that horse. I can't bear to know it.* Something rustled behind her causing her to look around.

"Hey, I'm over here," a voice croaked.

She whirled toward the sound. "Pike? Is that you?" A sense of relief surged through her whole being. "Where are you?" Her eyes anxiously scanned the debris.

Pike sat humped over on tree stump with his face in his hands.

There he was - her love - Pike! She vaulted off Clash and bolted in his direction. Dropping at his feet, she tried to assess his injuries. "You hurt your leg?" she asked. When he didn't answer she looked into his face and saw it was deeply pained.

"She's dead, Callie," Pike whispered. "She's gone and she was carrying Clash's baby, too. I got her killed. I'm so sorry. I shouldn't have tried to outrace the storm. I should have known better."

"Shush, now. You can't blame yourself. You were just trying to get home. It's a terrible thing, yes, but it's not your fault." Callie clutched him close to her, holding tightly. Her heart seemed to take over. "Pike, I can't tell you how much it means to me that you're still alive. I thought you were dead when I saw Gertie. I knew, then and there, I couldn't live without you. I just can't. I'd shrivel up and die if something happened to you." Tears sprang from her eyes. "You are my whole life."

Hugging her back, Pike squeezed hard. "Callie, I'm thrilled beyond words to hear that. I love you, too. You mean so much to me. I can't tell you just how much. I was so scared when I thought I might never see you again. You're the best part of my life."

"Oh, Pike." Callie drew back to gaze into his misty green eyes. Her lips were drawn to his without thought or words and she wrapped her arms about his neck.

A low moan erupted from Pike.

In all her life, Callie had never experienced such a thrill as this - being in Pike's arms.

A harness jingled in the distance and brought them out of their passion.

"Are you hurt?" Callie asked softly as they drew apart. She peered down the road to look for the source of the sound. As the chestnut mules and wagon came into view, reality brought Callie screaming back to the truth of the rift that divided her life from Pike's.

"Callie," Pike stuttered. "I'm sorry. I shouldn't have done that." He looked toward the wagon with Amos driving and the other men sitting in the back. "I'm glad the men are alive."

Callie couldn't find her voice, while so many emotions rampaged within her. Just moments before, all she could think about was how much Pike had meant to her. The kiss brought home just how much she loved him and she would treasure the memory, but the moment of passion was over. In its place, guilt now resided. She had just kissed her sister's husband. That wasn't right, yet she felt so confused. But now, it was time to stop thinking.

The wagon pulled up and the men piled out.

"Are you hurt?" Eric asked.

"I don't remember much after the twister picked us up. When I sort of came to, I found my ankle hurting. I guess I landed on it and twisted it. Otherwise, I'm just scraped and bruised." His voice dropped to a whisper. "Gertie wasn't so lucky." After a moment, he asked, "Is everyone okay at the mill? Did it get damaged?"

Eric shook his head. "The mill is fine. A few trees are down in the area. The twister missed us, thank the Lord."

"Let's get Pike in the wagon," Amos directed. "I need to get back and check on Rebecca and the kids."

"Here, I'll help you," Eric said to Pike.

Leading Clash, Callie trailed along after the men as they got into the wagon. *Pike kissed me as quickly as I kissed him. Did he mean what he said? That he loves me, or was it just the heat of the moment? Since he almost died and all. Guess I'll have to wonder. There's nothing we can do about any feeling anyhow.*

Pike looked at Callie with raised eyebrows. "Callie, what's happened at my place?".

"Well, Pike," Callie started hesitantly. "The tornado came straight across your land. Lucky it didn't hit your house with a direct hit. Your barn is destroyed. Sorry, too, but Bear was killed. He was in the barn."

"Oh, no," Pike said, as he closed his eyes. "I'm sorry to hear that. Bear is dead? You're sure?"

Nodding her head, Callie said no more about it. She changed the subject as her eyes lit up. "I've got good news for you. You have a daughter! She was born just after the twister came through. I got Maude there just in time to help. The baby is perfect."

Pike smiled. "Well, I never expected that good news. I can't wait to see her. How's Irene?"

"She's fine - just fine."

"Are we ready?" Amos asked, breaking into the exchange.

"Yes," Pike replied.

Callie hopped up on Clash to follow. She still had many emotions flowing through her as she trailed along and watched everyone congratulate Pike as he smiled, laughed, and shook hands with them.

Callie trotted along with the group as they crested the small rise near Pike's cabin. When they stopped at the top of the hill, all talking ceased. It was obvious that Frank's cabin was gone.

"I'm sorry, Frank," Callie offered. Looking at the other cabin with its damaged roof, she said, "Your cabin is going to need some work, Pike."

"You can say that again." Dismay filled his voice. "You sure everyone is okay down there?"

"Don't worry, everyone is fine."

Amos clucked to the mules and they started downhill.

When they arrived at the cabin, Callie lent Pike her shoulder.

"Thanks, sis," he told her, as they shuffled to the cabin door.

"I'm so glad you all are okay," Lyric blurted, as the men began to flow through the door. When Buster melded into the tightly-packed group, Lyric bolted to him. He wrapped his wife in a hearty hug.

"Come this way," Callie told Pike. "You want to see your daughter, don't you?"

"Let's go."

An infant's wail met their ears as they came into the tiny bedroom. Next to the bed, Maude rocked the blanket-wrapped baby.

"Can we see her?" Pike asked Callie.

"Sure," Callie replied, as they moved to stand next to Maude, who was beaming from ear-to-ear.

"Here's your daughter." She unwrapped the yellow blanket and exposed the small infant for Pike to see.

"She's lovely," Pike said in a fatherly voice, as he gazed at her squirming body.

"Come and sit," Maude directed, as she got up and let Pike rest in the rocker. After he was seated, she placed the infant in his arms.

He stared down at the baby and cuddled her close.

"Irene's been sleeping," Maude said. "I meant to ask her what she wanted to name the baby. Do you know what her name will be?"

All eyes turned to Pike.

His brow creased in thought. "Since she was born during a tornado, we could call her Toni. I like that."

Callie smiled at Pike, pleased to see his joy.

"Toni?" Irene's irritated voice blurted. "Pike Wheeling, you don't think we would put such a name on a girl, do you? What are you thinking? Or, are you thinking?"

Callie felt embarrassed for Pike. She noticed that everyone else had grown silent and watched uncomfortably.

"I thought 'Mary Lou' would be a pretty name. How about that?"

"Whatever you want, sugar," Pike amiable replied, stroking the baby's hair.

Callie wondered if that was how he truly felt but she knew it wasn't her concern. As she observed Pike holding his newborn, she was jolted by a fresh wave of pain. She had no place in Pike's world. He had a wife and a new baby to love. She didn't fit into his life in any way, other than as a friend. She had no right to expect more. *I don't really want my sister to be unhappy. I can't hurt any of them. I've got to get on with my life - time to move on.*

Second Wind/Lori Davis

Chapter 29

During early spring of the following year, Drisco and Rufus tried to find shelter from the cold wind blowing against their backs. Drisco kicked Pike's buckskin hard as he glanced at the recently-stolen gelding Rufus rode. Needing to get out of the weather, he remembered a small town from a previous visit. When the pair had been there before, they had not lingered in the town, since there wasn't much to hold the interest of a man like himself. But now, riding next to his cousin, he saw it as a refuge. He grumbled to Rufus, "Let's head into town for a snort."

"I could use one myself. How far is it?"

"I think Miami is only a couple of miles south of here. We stole enough from that family the other day to keep us fat for a while. I could sure use me a game of cards."

A little while later, trotting through the village, Drisco noted new homes and several buildings being built. He stopped at the hitching post of the local saloon. Dismounting, he grumbled at the stiffness in his joints. The days of riding had taken their toll and his legs balked.

Rufus pushed forward into the open door of the decrepit-looking saloon. "See you inside."

Squinting in the sun, Drisco scanned the main street - a habit that had kept him alive all these years. Ever vigilant for a hint of danger, he never knew who he might run into from his past. He trusted no one and had no friends.

His gaze drifted up the street to the general store. Several horses and wagons were tied out front. *They look like they're doin' a good business,* he told himself. *Might be a place to rob.*

- 351 -

At the other end of town, there wasn't much to see. Just a restaurant with 'Jo Ann's Place' painted across the false front. It looked new to him. Several other businesses were in different stages of construction. *Looks to me like this place is growing.*

Eyes turning back to the general store, Drisco noted movement. A tall, young woman and a redheaded man strode out of the general store with packages in their arms. The sight of Pike shocked him. *Well, well, well.* A snigger rose unfettered from within and his mind swirled with delicious plans for his enemy while he studied the girl. She looked familiar, and given time, he would place her, too.

As an idea took shape in his mind, a low rumble of laughter wanted to burst forth from him but he kept it to a low chuckle to avoid being noticed. Forgetting his stiffness, he tugged his battered hat low over his eyes, pivoted on his worn boot heels and purposefully thumped into the seedy saloon.

Being early in the day, only a few patrons sat scattered around the room. Rufus leaned against the rough boards of the makeshift bar and tilted his head back to drain a shot of whiskey.

Drisco marched to the bar, leaned over the counter on his elbows, and looked at the dirty barkeep. "I'll have what he's havin'." He hooked his thumb in Rufus's direction. "Cuz, looks like we need to find us a place to stay and hunker down here a spell. You'll never guess who I just saw." Drisco glanced at Rufus out of the corner of his eye to gauge if he was listening. He paused, reveling in his thoughts before he told him his plans.

Rufus turned to face Drisco with eyes seemingly alight with wonder.

"I saw that redheaded shit, Pike. Can you believe our luck? We're goin' to settle down here a spell and drink this town dry and while we're at it, we're goin' to get that rat and as much of the rest of his group as we can." He smirked, his eyes staring into space. "We can take our time. No rush. I want to enjoy this. We'll pick them off, one by one."

The bartender dropped a glass of liquor on the counter.

"Bring me another one," Drisco demanded. He took the swig in one gulp. Slamming the glass down, he said, "The first thing we need to do is find us a place to live. Then we'll locate where they live." He licked his lips as his groin twitched. "Can't wait to watch the women." Spit threatened to drip from his mouth as fantasies with his victims slipped into his mind.

"I can't believe our luck," Rufus belted out. He whacked his grimy hands together and rubbed them vigorously. A malicious grin formed on his grubby face.

"For now," Drisco said, voice full of laughter, "All I want is to get drunk. After that, we'll work on a plan. Damn! I can't believe how the heavens have smiled on us today. God sure is makin' up for all we suffered through as kids - sure is."

Both men chortled as they grabbed their second, full shot-glasses, only too glad to answer the liquor's call.

Drisco lingered around town to watch for the clan. He stayed out of sight in the saloon and surveyed the streets when new wagons and horses arrived.

One day, not long after that, he had spotted Nigger Boy with his delectable new wife. Drisco and Rufus then followed them home. Now, he knew exactly where they lived. It hadn't been long before they discovered the other cabins that belonged to the group and recognized some of the family members.

Meanwhile, Drisco had found an empty, deserted cabin deep in the woods, several miles west of town. Although the distance and difficult terrain made it problematic for them to get at Pike's group on the other side of the river, it had one major advantage - they would be able to escape detection more easily, since they had no neighbors for miles.

*

A week later, on a warm spring morning, long before the first rays of light, Drisco crept toward Pike's cabin and took up his favorite post behind a tall cedar bush, while a thrill passed through him. He had never expected that sneaking around and following Pike would be as stimulating as it was - a most delicious surprise.

Hope Rufus is enjoying watching Nigger Boy and his wife like I'm enjoying this, Drisco told himself as a shiver of anticipation shook him.

By this time, Drisco had recognized the girl from the ambush where Silas and Titus had gotten shot. He had all the more reason to have his way with her, since he had missed out the first time.

After the first rays of the sun bounced over the landscape, Pike exited the cabin with his brother and the girl. Just as they did every morning, they hitched up a mule team and jangled down the road.

The boisterous group irritated Drisco to no end as they happily left for the mill. While the last pangs of jealousy pricked him, Drisco sneaked along the tree line to peek into the cabin window. There, he spied the other young woman who had been abandoned from the ambush.

Her long, dark hair had been tied back from her face as she washed dishes in silence. A baby played in a rocker-crib not far from her.

Drisco never tired of his fantasies of raping this woman and bashing in the skull of the little baby. The familiar thrill of knowing he had this woman's life in his hands excited him beyond measure, filling his groin and making him itch to get inside. But he had withheld himself all these days, watching Pike and his group because he needed to know their habits intimately. If he and Rufus were going to be able to mount the plan of attack that he had devised, some sacrifice was required.

Crouching at the cabin window, he told himself, once again, that he needed a little more time to be completely familiar with these folks. He and Rufus also needed to collect some money so they could make it to Mexico after Pike's family was dead. That would take a little more time and planning.

Besides all this, Drisco had his daydreams, which now kept him alive and excited. He stayed so titillated, day after day, that he didn't want to destroy the fantasies by ending them but he sensed he would have to carry out the killings soon. Not only was the risk growing but Rufus was getting itchy and Drisco feared that Rufus might do something stupid and get them caught.

In a few days, he would take Rufus out of town and find a way to gather the money they would need to keep themselves comfortable.

It's time to follow Pike, Drisco grumbled to himself. After another minute of watching the dark-haired woman, he shuffled back to the woods. On foot, he trailed after Pike's wagon.

*

From another familiar hiding spot behind the lower branches of a bush, Drisco watched the work going on at the mill. Lying prone, he sharpened his ears so he could listen to the conversations.

The tall woman drew his most intense interest. She was a real beauty with her shiny hair, long body, and slender waist. The fire in her eyes stirred his lust, lifting it a notch. Drisco had heard her being called Callie. He desired to be the one to chat with her and join her in her work.

Pike's brother stood beside Callie, now, as they stacked lumber. The blonde-headed man whispered in Callie's ear and patted her on the back and they rocked their heads back to laugh.

Anger swooped over Drisco, turning his thinking into a cesspool of death and destruction. Everything in his line of sight turned red because being an outcast had left him bitter, once again. Because of this bitterness, he had to even the odds and give those people what they deserved.

As the intense anger waned, feelings of lust returned. Drisco knew he would get his chance with the woman as his tingling body sprouted new kernels of desire, fed by the attractive young face. He closed his eyes as the erotic fantasies threatened to drive him mad. Unable to stand his body screaming for release, he found himself rubbing his stiffened member through his pants and it felt good. The up and down motion urged his blood to boiling. He knew he couldn't tease himself like this much longer because he wanted something better, something more, like the tall wench. But, for now, this would have to suffice.

Unbuttoning his pants, he let his full erection pop from its confines. Drisco closed his eyes and let his fingers do their work as he gasped out loud. He grabbed his hard shaft tightly as his ragged breath intensified and his mind enacted luscious scenes with Callie. Her naked body groveled at his feet and blood dripped from her slashed arms as she cried out for help.

He bit down on his free hand to keep from screaming out his pleasure. *You won't forget me, girlie. I guarantee it.*

*

Several weeks later, Callie decided to stay home and work in the herb and vegetable gardens. She felt guilty for having neglected them for so long. The Bermuda grass had almost taken over. "What am I going to do?" she complained as she bent over in the hot sun to tug forcefully at the well-rooted grass. For an hour, she struggled with the weeds. Then, she plopped back onto the moist grassy soil and swiped her sweaty forehead.

Gazing vacantly at the new spotted colt across the field, her thoughts drifted to the same subject that always haunted her - the Wheeling brothers. Over the months since Mary Lou's birth, Callie had waged an inner war with herself over her persistent love for Pike. *Why can't my heart let go of you, Pike? Why do you still pervade my thoughts and dreams? I'm engaged to Frank, now. I do truly like Frank. He's so kind and thoughtful but my heart doesn't sing when I'm near him, like it still does for you. I know I can't go on like this - loving you. You're going to be a father, again. You're not pining after me. As much as I'm still drawn to you and as much light as you give my world, it can never be between us.*

Sighing out loud, Callie let her eyes drift back to the hateful grass. This time, she pulled at it more gently, removing a couple of handfuls and tossing them aside. *Why can't I get excited about my own impending wedding? Irene is like a schoolgirl with her excitement and planning. I need to show more enthusiasm. Frank doesn't seem to be skeptical of the feelings I profess for him, even though I don't feel more than fondness for him. He's going to catch on soon.*

The handholding and the stolen kisses were nice but they made her uncomfortable. She didn't feel like kissing him back and she hoped he just thought her shy. She had only one more week before the 'Big Day'. *I sure need to get my head on straight. Maybe everyone feels this kind of apprehension before they get married. It may be natural- yeah that's it. I'm just nervous and acting like a kid. It's definitely time for me to grow up.* She hoped Frank didn't intend for her to stay home to cook and clean. She couldn't give up working at the mill or hunting.

Candy blasted out of nowhere and hopped onto Callie's lap and she wriggled and licked Callie's face.

"You about ready to go and hunt up some quail, my dear?" She stroked Candy's bouncing head as she glanced around for Irene. Wherever Irene went, Candy was always close by.

Sure enough, Irene held the hand of her recently-walking little girl and ambled out of the barn. In her other hand, Irene clasped a feeding bucket. Her new pregnancy was just beginning to show, a constant reminder of Pike's attachment to her.

"Hey, sis," Irene said, grinning from ear to ear. "Isn't it just a lovely day? I was thinking, why don't we go and pluck a few ripe wild plums out in the pasture? I could whip up a pie for supper. How does that sound? I'm in the mood for something fresh."

"Sure, I could use a break from this mess." Callie stood and dusted off her dress. "I don't know if I'll ever get ahead of these weeds. Looks a bit hopeless. Anyhow, I'll fetch a horse and we can head out to the tree. Why don't you grab a bag or something?"

"Okay, I'll meet you back here by the barn shortly."

"I'll be ready." Glad for an excuse to get away from the weeds, Callie grabbed a halter and lead rope from the barn. She tripped out to the side pasture where Clash ran loose.

At her whistle, his head popped up and, with a flurry of legs, he flew across the pasture with his head held high and his tail flagging. He even threw a couple of exuberant bucks along the way.

He feels good too, Callie mused, as her pride-filled gaze drank in his graceful sight. She geared him up in the barn and cinched his saddle. As she led him out of the barn and back into the heat of the sun, Irene and Mary Lou were heading across the yard. Irene had a bag in her hand.

"You want to ride?" Callie asked.

Irene nodded.

Callie helped her into the stirrup. After Irene sat astride the horse, Callie lifted Mary Lou to sit in front of her mother. As she grabbed the reins, the stallion meekly lowered his head to bob along beside Callie as they meandered into the field toward the wild plum tree.

"Sis," Irene innocently asked, "Are you excited about next weekend? Rena is about finished with your dress. It's going to look so pretty on you. The light-green material will really set off your eyes. Frank will think you look beautiful, too. I can't wait to see his expression."

Callie wondered how Pike would like her in her wedding dress. Then, she caught herself. *Don't think like that anymore,* she scolded. *After next weekend, you'll be Frank's wife.*

Irene's voice took on a softer note. "Are you nervous?"

"Well," Callie replied, as she tried to think what would be best to say to her gossipy sister. "Frank is a good man. I'm lucky to have him."

"Yes, you are," Irene uttered in a conspirator's voice. "He's the catch around here, in my opinion. Wish my own husband was more like him."

The words shook Callie. Why would her sister like her potential husband better than her own? Callie would give anything to be in Irene's shoes. *Funny what life can do to a person.* She tried to comprehend the fact that both she and her sister were going to be married to the wrong men and she giggled out loud.

"What's so funny?"

Stopping herself, she said with a nonchalant shrug, "Oh, nothing. I was just thinking, in another week, I won't be a single girl anymore. I hope I'm not a failure as a wife. I was also thinking that Frank may not know what he's getting into. He may starve to death and wear dirty clothes."

Irene chuckled. "You're right about that. You may have to continue to eat with us. I'd like that anyhow."

"Thanks, sis, I'll keep that in mind but I guess I'm going to have to settle down into a more domestic kind of life. Here we are. Whoa, Clash." Callie looked up at the tree, heavy with fruit. An abundance of red plums dotted the long branches. She tilted her head back to gaze at the fruit near the top and wondered how to reach it.

Irene quickly snatched the more easily-acquired ripe plums and placed them in her satchel.

"I think I'll get on Clash," Callie declared, "and see if I can reach the top of the tree."

"Oh, let me try," Irene begged. "I feel like trying something fun today. I'd like to see the view from up there."

"I don't think it's such a good idea," Callie said. "With you expecting, you could get hurt - or hurt the baby."

Irene shooed her with her hand. "Oh, nothing like that is going to happen. I'm not going to get hurt. I loved doing that as a kid. Don't you remember how we used to take our horses out and pick fruit every summer? I never felt so free as when we did that."

"Yes, I remember." Callie felt a brief wave of grief over those lost days and the loss of her parents.

Suddenly, Mary Lou made a dash for the field on her newly-found legs.

As a natural reflex, Callie sprinted after her. She chased the child down and scooped her up. "You're getting fast." As Callie turned back, she noticed that Irene had already climbed up on Clash's back and stood plucking plums high up in the tree while Clash quietly chomped on the grass. "I swear," Callie blurted with irritation as she carried her niece, thinking, *Irene needs a good scolding.*

As Callie drew near, Clash's head flew up as he'd been spooked by something in the grass and he leaped sideways.

Irene screamed as she teetered, then fell from the saddle, landing with a thud.

Callie's heart plummeted and she quickly put Mary Lou down. "Oh, no!" she cried as she ran to Irene. *God let her be okay!*

Irene's vacant eyes stared out from her still form. A rock, jutting up from the solid ground, rested under Irene's head.

"No! Please no!" Callie felt for breathing on Irene's chest, but there was none. "No, no," she repeated as she bent low over her sister's mouth and prayed for a small breath. She dropped her head. "Oh, no."

Irene was gone.

Rocking back on her heels, Callie stared at her sister's pale face and bloody hair and tried to absorb what had just happened. *She can't be dead - she can't!* How could this be happening?

Callie heard a rustling sound in the grass to her right. She spied the undulations of a snake slithering away.

"Mama," a little voice quaked.

Callie grabbed Mary Lou's little body and swung her to her chest. She got up and trotted away from the grisly scene. With her mind nearly frozen, she couldn't decide what to do next. She stood holding Mary Lou for several long minutes while the breeze whipped Callie's loose hair.

Mary Lou began to fuss and the movement dragged Callie out of her shock, so she looked for the horse.

Clash grazed quietly nearby.

After she placed Mary Lou in the saddle and gathered the reins to make her way back home, a fog settled over her mind once more. She fought to keep her thoughts clear as her legs trembled and wanted to give out from beneath her. *I've got to take Mary Lou to Lyric. Then, I've got to fetch Pike. What's he going to say?*

As she plodded along beside the horse, her limbs didn't seem to be working right. They felt like lead weights, but she kept her eyes trained on the cabin to guide her steps. Without it, she didn't know if she could find her way back, while her stomach roiled. *Keep your eyes on the cabin. Keep your feet moving. You can make it.*

Suddenly, she felt the blood draining from her head.

You can't stop now! Come on feet - work. She set her jaw tightly and put her iron will to the test. *Remember, you've got Mary Lou to look out for.* Somehow, she kept her feet moving ever so slowly and after several more minutes of plodding, she gained some control.

*

Drisco and Rufus had spent the last few weeks in Nebraska. They had collected the large sum of money they needed to hightail it to Mexico after they finished killing everyone in Pike's group.

"Looks like we found us some rich pilgrims," Drisco said to Rufus, as they rifled through the contents of a wagon they had just held up. The wagon had started out with a family of four. The mother was the only one left alive, and she would soon join her family in heaven. But first, she would serve as entertainment for Drisco's depraved enjoyment.

Rufus pulled out a sack and counted some gold. "We've got us enough here to finance a quick getaway when we finish our business with Pike. The law's been trailin' us hard since Kansas. Think these nags will make it back?"

"Mine had better," Drisco answered sharply as he jumped down from the wagon and drifted toward the woman tied to a stump. He pulled out his knife. "We don't have much time," he said to Rufus, "so we'll have to have our fun quick, then high-tail it out of here - you ready?"

He already knew from the evil light in his cousin's face that Rufus was more than ready to practice on this poor woman some of what they had planned for the ladies back in Miami. Drisco let out a maniacal laugh.

*

A short time later, Drisco leapt onto the back of his tired buckskin gelding and kicked him viciously to keep up with Rufus. Drisco had been impressed with the toughness of Pike's old horse. He had never had a mount that had lasted as long as this tough gelding. The

scarring and beating of the animal had been pure pleasure - as good a substitute for Pike as Drisco could
manage.

A deranged laugh exploded from his throat as the
pair started the hard ride back to the Territory. Excitement rocketed through Drisco's veins, causing unre-
strained laughter.

Rufus joined him in the fun.

*Pike, here we come. Do you hear me, you redheaded
shit?*

Chapter 30

Head bowed over the freshly turned soil that now covered his wife and unborn child, Pike's tears dripped off his cheeks. Sniffles and tears poured from his friends and family around him. The new graveyard, about five hundred yards from Pike's cabin, had received its first occupants.

Amos had presided over the funeral and Buster with the mill-workers helped to shovel dirt over the grave. Now, the mourners began to drift away.

The incredulousness of his wife's death still rocked Pike. How would he ever come to terms with Irene and his unborn child's deaths? He just didn't know. He looked up at Callie, who stood next to Irene's grave, staring at the pile of dirt. He knew Callie suffered as much as he did, probably more.

Since Irene's death, Callie had been inconsolable. She either cried or she slept and at the funeral she had been quiet, her eyes puffy and red. Tears had streamed steadily down her pale, pretty face.

Pike drifted to her side and joined her in silence. After a time, he slipped his hand around hers and squeezed it several times. "You okay?" he inquired when she didn't respond to his hand.

She nodded her head once.

"Are you hungry? There's lots of food waiting for us."

"I'm not really hungry."

"I know it's hard, Callie," Pike continued. "It's torn me up, losing Irene and the baby. But we can't stop living. We both have to go on - somehow. Our lives will never be the same, now that she's gone. All we can do is try to live without her. Life will be different, that's all. We'll miss her but someday we'll see her again. I'll bet she's watching us right now. She wouldn't want you to quit living just for her - would she?"

Callie's eyes drifted slowly from the dirt to peer sadly at Pike. "I know you're right," she began, "but I can't help feeling so lost. All of my family is gone. What's going to happen to me now?" Her eyes began to water again. "I'll do my best to go on, but . . . I'm going to miss her so."

Doing what he could to provide her some comfort, Pike gathered her to his chest.

*

As Callie placed her head against Pike's solid chest, she drew all the solace she could from the man that she still held so close to her heart. She pulled his energy into herself to feed her chilled veins. Closing her eyes, she lived in the moment, forgetting all of her grief and pain. Drinking deeply of his scent, she drew comfort from the familiar, soapy-clean aroma of his clothes. He, alone, was the person who could give her the security she so desperately needed, so she absorbed as much as she could.

Her stomach suddenly growled and she pulled back to glance into Pike's face with a hint of a smile. "I think I am a little hungry."

"Here, hold onto my arm and let's go to the cabin. They're waiting on us."

"I'd be happy to," Callie returned. She wiped her cheeks one more time and slipped her arm through Pike's.

As they reached the cabin, Callie passed the outside tables, brimming with eating guests, and inside, the small cabin was filled to capacity. Callie mingled through the crowd and noted the ladies had made their most tempting dishes for the somber occasion.

As Callie gazed around, Frank suddenly stood in front of her, holding out a full plate of food. "Here, my darling, I brought you something to eat."

"Thank you," she said with a tiny smile. "Maybe in a little while. I'm not sure I'm really hungry yet."

Frank appeared a bit dejected by her rebuff but he

displayed patience. "Sis, you need to eat something. You look pale." He looked her in the eye - something he seemed to have had trouble doing since Irene's death.

Callie had likewise avoided Frank. She wasn't sure it was due to her grief but she didn't feel up to dealing with the reasons. She decided to accept his offer. "Okay, Frank, you're right. I'm ready to eat." She forced a smile.

His eyes lit up at her acquiescence. "That's great, hon. Let's head outside where we can have a bit of peace and quiet." He led her away from the tables to a spot by themselves.

Callie positioned herself so she could see Pike's back. She watched him briefly as he visited with Pumpkin, who had been working at the sawmill for the last several months and had stayed sober for that period of time. She wondered how things were going between Pumpkin and Maude. They seemed to have eyes for one another.

"I've been wanting to talk to you," Frank said. He seemed a little nervous.

Her stomach wrenched as she wasn't sure she wanted to hear what he had to say. It was probably about their wedding.

"Callie, I know that our getting married needs to be put off for a while, unless you think you can do it. I understand this has been hard on you but one thing is for sure, you can't live in Pike's cabin any longer. He's got Mary Lou to look out for. You can help him with her but you'll have to move into my cabin. If you think it's okay, we can go ahead and start living together until you are ready to get married. What do you think?"

Gazing down at her untouched food, Callie took a deep breath. She should tell him outright that she didn't want to marry him right now, and maybe not ever. But, when she collected the strength to look him in the eye, she found that she didn't have the fortitude or the heart to hurt him. There had been enough pain to deal with this week, so she decided it was easier to put him off. "I just don't know what I want Frank. I can't think about that right now. You're right, though, I will have to move out of Pike's cabin. I can stay in yours. You can live with Pike for awhile. I need time to think everything through.

My heart just isn't into a celebration right now, I'm sorry."

Frank, with his eager-to-please manner, replied softly, "I understand, sis. You can't think about *us* right now. That's fine. I'll wait until you're ready."

Callie's eyes drifted to Pike's back and lingered there while Frank spoke.

"It may work out sooner than you think. You'll be able to put your grief behind you. Until then, you're welcome to my cabin. I'll move my things into Pike's."

When Callie realized that Frank had stopped speaking, she quickly brought her eyes back to his face and spotted the anxious expression and guilt struck hard. She tried to brush off her staring at his brother by saying, "You want to help me move after I get packed?"

Frank reacted like a dog that had been thrown a bone. He jumped on the suggestion and instantly his eyes grew happier. "Sure, I'd be glad to help you. Grab me when you're ready."

"Okay, I'll see you later." As she rose, Frank offered his outstretched hand.

*

Later that evening, Pike sat in his rocker and stared out the open window. He drank in the damp, earthy smell of the fields. Frank and Mary Lou were sleeping quietly as he struggled to make sense of his life. *Where am I now? Where am I going?* He sure didn't know and just when he had been able to accept the fact that his married life would never be what he had hoped it would be, *bam!* The rug got yanked out from under him and he seemed to be back to square one, but now with the addition of one very special little girl.

Pike knew he would never have loved Irene in the way he had once loved Rebecca, and now loved Callie. Yes, he knew he still loved Callie, but being a man of God, he had never allowed his feelings to dictate his actions toward her.

Now, Frank was a consideration where Callie was concerned. Since she had become engaged to Frank, Pike had tried his darnedest to be happy for them. They both deserved all the happiness they could get. They were his favorite people in all the world so why should he, a married man, stand in their way? It certainly wasn't right - or fair. But his love for Callie, and wishing to be the one she would share her life with, plagued him to this day.

Not only did Pike feel lost because Frank and Callie were going to be married but also he felt he had been a failure as a husband to Irene. That guilt created a heavy burden of raw emotions and now he wouldn't have another chance to give her what she wanted.

With Irene buried and with the pain of the initial grief passing, it was time to face his true feelings for Callie. He didn't know how Callie felt about him anymore but he couldn't go on any longer without at least talking it over with her.

As so many thoughts played across his mind, he stopped himself. *First things first,* he knew he had to make amends with his Father, for he had let Him down.

I'm so sorry, Father. I wasn't the husband Irene wanted. Now that she is with You, I don't have another chance to make her happy. Maybe I didn't appreciate her enough because I still have feelings for Callie. That may have blinded me to Irene's best qualities. I guess I won't know. Lord, please forgive me. Help me make sense of it all. I need some peace. Hopefully, You can send a little bit my way. Amen.

Allowing his ruminations to drift back to Callie, Pike couldn't stop himself. *What does this mean for us both, now that I'm a widower? Will she go ahead and marry Frank? She may really love him. She may have forgotten about me - but I hope not. I don't know what else to do but wait and talk to her. I sure don't want to hurt Frank. If Callie wants to marry him, I'm going to have to accept it.*

Maybe it's not right to tell her how I feel. I'm going to make myself wait and see what she decides about her marriage to Frank before I open my big mouth. That's the only thing I can do. I'll leave it all up to her. Can I live with her decision? Well, I've got to. I have to let her go quietly, if that's what she wants. I need to do what's right for everyone involved and that includes Irene's memory.

As Pike settled matters on how he was going to handle the situation, poignant longing plunged deep within him. He wanted to jump up, race out the door, find Callie, and tell her that he loved her. He wanted to hold her forever but something within him clamped down on that urge and a few cleansing tears flowed. Pike never knew he could cry as much as he had over the last three days and he'd thought he had been cried out.

I must remember the promise to myself to let her go. I have to be strong, now. She can't be forced to make the decision I want. The tears flowed harder now. *God, I want her so much. To come this close and still not have her.* Silent sobs racked his frame.

*

Deep in the same night, Drisco and Rufus alighted by the corral at their crudely-made cabin. They dismounted the worn-out horses. Both animals dropped their heads in exhaustion, with their sides heaving and lather thick on their shoulders.

"Here, put them in the corral," Drisco ordered, as he shambled away toward the dark cabin. "We'll need 'em later on when we get our plan into action." He rubbed his palms together and stumbled over a rock. "Damn!"

Inside, Drisco lit a lantern, then threw himself onto the bunk and fell instantly into a deep, restoring slumber. In his dreams, he saw his devious plan under way. The reality of the dream brought him to familiar heights of excitement.

When he roused later and realized that it had been nothing more than a dream, his reeling mind took the opportunity to fine-tune his plan. His lust for blood drove sleep away for the rest of the night but that was okay with him since he enjoyed the quiet time alone.

*

Like every other day in July, Sunday morning presented itself to Callie as warm and steamy. Ready to rustle up breakfast for Pike, Frank, and Mary Lou, she burst through the front door of Pike's cabin and grinned at him.

Mary Lou hopped up from the floor where she was playing and shot headlong to her aunt. She hugged Callie's legs tightly. "Hi," her tiny voice squeaked.

Pausing to stroke the girl's dark-blonde curls, Callie beamed at her niece. "Good morning, little one. How are you? You want to help me make some breakfast?"

Nodding vigorously, the girl let go of Callie's legs and walked with her toward the stove.

"Whew! It's muggy out there," Callie complained.

Both brothers rested at the kitchen table and looked half asleep. Pike responded, "You've got that right, sis. We're going to have to get that stove shut down pretty quick or we're going to be run out of here."

"I'm just going to cook something fast, like eggs and bacon. How does that sound?" Callie turned to begin her cooking duties. *Sure miss Irene the most at this time of day.* Irene made the best pancakes and the idea of the tasty flapjacks made Callie's mouth water.

Forcing those notions from her head, she refocused on the task at hand - cooking. "Drats," she fussed, as she balefully glared at another egg after she had broken the yolk. "I broke another one. Who wants it?"

"He can have it," Frank directed as he pointed to Pike.

"That's fine by me," Pike said. "I don't mind them broken, hand it here."

Callie flopped the cooked eggs onto a plate and added a few strips of bacon. She placed the hot food in front of Pike.

"Thanks, sis."

"Someone's in a good mood this morning," Callie noted of Pike.

"I slept well. Mary Lou slept through the night - finally." Pike beamed at his daughter, who had already eaten her egg and had gone back to playing on the floor. Candy slept nearby.

"You know," Callie said, "I'd be happy to keep Mary Lou for you at night." She placed Frank's plate of unbroken eggs in front of him before cracking a few eggs for herself.

"Callie, I appreciate it, but having little Mary Lou around eases my depression about Irene's death. Thank you, though."

The mention of her dead sister brought Callie a moment of pensiveness. Each night, sitting out under the black carpet of heavenly lights and listening to the sounds of the land around her, she had spent long hours in heavy thought. She had shed many a tear for Irene and she also had contemplated her own future and what she wanted to do with it. Just last night, she had made one decision and that was to not marry Frank. Even though she didn't know how Pike felt about her anymore, she knew she couldn't marry Frank. It just wasn't right, she didn't love him. It wouldn't be fair to him, but, more importantly, it wasn't fair to her. She wanted to be with someone she loved.

She still longed to be with Pike. She had never stopped loving him and she finally accepted that fact once more. She had tried to bury her feelings but had never been completely successful. Now she had the opportunity to tell him just how she felt and she meant to tell him at the first opportunity, but first, she had to deal with Frank. It was only right.

Today, after church, she hoped to tell Frank that their relationship was over. Maybe then she would be free to divulge her true love for that lanky, redheaded man that sat across the table from her. He was close enough to touch, close enough to kiss.

Instantly, inklings of the old guilt washed over her. *How can I have these feelings toward my dead sister's husband? It isn't right, people will talk.*

Did it matter? Well, not to her now. She finally felt at peace with herself. She had learned a valuable lesson - always be true to your innermost feelings. If they were denied, she would be in big trouble and she knew that now.

Pike spoke up. "Someone else seems to be in good spirits as well."

Realizing she was smiling, Callie said, "Yes, Pike, I am feeling grand this morning. I slept hard. I'm ready for church and then ready to get back here to work in the garden. That is, unless Maude wants to get together for a while. You know Sunday is our girls' day. I'll wait and see what she wants to do."

Pike continued to eat contentedly when Frank's head shot up.

"There's a wagon coming," Frank said. "It must be Amos, or maybe Eric. I'll go see." He stretched as he got up from the table, then trudged out of the cabin.

Pike heard voices outside.

Patrick's cheery voice called out, "Pike, where are you?"

Pike turned to face the door as the lad burst through it. He rushed to hop on Pike's lap and to give him a big hug. "Looks like you've grown a foot since I saw you last week," Pike said, eyes shining.

Patrick, afire with youthful energy, fixed his green eyes on Pike and smiled. "Can we go hunting today after church?" His eyes brimmed with hope.

"I would love to see if we can rustle up a few quail for supper with Candy. How does that sound?"

"Yippee! I can't wait! Can I shoot some today?"

"We'll see about that." Pike watched the rest of the group shuffle into the cabin.

"Hi," Rebecca and Amos said in unison. Rebecca asked, "Are you ready for church?"

"Yes," Callie responded as she jumped to her feet and deposited her plate to wash later. "I'll start getting the mules hitched." She turned to leave.

"No," Pike said, "let me do that. You can stay here and rest with Mary Lou."

"Whatever you say, boss."

Rebecca, Amos, and their two girls followed Pike from the cabin and visited while he prepared the mules.

Amos said, "We'll go on ahead and meet you at the church. Do you mind bringing Patrick?"

Pike had noticed, of late, that his surly brother had been a lot friendlier toward him and Amos didn't seem to mind if he had Patrick with him anymore. He and Amos had never talked over the whys and wherefores of Amos's past behavior but he felt relieved that Amos no longer distanced himself.

Amos clapped him hard on the shoulder and said a bit loudly, "I'll see you at church. Don't be late like last week." He laughed.

Caught off guard by his brother's teasing, Pike responded with a big-hearted laugh. "I'll try real hard not to make a scene while you're driving home a point to the congregation. Sorry about last week. Remember, the cow got out."

"Yes, well, I see they're all in now, so there are no excuses. And Pike, could we spend some time together - maybe this afternoon. I'd like to talk to you. I need to tell you some things."

"Sure, brother, I've always got time for you. I'd enjoy an afternoon with you. It'll be just us boys - like old times, huh?"

"Yes, like old times," Amos responded, still grinning. "Well, we've got to go. Don't be late."

*

Rebecca helped the girls find their seats in the wagon and watched her husband step into the driver's seat. "Is everything all right?" she asked,

Amos clucked at his prized pair of chestnut mules. "Yes, sweet, everything is just great."

"Okay, just checking." She shifted Hope in her arms. The small child loved to ride up front so she could see where they were going. She was a handful, squealing and bobbing her legs while her mother held on tight.

The day was as perfect as any Rebecca had ever spent with her family. Sundays were their special times together. Listening to her husband's weekly sermons had helped bring Rebecca understanding of the place within her marriage she now resided. It had blossomed into the special bond Amos had spoken of in several of his Sunday instructions.

Amos had discussed the way a marriage was a gift to a couple - something that aged well and got better with time, like a fine bottle of Chardonnay. Of course, he admitted, the excitement of the new relationship waned over the years. But, in its place, came something much sweeter and deeper. It was a bond that could only come from two people sharing a life together through time and tribulation. The comfort from that intimate bond was immeasurable. Having a safe place to fall, through the true love of another, was the rarest and most prized possession a person could have.

Rebecca knew that she had such a marriage, even after its difficult start and she reveled in it these days. Since she would have never thought that her love for Amos would ever surpass what she had experienced for Pike, she was surprised when it had. The fact still surprised her, even now. She loved her husband deeply, and respected him as no other in her life. No one could take his place in her heart - or in her world. She reached out, cupped his warm hand with hers, and squeezed lovingly. "I love you," she whispered, her voice suggested a few tears.

"I can't begin to tell you how much I love you," Amos responded. "Don't ever forget that."

"I got it." Rebecca giggled like a schoolgirl.

Rebecca shifted Hope in her arms, then looked up to suddenly note two strangers mounted on gaunt-looking horses up ahead in the trees. A quick shiver raced through her as she heard the flap of grim messenger's wings, causing her to freeze and a lump to come into her throat. Maybe it was the way the strangers wore their hats - low over their eyes. Maybe it was the ratty, grimy clothes. She couldn't put her finger on it, but as she caught sight of them, she said to Amos, "Look, there's trouble ahead."

Amos pulled on the reins and instructed, "Whoa, mules," as fear came into his straining eyes.

The first bullet rang out, ripping into Amos's chest. He slumped over.

Rebecca felt a scream explode from her throat and Hope and Hannah screamed with her.

Rebecca felt a sharp jolt to her neck and then the world quickly faded. Next, she saw her first glimpse of a brightly shining light and she knew all of her fear was gone.

*

An alarm bell tolled within Pike's head as he heard the shots. "Get up there, Dunk and Don!" he shouted, slapping the reins. "Hold tight!" he hollered to the passengers. As the mules stepped up their pace, he saw Callie grab hold of Patrick. Over his shoulder, Frank held tightly to Mary Lou and to the sideboards.

Pike kept his eyes on the horizon, searching for the cause of the shooting. As they rounded a bend in the well-worn road, he spotted Amos's wagon and two strangers on horseback. *Where's Amos and Rebecca?*

Suddenly, reality struck like a bolt from heaven - Amos and Rebecca could be hurt! Struck by a white-hot rage, Pike screamed, "Hang on! Keep Patrick from looking in the wagon when we get there!" He urged his mules into a headlong run.

As he drew closer, Pike began to make out the details of the gunmen's faces and an icy blast struck as the round, pocked face became clear. It was Drisco! Beside him was Rufus.

Pike gaped at the mangy, dirty horse under Drisco's saddle. The recognition of his long-lost gelding blasted him. *It's Hank!*

The gunmen whipped their horses and fled in the opposite direction, soon enveloped by the woods.

"Whoa!" Pike screamed as he jumped from the still-moving wagon. He stumbled once but managed to maintain his balance. Terror at what he was about to find gripped his mind and his soul but he couldn't stop now. He raced on, his heart thundering like a frightened herd of mustangs. *Please, God, no - no.*

Eyes coming to rest on the crumpled bodies of Amos and Rebecca, Pike's breath caught in his throat as the river of blood told its story. He gaped at Amos, who was slumped on the opposite side of the wagon. Pike placed his hand on Rebecca's shoulder and tugged her over. The expression on her face, grisly and set, told Pike she was gone. Her sweet young life's work had been completed; now she had her angel wings.

"Are they hurt?" Frank gasped as he flew up behind Pike. He instantly fell silent as his eyes took in the scene.

Still gaping, Pike stared at Rebecca's pale face.

Frank skirted around him and ran to the other side. Gawking at the ground, he stood without saying anything.

Pike's eyes moved slowly to Hope's little body dropped coldly not far from the wagon, and he knew she must be dead.

Frank walked in slow motion to Amos, to his brother's limp body. He asked quietly, "Amos, can you hear me?"

Amos's head lifted ever so slightly as a small groan escaped him.

Frank yelped, "He's alive!"

Flying into action, Pike gaped around. "We've got to find Hannah and get Amos back to the cabin." He checked the back of the wagon and saw nothing but a bundle of blankets. A new bolt of fear shot through his spine. *Please don't tell me they took her.*

Suddenly, the bundle moved.

Pike scaled the side of the wagon, tossed back the covers and scooped up the cowering child. "Hannah, you're okay. You're safe." He clutched her to his chest and hopped out of the wagon. He raced her to Callie's arms, then ran back to help Frank.

Together, they lifted Amos from his seat and carried him to their wagon. Covering Amos with a blanket, Frank hopped in beside him before Pike reined the mules around.

Along the way, they met Buster, Lyric, Rena, Herman and Eric. Pike wasted no time with explanations but told them to meet him at the cabin and panic raced through him as he urged the mules to hurry.

Chapter 31

Callie held the children in the main room of the cabin until the other ladies arrived. Buster and Eric, along
with the professor and Effie, soon clustered nearby.

"Callie, please tell me what happened," Rena
pleaded, her face flushed white. "Where is Rebecca?"

"Help me get the kids over to Frank's first," Callie
replied, evading the direct question, as she handed
Hannah to Lyric. "Then, we can talk."

Once inside Frank's, Callie hugged both the little
ones. Hannah still appeared shocked and Patrick was
unusually quiet.

"Lyric, Hannah has been through a terrible event.
Would you please wrap her up with a blanket and hold
her tightly."

To her credit, Lyric followed orders and didn't ask
what she had to be dying to know.

"I'm going to leave Mary Lou with you, too. Can you
manage?"

Lyric bobbed her head.

Callie turned to gaze at Rena's petrified, misted eyes
as she clutched Herman. Callie's heart sank. "Come on,"
Callie said as briskly as she could. "Let's go outside."
She clasped Rena's solid arm and guided her.

When the door shut behind them, Rena turned and
implored, "Please, I have to know. Where is Rebecca?"

Swallowing hard, Callie collected her courage and
began to speak. "I wish," she stammered, "I didn't have
to tell you this." She grabbed for the right words to say
as she put her head down a moment. Then, she looked
up again. "Rebecca and Amos were ambushed by a
couple of bandits. Both Amos and Rebecca were shot

and so was Hope. Amos and Hannah are the only ones still alive." Callie clasped Rena by the shoulder, studied her eyes and tried to determine if her words had registered.

Rena stared straight ahead with a blank expression on her face. Inch by inch, the powerfully-built woman began to sink downward, her knees shaking and growing too weak to hold her.

Callie quickly reached for Herman.

Rena dropped to her knees. "No, no - she can't be dead." The whisper floated from Rena's mouth but her eyes remained fixed in front of her and her head began to shake from side-to-side.

"I'm so sorry," Callie stuttered as she attempted to comfort Rena, knowing there was no comfort to be found. She knew well the depth of pain that Rena faced in losing her sister.

"I want to see Amos," Rena said woodenly, as she rose back to her feet. Stumbling, she headed toward Pike's cabin.

Callie, clutching Herman, trailed behind her.

*

"Can you hear me, Amos?" Pike breathed into his brother's ear as he knelt by his head and gripped his hand.

Collin sliced off Amos's shirt and bared his chest for all to see. Effie stood beside him with rags in hand. The blood still dripped from Amos's wound as Collin gazed at it. After a few moments, he lifted his troubled eyes to Pike and shook his head once, telling him volumes.

Pike's heart sank as he accepted his brother's fate. Tears sprang to his eyes as he lifted his gaze to look at Frank, wanting to share this solemn moment with him.

"Pike," Amos said, just above a whisper. "Is that you?"

A sob threatened to overpower Pike when the words registered. As he turned to look at Amos, a painful wave of emotion struck him. He couldn't stop the waterfall of tears that flowed but after a few seconds, struggling to find his voice, Pike replied, "Ye-s, A-mos . . .I'm he-re with you."

"Pike," Amos strained to say. "Please forgive me. I've been a terrible brother. Please - forgive . . . " He lost his voice as his chest heaved.

"No, Amos," Pike said anxiously. "Don't feel bad. We'll always be brothers. We'll meet again when we're with God. Save me a place by His side. Go to His glory with all of the love I possess held in your heart. You're a wonderful brother. Rest now. I won't leave you." Bending his head forward, pressing it to his brother's temple, sharing the last scrap of earthly warmth they had together, he let the tears flow freely.

Amos found his voice again. "I love you all. I'll see you again - soon. Where's Rebecca?" His strength faded.

"She's waiting for you. Her arms are open. She's already with our Father in heaven." Pike squeezed out the words through his tears. "Go to be with her, brother, leave behind your earthly pain."

Everyone joined him in weeping.

A serene expression glided over Amos's face as he visibly relaxed and let go.

As soon as his chest stopped rising and falling, Pike said his last goodbye, sharing the moment of Amos's passage from his physical life to his spiritual one. Pike laid his head against his brother's chest and he allowed the mountain of grief to flow unbridled and unheeded while sobs racked his body.

After a few minutes, he could feel Frank place a hand on his shoulder and he could hear his brother's sobs. Pike managed to croak, "Why, Frank? Why is our brother gone? Why did that scum Drisco kill our brother? I should have chased that bastard to the ends of the earth. Now, look what he's done." Another wave of emotion overcame him, rendering his voice useless.

*

Callie brushed away her tears as she lit the stove. She hoped some coffee would help everyone. There were things that needed to be tended to, such as bringing Rebecca and Hope home. *Where will we put them?* she wondered, as she numbly moved about the cabin until she stood next to Buster in a corner of the bedroom.

Face filled with shock, Buster turned his worn hat in his hands and stared off out the window.

"Buster," Callie whispered. "Do you think you could go back and bring poor Rebecca and Hope home? We need to do that. It might be a good idea to put Amos, Rebecca, and Hope over in your cabin until we can bury them. Some of us will need to clean and dress them. Can you do that?"

Tilting his head down toward Callie, he nodded and said sadly, "Yes, I's fetch them. It's be best if'n I did. Eric need to stay wiff Miss Rena. Once I's got the girls over to my place, I's come and fetch Amos. It would be better if'n his brodders couldn't sees him no mo'." He turned on his heels and walked out the door, shutting it quietly behind him with care.

Callie struggled with what to do next. Knowing the trauma of the day would have taken its toll on the children, she needed to check on them. Tears threatened as she experienced their pain over losing their parents. *Poor babies,* she thought as she turned back to the coffee.

The professor and Effie stepped into the room. Holding each other tightly, they each looked lost. Collin voiced his thoughts. "There's going to be hell to pay for this deed, if I know Pike and Frank. They are so racked with their hurt right now, they aren't thinking about getting Drisco. But soon, the idea will strike and heaven help them when it does. We can't let them go off half-cocked after those two. This needs some careful planning. How are we going to stop them until we can get a group of riders together? We should talk to Lincoln first."

"We'll do it by force, if we have to," Callie replied breathlessly. "We have several strong men in our group that can keep them in check. You're right; we need to get the sheriff on this, and anyone else he can find. I don't want these men to escape any more than you do, but we need to make a plan. As much as I know about those two animals, they are killers of the lowest sort. I'll be happy to lend my hands to stalking these bastards. Sure will!"

The vehemence of her words seemed to surprise the professor. He readjusted his glasses and rocked back on his heels and he offered a few careful words. "Well, we'll wait and see what the sheriff wants to do. He may be happy to have you along."

"Let me help you with the coffee," Effie suggested, with a raw voice strained from emotions.

"Yes, please do," Callie replied as she turned to collect the pot and help Effie gather the mugs.

In the bedroom, Callie saw that Rena was being held by her burly husband. No tears showed, but pain-filled eyes stared at Amos.

"Here," Effie offered. "Let's share a warm cup of coffee. It might help you feel better."

Eric reached out and took the offered mug. As he held it out to Rena, he said, "Hon, drink this. You'll feel better."

Frank and Pike both sat on the bed with their eyes locked on their brother's dead body.

Reaching out and patting Pike's back, she said, soft and low, "Pike? Think you could drink some coffee? I know you're hurting but it would help if you could walk into the other room for a minute or two and drink some coffee – take a break. Amos wouldn't want you to suffer so."

Pike lifted his eyes but he didn't appear to understand what Callie had said.

Patting him again, Callie tried, "Pike, did you hear me? Think you can get up?" It broke her heart to see the attempts he was making to turn up the corners of his mouth, only to tremble and fall. "There, there. Come on, now," Callie crooned to him like a baby. "Here we go." She guided him to his feet and out of the bedroom, away from his dead brother.

Effie managed to get Frank to do the same. They guided the brothers to chairs by the kitchen table and placed cups of coffee in front of them.

"We can't let those vermin-ridden, whore-masters get away with it, Frank," Pike cursed in a wrath-filled voice. "They've killed too many people. Not any more, they won't! We'll get them once and for all. You ready?"

Eyes snapping with fire, Frank's grief took on a look

of determination. "I hear you! Let's go!" Frank shot to his feet and searched the room for a weapon.

Pike rose with him, a wild expression on his face.

"No!" screamed Callie. "Listen to me! You can't run out of here and try to hunt down those men. You'll get yourself killed, for sure." She rushed to stand toe-to-toe with Pike and hoped her presence would block him long enough for her words to register. "Professor! Eric!" Callie shouted. "Help me!"

The men were instantly at her side, trying to block the enraged Wheeling brothers as they attempted to run out the door. Eric's stout presence barred the way, giving Callie enough time to try to get through to Pike.

"We're going to send someone after Sheriff Edwards," Callie said. "Once he gets here, we'll be able to devise a plan to round up those killers. Don't worry. We don't want them to get away any more than you do but we need to all work together. Now, drink your coffee and I'll fix everyone something to eat."

Reason seemed to slip back into Pike's eyes because he dropped his shoulders and sat down. And then, Frank followed suit. Eric and Collin stepped back.

"Good," Callie continued. "We'll fetch Lincoln. He'll know what to do."

*

Resting in the cabin, Drisco oozed with pride. He relived the day's events. And if it hadn't been for the other wagon, he knew he could have done a little more damage.

Rufus had gone outside to fetch some whiskey bottles they had stashed in a little underground storage room.

While Drisco waited, he enjoyed being alone with his thoughts as he reveled in the killing, especially the parts where he had shot Amos and Rebecca. Those moments had left a sweet taste in his mouth. The baby had added to his pleasure. He tossed back his head and crowed aloud at the memory, just as he had done earlier on their way back through the woods. Out of sheer glee, he had kicked the buckskin hard with his spurs. The gelding had stumbled but didn't fall.

Drisco chuckled to himself now. The gelding got him back home, all right, but there would be no one on their trail. The devastation would keep Pike and his brood occupied for a while. It would give Drisco time to plan his next move on the family. *Yes, sweet memories,* Drisco thought.

Rufus bolted through the door with a big smile on his face. He seemed unable to help but hoot loudly as slapped a couple of full whiskey bottles on the table. "We sure got 'em, Cuz. Did you see the looks on their faces?"

"I'm glad we got the jump on 'em," Drisco said bluntly. "Just wish we hadn't gotten caught and had to run off. They may have had something good in that wagon. Wish I'd been able to wait around and watch them up close when they seen what we done. I sure wanted to see how they took it. I hope bad." He popped the cork on a bottle and guzzled down a mouthful of liquid. Wiping his lips with his ragged sleeve, he laughed. "It's what Pike and those others deserve. No one messes with us and gets away with it. They're all goin' to pay. Can't wait to get the rest of 'em, especially them girls. We need to keep one of 'em here for a while and use her up real slow."

"You've got that right," Rufus chortled in a conspiring tone.

The two men grinned at one another.

Drisco's mind raced with new demonic fantasies. "Let's eat. I'm starved! How about another drink to celebrate?"

"Sounds great to me." Rufus lifted his bottle and joined Drisco in taking long swigs.

After several hours of celebrating and drinking, Drisco couldn't keep his eyes open. He fell into a deep sleep.

*

Now that it was dark, Pike rested in a chair and stared at the wall. He tried to devise a plan. *It's too much to bear,* his mind screamed over and over. This day was the longest in his life.

Sometime during the afternoon, the sheriff had vi-sited. He and the others had come up with a plan to go after Drisco and Rufus but Pike had been too upset to participate. He wanted to go after them right then and there, so he kept himself away from the planning, know-ing he would be of no help.

They are all dead - dead!

Several people from the area had come by to pay their respects but he couldn't face anyone just yet. He stayed in the room with Amos and held his hand for hours, thinking of the past and what would never be. All the while, he stewed on his own plans for revenge. *I'll get them myself.*

Later that evening, Pike couldn't face the ham and beans the ladies had placed in front of him. He stared at the plate as his hate-filled heart helped him hang onto his sanity, which was clinging only by a gossamer thread. He was grateful when everyone finally left after Amos's body had been removed and only he and Buster remained in the cabin for the night.

Buster rested nearby. His presence provided Pike a measure of comfort because he knew Buster understood what he was feeling. Buster had lost a loved one to the same men. Breaking the silence, Pike asked quietly, "Do you think about your dead wife often?"

Shooting him a pensive look, Buster said, "Yes, I's do. Daria will always have a place in my heart. I loved her so. I's never thinks I get over her, but I's did. She's still in my heart, as always, but the pain go down some. I's happy again. You's be, too. I feel you's pain. It's you's, but it's mine, too. That's the one pain that binds us all together in this world. If'n we live long enough, we's all knows this kind of pain. You's have to find you's way back from grief. You's strong. You's find the way. Jus' takes time, that's all. The Lord will give you's the time you need, and this time, I jus' knows he's going to let us get that stinkin' rat Drisco." With wise, saddened eyes, Buster gazed at Pike. "Why don't we's lay down now. We's needs our strength tomorrow to chase that snake."

Pike couldn't help but try to lighten his friend's bur-den. He bobbed his head and worked his stubbornly stiff jaw, tugging up the corners of his lips, hoping it looked like a smile. "Thanks, Buster, for being here with me. You're a good friend. I know what you've told me is right. My heart just can't accept that I can be happy again. I'll take your advice and turn in. We could both use some rest."

Not able to face going to his bedroom, Pike rolled out a blanket and rested on the floor. The wide-open door and raised windows allowed a breath of cooling air to flow over him. His emotional exhaustion pushed him to sleep. His eyes closed as a disturbed slumber possessed him.

Soon, his troubled dreams jolted him awake and he bolted upright, gasping. How long he had been asleep he didn't know but he could feel the wet sheen of sweat across his back and chest and his heart hammered against his ribs and throbbed in his throat. His vision cautiously scouted the dark room and noted that Buster was sleeping soundly.

Shaking his head to clear the cobwebs from his brain, Pike eased to his feet and padded silently through the familiar room into the darker folds of his bedroom. Fresh grief wafted up and settled on him like a quilt and he quickly tossed it off as he searched for the Colt.45, stashed in his bedside table.

The drawer silently slid back as he reached for the gun and wrapped his fingers around the cold metal. *Tonight's your night, Colt. Drisco and you need to meet.* Silently, he pivoted and wound his way out of the bedroom, through the front door and toward the barn.

All his senses seemed fully alert. The comforting sounds and smells of the barn assaulted him when he opened the door and he could hear the animals munching on hay. He even heard the baby foal suckling on its mother.

Feeling determined and steady, Pike lit the kerosene lamp to saddle his new black gelding. The horse gently nudged him as he approached, giving him a small measure of peace. As Pike rubbed the gelding's nose, tears threatened once more. *Not now! Come on!* He pushed away his thoughts and forced himself into action.

Pike led the gelding out of his stall, found his saddle and bridle, and put them into place. He stuck the Colt into his saddlebag and took the mount out of the barn.

Luckily, the moon was full so Pike could easily see the road as he mounted the horse and headed away from the cabin. *I'll be able to track those killers for sure,* he told himself as he began to lope forward. The horse's night vision was much better than Pike's, so Pike felt confident in the horse's stride. *I hope Hank will be glad to see me.*

*

Callie hurried to gather her equipment, mainly her rifle and knife because she had to trail after Pike. She had been resting outside Frank's cabin to get some cool air. After gazing up at the stars and talking with God, she had spotted Pike trotting to the barn and she knew exactly what he was up to.

Moving quietly and taking care not to wake Frank, Callie changed out of her dress and into her thickest pair of pants. The sound of horse hooves clopped away in the distance as she tiptoed through the cabin and shut the door softly behind her.

Once outside, she bolted to the barn to saddle Clash. Pike had left the lantern lit, so it took her only a few minutes to get the horse ready.

Clash's hooves rumbled over the road as Callie put her top-notch tracking skills to the test.

*

Even though it was night, Pike found it easy to pick up the trail left by Drisco and Rufus. The clumps of dirt from the torn earth could be seen, even from the gelding's back. But Pike was forced to walk his mount as they entered the woods with its thick, prickly trees. He followed the trail which seemed to be heading toward the river.

The summer heat and lack of rain had brought the river to its lowest point of the year. Pike could ride the horse across without having to dismount.

As the horse struggled to descend the steep bank into the water, Pike kept his eyes focused on the task at hand. He allowed nothing else to enter his mind. Once finding that the renegades' tracks hit the water's edge, Pike nudged his horse onward into the welcome liquid. He took a moment to wipe his sweaty brow as the horse carried him across.

*

Following the trail for a couple of miles on the other side of the river, Pike spotted the outline of a rough cabin hidden in the woods. For a time, just seeing the cabin rocked him to a standstill, as his world spun out of control and his tears flowed. His hurt seemed insurmountable. But after a time, once his tears were stemmed, he dismounted and tied his horse to a tree. Removing his Colt, he began the careful crawl toward the rear of the cabin.

Hearing a horse snort and noting the corral to the side, Pike searched the darkness for his gelding. *Please let Hank be okay, Lord.* He caught an outline of a horse and his heart swelled with excitement because he knew it was Hank.

Cautiously making his way along the cabin, Pike slipped through the brush corral.

The horse's head went high, warily eyeing him. Another horse, also wary, huddled at the far end of the corral.

Even in the darkness, Pike could see that his favorite horse was not the same animal. As Pike approached, the horse laid his ears back and took a swipe at him. "Easy there, Hank," Pike said quietly, hoping the horse would remember his voice and settle down. "Take it easy, boy. Do you remember me? Huh?"

The gelding's ears twitched as he pawed the ground, until Pike's voice registered. After a few moments, the horse dropped his head and hobbled to Pike. Hank placed his nose against Pike's cheek and blew softly.

Tears sprang into Pike's eyes as he felt the warm breath on his face. He checked the horse's muddy, scarred body and felt the horse's ribs sticking out and anger welled up in him, pushing out his hurt and taking full control. *I'll kill that son-of-a-bitch!*

Feeling no fear, he wheeled around to finish what he had set out to do. He ran to the front door and blasted it open with his boot. The hinges of the door screeched from the onslaught.

As the moonlight filtered through the room, Drisco and Rufus leapt from their sleeping cots. Drisco held a blade in his hand while Rufus fumbled for his gun.

Pike took instant aim and released a bullet.

Rufus crumpled into a heap on the dusty floor.

Drisco came at Pike like an animal gone crazy and his knife flashed in his hands.

Feeling the sting of the blade in his side, Pike brought his hands up to defend himself, hoping to hit Drisco with his pistol. Instead, Pike got one hand around the shorter man's arm. The struggle caused Pike to drop his Colt into the shadows of the dirt floor and he managed to get his other hand out against Drisco's body to shove him away.

Drisco instantly came back at Pike and wrapped his arms around Pike's waist, knocking them both to the ground.

Seeing the knife sticking up from his side, Pike felt it being yanked from his body. As the blade came out, a feeling of sickness passed over him. Now, too weak to move, Pike watched the knife being lifted up over Drisco's head to soon be plunged into Pike's chest.

*

Callie dashed into the room and kicked the man's arm with her long, booted leg. She knocked off his aim as the blade went flying to the side of the room and Callie glanced at Pike.

His head flopped back as he passed out.

The killer grabbed Callie's legs and knocked her off her feet. The air whooshed out of her lungs as her back banged against the hard-packed floor beneath her. She struggled to catch her breath.

The foul-smelling man climbed onto her chest with both his legs spread, riding her like a horse. His crotch was close to her chin, pinning her to the ground. He latched onto her arms with his massive hands to prevent her from moving.

Callie struggled to breathe and she could hear the man panting.

He hovered over her face.

Even in the dim moonlight, Callie could see a wet leer gliding across his ugly mug. A shaft of sheer terror shot through her as she screamed inside, *God help me! It's my dad's killer!* She averted her eyes from the evil glare of the dirty pig's face. She screwed up her courage, as she had done once before, and turned her face back to look straight into his malevolent eyes.

A craze-filled laugh erupted from deep within the man's throat. Spittle dripped from the corner of his mouth. "Oh, yeah, sweet one. I've been waitin' for you. Yes, I have. I been watching you for months. I trailed you like a bitch in heat, I have." He laughed wildly and cruelly. "Now, that you showed up on my doorstep, I'm going to do everything I thought of doin' to you and that will take some time. Hope yer ready for a long, long night."

Drisco's spit sprayed Callie's face, causing her to avert her head again. Closing her eyes, she bit her lip and prayed for God to save her from this madman.

The vile, stinking man bent over her exposed throat. He flicked it with his tongue several times, then sank his teeth into her soft flesh.

A scream formed in her throat but only a low moan escaped.

Suddenly, the man got off of her. Confused by her temporary release, Callie opened her eyes and started to move. Someone else had entered the cabin. The evil man was now falling to one side and she rolled the other way, out from beneath him and rocked to her heels, prepared to fight as she took in the scene.

Buster's massive body stood over the man. His monstrous foot resided squarely on the killer's neck, crushing it with all his strength.

Drisco flailed, fighting and pushing at the boot with his hands but his strength began to weaken and he finally dropped limply and ceased his struggle.

Moving his foot, Buster rolled the man over. He gazed into his enemy's face and said quietly, "I's been waitin' a long time for this. I prayed to God to give me this chance." Buster suddenly pounced on the man, latched onto his throat with his meaty hand, and lifted him off the floor.

The man's eyes began to bulge and his tongue dropped from his open mouth, gasping for air.

Buster bore down more as the man's face turned the color of ripe plums.

Even though hearing the bone crack, Callie watched as Buster kept squeezing and squeezing, as though he did not know that the man's neck had snapped. Tearing her eyes away, she turned to Pike.

Pike lay on the floor with blood pouring over his shirt.

Please don't let him die, too! Desperate to see his wound, she knelt beside him and tore at his clothes. She tried to determine the severity of the wound to his lower left side. All she could see was blood - everywhere. *We've got to get him out of here.*

Callie leapt to her feet and bolted across the space separating her from the black man. She tugged on his arm. "Buster, can you hear me? Stop that now! The man is dead. You've got to help me get Pike back to Maude's. It's not that far. She can help him."

When her words did not seem to register, she pounded Buster on his arm and back.

Finally, Buster turned his head and glanced down at her. Still holding onto the man's throat, sanity seem to return and his eyes focused on her.

"Buster, we've got to get Pike some help. He's hurt bad. Please put that man down and help me. We can take Pike to Maude's house. It's only a couple of miles from here."

Quickly dropping the lifeless body, Buster rushed to the side of his dear friend. Sweeping Pike from the ground, he turned and ran out of the cabin.

Shooting ahead, Callie gathered up the horses. They placed Pike astride Clash and Callie jumped behind him on the saddle.

Buster mounted his horse and gathered up the reins

of Clash and the other gelding, then they hightailed it toward the town.

Holding on with her whole being, Callie clutched Pike and she prayed for all she was worth. She chided herself for not telling him of her love, now that Irene was gone. She might never have a second chance. Even with her sinking heart, she continued to fire a tearful prayer to God to please save Pike's life.

Chapter 32

Sitting next to the bed, her head resting on Pike's rising and falling chest, Callie listened to the thump-thump-thumping of Pike's strong heart. The sound gave her comfort as she waited for him to wake up. She doggedly held on to her hope that his life would be spared. A whole day had passed since Pike had been put in Maude's bed and Maude had tended to him. Now, all Callie could do was wait.

Frank and Buster remained with Callie in the cabin. The rest of the clan had taken the children back to their homes to wait on word of Pike.

Maude quietly moved in and out of the bedroom at regular intervals as she tended to Pike. She also checked on her close friend. "Are you okay?"

Callie lifted her weary head and nodded. "He's still hanging in there. He can't leave us now, can he? Please tell me he won't die - please!" Tears misted her vision and her chin trembled. The notion of losing the last person in the world that she deeply loved seemed almost more than she could bear. *No,* she instructed herself. *You have to be strong for him. He can't hear you sniveling. You've got to let him know he's going to be okay.*

Callie reached out and clasped Pike's hand in hers. She bent over him and smiled through her tears and started spilling out her heart. "Pike, I hope you can hear me. Don't worry about anything. I want you to know I'm here for you. I'll be right here by your side until you get better. I won't leave you – I promise." Her words began to waver in her grief-stricken throat as the fear of losing him overwhelmed her. "You just think about getting well. I can't wait to go for a ride with you. Doesn't that sound grand?" She stopped speaking, trying to rally him and keep him fighting by squeezing his hand and letting him know she was there. She rested her ear against his chest and merged with the sound of his internal rhythm.

*

Lying unconscious, Pike's mind tumbled and turned with thousands of images from his past. His childhood flooded back to him. He saw himself as a boy; fishing the ponds in the woods, running through the hills around his home near Baltimore, singing in the church, learning to play his guitar.

Rebecca floated into his thoughts and her pretty eyes smiled at him. Her velvet hair brushed against his cheek, and he felt her soft warmth encased in his arms.

The battlefield raged through his memories, breaking his home life, bringing dark shadows. Andersonville loomed large, recreating all the ugly pictures of death and disease. Yet, gentler memories of friendship and time spent with his band of close-knit brothers tempered the horror. Then, came the sweet day he had stepped through the gates as a free man.

A new perspective on life came alive and burned within him as he watched himself journey to a fresh start in the Indian Territory, away from the atrocities rendered by the war. Pride filled his heart over his success at survival and the many months of struggle to build a new life.

Pictures of the many folks who meant so much to him flashed one on top of the other. Irene's image passed before him and the faces of his precious son and daughter. Then came Frank and Amos, Buster and Collin. The line of his extended family grew as each passed.

Then, there was Callie and every fiber in his body hummed as his soul fed on her strong young face, her golden-streaked hair, her alert hazel eyes. Pike allowed his mind to have its head and gallop away where it willed. He set free all his pent-up feelings and let them fly, soaring in the warmth of the one he loved. A warm coat of comfort engulfed him and he floated upward into a pool of light.

"You are going to be okay."

Callie's sweet voice seemed to softly drift into his thoughts. He strained to pick up every blessed word.

"I'm right here. I won't leave you, I promise."

That voice urged him to turn away from the warm and inviting light and run back toward Callie's voice. He pumped his legs for all they were worth. *I've got to find her!* His mind clung to that thought as he struggled to locate his love. *Callie, where are you?*

"I'm here, Pike. I love you."

Fighting to see through the fog, his eyes fluttered open and the images blurred. A weight pressed upon his chest and he couldn't move his arms or legs. He blinked several times, trying to bring the world into focus and get his bearings.

Where am I? he wondered, as he stared up at the ceiling. The cabin didn't look familiar.

Then, his eyes fell on the silky hair of Callie as her head lay against his chest. A huge measure of comfort passed over him because Callie was here with him, nothing else mattered. Gathering strength in his stiff, heavy arm, he slowly lifted his hand to brush the top of her head.

Jerking her head, Callie peered at him through her tear-stained eyes. Her hazel eyes flashed with an inner glow that lit up her whole face. "You're awake," she cried, as she threw her arms around his neck and buried her face against his cheek. "Oh, Pike, I've never been so scared in all my life. I just can't lose you. I prayed and prayed you'd live, and my prayers have been answered. You're back - I would've died if you'd left me."

Callie's words fell on Pike's ears like a tonic, soothing his reentry into the world as the waves of pain erupted from his side. The words he had longed to hear had been uttered. He drank up every one of them, locking them away to remember, always. He moved his lips, struggling to speak.

Callie leaned back and gazed at him with love shining in her eyes.

Pouring out his heart, Pike said, "Oh, my sweet love. How I've longed to hear those words. You don't know how many days and nights I've spent thinking about you, and how much I love you. It feels wonderful to be able to say that. Please tell me you'll stay with me forever. Don't ever let anything separate us. You are associated with every thought and every action of my existence. The Keeper of the Heavens bestowed on me the greatest gift when He sent you into my life. I can never thank Merciful Providence enough. But, I'll spend eternity trying. Our paths through this world are now forever linked. Please tell me you'll be my wife!"

Callie gasped as a new crop of tears dripped, and she said, "You don't know how I've longed to be able to say this to you. Yes!" Another tidal wave of tears began.

Pike grinned and let his own tears run free.

*

Gazing down at Rebecca's headstone, Pike thumbed the long-treasured fob of her locks. He felt close to her and his brother Amos at this moment and wished for one more minute with them.

Hearing a horse approaching, he looked up. As Frank came abreast of him, Pike said, "Brother, are you scudding out?"

Frank released a tight smile from his saddle and nodded his head. "Yes, I've got a ways to go before I can hop a train. Do you want me to tell Mother and Father anything when I get home?"

"Are you sure you want to go?"

A cloud passed over Frank's face as he replied, "I need to go home for a while. I need to get away from here and all the recent pain. Don't worry, I'll be back. I just need some of mom's good cooking and dad's sermons to get me right as rain. I just need a little time."

Pike nodded. He understood Frank's hurt and his reasons for leaving. "All of us will miss you. I hope you can find it in your heart to forgive Callie and me. We never meant to cause you any pain."

"But you did," Frank said, as he tried valiantly to smile and soften what he had said. "You and Callie were meant to be together. I know that, but I need some time to heal. I'll write you soon to let you know how I'm doing."

"Things won't be right until you get back, but, we'll muddle through. Here, take this letter to our folks for me. Would you mind?" He handed the folded paper to Frank.

Frank slid it into a pocket inside his jacket. "Sure thing, brother. I don't mind at all. Well, I guess I'd better hightail it out of here." Frank clucked to his horse and urged him into a ground-covering trot.

Pike watched as long as he could, but Frank never looked back.

Eyes traveling across the pasture, Pike spotted Hank grazing on the grass. *At least I have him back,* he said to himself, feeling pleased to see the weight coming back on his old friend. Sighing deeply, he turned toward the cabin and started on his way home.

Callie's long hair fluttered in the wind as she stood in the doorway and shaded her eyes.

Pike couldn't help but grin at her.

Picking up the signal of comfort sent her way, Callie responded in kind.

Thoughts turning heavenward, Pike marched across the grass. *Wild dreams and real facts are but brothers. This day I have realized all of my dreams. Lord, thank You for Your wisdom in bringing this perfect woman to me. I followed the pathway You designed for me and the end result is that I couldn't ask for anything more. Callie is the wonder in my life that will forever fill my soul. You have blessed this son with more than I deserve. But, I will be grateful for Your grace upon Your child for all the days of my life.*

Pike began to hum to himself as his mind flitted to the letter he had sent with Frank to his parents.

I know that losing Amos will burden your heart, gripping you tightly with your grief. I want you to know that Patrick and Hannah are well and living with us. Mary Lou and Herman are growing like little weeds. I hope you can visit us soon. I wish I could be there to help you when you find out about losing your son, daughter-in-law, and grandchild, but, I can't. Know that I am with you as I hold you in my thoughts and prayers.

I am to be married soon to the most wonderful person God ever placed on this earth. It is my hope that you will be able to know her. I feel you'll find her as special as I do.

I will end with this verse, that I hope can provide you

a glimmer of hope in the troubled times ahead of you:

Yet I am always with you,
You hold me in your right hand.
You guide me with your counsel,
And afterwards, you will take me into
Your glory.
My flesh and my heart may fail,
But God is the strength and my portion
Forever.

Calling on the comfort of those words for himself, Pike stopped in front of Callie. His eyes rested on her as she returned his love with her own hazel gaze. Pulling her to his chest, he whispered in her ear, "Every moment of the rest of my life will be lived to the fullest because God saw it within Himself to bring you to me. I'll cherish you for the rest of the time He gives me on this earth and beyond - for eternity. Know that having you in my life brings me the greatest of joy and the deepest comfort to my soul. I love you, we are truly blessed.

Made in the USA
Charleston, SC
06 January 2013